Revenge in Rochenoir

By the same author

Peril in Rochenoir

Revenge

In

Rochenoir

Bernard Spencer

Revenge in Rochenoir

Published in 2009 by New Generation Publishing

First Edition

British Library C.I.P.
A CIP catalogue record for this title is available from the
British Library.

Foreword

The two policemen were on edge, having been warned to expect possible trouble. After all, there was thought to be a considerable amount of missing money or gold at stake and it was believed their prisoner knew where it was hidden.

Machine pistols in their laps, they sat with the driver in the front of the prison van and there were two further armed guards in the back of the van with the prisoner. One of these guards had a light machine gun. None of them spoke to the prisoner whose only restraint was the handcuffs joining his wrists.

The driver, moving as fast as he dared through the busy streets of Pau, was relieved to be turning into the Rue d'Etigny; they were almost there. It was the last thing he remembered before a large lorry, with a tough grid reinforcing the radiator, approaching from the opposite direction, suddenly turned across the road and went head on into the prison van.

A car following the prison van screeched to a halt and three hooded men, dressed all in black, jumped out, each armed with a pistol, two of the men firing into the air or at shop windows. Cars swerved in all directions, drivers diving for the floor and pedestrians scattered or ran for safety in the shops.

The back door of the prison van was flung open from inside and the third hooded men entered. Inside, one guard was trussed like a chicken, the other jumped out of the van and into the gangster's car.

The hooded man approached the prisoner who held out his manacled hands to be freed.

The intruder laughed and said, 'Au revoir Renauld Coutard,' then shot him twice in the head

Resumé

What Happened?

In the previous adventure "Peril in Rochenoir" Sam Elliot, an unassuming, retired bank manager on holiday in Rochenoir, Pyrénées, was intrigued by the burnt out ruin of Le Manoir du Roche du Diable. When he made enquiries in the town his curiosity was rebuffed by a wall of silence.

He enlisted the help of a young, attractive girl, Claudine Pepin, who worked in the Tourist Office, and her two friends, Jean Dubois, a reporter with the local radio station, and Alain Mercier, also known as Egg, an IT expert working for a computer magazine.

The web they unravelled led them to a trail of wartime smuggled gold and murder. Involved were Renauld Coutard, owner of the local wood yard whose fate you have just learnt, Bertrand Duval, owner of a local restaurant who died under a roof fall in a tunnel while trying to recover gold from the Manoir, and a greedy gendarme, Gerard Vachon, who died in a shoot out with the police. During this exchange Sam Elliot was also fatally wounded, later dying in hospital.

In England an old school friend of Sam's, Graham Rush, some kind of financial investigator or spook, was of great help to the friends, Claudine, Sam, Jean and Egg, who jokingly called themselves the Four Musketeers.

With Graham's help the above mentioned crooks were brought to some kind of justice.

What no one knew was who else was involved. Perhaps the hospital doctor, Noel Abrano, or a property owner, Yoland Ferrand, who seemed to know too much. A known suspect was Paul Vachon, brother of the crooked gendarme, Gerard Vachon.

Oh! And there was another member of the crooked group, Daniel Pierront, who was shot down in Dorset by Graham. Naturally, he is no longer part of the story.

<u>Who started it all?</u>

A beautiful woman called Josephine Sayers whose burnt remains were found in the ruined Manoir.

Her friend Mark Billington who is buried in Pau cemetery, supposedly as a result of a car accident.

And, Josephine's elderly aunt, Lady Sophie Grant, who is determined to discover the truth about the death of her niece.

<u>What happens next?</u>
Read on-

Prologue
Making Plans

Lady Sophie agreed to attend the double funeral which it was also agreed unanimously should be in Rochenoir. Her permission for Josephine's remains to be buried next to Sam was more difficult, consent only forthcoming following a plea to Lady Sophie from Claudine that it was right Josephine and Sam should be together. After all, he had been killed while trying to solve the mystery of Josephine's disappearance.

Graham had been a tower of strength to everyone following Sam's death. First he sheepishly produced Lady Sophie's unlisted telephone number in London. 'Of course' he explained, 'when she came on the scene we naturally checked up on her;' without explaining to whom the "we" referred. He admitted in answer to a deluge of questions that she was the widow of a diplomat, but respected her privacy by saying nothing more. 'You will have to ask her yourself when you meet her,' was his response to everyone's curiosity.

The Pyrénées put on their best face for the day, with a hot sun shining from a cloudless sky. Joining the chief mourners, Lady Sophie, Claudine, Egg and Jean, there was quite a local crowd led by Jacques Feron, the Mayor of Rochenoir; Commissaire Ramel of the Pau police and an assortment of other dignitaries amongst whom could be seen a couple of figures who looked suspiciously like Intelligence personnel. There was also a delegation from the hospital including a tearful Nicole who had cared for Sam in his last days. Graham's friend in the Compagnies Républicaines de Sécurité, Comte Brigadier Marius Bertin made it at the last minute having landed on the sports field in a helicopter, and, of course, Egg's parents, Brigitte and Albert.

Graham was there, with a sympathetic word for all, but the surprise missing guest was Claudine and Sam's friend, Hélène.

Claudine apologised to Lady Sophie on her behalf and explained she had suddenly flown to England, adding that Hélène suffered mixed emotions about the day for she wanted to attend the funeral, but also dreaded the moment. She phoned Claudine the day before to say it was impossible for her to be there and was leaving at that very moment to fly to England.

When told, her friends were surprised at the news for Hélène and Sam had appeared to be developing a certain rapport

An extra special guest at Claudine's request was the owner of Rochenoir Garage, Louis Lafolie, who had protected Sam and offered unqualified support when Sam was attacked by Renaud Coutard.

Chauffeur, James? attended Lady Sophie and stood discreetly a few feet to one side during the ceremonies.

Egg, in a quiet moment, expressed to Claudine his surprise that Hélène had not delayed her trip a day so she could be with them.

'Perhaps they were closer than you think,' she replied enigmatically.

Graham whispered to Egg that James' name was really Richard and that he had been a chauffeur and security guard for Sophie's late husband, Anthony. He had volunteered to stay with Sophie and Anthony after Lord Anthony retired from the diplomatic service.

Claudine's eyes were not the only ones filled with tears as the elegant black horses, tossing plumes of red on their heads, pulled the gleaming black carriages to the graves. While they waited for the coffins to be unloaded, Claudine explained to Lady Sophie that, 'Graham was insisting on paying for everything including a full sized coffin for Josephine and not something smaller just to take.......' Here Claudine faltered, unable to say "bones" in a steady voice.

Sophie gently took her hand, 'Don't upset yourself on my account, my dear. I have long dreaded this moment and have lived it in my thoughts so many times I am prepared. In a horrid sort of way there is a relief it is all over and I now know what happened to Josephine.

When Sam had described Claudine, Egg and Jean as his new family he must have been right for that was exactly how they behaved and mourned. Josephine and Sam would have been astonished at the crowds of well wishers who attended their joint funeral kept, by the Mayor's staff, a short distance from the official party.

Φ   Φ   Φ

Everyone cheered up a bit at the reception afterwards and all were surprised when Lady Sophie gave a little speech making a fine tribute to Sam. She confessed her early doubts regarding Josephine's involvement in the hunt for her friend, Mark Billington, and the suspected hoard of gold. Expressing regret that she had not given more help to both Sam and Josephine, she explained her knowledge of the affair had been minimal. Her short discourse ended with, 'I cannot find the words to convey my admiration for Sam's Musketeers, Claudine, Jean and the brilliant Egg. They selflessly did more than give up their time to help Sam find the answer to the disappearance of my niece, Josephine, and her friend from the security service, Mark Billington. They also risked their lives. That was beyond the call of duty and I want you all to join me in a toast to their bravery.'

A little later, Graham, who was talking to Richard, the chauffeur, observed that Sophie and Claudine were in animated conversation. He said, 'Those two are getting on fine.'

Richard replied, 'The resolution to the mystery of Josephine's disappearance has done marvels for Lady Sophie. I would not be exaggerating when I say it has given her a new lease of life. I gather she has taken to Miss Claudine and intends inviting her to London for a visit.'

Almost the last words came from an emotional Claudine who announced, 'Sam asked me to settle down and stop doing foolish things when our adventure was over. Well, sorry Sam, you showed me a new world that I want to explore. Yes, I will take care, but Egg, Jean and I will continue our investigation into the story of the hidden gold and we have two places in mind. Sam was the only one who listened to me when I said there might be more gold hidden, even before Vachon was seen in one of the places. We will call our activities, 'The hunt for Sam's gold."

And the last words?

They came from Graham who called the three together after the reception. He announced, 'Now look here you chaps, I won't try to talk you out of this dangerous and foolhardy mission because it would be a waste of breath. Just remember you can, without saying, call on me at any time of the day or night. Don't even attempt anything risky without talking to me first.

I've just had news from Commissaire Ramel that the prison van taking Coutard to court was ambushed and Coutard executed in cold blood on a street in Pau. Is that enough of a warning that you are out of your depth in tackling this gang? Please, please, if you must look for the gold, do just that and abandon any plans to clear up the loose ends from the mystery and leave that to the police.'

Claudine interrupted, 'We owe it to Sam to do all we can.' Then added to laughter, 'Anyway we were just promoted by being called, "You chaps!"'

Egg and Jean agreed.

Graham sighed, 'If you really must go on searching keep me posted on what you are doing and here's another warning. Vachon's brother, Paul, is still out there somewhere and don't ever underestimate him or attempt to follow up any lead connected with him. Please do not believe the local police thinking that he had nothing to do with it and keep away from him. I believe he is just as dangerous as Pierront. In other words, he is a ruthless mad dog.

Most of all, something I knew nothing about until I read Mark Billington's notebook. I was shocked by only one item and it is something none of you has considered. I know the exact words because they are burnt onto my memory. Josephine added to Mark's notes-

"In the event of my disappearance, the appropriate person has been advised of my intentions."

That person must have been someone Josephine trusted implicitly, yet they never came forward. Why, what will be their next move? I urge all three of you, and I don't apologise for repeating it again and again, be very, very careful.'

Later, as Graham left for the airport, he turned to the musketeers and asked plaintively, 'When am I ever going to meet the exotic Hélène?'

Φ　　　Φ　　　Φ

Of course, Egg, Claudine and Jean soon had a meeting to make plans for the gold hunt. It led nowhere except for a loose arrangement to spend a few weekends hunting in the gorges. With Coutard, Duval and Vachon dead where could they start? And, of course, the shock of Sam's unexpected death had upset them all, especially Claudine who still blamed herself and was desperately unhappy about the loss of Sam's life.

Graham also blamed himself and wished he had done more to stop the Musketeers, 'Not that they listened to me,' he told himself ruefully. However, he had another problem. Sam had made a will on his last visit to London and had made Graham Executor along with Sam's solicitor. Although capitalising Sam's estate they had agreed to do nothing about distribution pending legal arguments.

So you have in the previous pages read an outline of the first story, "Peril in Rochenoir." If you read the previous adventure you are familiar with some of the characters and of the circumstances before reading the following tale.

The new story will start with the arrival of two strangers from England.

Harry and Rebecca, on a protracted, working holiday, rented the flat immediately below Egg's. Rebecca, in trouble with making her computer do what she wanted, contacted Egg for help and she recounts the result.

Revenge in Rochenoir

Chapter One
Rebecca

My name is Rebecca and I'm a geologist. My particular field is in photographic recording. Like my husband, Harry, I am English. He specialises in a complementary line, archaeology, and you won't be surprised to learn that's how we met; at university.

I'm 26, tall, slim with the right proportions and not bad looking with shoulder length, auburn hair. My venture into probing strata came after a brief skirmish with a job in commerce, a line of work that did not appeal to me one little bit. Harry's passion, hopefully after me, is pure archaeology. By the way, those of us in that trade refer to our profession as "arc" or "the arc."

What was wrong with commerce? The job! nothing. I enjoyed the work but not the brain dead men in the office who could not keep their hands to themselves and thought anyone of the female gender was fair game. A friend who was interested in Martial Arts showed me a neat trick where with a twist of the wrist you could capture a man's finger and twist it back until they screamed. I only tried it once, they left me alone after that, but I pursued classes in unarmed combat and Judo. I really enjoyed the art and it kept me slim. Things went well until one day, in a crowded lift at work; I felt a hand caress my bum. Whirling round, the culprit was not hard to detect from among the three smirking faces behind me. I had him down on his knees in a flash and thrust his face into a nearby man's crotch. I screamed 'If you like trying sexual harassment see how you get on with that.'

I shall never forget the face of the man I pushed the toad's head into. The next time I saw it was over the Managing Director's desk when he sacked me for unseemly behaviour.

After that my father paid for me to study and qualify as a geologist. My first job was doing fieldwork for an oil company where the men were real men and all, without exception, treated me as an equal. Of course there was banter and leg pulling, but nothing like some of the sick jerks I'd met as an office junior. I really enjoy the fieldwork and turned down promotion because it would have moved me back into an office.

Φ   Φ   Φ

My first meeting with Egg came a few weeks after Coutard's funeral. Harry and I had decided to take a break after our wedding by taking an extended holiday of a few months to relax in the Pyrénées while I bashed the odd rock when I felt like it. Renting a flat in the "Emile Zola" apartment block in Orthez is how we got to know Egg.

As I said, my interest in arc tended to be more in the line of photographic recording so I had purchased a digital single lens reflex camera and a laptop to take on holiday. This purchase had a dual purpose originally, practice for arc and geology recording and for our holiday snaps. However, in my thoughts the camera turned to a third purpose when Harry and I started to make arrangements for our break and we decided on the Pyrénées. Why did that alter my plans? Because he mentioned that glorious seaside resort of "St Jean de Luz" home of a beautiful, hot sandy beach, so I added "topless photography" to basic "holiday pics." Not, I hasten to say to titillate Harry, as it undoubtedly would, but to advance my theory there is more money in pulchritude for magazines and newspapers than for photographing rocks.

It came to pass that the first time I needed to download my camera onto the laptop, it didn't. The computer adopted an indifference to my camera that extended to ignoring it completely. According to the word around Emile Zola land, the best way to sort out that kind of problem was to talk to Egg. Our meeting was as simple as that and although I obviously didn't know it at the time, an extra plus was the dubious experience of being pushed off a cliff. But I get ahead of myself.

I knocked Egg's door and a medium height, thin, fair complexioned man opened it with a smile, 'What can I do for you?'

He spoke in French, as he would, which I just about understood, but seeing over his shoulder a rather beautiful girl sitting in an armchair embarrassed me slightly. I blurted in English, 'I am sorry to disturb you, I will call again another time when you are free.'

'Oh! Don't worry,' he replied in perfect English, 'that's Claudine, a friend of mine. Please come in,' he added, opening the door wider. 'You won't understand why but we are happy to hear an English voice.'

And, as I was to discover, in such a trivial way a lifetime's friendship began.

I explained my problem of how to make my computer talk to my camera which fazed him not one iota.

'Pas de problème, I'll go down and sort that out now,' he offered.

I was aghast, 'You can't leave your guest for me, etc.' All of which ended with Egg and Claudine agreeing to visit our rooms and meet Harry over a bottle of wine.

We all descended to our apartment and introductions were made with Harry, who I could see from experience of the man, was enchanted with Claudine.

Egg had been studying Harry intently and suddenly exclaimed, 'Harry, I am sure Claudine will agree with me you are like a younger version of an English friend, Graham, who I once heard described as looking like a television advertisement for after shave. If I can say that to you without offence.'

'Well!' he replied, 'it sounds very much like an undeserved compliment.' To laughter all round and agreement to his "undeserved" opinion from me.

My age, I discovered, is a couple of years older than Claudine's, and my figure almost a match for hers, except her hair is an attractive brown, and differently styled. Both of us – this is simple fact, no boasting – are of the type that make uncivilised men exclaim "wow."

Hair became a short topic of conversation when Claudine said, 'Rebecca, I love the colour of your hair. Are you from Scotland?'

'No, but I can't speak for my ancestors,' I replied. 'But you are not alone with the question for most people think a red haired woman is Scottish.'

I sensed the casual intelligence of Egg and commented on his slim, sporty appearance, which made him laugh.

'Sport has never been a part of my life,' he explained. 'I am slim not so much from exercise as forgetting to eat while concentrating on my work for a computer magazine.'

After explaining about Harry and myself, I turned to Claudine, 'Is it considered polite in France for me to ask what you do?' I asked

'Not at all,' Egg replied for her, 'Claudine is the backbone of the French tourist industry.'

'Don't listen to his boasting,' she laughed. 'I just work for the Syndicate d'Initiative in Pau. You would call it the Tourist Office.'

Egg sorted out my problem in about five minutes while Claudine and I hardly stopped chattering. We seemed to become soul mates in no time at all and were soon making arrangements for a ladies only shopping trip to Pau before their visit to our flat was out.

After finishing the bottle of wine we parted with an invitation to have supper in Egg's flat the following Saturday evening and to meet their mutual friend, Jean, who worked as a reporter for a Bayonne radio station.

'Do you think they are an item?' Harry asked me after they left.

'No! They are not at the moment, 'I replied, 'but there is something there so don't ask me to bet on it.'

Φ   Φ   Φ

Another subject that intrigued Harry and me was a burnt Manoir in Rochenoir, although we had been careful not to mention it to Egg or Claudine. We had heard something of past events involving Egg, Claudine, Jean and the Manoir, so were proceeding cautiously.

However, there was no reason why we should not make a personal inspection, so having picked up a hire car, drove to Rochenoir. We were charmed with the town astride the river Oleron. Admired the quaint streets and old houses, not to mention the flowers everywhere in countless window boxes. We wandered through the streets savouring the atmosphere, made a couple of small purchases and had a beer each at an attractive riverside restaurant called, "Les Artisans."

Whilst we regretted not making Rochenoir the base for our holiday, there were good reasons for our choosing Orthez.

The ruin of the Manoir affected me profoundly. What a wonderful building it must have been, but was now just a fire gutted shell.

Driving through the open gates, we stopped not far from the front of the building. To say the gardens were overgrown would be an understatement, but an area near the front of the Manoir had been cleared by workmen and deposited there were piles of charred timber and rubble. All, presumably, from the interior of the Manoir.

I looked at the dead and empty windows and felt an overwhelming feeling of sadness. Almost, I didn't want to go in and remarked on my reluctance to Harry.

'I know what you mean,' he replied. 'There is a feeling of great sadness here; perhaps because we know there was some desperate wrong; but there is also an aura of peace.'

'Well I don't feel that,' I replied. 'There's evil I'm sure. Are we doing the right thing in coming here? Should we walk away from our plans?'

'Don't be silly, come on.' Harry headed towards the building, climbed the steps and disappeared through the gaping doorway.

Following him up the steps, I paused at the door suddenly aware of the turmoil inside. I looked up at the teetering remains of the roof and, at one end, items of furniture balancing on part of a wrecked floor that although sagging where unsupported, somehow clung to the walls. A sort of horror came to me and I ran back down the steps where I struggled to compose myself.

Just as I had managed to pull myself together and was about to follow Harry, having once again reached the doorway at the top of the steps, a woman's voice stopped me. 'Qui êtes vous? Et que faites vous ici?'

I turned to see a smartly dressed, dark haired woman of about fifty who was also wearing a belligerent expression.

My reply was in English. 'Sorry if we are trespassing, we thought it a ruin, who are you?

Her answer was in very good English. 'I am Arlette Coutard, owner of this ruin as you call it. A ruin perfectly marked with a large sign attached to the gate explaining it is private property, including a police notice explaining that it is also a restricted crime scene.'

I walked back down the steps, noting as I did so that there was an attractive middle-aged woman behind her scowling face.

'Je suis desolé' I answered, 'and now you know almost all my French and also the reason why I am usually in trouble.'

She took stock of me for a moment and then smiled. 'Then it is fortunate, Madame, that I speak English.'

I held out my hand, 'My name is Rebecca Tilsley, a geologist; is there any chance of you showing me round your ruin?' I grinned at my use of the word ruin again.

My tenuous thread of contact was then placed in peril when Harry appeared in the Manoir doorway and called, 'I wondered where you were all this time and find you are still out there chatting with one of the natives.

I turned back to Arlette, 'That's my husband, Harry, he is not very tactful, but is a good sort really.'

Arlette laughed, 'Can I make a guess that your husband does not work in public relations?'

This reply pleased me enormously. If Arlette had a sense of humour then she was not all bad. I called Harry down to join us and made the introduction.

'I am sorry about your husband,' I commented, 'it was in the newspapers.'

'We were not close,' Arlette shrugged, 'but he was involved in crime and of course the brush paints me as well.'

That was an interesting version of our well-known saying, but I didn't want to explore that and replied again, 'Can we look at your Manoir?'

It seemed to amuse her to show us round and we went inside. Although a large part of the ground floor had been cleared - hence the rubble outside - it was still a wilderness of destruction. Nothing had been done to clear the section of fire damaged floor which seemed about to fall from above, or the loose, burnt timbers on the tops of the walls.

'In England,' Harry remarked, 'workmen would not have been allowed to work under such a perilous threat.'

I asked where some steps going down from the ground floor led and Arlette explained to a cellar, but the police had sealed it off.

Harry and I studied the masonry and explained the reason we were so interested in the Manoir was that we were geologists.

'You mean my ruin,' she laughed.

We agreed and I explained the stone used to build the Manoir was not local and Arlette replied she had heard it was from the Gaverne region of the Pyrénées.

Our comments on the stone appeared to have cemented our authenticity with Arlette and she visibly relaxed in her attitude towards us.

Indeed, we all went to Les Artisans restaurant for a coffee in the riverside bar and, as they so commonly say, "got on well together."

Arlette explained a little about the history of the Manoir, but said nothing about the hidden gold or the police gun battle when Sam was killed.

In exchange, we said nothing about Egg and Claudine.

Chapter Two
Talk of Gold

We arrived at Egg's flat to a warm welcome. 'You have yet to meet the third Musketeer,' Egg announced almost immediately. 'This is Claudine's friend and regular companion, Jean Dubois. Jean, this is Harry and Rebecca Tilsley who are temporarily renting a flat downstairs.'

Jean, I thought appreciatively, was a rather handsome man, about my age and tall with fairly light coloured hair so it was a slight surprise to be looking into a pair of brown eyes.

'Hello Jean,' I said as we shook hands, 'I'm sure Egg has told you all about us.'

'All he knows except why you chose to come to Orthez,' he answered.

This was a question I was expecting from someone, so was not surprised, except it seemed a slightly rude response to my friendly greeting.

I answered, 'Because we didn't want to stay in Oleron. Oleron might have been ideal for us, because we had been told that, like Pau, there are a lot of English there. However, we want to try and absorb some of the French culture. We also thought of Rochenoir, but it seemed the sort of place where nothing ever happens, so Orthez looked to be a fine compromise.'

The three Musketeers all exchanged glances when I mentioned Rochenoir but Harry cut in swiftly with, 'Rebecca! When are you going to stop talking so I can be introduced.'

I had hoped Jean would bestow a kiss on each of my cheeks as Egg had done, but Jean simply answered, 'I'm afraid you will find there are a lot of English in most of the towns in southern France these days.'

'Boy! What a charmer he is,' was my thought.

A mildly plaintive voice asked, 'Who is going to introduce me?'

I swung round and saw a young, very pretty, dark haired girl standing near the window holding an untouched drink. She wasn't one of the world's great beauties I acknowledge. Certainly as good looking as Claudine although not as slim, not plump either, more of a Marilyn Monroe womanly shape. But her effect on Harry was a surprise. He stared to the point of rudeness.

I took his arm and walked towards the girl as I whispered sharply to him, 'Your eyes will pop out of your head in a minute.'

Egg beat us to her side by a fraction, 'Harry, this is Nicole,' he introduced. 'Nicole is a long time friend of mine and a dedicated and caring nurse.'

Harry's speech seemed to have deserted him. I sensed his thoughts were in total disarray. He shook her hand and mumbled, 'I don't know what to say to you.'

'You could start by giving me back my hand,' Nicole replied, then bestowed a smile upon him that froze my spine.

'Hang on a minute,' I thought, 'This is my husband.'

At the same moment Egg realised he had not included me and exclaimed, 'Nicole, this is Harry's wife, Rebecca.

I - hopefully - smiled sweetly and explained to Nicole, 'Harry has a weakness for both dark hair and dark eyed women; to meet the two together in one person has probably turned his brain to jelly.'

Harry found his voice at last, 'Don't listen to her, Nicole, Rebecca misunderstands my friendly nature.'

'I think I hear that before,' she replied with a laugh and Claudine, who had also joined us, said, 'The reactions of men to women are surely one of the delights of life.' She turned to Harry and said teasingly, 'I can't wait for you to meet Hélène.'

A promising conversational opening, which ended when Egg called us to be seated. 'Who's Hélène?' I muttered darkly to myself, another rival?

A superb meal followed matched by unstoppable chatter. Once I looked up and caught Nicole's eyes upon me. She looked away a little too quickly.

Noting that Jean seemed quiet compared to the others I directed a question to him, 'Jean, we have heard the legends of the Cathar Treasure and that the Cathars hid their gold before the fortress of Montségur was destroyed. The story is that it was so well hidden, it has never been found. Do people still hunt for the gold or whatever the treasure is?'

He looked startled and did not reply immediately.

An absolute silence fell over the table.

Harry looked round from one face to another and asked, 'Has Rebecca spoken out of place or said something to upset you?'

'Sorry,' Egg replied. 'We are being unpolite, you just surprised us, that is all.'

'Well!' I said cautiously, ignoring Egg's mistake in English, 'We heard about the legend and thought of it as an entertainment for our holiday. You see we could use my knowledge as a geologist to look for strata that would provide the right possibilities for forming hiding places like underground caverns.'

Harry joined in, 'We were especially interested in the story that the location of the treasure is hidden in a code formed by the carvings of Oleron church. I thought, maybe, we could photograph the carvings and superimpose them on the computer to see if that produced any hidden clues for us to follow. Now I am worried that we might offend you before we have even properly become friends. Is there something we should know and avoid about the Cathar legends?'

Claudine laughed and Egg did too but Jean was slower to respond. He is against our interest in the treasure and possibly in our association with Egg and Claudine was my very positive conclusion.

Putting down her knife and fork, Claudine laid her hands on the table and spoke earnestly, 'We are being unpardonable rude. Of course you can search for the Cathar treasure, hundreds of people do so every year. It's just that you touched what I think the English call a raw spot. Our own thoughts and joking about any hidden treasure is inex...inext...oh no, what am I trying to say?'

'Inextricably,' I said softly and realising she was becoming emotional, reached across the table to put my hand over hers.

'It's just that,' Claudine explained with the wry sort of smile that can only pass between two women, 'well Sam.....' and a tear or two ran down her cheek.

'I understand.'

Egg explained, 'We have almost daily for two or three months discussed the gold we think a Rochenoir man named Coutard, and his smugglers might have hidden away.'

Jean, who had been sipping his wine, put the glass down with a bump and interrupted Egg almost violently. 'I don't think we should be discussing this,' he said abruptly.

Egg looked surprised and replied to him, 'This is no secret and we are among friends.'

He continued, 'At one time, before we found out about the smuggling, we thought a group of Rochenoir men had found the

Cathar gold and Claudine was cross because it is her ambition to find it for herself.'

I didn't dare look at Jean as I answered, 'and in we come like blundering buffoons. I offer you a bargain, Claudine, if we find the Cathar treasure we will give you a third.'

'No,' Harry interrupted, 'she will have a half, and if Claudine finds it first she keeps it all.'

'All right,' I turned my hand for her to shake, 'agreed. You have half of what we find. Harry's folks are well off, they can afford to support us.'

When the laughter and protestations had died down, Claudine raised her glass of wine, 'I thank you for your consideration, Rebecca and Harry, and propose a toast to your kindness along with a promise to share my spoils with Egg,' and after a fractional pause,' and, of course, with Jean as well.'

My brain instantly registered the minute delay and I remembered my qualification to Harry's question about Claudine and Egg. 'I may be right,' my thoughts polarised. 'I don't think all is well between Claudine and Jean. But, where does that leave Egg and Nicole?'

'I like Claudine very much,' I commented as we returned to our flat.

'I like them all,' Harry replied.

'I know that from your performance tonight. Don't think for a moment I didn't notice the way you looked at Nicole; watch it! There's too much at stake.'

.

Chapter Three
Trouble with Jean

Returning from a laundry room on the same floor as Egg's apartment, I thought I could hear raised voices from his door and hesitated. Then shrugged, 'Nothing to do with me, I thought,' and continued downstairs to the hallway. Curious, I took my time as I stood, slowly opening my door, when I stopped at the sound of a door slamming. It then slightly shocked me when I heard steps coming at some speed down the same stairs and Jean pushed past without a word. I called a greeting, but he did not reply.

Overcome with curiosity, I threw my laundry inside the flat and went upstairs to tap gently on Egg's door.

The door was opened quite quickly to reveal an angry looking Egg, who looked at me and burst out laughing.

'Well! I didn't think I looked that bad.'

'No, sorry Rebecca, I just laughed out of relief. You are easing the tension after I have just had an argument with Jean.'

'It was Jean brushing past me in the hallway at great haste and without a reply when I greeted him that concerned me, so I came up to see if all was well.'

Egg smiled. 'Nothing to worry about, but I would be concerned if he had been rude to you and if he has, Rebecca, I apologise on his behalf. He came with Claudine for a meal last night so that the three of us could discuss what next moves we could make in our investigations. There are a few questions to be answered that were unresolved after Sam's death and Jean and I had a few words, while Claudine played what you call a referee.'

'Don't be embarrassed to be open about it, Egg. I'll wager the row was because Jean does not want us to join you and be involved in your investigations.'

'There are no investigations at the moment. We have done nothing since Sam died. We need someone like you and Harry to give us a bit of a push.'

'What does Claudine think?'

'Rebecca, she likes you very much, as I do, and we would both be unhappy if you dropped your association with us. Jean, Claudine and myself worked closely with Sam to hunt down the crooks and search for the gold. We were very close to each other and Sam's death shocked us all. Claudine and I are adjusting to the present situation, but Jean is still living in the past.' Egg suddenly looked distraught. 'Rebecca!! I am so sorry talking to you in the doorway. I am so rude. Can you come in for a coffee?'

'Try and keep me out,' I thought, but said instead, 'Thank you Egg,' and followed him inside.

Settled with our coffee, sitting one each end of Egg's long sofa, I circumspectly folded up my legs so I could face him while he spoke.

'Sam was on holiday, like you, and during the times he walked from his cottage into town he became suspicious of why nothing had been done to the burnt Manoir. Claudine and I gradually became suspicious as well when we tried to help him. It took time for us to find out what was happening because no one wanted to talk about the past. Eventually, an involved story of smuggling that went back to the Second World War emerged. Sam's questions round the town generated violence from four local men including Vachon, the gendarme who eventually kidnapped Claudine and shot Sam. The owner of the wood yard, a man named Coutard, who was recently shot in a prison van on a street in Pau, and who seemed to be their leader and Duval, who owned the Pont du Rochenoir restaurant. The big puzzle is why these men reacted so violently to our enquiries. Any crime to do with possible hidden gold remaining from illegal operations during the war must have been the responsibility of people long dead.'

'They were probably afraid any gold they had found would be confiscated.'

'That's true. Sam found some gold in the sawdust pit of the wood yard, but the crooks took that away. We found traces of where some gold had been hidden in the cellar of the burnt Manoir, and, in the tunnel behind the Manoir where a roof fall killed the restaurant man, Duval, one of the four men. Six gold bars were recovered from under the roof fall in the tunnel. The police say Duval must have been carrying them.'

'Phew!! What a time you have had.'

'Rebecca, that's the least of it, there have been attempts on all our lives. You and Harry should think carefully before you become involved.'

'But if all four of the men involved with the gold are now dead, what is the danger? Surely it's normal for you to try and find any gold that is now hidden and lost.'

'Vachon had a twin brother, Paul, who disappeared and is missing. Our English friend, Graham, who has been such a big help to us, thinks Paul Vachon is the organiser, or what I think you would call a "Ring leader," and he is still a threat, especially to Claudine.'

'Egg, if you and Claudine are in danger, then we are willing to support you in every way possible. Count on it.'

'I know we can and it makes me feel easier in my mind. It's Claudine who worries me, I cannot bear the thought that anything might happen to her.'

'Then marry her.'

Egg looked quite shocked at the suggestion. 'Rebecca, we are just friends.'

'Of course you are.'

Φ   Φ   Φ

'Do you want the car?' I asked Harry over breakfast. 'I want to go over to Rochenoir and meet Claudine for lunch. I am to be introduced to her friend Hélène today.'

'Golly, I'll certainly look forward to that.'

'You're not invited, this is a girl's thing.'

'I'd like to meet her, don't you think it's a good idea that I should?'

'Sometime, maybe but not today.' Then seeing Harry's obvious disappointment, I relented slightly. 'Tell you what, you could drop me off in Rochenoir, and lose yourself, keeping away from the Pont du Rochenoir restaurant in the square. If you have your lunch in the Artisans then walk down to the square about three, and if I think the time is right, I'll see if we can run across you accidentally. I will park somewhere near the Spa. When you go back to the flat, use your key to take the car back to Orthez. If we don't make contact just go on home and Claudine will give me a lift.'

'All the more reason for me to keep the car if you are going to start running across people accidentally.'

'Ha-ha, almost droll'

Claudine and Hélène were waiting at the restaurant bar so introductions were swift and I really felt the warmth of their greetings. I sensed an immediate rapport with Hélène on a subtle and different level from my growing friendship with Claudine. I was also impressed for Hélène is a real beauty with long fair hair and a perfect complexion.

I simply could not resist being a bit naff and asking her, 'Are you a model?'

She laughed and replied, 'No! that would be no good at all for me because I would not want to give the clothes back.'

We had a marvellous time, merging smoothly from a twosome to a threesome. Hélène charmed me and, according to Claudine, when we spoke of it later, vice-versa. Claudine introduced us to the new owner of the restaurant, François Duval, a cousin of the late Bertrand Duval who was one of the crooks who had attacked the Musketeers. Indeed, François flamboyantly kissed Claudine's hand and apologised profusely over his cousin's part in the affair.

After he had gone, she explained the police had introduced her to François and assured her he had passed all their checks and they were sure he had nothing to do with the evil group of smugglers.

'Are you still in contact with the police?' I asked curiously.

'Oh yes, one of the bandits is still at large and they are concerned he might make another attempt to harm me in revenge. His name is Paul Vachon and it was his brother Gerard Vachon who kidnapped me. I don't see what good it would do him to come back, it seems he must have managed to move most of the money away. He's probably in somewhere like Réunion by now.'

She rummaged in her shoulder bag and produced a phone. 'They gave me this specially programmed and all I do is press 77 and it automatically alerts Commissaire Ramel, an elite car squad in Pau, plus certain police cars who are always on the road. I am well protected by the gendarmes.'

I leaned forward, 'Claudine you must wear that phone on your person, in a pouch on your belt or any way you can. It took you a couple of minutes to find it. In that time someone could knock you unconscious and drag you into a car. Please promise me you will never put it in your handbag again but always have it to hand.'

'Something like this.' Hélène displayed a small pouch attached to her belt, then, on an impulse, removed the pouch from her belt, extracted her phone and handed Claudine the pouch. 'Here, take it, I have another at home.'

Claudine made only a nominal protest and in a matter of minutes had the pouch installed and was ready, as she laughingly explained, for a 'quick draw phone call.'

'Have you ever met Paul Vachon,' I asked.

'No! never.'

'What!!!'

'It's all right, Rebecca, I know how he looks because he and his brother, the gendarme, were jumeaux, you would say twins, vrai jumeaux, identical twins.'

I relaxed a little, but felt a mounting concern for her safety and could see why Graham was genuinely worried about what had been Sam's little band.

A little provocatively, Hélène asked, 'Aren't you tempted to make a mistake with the phone and be a swooning damsel waiting to be rescued by the gendarmes? They all seem to be universally handsome.'

'She wouldn't get away with it,' I answered, 'I don't think they would believe she is the swooning type.'

Claudine agreed and explained, 'Instead, I would become a guest in one of Commissaire Ramel's cells.'

Hélène accepted with delight an invitation to join Claudine and me on a shopping trip to Pamplona. Then there was a surprise to come when we attempted to pay the bill and François announced with a flourish there was nothing to pay as a small compensation for the acts of his relative. And also, 'It was an honour to have three such beautiful ladies to lunch in his restaurant.' Then the businessman came to the fore when he added, 'We would be allowed to pay the next time we dined.'

We left the restaurant laughing at his commercial comment and were distracted, almost making my recent fears come true. We failed to see a man run towards Claudine until he pushed her off balance and snatched her shoulder bag. As the man turned to run away, I swung my small, sling bag and hit him in the side of his head. The bag-snatcher staggered. Dropping my bag I jabbed him in the throat with the fingers of both my hands. As the swine threw his head back gasping and choking, I chopped him smartly in the back of his neck with my right hand. He went down on the ground as if he had been pole axed. He feebly put his hands down on the pavement as if to push himself up and I kicked his arm away from under him.

As the man sprawled, still gasping, with his legs apart, Hélène stepped forward and pressed hard on his heel with her foot, so twisting his leg and his knee. His anguished scream was probably heard on the other side of town.

Claudine, who in the few seconds the attack had taken, had triggered her special phone, cried, 'Wait, I didn't do anything,' and stamped on the man's outstretched hand provoking another scream of pain as the man rolled into a ball and lay groaning. She turned to me in admiring wonder, saying, 'What do you have in your purse, Rebecca, a brick?'

'Don't ask,' I laughed.

Almost in a minute or two a police car came screeching to a halt and two gendarmes came running towards us, closely followed a few minutes later by another car with two more. The leading gendarme looked at the man on the pavement and then at us three girls and said in wonder, 'Mon Dieu, the poor devil never stood a chance.'

Questioning produced nothing from the man and there were no papers on him to provide any identification. 'Just a common thief,' one of the gendarmes remarked.

'No!' I disputed, 'Claudine must have had something he wanted. He took too big a risk for the small amount of money he may have stolen.'

'I would guess,' Hélène suggested, 'he may have been after a diary with the addresses of her friends and contacts.'

The radio of the senior gendarme gave a soft tone; he lifted it quickly to his ear and answered respectfully, 'Yes sir, immediately.' He looked at us and asked equally respectfully, 'Which of you ladies is Mademoiselle Pepin?'

When Claudine acknowledged, he gave a little salute (to the quiet mirth of Hélène and me) and said 'Commissaire Ramel asked if he could speak with you.'

Claudine took the hand radio, 'Yes, we are fine. The two friends with me do not think he is an ordinary thief, but was after my diary for any addresses that it might contain. Yes. Thank you a million times. No! I assure you Commissaire I am fine and your men are terrific.'

She handed back the radio and the gendarme looked even more respectful as he took it. 'Thank you for your compliment to my men,' he acknowledged.

He put the radio to his ear and listened for a while with his part of the conversation consisting mostly of 'Yes sir' then turned to the other gendarmes. 'Why isn't that man in handcuffs? Take him to the

Gendarmerie, not the police station, immediately! The Commissaire is sending two men over to collect him.'

'No!' the man was almost hysterical. 'Please, I'm only a thief, let me go.'

The gendarme laughed sardonically, 'The CRS are interested in you mon ami. Don't make any plans for the next few years.'

A small crowd had gathered attracted by the two police cars which had been left with doors wide open and with lights flashing, thus bringing traffic to a standstill. Not to mention four gendarmes, three pretty girls and a man being handcuffed as he lay groaning in the road.

The compiler from a Press agency across the square had not unnaturally noticed all this and ran across with his camera. 'Can I take a picture before you take him away?' he asked.

A request that received short shrift from the gendarmes.

'No,' Hélène called to them, 'we don't mind posing, do we girls?'

We stood around the recumbent figure in a variety of stylish poses and I placing my foot on the man's chest.

After a brief visit to the police station to make a statement, I eventually reached our flat, Harry was looking most impressed.

He kissed my cheek and said, 'When I arrived in the square and saw the three of you posing, I thought, 'My God; it's Charley's Angels!'

Revenge in Rochenoir

Chapter Four
Graham Flies In

Egg, working with his assistant on a magazine page layout, had just stopped for a coffee break when his phone rang. He picked up the receiver, 'Oui, Mercier.'

'Hello, old bean, how's the weather in the Pyrénées?'

'Graham!'

'Who else! How's the favours department?'

'Anything!'

'I'd like to stay a couple of nights with your parents at Labaraquette if it can be arranged?'

'Pas de problème, when?'

'Tomorrow any good?'

Egg laughed, 'You certainly do not waste any time or words. Yes, of course it is fine. Would you like me to pick you up from Pau airport?'

'No, but I'd appreciate being collected from Pau police headquarters about four o'clock.'

'Will I need any bail money to pay for your release?'

Graham laughed, 'Not this time, old man, but you never know in the future. Could we have a meeting with the Musketeers tomorrow evening?'

'I know Claudine is free, I'll find out about Jean.

Graham, there's an English couple taking an interest in us. Harry and Rebecca Tilsley, who are renting the flat below us. They are professional people and are on a long holiday. As a precaution, in view of our situation, I sent you an e-mail asking if you knew anything about them.

Would it be of any use to ask them to join us?'

'Is Rebecca good looking?'

'She's been described as looking like a Charley's Angel.'

'Sounds the perfect dinner guest to me, give them a ring. I did follow up your e-mail and they check out ok and are who they say they are. I'll look forward to seeing you all tomorrow.'

Φ   Φ   Φ

Egg came down to our apartment and recited the above conversation to us and we, of course, agreed to join the party. More, we offered to drive Egg to the police station and collect Graham so we could all go together to Egg's parents at Labaraquette

We had to wait half an hour in the police station reception for him and I easily picked out the rather handsome, well built man, I guessed, in his early fifties who walked towards us. He apologised for being late when he did appear. If he was surprised to see Harry and me he did not show it and, in any case, Egg quickly introduced us. While being introduced to Graham I froze when he remarked, 'Haven't I seen you before somewhere?'

I answered in my steadiest voice, 'I doubt you would have remembered if you had,' and gave him one of my sweetest smiles.

He laughed and said, 'Jolly old plane was a bit late. A cloud in the way or something, but we're all sorted now. Absolutely top hole to see you again, Egg, and I can't wait to see the others. Can we stop somewhere to buy your folks flowers or chocolates, what do you think?'

Egg laughed, 'You do not change one little bit and all the thanks for that. My mother and my father adore chocolate, but you really do not need to for they are delighted you are coming to stay again.'

Needless to say Graham purchased enough chocolates to last them until Christmas and we were soon having an enthusiastic welcome in the rambling farmhouse home of Egg's parents in Labaraquette.

Brigitte industriously waved her arms about then kissed Graham on both cheeks saying, 'Bienvenu, bienvenu.'

Albert pumped his hand and held a corkscrew ready in the other.

They next turned to us and the introductions did not take long. It was clear I was an immediate hit with Brigitte. Once more I marvelled at my ready acceptance by other women. Life can sometimes be difficult due to the jealousy felt towards younger women, but my instinct seemed adept at handling such problems. 'So is Claudine's,' I suddenly realised.

Sam, the family brute of a dog, ran into the extensive lounge/hallway at the sound of Graham's voice, wagged his tail a little, sniffed all round the room, then retired to the kitchen.

Graham called after him, 'I say, old sport, that's not much of a welcome.'

'He is very quiet,' Albert explained. 'He is not his normal dog.'

'Not his normal self,' Egg corrected.

Brigitte gave what can only be called a snort and said, 'I keep telling them; he misses Sam and is restless and sometimes leaves his food. What is it called Alain?'

'You mean he pines for Sam.'

'That's it,' Brigitte said triumphantly, 'he pines.'

'But I thought he always growled at Sam.'

'He misses having his growl,' Albert added with a chuckle.

Brigitte rounded on her husband, 'Don't you make jokes about it, we all miss Sam. It was a terrible thing to happen.'

'Yes, you are right,' Albert answered. He turned to Graham, 'We had to change his name back for we had called the dog Sam in honour of Sam the man when he was alive, but now that one Sam is not with us, the other Sam wants to know why.'

He puzzled over his comments, and then shrugged.

'What I am saying is that we had to change the name of Sam the dog back to Marmite because when we called Sam the dog he thought Sam the man had arrived and came rushing to see him. I think I make a mess of this explanation.'

Graham laughed, 'I understand perfectly what you are saying. But why do you call him "Marmite", does he like to eat it?'

Albert looked even more puzzled at the question, 'Que dites-vous?' he asked Egg.

It was my turn to laugh, 'Graham, in French marmite means a big pot or a big container.'

Egg explained the misunderstanding to his father and mother. 'Our family like odd names for the animals, you should have heard the names of some of the cows when we had a dairy herd.'

At that point Jean and Claudine arrived and all thoughts turned to food.

Graham took both Claudine's hands and asked anxiously, 'Are you all right. My heart jumped a beat when I heard the news.'

She looked puzzled, ' What news?'

'This man attacking you of course.'

'How did you know?'

'Ramel keeps me informed. And on our way here, I spoke of it to Harry in the car.'

Claudine kissed him on the cheek. 'Oh Graham, I am flattered that you have concerns for me but I have friends who help me.' She triumphantly held up the local paper and there on the front page was an excellent picture of Claudine, Hélène and me standing over the man prostrate on the pavement outside the Rochenoir Restaurant.

Of course the paper was passed from hand to hand with all admiring the exploits and photograph of the three girls.

Well! All except Graham who said, 'This is not what I would describe as low key.'

His words were stopped at that point by Brigitte who wagged her finger under his nose in a markedly similar manner to Claudine and said, 'It is time to eat, no more talk about investigations until you hold a coffee cup.'

He laughed and turned to Harry. 'I hope you can be a stabilising influence on these young hot heads. They had some hectic adventures in the past and I am trying to get them to settle down.'

'I'll do what I can,' Harry replied, 'but you can see how difficult that might be.' He waved the newspaper with the picture.

Graham grinned again, 'Especially when your wife seems to be the ringleader.'

The laughter of the others was interrupted by a low "woof." Marmite had crept up behind Harry and stood, his body rigid, and his nose inches from his leg.

'Oh Marmite!' Claudine wrapped her arms round the dog's neck as she reproached him. 'Harry is a friend.'

Φ   Φ   Φ

Brigitte put on a superb meal and Albert delved deep into his cellar to find a few bottles of Navarre wine, red and rosé

Graham lifted his glass and said 'Cheers!' prompting an echo round the table.

Claudine next lifted her glass of rosé and explained, 'The last time I drink this wine was when I joined Sam and Hélène having lunch together.'

The table fell silent.

'Oh!' Claudine exclaimed, 'I cannot help having so many memories of Sam.'

'And so you should have memories'; I said firmly. 'It is good for all of you to talk of your sadness. You have so much right to congratulate yourselves, not only for your past actions, but also for being such good friends to Sam and he must have been very fond of you all.'

I lifted my glass and said loudly, 'Cheers, Sam.'

Harry quickly did the same and the cry went round the table.

Graham, who I swear had a glisten in his eyes, looked round the table, 'If we are going to talk about Sam, I thought he was playing detective, not wining and dining this Hélène. And, according to your newspaper, Hélène is the type who goes round attacking the local population. When can I meet her? I can't wait.'

'Stand in line,' Harry interjected, 'I also have yet to meet the lady.'

This caused laughter and a promise from Claudine to introduce Graham and Harry to her friend one day.

Over coffee, Graham wanted to know all about the attempted bag snatch and if anyone had any new detail to add to the account.

Claudine and I between us covered every angle but there was nothing new to say in the story except when Harry complained missing an introduction to the famous Hélène because the police would not let him through the crowd, adding that when he explained one of the three girls was his wife, the gendarme who could speak English laughed derisively and told the other gendarmes to arrest the Don Juan if he caused any trouble.

This provoked some leg pulling about the possibility Harry had a criminal face or maybe his photo was already on the police station notice board.

When all had calmed down Graham said, 'What I can tell you is the thief claimed to have no knowledge at all and that a man he swears is unknown to him sought him out and paid him just to snatch Claudine's bag. This man was with the thief and he pointed her out. The thief's role was to snatch the bag and pass it on before escaping.'

'Now this is interesting because the thief had been briefed for some days and the attack was at short notice after the thief had a telephone call telling him to come immediately and told him where to meet the man who had recruited him. Someone must have alerted this chap to where you were having lunch. Remember, the girls were dining at the Pont du Rochenoir Restaurant which, as we all know, is run by François Duval.'

When the murmur in response to his comment had died down he continued, 'We are not naming the thief, or releasing him for the time being but frankly, I think he is telling the truth.'

He looked sternly at Claudine and me. 'Either of you ladies could have been standing a few feet away from the man who organised and paid for this attempt and that should give you a chill. If it does not, then when I tell you this man could well have been Paul Vachon that should keep you alert to the potential danger.'

Claudine and I had a whispered conversation and she stood to speak. 'Rebecca and I thank you for your concern and your warning, Graham, but we are determined to live our lives as normally as possible and while we are together we are not afraid. I am absolutely certain that Hélène would support me in that. I hope it was Paul Vachon who was standing near so that he could see we are not afraid of him.'

She sat down to a round of applause that had Graham snorting and tut-tutting and everyone else laughing.

He held up his hands as if in surrender and said, 'Alright, I know you are all foolhardy and obstinate, but just tell me, have any of you been making any kind of move towards these crooks?'

As Egg said, 'The answer is no! we don't even know who the new enemy is.'

'Is there anything else I should know?'

Egg told him about the farmer Hélène said had spoken about German gold.

Jean suddenly said angrily, 'I don't think we should be speaking about such things in front of strangers.'

'Strangers?' a note of enquiry in Graham's voice.

'He means Harry and me,' I answered. 'Would you like us to wait in the other room while you talk?'

'Oh! Come on, old bean,' Graham spoke I thought a little sharply to Jean, 'it looks as if Rebecca is already one of us. And young lady,' he turned to me and raised his hands as if in supplication, 'you have even had your picture spread across the papers standing beside this well known gold hunter, Claudine. Although I will say again to all of you, be careful, keep your eyes open everywhere until we know who the enemy is.'

'What do you recommend I do when I am seen by the enemy?' I asked with, hopefully, a twinkle in my eye.

'Scarper,' he replied with a laugh.

It was Jean who then stood and exclaimed, 'I don't think it is a laughing matter. We have seen what has happened in the past. Introducing strangers increases the risk to us all.'

Graham looked angry. 'Jean, what increases the risk when working undercover with other people is a weak link in the organisation. You must all work together as one and support each other at all times. It is not up to me whether you work with Rebecca and Harry, but for your companions, Egg and Claudine, to decide. If it was my decision I would welcome them with open arms and say to you either you are a wholehearted supporter of your group or you must leave. Sorry about this, Rebecca and Harry, but I have checked that you are who you say you are and that you have no police record.'

I jumped up and said, 'Harry and I have no desire to cause trouble in your group. We are willing to help where we can, but if Jean says "No!" then obviously we will stand aside and keep out of the whole thing including the Cathar gold.'

'No!' Harry was immediately on his feet. 'I think Claudine is in danger. Damn it! We have seen she is in danger and I am ready to be by her side when she needs me whatever Jean thinks about it.'

Albert next jumped up, 'Sacré bleu! You young people all mean well, but you must cool your feelings for a little while you give reason a chance. Come, all settle down while we produce some more coffee and a cognac.'

After Graham's remarks, Jean had sat glowering at the table and he then stood and throwing his napkin on the floor, almost shouted, 'Too much has changed since Sam was shot, I think it is dangerous to take strangers into our group.'

Jean strode towards the door and Graham called after him, 'Don't be hasty, come back and discuss your fears.'

The only response was the door slamming behind Jean

Claudine leapt to her feet, exclaiming 'Oh no!' and ran after him.

The room seemed eerily silent as the second bang of the door slamming died away.

Graham turned to Brigitte and Albert who were still standing poised to go for more coffee and brandy, 'I am sorry that this had to happen in your house. I apologise to you without reservation, it was my fault.'

'No,' Albert had a sorrowful tone to his voice, 'this strange attitude of his has been growing since Claudine was kidnapped. We do not know the cause, but it certainly is not you. Sit down my friend, you are welcome in my house.'

Egg agreed with Albert and said that he had an idea to suggest if Harry would listen until he had finished.

Harry was astonished at this comment and protested he was the world's best listener.

'No, you are not,' I countered.

'Take no notice, go ahead Egg.'

Albert turned away as he explained, 'Brigitte and I will bring more coffee while you young people talk.' He inclined his head to Egg and turned to Harry and me, 'Please listen to what Egg is going to suggest for he discussed it with me and il y a bon sens dans ce qu'il dit.' He then turned and they walked into the kitchen.

'Fire away, Egg.'

'Since Sam was shot,' he hesitated, 'we have really done nothing about clearing up the remains of the mystery of the lost gold and even of finding out who the new bandits are.'

'Good,' Graham interrupted, 'that's probably why you are still alive.'

Egg grinned and continued, 'The reason is because we are all working with our jobs and there is no one to lead us. You understand it was Sam who kept us all together and quietly organised our investigation. Harry, we need you to take Sam's place and advise us and argue with us and take us to a time when all the bandits are punished for their crimes. Except, I have no right to ask of you this help for it will put you in danger.'

I had heard the door open as Egg spoke and then Claudine's voice when he finished.

'I'm sure Harry agreeing is the best way we will really avenge Sam's death.'

All heads swivelled to her, she had returned and was standing in the doorway.

Harry stood and looked a little embarrassed. 'You do me a great honour and I could easily say yes, but,' He stood silently for a while clearly deep in thought as we waited. He suddenly exclaimed, 'If you want the best possible chance to catch the crooks you should ask Rebecca, not me,' and sat down quickly.

The group round the table was as silent as me.

Claudine walked up to Harry and kissed him on the cheek. 'That gesture took a lot of courage and I'm sorry to be the one to say I agree with you. I vote Rebecca.'

'If Harry really doesn't mind,' Egg paused.

'Go ahead old chap,' he prompted.

'Then I also vote Rebecca.'

'Fine by me. We need someone good at the rough stuff,' Graham practically beamed.

'And it's fine by me,' Harry agreed, 'You all forget I'm just an archaeologist.'

'End of argument,' I laughed, 'that settles the question. I thank you all for your confidence. You can all rely on me totally.'

'What happened with Jean?' I next asked Claudine.

'He would not come back. I will talk to him tomorrow.'

Albert returned with brandy and Brigitte with a pot of hot coffee. They both looked round at our faces and exclaimed almost together, 'That's good, you have made the right move' and Brigitte added, 'You have made the right decision, Mr Harry.'

'Just a minute,' he protested, 'it's Rebecca we have elected.'

I looked up to Brigitte's smiling face and thought no, words aren't always necessary. She had guessed what was going to happen.

Graham gave Harry and me his card. 'Keep in touch constantly. No disrespect to Egg and Claudine, but I feel slightly easier in my mind that someone who is not personally involved will be with them. Keep them safe for me Rebecca.'

As we left after dinner, Brigitte pinned me to a corner. 'Mrs Rebecca, it would do my heart good if you and votre homme would keep a watch for Claudine. Je m'ai pris d'affection pour her; my happiness would end if anything happened to harm her.'

I took both her hands, 'Brigitte, Harry and I will do all that is possible to keep her safe. A promise that I am sure Sam would have made and you can rely that we will too.'

Φ   Φ   Φ

There was no doubt that Jean went off in more than a huff after dinner and I am sure he bent Claudine's ear, but it worried me not a scrap. I agreed with what Graham was suggesting, that he had become a weak link.

Over a hot drink before going to bed Harry raised the subject, asking what I really thought.

'Well,' I answered, 'He is clearly furious about Claudine transferring to the Pau Tourist Office and apparently became even more angry when she discussed taking a room or a flat in Pau to be nearer her work. As for the possibility of her accepting the invitation to visit England and stay with Lady Sophie at her house in London it is a taboo subject.'

I sat playing with my cup, swirling the liquid while watching it intently, 'Do you know, she stays the occasional night in Egg's apartment when working late. I'm not for one moment suggesting there is anything going on, but I would bet that Jean doesn't know. But, just remember I once said watch this space.'

'Good for her if she is, she should enjoy life.'

I threw the magazine in my hand at Harry's head. 'Another warning for you,' I exclaimed. 'Don't get up to any mischief or make me angry. I know I can trust Claudine, but there are two more attractive girls coming into your sphere, Nicole and Hélène. Just remember you are married and behave accordingly. There is too much at stake here for games and lives are at risk. My previous comment about Nicole when your eyes nearly popped out of your head was, Watch it! Let's upgrade it to, 'Don't even think about straying over the line because if you wreck this operation, it will be the very Devil you have to pay.'

Chapter Five
Farming Times

I had arranged with Graham for us to go up into the mountains to interview the farmer that Hélène had discovered. Claudine, disappointed that she could not be with us due to pressure at work, had suggested we take her. She reminded me it was Hélène who had previously talked with the farmer and thought he might know something that would help with our investigations. Accordingly, I arranged to meet Graham for breakfast at Labaraquette. Harry had some research to do at Pau University so I was free for the day.

I asked Bridgett for only a coffee and a couple of croissants. Graham, having slept overnight at Labaraquette, stood at the breakfast table looking a little sheepish.

'With all the talk last night I forgot there was something to ask you.' He looked from one to another of his hosts as if wondering whom to address.

Albert looked up and laughed. 'You have no need to ask, my friend, you can stay as long as you like and welcome.'

'I say old man, how did you know?'

'I think you English call it Second Sight.'

'Oh!!' Brigitte scolded, 'take no notice of him. Albert makes jokes with you. It is simple, for you told Claudine you needed help to see someone and she had suggested a friend. She was so pleased to be asked for help she could not résister telling Albert.'

'Gosh!' Graham laughed, 'I'll have to sign him into the investigating team. It seems Claudine is going to ask her friend Hélène if she will take us to a farmer she knows in the mountains.'

'I'll find my coat,' Albert said hopefully.

'You will do nothing of the kind,' Brigitte responded firmly. 'You are not joining anything where they shoot each other. It is not healthy. Now, Mr Graham, sit down and have your breakfast before Albert has any more bizarre ideas.'

Over breakfast Graham became concerned about Hélène being drawn into our activities. He said as much to me and included Albert and Brigitte. 'Claudine and Egg have some experience in the situation we face,' he explained, 'but she might be vulnerable. Perhaps it's not such a good idea to involve any of the girls. Perhaps I should go alone or just take Rebecca.'

'Thank you, does that mean I am expendable?' I asked.

He grinned, 'No it means I think you are well able to look after yourself.'

After a question from Albert and an explanation of what "vulnerable" meant in Graham's sketchy French, it was decided he ought to ring Claudine and ask her opinion.

He was left in no doubt. 'There is no question,' she said immediately, 'Hélène should go with you because her word is the only proof you have that the farmer knows anything at all about the wartime activities.'

Graham chuckled. 'Well! I'm not going to argue with that. But will she go alone with Rebecca and me into the mountains? I'm thinking it's an unnecessary risk to take any of the weaker sex with me.'

We could all hear the explosion of sound from the telephone as Claudine registered her objection to his sexist comment. She went on to say, 'It's a pity I cannot go with you as well for the farmer is almost certainly Basque and if he does not want to talk to you that is the language he will use.'

'Didn't someone say Hélène is an expert with languages?'

'She is a city girl. You will need someone close to the country. As you English say, in a word, it is me you need, but I'm not available.'

Graham laughed outright, 'That's five words, but I'm not arguing. I will be happy to have Rebecca and Hélène along.'

'Hélène will wait for you outside the Tourist Office. She will be wearing grey trousers and a red jacket, but if Rebecca is with you she knows her.'

As Graham pulled up alongside Hélène I could almost feel his temperature rise. Claudine is a very pretty girl, but Hélène is something else. She is simply stunning. I doubt Graham would have been able to describe her stylish clothes, but the aplomb with which she wore them showed chic in its truest meaning. He just stared at her for a few moments.

'You have to be a fashion model or a film star,' he finally greeted her

I tut tutted, 'These days an excess of compliments will not impress, we are aware of the wiles of men.'

'No!' Hélène said, 'I like the compliments of men. Thank you Graham.'

'Take no notice of Rebecca,' he explained, 'I really meant what I said.'

Hélène sat in the back and as I slipped into the passenger seat beside him, Graham turned to me and said, 'You're not bad yourself.'

'That's far too late. I am now jealous'

So, an hour or so later, we drove up a winding mountain road that spiralled as if it were to end at any moment rather than be access to a farm. When we did arrive only Hélène, who had been before, recognised the sprawling, tumble down collection of huts and sheds as a working farm.

As soon as Graham stopped the car, two large, rough looking dogs came hurtling out of one of the sheds and circled the car snarling. 'What do we do now?' he asked.

'Un moment' Hélène responded, opening the car door and writhing her slim, immaculate, form through the opening.

As both dogs moved towards her, one drooling, she simply stood upright and commanded, 'Chien, ici!!!' pointing to a spot just in front of where she stood.

Both dogs stopped and looked at her uncertainly.

'En bas!' she raised her voice slightly.

Both dogs sat obediently in front of her.

Graham and I emerged from the car.

'This is my day for being impressed in more ways than one,' Graham said to Hélène admiringly. 'How did you learn to do that?'

'I did not learn. Dogs are like men, they respond to firm handling.'

'Sounds a fair bargain,' Graham replied. 'When do we start?'

All Hélène did was laugh, but I looked up sharply at her. 'Oh ho!' I said quietly under my breath.

A very old, but upright man came out of the largest shed and said something unintelligible to the dogs who both returned to their hut.

'Qu'est-que-c'est?' he asked Hélène.

This generated a short conversation in French, which resulted in an invitation inside the man's untidy, cluttered home.

Hélène introduced us to Monsieur Bruno Laurade, a sheep farmer and smuggler.

'Did you say smuggler?' Graham asked.

'Bien sur, it would be difficult to earn a living from just sheep on a farm as small as this.'

'And he admits he smuggles?'

'Of course, why not, who cares?'

He shrugged. 'Ask him if he has seen Gendarme Vachon recently.'

'Are you sure?' I interrupted with doubt in my voice.

Graham nodded.

Hélène posed the question.

Bruno smiled for the first time. 'No not for a number of weeks.'

'Is he expecting to see him?'

It seemed the farmer did not know. Very occasionally Vachon called, but he had no reason to come other than that they once worked together.

It appeared Bruno did not know Vachon was dead so would obviously not be in possession of any recent reliable information.

'Ask him if he is sure he has finished working with Vachon?"

When Hélène posed this question the farmer looked suspicious and noticeably withdrew, leaning back in his chair.

Hélène interceded quickly, decrying Claudine's earlier opinion by speaking to the man in Basque. A short conversation followed as the man relaxed to her smooth, soothing manner, responding easily to her questions. Once when Graham attempted to speak, Hélène waved to him to be quiet. Eventually she turned to face us. 'I have explained that you are not looking for Vachon, but merely curious because you have not seen him for a long time and are concerned something might have happened to him. He has known Vachon all his life and agrees the gendarme has some dangerous friends and something bad might happen to him. When that happens he will deny he knows him.

I think, Graham, it would be better if you told me what you want to ask and leave it to me. He is now very suspicious of you and your questions and I am certain he will not speak freely while you are here.'

'Tell him we could have him arrested and it would be better for him to talk now than in the police station,'

'If I do that you will learn nothing. He is an old man who cares nothing for you and nothing for his life.'

I supported Hélène. 'Our approach was clumsy. We should have spoken of other matters before asking questions. Graham and I should leave and wait in the car.'

'No, I'll go,' he agreed. 'Rebecca knows the sort of thing that concerns us.' He rose, politely said good-bye to the farmer and left.

Hélène moved and sat close to the farmer, her expensive, but subtle perfume calming him more. She said softly to him, 'You must not be offended by my English friend. He lost a close relative during the war, lost somewhere in the Pyrénées.'

Bruno grunted with interest, 'Was his relative an English agent?'

'Yes!'

'Many died in the war.'

Hélène leaned forward and placed her cool hand on the farmer's rough hand. 'And, many escaped helped by men such as yourself.'

Bruno used his other hand to pat hers. 'Yes, I helped both English and Germans to escape. I helped willingly until my only son was killed.'

'I am sorry,' Hélène spoke quietly, 'Do you know who was responsible?'

'No! He was missing. It took me two days to find him. I don't know who shot him. I buried him near to where he fell. It was all I was able to do. My feeling was that my own life had ended.'

A couple of tears ran down Hélène's cheek and she wasn't acting. 'I'm so, so, sorry,' she whispered.

'My life ended with his,' Bruno repeated without emotion.

'Would you rather we left you,' she asked gently in Basque.

'No!'

'Do you have any idea who killed your son?'

'No, it could have been English or German agents. The Vachon brothers may have become involved in a fight with either and then someone killed my son in revenge.

There were all kinds of trouble and although the mountain slopes were strewn with beauty that summer, none saw the flowers, only the money. Gerard Vachon and his brother collected heavy payments as guides helping others to escape through the mountains.

My son had spoken angrily to the brothers about their activities reminding them they should be working for the good of France, not their own pockets.'

Hélène guessed what I was about to say next and put her finger to her lips.

As we left she said to me, 'Sorry to stop you, Rebecca, but some things are better left unsaid. It would hurt him even more if he thought a man he considers his friend had killed his son.'

We gave Graham an account of our conversation with the farmer and although he looked disappointed at the outcome, he acknowledged the farmer probably didn't know whom the Vachon's had been working with so it looked to be the end of this particular line of enquiry. Hélène agreed, but said she and Claudine had another card to play.

'I have promised Bruno Claudine and I will call to see him again. I think he is lonely for he agreed without argument. I think it possible he may know important things without realising.'

Graham looked very dubious about that. 'If Vachon's old contacts approach the farmer they will know about Claudine. I think it's an unnecessary and dangerous enterprise.'

'If she agrees, as I am sure she will, I will go with her,' Hélène offered. 'If I tell of my history connections, and that I am to write a book about the hard times hill farmers have always had to endure, that would be a legitimate reason to speak of the old days.'

Graham reluctantly agreed. He turned to Hélène, 'You are gradually being drawn into this mess and the danger it brings. I implore you to take a step back and think carefully about the commitment you are proposing.'

'That's sweet of you, but I am determined to stand up beside you all and be listed,' she replied.

'Now I know when I'm beaten,' Graham sighed. 'No one's ever called me sweet before.'

Hélène and I laughed. 'Well!' I said, 'I can count on Hélène now she has been listed.'

She put her hand to her mouth and giggled, 'Oh! I make a mistake."

It was a more light-hearted trio who drove back to Rochenoir. On the way Graham suggested we stop at Duval's restaurant for a drink because he had not yet met the new owner. 'I want to assess what sort of character the little creep is.' he explained.

Hélène and I laughed again. 'Oh Graham,' Hélène leaned forward from the back seat and squeezed his shoulder. 'What a time Rebecca and I could have analysing your thoughts if that is your neutral way of assessing someone you have never met before.'

'What did I say?' he protested to even more laughter.

'Never mind,' she consoled, 'I fancy you are probably more right than wrong.'

There was still banter as we pushed the doors of the restaurant open and I paused at the sight of an undeniably important man, who exuded power, sitting at a table in earnest conversation with two other men.

Then surprised when from behind me Graham's urgent voice whispered' Take no notice, move on.' He also gave me a little push.

The man at the table looked up briefly, but took no notice of our group.

I walked to a table as far away from the stranger as possible and as we settled in Hélène could wait no longer, 'What's wrong,' she asked, 'who is that man?'

'He is the Comte, Brigadier Marius Bertin, of the Compagnies Républicaines de Sécurité' Graham replied.

I turned to him, 'Did you know he would be here?'

'No, I did not. He said nothing to me about a visit. He might be here on police business.'

'Oh yes! I remember,' Hélène exclaimed, 'I briefly met him at the hospital. He looks so different in ordinary clothes. He was charming and flattered me.'

'Every man flatters you,' I grumbled, 'even Graham.'

'Only once,' she pointed out.

Graham grinned, 'There's still time Miss Retour.'

'How did you know my name?' Hélène countered.

He looked discomforted, 'Wasn't it mentioned?'

'No!'

I laughed, 'You have caught him out.'

Hélène also laughed, 'Have you been checking up on me Mr Rush?'

'Not checking, just asked the question,' he admitted, his ears going a bit pink.

Any further comment was drowned by the arrival of a gushing François Duval.

As we parted outside the restaurant Graham admitted he should not have called François Duval a little creep. 'He's really a fat, little creep,' he explained.

Hélène went on her way and Graham walked back to the car with me. 'I don't want to impose on your time Rebecca,' he explained, 'but I aim to fly back to London tomorrow afternoon and before I do would like to visit Sam's grave. I'd prefer not to go on my own, is there any chance you have time to come along?'

I stopped and searched his expression, but his face was impassive.

'Early tomorrow there are a number of things I have to attend, but I could join you at eleven, would that be too late?'

The arrangement was made and Graham said he would pick me up in his hire car.

Φ   Φ   Φ

Next day was one of those clear, cloudless, sunny days that is perfect for a happy mission and lightened even our sad one.

'What do you really think of Hélène?' I asked on the way.

'Why do you ask?'

'I like her very much, but worry she seems too good to be true. She would fit in perfectly with our operation and she has skills and knowledge that would be useful in our battle with the bandits.'

'I rather like that description,' Graham replied as we pulled up at the cemetery, 'Battle with the bandits.'

'You have not answered my question.'

He laughed, 'Ask me again next time you see me.'

As we approached the grave we could see a figure sitting on a nearby seat. Closer inspection revealed it to be Hélène reading a book.

Graham stopped. 'Maybe we should not intrude?' he suggested.

I pulled his arm. 'Sam and Hélène were just friends, she will be pleased to see us.' We walked forward and in doing so attracted her attention,

Hélène, in fact, did not greet us, sitting motionless as we approached.

'I'm sorry if we are intruding upon a private moment.' Graham said.

Hélène produced one of her men melting smiles as she laid down her book. 'Nonsense, I am delighted to see you both. I sometimes come here and sit with Sam and Josephine for a peaceful hour. I have only happy memories of Sam.'

Graham sat beside her and explained. 'I feel a deep grief at Sam's death and agonise that I should have done something to prevent it.'

She looked thoughtful, 'No one can foretell the future. Sam told me himself that some of his happiest times were with Claudine and Egg. I was ready to be a little involved in their dangerous activities and prepared to ignore the danger. I too, feel a deep sadness over Sam's death, but also have a feeling of pride that I can claim to have been a friend of this man who gave his life to save Claudine.'

Chapter Six
Scent of Danger

Harry was engrossed in trying, fairly unsuccessfully, to read the local French newspaper and took little notice of me as I returned from the supermarket with the shopping.

'Get all you wanted?' he asked casually.

'More than I bargained for; would you believe, a man threatened me?'

As the information gradually percolated into Harry's brain, he looked up with a modicum of interest. 'What happened? You haven't been arguing over the only trolley without a wobbly wheel? Was it serious?'

'No! I suppose not.'

It was probably difficult for Harry to tell if I had been frightened by the encounter because I was also amused, although not smiling.

Harry looked back at his paper.

'Don't think I've ever been threatened before,' I added, 'but, in a funny sort of way, it was quite thrilling.'

Thus far Harry had not taken my shopping story very seriously. Engrossed in his newspaper he was thinking it some minor contretemps with a shopkeeper. My next words put him bolt upright in his chair.

'The man said - in English - he was a friend of Paul Vachon.'

Shocked, Harry demanded, 'Tell me exactly what happened and what was said.'

'Well this tall, fairly handsome bloke passed the time of day in the supermarket, full of smiles, you know, not on the make but flirting a little. Just as I was wondering what old line he was going to try next he said, 'You're Mrs Tilsley, aren't you?'

'How did you know that?' I asked him in surprise.

He shrugged and said, 'Oh! Somebody told me.'

Then he looked quickly around and suddenly caught hold of my arm by the elbow and told me it might be good for our health if we left Orthez and tried to find treasure elsewhere. A long way elsewhere.'

'Then, by the time I recovered from my surprise, he was gone.'

I had made light of it but it caused Harry great concern. 'We'd better talk to Egg about this; it's obviously something to do with their adventure with Sam. But why is the man interested in you and how did he find out our names and where we are? Most of all, why did he mention treasure? It's a concern that he must have been following you.'

'One thing is certain,' I answered, 'his knowledge - or what he thinks he knows - is not from Claudine and Egg, of that I am sure. You know the only other person who had any kind of information is Arlette Coutard, but I can't believe that either for she seemed so nice.'

'Sadly,' Harry answered, 'now that we have agreed to join in with Egg and company we are going to have to stop thinking "nice" in regard to anyone we don't know. God! Somehow, somewhere, we have unintentionally hit a spot. We have brushed against people who must be very touchy indeed. Perhaps we are close to finding the enemy.'

Egg was very concerned to hear our story. 'I can't believe it,' he replied. 'It's the sort of thing we have had in our past investigation, but that was nothing to do with you and why should anyone even think so. I am so very sorry if this is any kind of response to your meeting us and we would quite understand if, for your own safety, you wanted to end our association even though it would make me very sad.'

Harry exclaimed, 'Don't talk tosh we are not fair weather friends. We may not merit the high honour of being a Musketeer, but a friend is a friend.'

Egg laughed. 'There is no honour in being one of our Musketeers, only greater risk and I thank you for your confirmation of friendship. Indeed, it is Claudine and I who are honoured. But, tell me, what is "tosh?"'

It was my turn to laugh, 'Something from Harry's schooldays Egg. Schoolboys used "tosh" in reply to something that was completely wrong, or against information that was rubbish, but always meant in a friendly way. He was not insulting you.'

'Rebecca, I never thought for a moment that he was. Our English friend, Graham, who you met at Labaraquette, uses what Sam said were schoolboy expressions like "old man" and "old bean" and when he referred to Claudine and me as "you chaps," Claudine said he had promoted us.'

We grinned and out came the cognac.

As we left Egg's flat my musing was that, so far, in two instances when Egg had referred to the Musketeers he had not mentioned Jean's name.

Φ   Φ   Φ

On Harry's insistence we went to see the local police and reported my encounter at the supermarket. They were sorry I had an unpleasant incident, but did not think it very serious.

I pretended to explode and be very angry, saying how could they describe a threat to a foreign visitor as not very serious and insisted on seeing someone more senior or I would drive straight to the British Embassy in Pau and lodge a formal complaint.

While all this was going on, a man who was obviously a senior police officer walked into the station and asked if we had a problem. Harry's answer resulted in his asking us to step into an office where he explained he had heard me mention Pau and he was, in fact, from the police headquarters in Pau. 'My name is Commissaire Ramel,' he introduced himself.

We explained what had happened but made no mention of Egg and Co. I showed paperwork that confirmed I was a geologist and explained that although we had talked about the Cathar treasure, we understood hundreds of people searched for it so could see no reason why that should cause any problem.

I have to say that he did take all we said seriously and called an officer to show me, on a computer, photographs of known criminals to see if any were the man I had seen and when that was unsuccessful, I helped make up a photo-fit picture using a computer programme. Then Ramel gave us a copy of the resulting picture and I announced it was my first pinup. A comment that drew the first smile from the Commissaire

While I was busy with the picture, Ramel also had a long talk with Harry explaining that there had been a recent case involving smuggled gold and an Englishman had solved the mystery. He was concerned we might, through a misunderstanding, have been suspected of being involved in that crime. He would do all he could to sort it out, but it might be advisable if Harry and I were careful in our actions and if we had any suspicions about anyone to telephone him personally. He gave each of us a number for Pau and a mobile number for him if he was not in his office.

I said to Harry as we walked home he had been helpfulness personified and there was nothing more he could have done.

'On the other hand,' Harry answered, 'he did not say that Sam had been killed or tell us of anyone else who took part like, for instance, Egg and Claudine.'

Φ   Φ   Φ

On an impulse I suggested we drove to Rochenoir and made ourselves known to Louis, the garage owner. He was busy serving petrol so Harry parked by some second hand cars that were for sale and we pretended to be interested. Harry noticed one was English and he was sitting in it when Louis joined us.

He smiled and remarked, 'You are both English and already have a hire car. Do you want to buy this English car to take you back home?'

Harry smiled back, 'Just surprised to see it here. My name's Harry, a friend of Egg and Claudine. Did the car belong to a man named Sam?'

Louis held out his hand to shake Harry's and mine. 'Graham telephoned me to say a woman named Rebecca who would be with a man named Harry might come to see me. Come into the office.'

'What's going on?' I asked, then turned to Harry and demanded, 'You two seem buddy, buddies; is there something you haven't told me?'

'Wait until we are inside.'

We settled in the office and Louis put his battered saucepan on for coffee and joined us.

Apologising to me for not mentioning it before, Harry explained that Graham had told him if ever Egg and Claudine were in trouble we could rely on Louis for help. Graham also suggested Louis put Sam's car on the forecourt and Harry would sit in it and use the exact words, "Did the car belong to a man named Sam?" He would arrange the code as a confirmation we were who we said we were and that we could be relied on.

'You arranged a code sitting in Sam's car?' I said, mildly stunned.

Seeing I was either shocked or annoyed to be left out of planning the code, Harry turned hastily to Louis and said, 'Egg and Claudine are fine,' and that he just thought it a good idea to make contact as soon as possible.

'Sam left the car here some time ago,' Louis explained, and said he was pleased we had introduced ourselves and asked how everyone was. It seemed he had seen no one since the funeral.

'Are you both secret agents?' he enquired.

'No we're....' was as far as I reached before he held up the palm of his hand towards me. 'Save your breath,' he ordered, 'I know you are just tourists on holiday,' and laughed enough to burst except the kettle boiling distracted him.

Louis returned with the coffees and a beaming smile. 'I will commence to call my garage a new name, "Le rendezvous des agents provocateurs."'

I thought it best to laugh then told him about my supermarket incident.

His face took on a more serious expression. 'You are too beautiful for an undercover profession,' he then said to me in a confidential tone. 'Les chasseurs d'espions will notice you, how can they not?

'I am on holiday,' I replied firmly.

'Of course, who would doubt it?'

He looked at us from one to another and asked, 'Are you looking for anything in particular?'

I told him Claudine and Egg were to continue with their enquiries and we would help them if we could.

He gave us the same searching look as he would if puzzling his next move. 'I hoped to see the man Graham again,' he said eventually, 'I have an idea that might help.'

I leaned forward in a confidential gesture towards Louis and said in a lower voice than I intended and consequently must confess, a voice that was sexily husky. 'You can trust us so explain your ideas to us and we will discuss it with Egg tonight and leave it to him to speak to Graham by using a special code on his computer.'

Louis stood up to make more coffee and I motioned to Harry to be quiet for I realised Louis wanted a little thinking time.

He returned and shared round the inky black coffee and as we sipped, explained.

'The Casino closed just after Sam was killed and there were rumours it had been sold.

When nothing happened I became curious and then more curious when someone who used to work there told me it had a very large strong room. That alone will interest Egg very much, possibly you as well even though you are both on holiday, like Sam.' This merited a big grin.

'The Casino remains closed with no other word on its future. I have asked more questions without result and was losing interest when one day a car pulled in for petrol. It contained two men I had not seen before dressed all in black. One paid me the monnaie and the other suddenly stepped forward so they both had me trapped between them then they pushed me back into la pompe d'essence, the driver of the car saying, 'Your interest in the Casino is unhealthy, mind your own business.'

He paused, regarding us. 'I stamped hard on his foot and they left quickly. Well! As quickly as he could on one foot.' Louis grinned from ear to ear.

'Tell Egg that I made some more enquiries and was unable to find out who had purchased and closed the Casino, but it was paid for through a bank in Madrid.'

Harry replied, 'This is very important information, but you must not take any risk because if this is anything to do with the gang Sam was chasing you must know very well they are dangerous men. Did you know Coutard was shot by men in black, these could be the same men?'

Louis said he did know and was not afraid. He was determined to help the young people and avenge the death of Josephine and Sam. His life was of less value than the lives of Claudine, Egg and Jean for they had the rest of their time on earth still to live.

When we left, I thanked him and gave him my mobile number.

Φ   Φ   Φ

We went straight to Egg's apartment for it was then early evening. Egg was bursting with news and was so anxious to impart it that he stuttered and stumbled over the English words. A voice I immediately recognised floated from the kitchen, 'He's trying to tell you that we have found out that a woman named Yoland Ferrand owns this apartment block and she would know who stays here and is almost certainly the one who passed on the information that you were here.' Claudine then walked from the kitchen and gave me a sort of hug with her outstretched arms as she kissed both my cheeks.

'How about me?' Harry asked plaintively.

'My hands are preparing Egg's supper,' she waved her flour covered digits in front of Harry's nose.

'Then who is Yoland Ferrand?' he asked.

Egg and Claudine looked at each other and roared with laughter. 'Of course,' Egg answered, 'you don't know. She owned the holiday cottage that Sam rented and we suspected her of passing information about us to Coutard, but now she must be telling someone else.'

Claudine expanded her cooking to enough for four and we had wine while we waited. We told them about the Casino and Louis's comment on the strong room.

'We must investigate this as soon as possible,' Egg replied.

'Just what I was thinking my dear fellow,' Harry replied.

Claudine and Egg burst out laughing again and Egg replied, 'My dear chap, are you sure you want to become involved in the break-in of a casino?'

'Touché' Harry answered.

Chapter Seven
The Casino

Harry and I had just finished breakfast and were lingering over coffee when a discreet knock on the door announced the arrival of Egg.

'Are you doing anything special today?' he asked. 'I would like to see if we could get into the Casino building and find out if Coutard and his crooks were using it in their smuggling operation.' A question clearly aimed at Harry but answered by me.

'I would be delighted to join you,' I answered.

'Oh!' Egg looked a little embarrassed, 'Sorry, Rebecca, I really meant Harry, it's too dangerous for a woman.'

'What! Really Egg you're the last one I would have thought to be a male chauvinist. Didn't you read about how Claudine, Hélène and I sorted out that thief who tried to snatch Claudine's bag?'

Egg looked even more embarrassed and stuttered, 'I didn't mean to offend you.'

Harry came to his rescue, 'I think it's a whiz idea and all three of us will go. That is if the new boss approves. How about it, Rebecca, can I join your Irregulars?'

'Of course you can,' I laughed. 'Providing you obey orders.'

'Please,' Egg asked, 'what are Irregulars?'

'A disorganised army.'

'Don't listen to him he will mislead your English. It means soldiers who are not part of a military unit or an organised non-military force. For example, guerrilla's could be described as Irregulars.'

'It is like us then.' Egg grinned.

Φ   Φ   Φ

Fortunately, the old casino building was in its own grounds so we were able - as they say in all the best thrillers - to case the joint before trying to break in. Although the entire property was fenced, it was not secured in any way. An open drive allowed us simply to walk in. We found it a large building, extending to three floors which surprised me until I realised it would also have been a hotel. "Another cover for hiding people," I thought to myself. The building was clearly empty but unlike the Manoir, was not a ruin. Indeed, the paint work looked in good condition, although the windows were dirty, enhancing the air of abandonment.

The grounds were a different matter; the lawns at the back looked like a hayfield and bushes were overgrown. The decorative beds that should have been a riot of colour were full of dead flowers.

'Are we really going to break in?' I asked.

'No,' Egg replied, 'we must not show any sign we've been here.'

'Let's find the kitchens,' Harry suggested, 'they're always a weak point.'

They were not difficult to find with a stainless steel extractor tube running up the rear wall. There were two likely looking doors, one on each side of the steel tube, but they were impossible to open without smashing our way in. Then Harry saw the top of the large kitchen window was capable of tilting inwards for ventilation. He looked at it for a moment then remarked, 'I reckon Rebecca could squeeze through there and let us in by one of the emergency exit doors'.

'Oh yes' I said, 'and how do I climb back out on my own if you're wrong and the doors won't open?'

'We'll go into desperate mode,' Harry answered, 'and smash the kitchen window.' 'Perhaps we should break it after all,' Egg said with a worried tone. 'I think it's a bit risky for Rebecca to climb in.'

'Rebecca will be OK.' Harry took a strip of plastic from his pocket and fed it between the window and its frame wriggling it backwards and forwards until the catch snapped open. The top of the window tilted inwards onto its retaining brackets.

Pulling himself up using the now open frame Harry knocked the left hand bracket clear with a heavy stone, intending to do the same with the other end after securing the window in some way. However, the remaining bracket was already bent and was not strong enough to hold the weight of the tilted window on its own, which dropped down with a crash. By some miracle it didn't break the glass but we all stood still holding our breath in fear that someone would investigate the noise.

Nothing happened.

In a flash, I swung myself up and snaked my way through the frame like an acrobat.

'She used to be a cat burglar,' Harry joked with Egg.

Egg then almost caught Harry wrong footed when he replied, 'I believe you, but how did you learn to open windows like that?'

Harry was saved an answer when I, from my less than elegant position standing in a large sink partly filled with water, called, 'Will you two keep quiet so you can hear if I'm in trouble.'

It had occurred to me that from the instant I had climbed inside the building until the time I was able to open an outside door; I would be very much on my own.

Dropping down from the sink, while cursing my wet feet, I took time to empty the water out of my trainers

Standing with my back to the rear kitchen window there were two doors to my left, double swing doors to my right and double swing doors ahead of me. First I walked to the double doors ahead of me, therefore at the back of the kitchen. Carefully, I opened one. It led to a very wide sort of carpeted promenade that ran from one side of the building to the other. It was sumptuously decorated and furnished with a few scattered chairs.

Next I opened one of the left hand doors that I could tell from the type of lever handle was a cold room. Nothing was stored inside, the racks gleaming, but empty in my torch light. As I shut the door there seemed to be an echo of some kind. I stood still as a mouse listening.

Not a sound, but a sixth sense made me uneasy and instinct told me all was not well. It was a feeling I had felt in the past when, in much the same way, you can sense when someone is standing behind you. In fact the feeling was so strong, I automatically looked over my shoulder, then cursed myself for a fool.

Question was what should I do next, go on, go back?

Conscious of Harry frantically waving through the window and pointing to the outside doors I moved to check. The outside door in the kitchen was screwed up and immovable. I felt a chill run through me. This was serious stuff; no admission or exit tolerated.

I turned back to the second door in the left hand wall and found it protected a large storeroom, empty of goods, but also containing the other outside door.

That door was also screwed to the door frame.

I returned to the kitchen and could see Harry outside; still gesticulating, pointing frantically to where I knew the other door we had seen was situated. I shook my head. Of course, Harry didn't know I had found out about the screwed up door so was hopping up and down like a madman.

I went cautiously to the double doors on the right hand side of the kitchen that I had already guessed must be the dining room and noticing the swing doors could be hooked back, I did just that, so that if I had to make a fast return, I would not be delayed. My hand was still on one of the doors when there was an indefinable but positive noise from above.

I froze, my fears realised, there was someone else in the building. I felt in control but was also aware panic wasn't too far away.

Did I hear it or was it my over stressed imagination?

Moving cautiously into the room, I was astonished to see all the tables still had white tablecloths. Surely the owners either left in a hurry or did not intend to be away long.

Ignoring the dining room's double doors to my left for they obviously led onto the carpeted central promenade, I headed to the far right hand corner of the room where I could see an emergency exit door. Gently pushing the door it opened easily to what I expected to be the outside world but it was instead a pitch black nothing. My torch revealed it to be a long corridor with a door at the far end. Hesitating, with memories of university games of Dungeons and Dragons, I felt uneasy about taking the risk of being trapped in a dark, windowless space. I fetched a chair from one of the tables and jammed the door open then entered the corridor cautiously walking carefully to the far end. Arriving, eventually, at the far door, I passed through into what seemed to be a staff room.

Joy of joys, there was an authentic looking emergency door in the back wall, but after finding so many doors screwed tight, would it open? I took a deep breath and pushed the bar. To my amazement the door did swing open. As I breathed again, an irate, red-faced Harry appeared, 'Where have you been?' he demanded.

'Safety door,' I announced nonchalantly, 'just push the bar in an emergency.'

He was not amused.

I led them inside showing the staff room and its little dining room adjacent the corridor, then back to the kitchen via the corridor, dining room and kitchen softly explaining the layout as we went.

While checking out the kitchen, we found the main power supply and the water had been disconnected. Again it was fortunate we had each armed ourselves with a powerful torch to use in any room without windows, including the hoped for strong room.

'It's time we found the real casino,' Harry exclaimed impatiently. 'We didn't come to inspect the servants quarters.' He marched back into the dining room and threw the doors I had left alone open, exposing, right ahead of us, a rather opulent foyer and beyond that what appeared to be the front doors to the building.

'Harry,' I protested, 'don't make so much noise, if there is anyone here they now know we are here too. I thought there was a noise upstairs just before I let you in.'

To left and right was the really wide corridor that I described as a promenade. The foyer was beautiful. We walked to the far end by the front doors and looked back. On each side two matching stairs, with gold and white wrought iron balustrades curved up, from the area near the front doors, in sweeping arcs to where they met again on the first floor. On one side a curved counter of polished wood formed an elegant reception desk and there were deep, easy chairs everywhere. Opposite the reception desk was a bar also matching the curved decor. I think we all, at least, thought "wow!"

From the foyer, archways, on the reception desk side, led the way into a very large, palatial gaming room. On the opposite side of the foyer more archways opened the way to a big lounge and another bar. We moved first to the grandly furnished gambling area. The room glittered with glass chandeliers.

Egg looked in wonder at the white, blue and gold carvings topped by ornate wall lights and chandeliers dripping with glass. 'Why would they shut away all this fine, expensive furniture and equipment and not make use of it?' he asked in wonder.

We lifted the dust covers on several tables and they were all that one would expect them to be, high quality gaming tables catering for various card games, dice and including a magnificent roulette wheel. 'So many ways of losing your money,' Egg breathed.

'There's nothing out of the ordinary here,' I announced regretfully. 'It is just what it's supposed to be, leaving us with Egg's question, why is it all empty of gamblers?'

A search of the ground floor produced no sign of a strong room or cellar and nothing else of note except that the doors Harry had thrown open from the dining room were faked to appear concealed from the foyer side. We also found the doors to the kitchen were the same. Further down the promenade from the dining room a door opened into an interesting room with a grilled counter facing across the foyer into the gambling area. Obviously it was the chips and cashing in room.

So we turned our attention to the cashing-in room. There we found a large, locked cabinet presumably made from steel that looked invincible. Harry told us it almost certainly held the stock of gambling chips. There was a fairly big safe, but not big enough to hold a very large stock of gold. On one wall a floor length board listing the odds on various games and special awards.

'Not exactly brilliant odds,' Harry remarked. 'Gambling is unlikely to tempt me.'

A room, to the left and next door to the chips room, also with a counter, we found to be a cloaks room and someone remarked it looked no larger or smaller than the chips room, but no one thought that was significant.

As we left the room heading back for the wide, sweeping stairs to the upper floors, I had the same feeling as earlier and suddenly stopped and shivered. 'There is someone here,' I exclaimed. Can anyone feel a presence? We are being watched, of that I'm absolutely certain.'

We looked round but could see nothing. 'It's just nerves,' Harry suggested.

I was unconvinced.

Egg shrugged, 'I feel nothing, but it occurs to me we have not protected ourselves by telling anyone we are coming here,'

On the next floor we found a few suites that were presumably for party or business hire, a number of bedrooms, and what was presumably the nerve centre of the whole operation. A large accounts and general purpose office as well as smaller offices. A control room with a bank of monitor screens covering all parts of the ground floor and remote controls for cameras and recording equipment. This office also had wide, tinted windows that overlooked the upper corridors and the tops of the two stairs.

There was another door, which we assumed was the manager's office. It was as we were about to enter the office that Egg suddenly stopped, putting a finger over his mouth and signalling us to go back.

As we stepped quickly back into the main office a door banged somewhere and I cried, 'I told you there was someone here. Did you see that fleeting black shape go past the window?

'I didn't see anything,' Harry replied asking Egg 'Did you?'

He shook his head.

'We'll make a quick search of the rooms on this floor. You're just a bit jumpy Rebecca.'

'No, I told you there is evil here and we are trespassing. You heard that door bang. Let's get out now. Why not simply ask for permission to look over the place? We could explain we are archaeologists and interested in the history and construction of Rochenoir's buildings. Come on, let's leave, I really don't like it here. I tell you, there's something wrong.'

Harry shrugged, 'It's better we remain low key and not attract attention to ourselves." An ambition to be destroyed sooner than I expected.

We searched the floor again but could find no one. Taking the next flight of stairs to the third floor took us only to more bedrooms. 'All empty of black shadows,' Harry remarked with a trace of sarcasm.

We turned back down the corridor towards the stairs and this time I screamed.

Egg looked pale, 'I saw it this time, Rebecca's not seeing things. It was just like a black shadow.'

We hesitated, considering our next move.

I turned to Egg, 'What did you see in the manager's office that made you back out?'

'There was a computer on the desk and its red standby light was on.'

'What's so unusual about that?'

'Rebecca, the main power supply is off. If there is some other arrangement for power to the computer in an otherwise empty building it must be for surveillance, they could be listening to us now.'

'We've come this far,' Harry said. 'If the computer is powered, there might be a chance of seeing what information is on it. I'll go back to the office and check it out. Egg, as a precaution, would you take Rebecca outside and I will follow in a few minutes.'

'I'm not leaving you,' I answered.

'Let's get on then.'

As we entered the manager's office Egg dived under the computer desk in search of power supplies. I kept watch by the door.

Harry did not need to switch on the computer, the screen lit up as he approached, and a few seconds later a man's face appeared.

'My name is Paul Vachon. This is a security announcement,' the man displayed on the screen said clearly, repeating the message in English and German. 'You have gained unauthorised admission and put yourself in danger. Stay where you are and do not move until escorted safely from this building.'

I realised instantly whoever it was speaking probably did not know about Egg and me. It was also obvious the only purpose to such a conversation was an attempt to delay anyone present from leaving the building, for there was no reason to talk at all. Someone would already have been sent to catch us on the property.

Harry answered the screen, not expecting a reply, 'I must have taken a wrong turn somewhere, and I'm lost.'

To our complete surprise the screen picture changed, still with the same man, and a voice answered. 'That does not amuse me. Are you the man named Graham?'

'Who?'

'I think it is time to teach you a lesson..........'

The screen went blank. Egg had disconnected the power supply.

Harry raised his hand impatiently, 'Gee, thanks, he was about to teach me a lesson.'

'Is it a bluff, do you think?' Egg asked.

I didn't think it was and from the expression on Harry's face he didn't either, but I put on a show of bravado. 'Whoever he sets on to us has to find us first, so the best thing to do is to hide.' I then copied Egg by putting my finger over my lips. They both realised my comments were to mislead in case the crooks were still listening for us.

We crept out of the inner office and ducked behind some filing cabinets where I handed out an emergency kit I had prepared and brought with me; very dark glasses for each of us and a small flare which I tossed to the middle of the office.

'I thought that was just a haversack for your lipstick you were carrying,' Harry said with a chuckle; a joke only he thought funny.

Signalling a warning to the others, I triggered the flare so the intense light would knock out any video cameras the crooks might be using.

We ran along the corridor to a fire escape door, but as Harry was about to open it Egg voiced a warning. 'We will be exposed on the side of the building, all the way down to the ground. Suppose they are armed?'

'We'll have to chance the stairs,' I said quietly, 'come on.'

I left them behind as I raced along the corridor and leading the way was almost at the top of the stairs when we had the shock of our lives. A black figure leapt from nowhere seizing me from behind with an arm round my throat. Only it was no shadow but a man dressed all in black, his face also darkened with make-up.

'Mettez-vous en bas!' he shouted at Egg and Harry

There was no way they were going to lay on the floor, but the issue didn't arise because when the man in black had raised his right arm – which presumably included a gun – he weakened his grip on me and I instantly turned into a whirling dervish which ended with my gripping the man in a judo hold that rendered him helpless as I propelled him towards the top of the stairs.

Realising what I was going to do, Harry shouted, 'No! Rebecca, No!'

I hesitated, which gave the rat I was holding another chance and he kicked me.

'You bastard,' I screamed and in a second twisted him off balance and sent him head over heels rolling down the stairs to the hall where he lay in an inert heap on the Foyer floor.

We ran down after him and I was relieved to hear him groaning as we passed on our way to the kitchen. Harry hastily put the swivel window back in order to cover our tracks and we raced for the emergency exit we had used to gain entry.

It would not open.

'It's been wedged on the outside,' Egg cried. 'What shall we do?'

'Go for the front door quick before anyone comes. It's our only chance,' Harry called urgently and we ran helter-skelter back to the Foyer and past the still inert man. Thankfully, the front door opened from the inside, and in seconds we plunged into a thick shrubbery.

We were only just in time for, even as we glanced back through the bushes, a car screeched to a halt outside the open front door and three men dressed in black ran inside.

None of us spoke until we were safe in Egg's armchairs, each of us holding a large cognac, as we waited for the black coffee and I nursed a bruised leg.

'You know,' Harry opened. 'If those men were the ones who hijacked the prison van and killed Coutard without mercy, we just had a lucky escape.'

Egg had serious thoughts on his mind as well. 'From what I've observed today of how you two handle yourselves, I think it might be time you took me into your confidence if we are to work together. Just exactly who are you?'

Revenge in Rochenoir

Chapter Eight
St Jean Pied-de-Port

I thought rapidly but could see no easy way to avoid Egg's question. 'Yes! You do have a right to know but our hands are tied. Yes, I am a working geologist and yes Harry qualified as an archaeologist. I think I told you we met at university. So you have my word that we have not lied to you about anything important in the quest for Sam's crooks. What I can't tell you is why we are here and I really hope you will take my word that we are on your side. I have already given your mother, Brigitte, my promise I will do all in my power to protect Claudine. I like and respect you and fervently hope we can work together.'

Egg grinned, 'That was quite a speech. I have never had any doubts about either of you. I suppose my fear was that you didn't trust me.'

I breathed a sigh of relief; he hadn't asked anything more about me.

'Anyway, I am the fool for it came to me as we drove back from Rochenoir that I had missed the anomaly for which we searched. We looked quite a long time at the chips room and the cloaks room next door and even remarked on them being the same size when we should have remembered the staff dining room'.

'Yes, I remember,' Harry agreed, 'but we found nothing there.'

'Ah!' I suddenly grinned like a Cheshire cat, 'I'm with you Egg, and we are all fools.'

'Someone better tell the biggest fool," Harry responded. 'What did we miss?'

'Don't feel badly,' I grinned again, 'instead remember that the staff dining room was square. So just tell us what was on the other side of the dining room.'

'Well it must be the back of the library, but we only had a cursory look in there. and,' as realisation dawned, 'the library can't fill the hole behind the chips room!'

'Trouble is,' Egg ventured, 'not only did we fail to realise the chips room and the cloaks could not possibly be the same size without leaving a space at the back, we even remarked on it. There must be something to fill the square bordered by the chips room, cloaks, back corridor and the two dining rooms, but we saw no door.'

'I claim back my intelligence,' Harry announced. 'How about the floor length gaming odds board that is on the back wall of the chips room? That undoubtedly covers the door into the strong room.

Our silence as we sat looking at each, other numb with the realisation we may have walked past the very object of our, well! burglary, was broken by the sound of the doorbell.

'That will probably be Claudine,' Egg leapt to his feet. 'She said she might stay if late leaving the tourist offices.'

As Egg opened the door, she looked surprised to see us, but immediately smiled in welcome. 'Fortunately,' she called, 'I come armed with all that is needed for guests.' She waved a bottle of rosé and, in doing so, dropped some of the packages of food clustered under her arms.

'Oh no!' I stood up quickly, 'we must not intrude on your evening. We were simply relaxing after our adventures.'

'Then you must stay, for I will certainly want to know all about those adventures.'

'Of course you must stay,' Egg added. 'What purpose is there in going down to your flat to cook when we have a willing volunteer here?'

He put his arm round Claudine and kissed her cheek. I don't know what it was about his gesture of welcome, but even a mere man like Harry detected the warmth. I turned away from them to open the kitchen door for her. Unseen by Egg or Claudine, Harry raised his eyebrows to me in a somewhat theatrical gesture as she passed, so clearly we were on the same wavelength.

Egg and Harry sat down chatting as Claudine and I produced a meal in a surprisingly short time. After friendly recriminations from us girls about the men drinking most of Claudine's wine while we worked in the kitchen, Egg produced a bottle of Chateneuf du Pape to round off our meal.

Although it was clear Claudine had something on her mind, she obeyed Egg's rules of no discussion of our adventures until the coffee and then Egg himself jumped in first when he told her we had been to the Casino that afternoon.

'Oh!' she replied, 'I wanted to come with you.'

He grinned, 'You'll have another chance I am certain. We think we have found the strong room and that news will probably have Graham flying out. He will let you join us for sure.' Egg then went on to give her a brief description of our activities and our narrow escape on leaving the building.

'Oh! Rebecca,' she exclaimed, 'do you think the man who fell down the stairs is dead?'

After assurances the man was still breathing when we left, Claudine could wait no longer. 'I wait for the coffee before I tell you my news and I burst inside from waiting because it sounds important.' Having thus gathered our rapt attention, she explained that a Spanish tourist office representative had told her it was possible to buy certain substances in St Jean Pied-de-Port. Claudine added that she had not realised at first the man meant drugs for they were not a problem in the area. When pressed he said he thought it might be cocaine and he had reported it to his superiors.

'Surely that's normal these days,' I exclaimed.

'Not here,' Claudine exclaimed, 'and we don't want drugs to become common, or for the tourists to learn that such things are easily available. What did my boss say? Oh yes! "It is bad for our image."'

'Well it would be easy to smuggle so close to the Spanish border,' I commented.

Egg looked puzzled and explained, 'Penalties are very high in France and Spain so it is a big risk and where would be their source? The nearest likely place is as far away as Bordeaux.'

'And Toulouse,' I added.

'That's true.'

'Anyway, you do not wait for the best part of my news. When I asked where he had been told was a likely place where drugs could be obtained it was to go to the Uharte car park, around the middle of the day, and look out for two men sitting in a car.'

'That's not much help.' Harry commented.

'Two men dressed all in black, sitting in a car.'

We played around with this for a while without reaching any conclusion. It was accepted the men were very likely to be connected with the ones we had seen, but all thought it best to steer clear of them for the moment. Egg couldn't have put it better.

'If the matter has been reported, leave it to the authorities.'

'Have you seen Jean lately?' I asked.

Claudine shrugged her shoulders and displayed a face without expression.

Egg poured some more wine, then paused. 'I think elle fait la tête. You know, bouder.'

'I am not sulking,' Claudine replied.

'Of course not,' Egg winked at Harry and me.

'Perhaps Rebecca and I should ask you all to a meal with us and see if Jean will come.' Harry suggested.

'Worth a try.' Egg replied, 'It's a shame to have this discord after we have known each other so long. But, it's Jean who is completely in the wrong.'

Claudine suddenly interrupted the conversation. 'Rebecca, I want to ask you a favour, but I don't know how to ask or if you will understand what I want to do.'

I'm sure I looked surprised and asked, 'Is it confidential, do you want Harry and Egg to leave the room?'

Looking a little embarrassed, Claudine said, 'Oh no! I want you all to know so there is no misunderstanding, but there is something my instinct tells me is right for me to do and I want to borrow Harry for the morning to help me.'

Laughing, I answered, 'I thought you wanted to borrow something valuable, of course you can have him.'

'I don't want to explain because I'm sure you will all laugh, but this is something I really feel I have to do and it is very important to me so I must ask you to trust me.'

'Dear Claudine, I would do so much more for you than lend you my husband. Of course I trust you and the answer is yes. How about Egg, does he mind?'

'Why should I mind?' Egg replied, 'Claudine is a free woman to do as she pleases.'

'Egg,' Harry intervened, 'you introduced Claudine to us as a friend of Jean, but I doubt there is anyone I have met who is closer to her than you.'

'Do you two men mind.' Claudine frowned at each of them in turn, 'This is something between me and Rebecca, we are old enough to make up our own minds.'

'Hang on, Harry protested, no one has asked me if I am prepared to go and I'm the sacrificial lamb.'

I thought to fall off my chair with laughing, 'Oh Harry, I don't know which is more funny, you describing yourself as a sacrificial lamb or the notion that you would turn down the chance of spending the morning with the prettiest girl in Rochenoir.'

Φ   Φ   Φ

Harry even put some aftershave on the next morning as he prepared to meet Claudine and his disappointment was comical when she phoned to change the plan. Fortunately, I answered the phone and she expressed relief. 'Oh! Rebecca, all night I have been thinking about what I want to do and have come to the conclusion I should not have asked Harry. I think it would not be right and I don't know what to say to him.'

'Don't worry, I can tell him for you. Do you want me to say anything in particular?

'Just tell him I am sorry and that you will explain later.'

'How will I do that?'

'I would like you to come with me instead, if you will.'

Φ   Φ   Φ

I drove over to Rochenoir and picked Claudine up from her home. She was waiting outside and jumped quickly into the car.

'If my mother saw me get into a car with someone she does not know it would, how do you say, stir her up, that I am arranging to meet a new boy friend. She is constantly trying to make me married. That's one of the reasons I asked you to come instead of Harry.'

Under instructions to drive to St Jean Pied-de-Port, Claudine quickly explained it was nothing to do with our discussion on the drugs. 'That simply reminded me of something that I really must do to,' she searched for the right words then triumphantly said, 'clear the air;' except she did not smile as I would have expected.

On the way I glanced at an obviously tense Claudine and explained, 'Look, I am not going to ask you any questions at all. I will do whatever you say and leave it to you to tell me as little or as much as you wish.'

'Thank you, Rebecca as I have said before you are very understanding. There is a ghost in my mind that I must put to sleep. I may be upset, but you must not notice, I will tell you more about why we go when we are there.'

I glanced at her curiously and was surprised to see her eyes already looked close to tears. I changed the subject quickly by asking her about St Jean and the route de Compostella.

When we reached the town Claudine directed me down a narrow street that led to the river where there were grassy banks on both sides with bench seats and picnic tables dotted about. After asking me to park Claudine sat silently and I did too.

'We have spoken about Sam,' she said suddenly. 'You know I blame myself whatever everyone says.' She held a hand up to quell an expected protest from me.

Realising she was still very close to tears, I kept still and quiet for a while.

Eventually, without looking at her, I said softly, 'It seems clear that this place has a special association with you and Sam. That surely is a happy memory?'

'There is only a mental association, for we were never here. The last promise I made to Sam was that we would come here for a picnic so I could show him the Roman bridge. I made many plans because for me it was going to be a very special picnic to thank him for all the help and support he gave me. That chance never came. It's simply that to think of this place now reminds me of my ghost and of what I might have done to avoid that awful situation when Sam was shot and that he would now still be alive.' I sensed rather than saw a tear or two trickle down her cheek.

'Oh Claudine, you must not think like that. As soon as Vachon took you away from everyone who loves you events were out of your hands. You would not have been freed. In almost every case a kidnapper kills his victim. Vachon would have killed you whatever happened that day. Think instead that Sam's regard for you was so strong that he was prepared to risk his life to save you from harm. Don't waste that heroic sacrifice by your own regrets.'

I twisted round in my seat. 'Instinct tells me you want me to help the spirit of Sam to understand so that you can feel at peace. There must be something else you have to tell me. Oh! Claudine, I am honoured you have asked me to accompany you to this special place.'

We sat quietly in silence for a while. Finally she stirred and vaguely dabbed her cheek with a tissue, then said simply, 'Come.'

I followed her along the river to a lovely old stone bridge. 'This is Roman,' she announced waving an arm towards the bridge. She paused then continued in quite a calm voice. 'On one of my happiest days when in the mountains with Sam, I promised to bring him here to see the bridge. That never happened because he was killed, and somehow those things focus together in my thoughts. Already, just by coming here, I feel easier in my mind. I could never have come here on my own and visiting the bridge has broken a spell. I think now that only the happy times will be my thoughts.'

'Always think that, Claudine,' I answered. 'Only the happy times are important.'

When I dropped her off at the Tourist Office, she leaned across and kissed my cheek. 'Thank you, Rebecca,' she said simply. 'I will never be able to tell you how much this morning meant to me, but I will never mention it again. I now feel able to live the rest of my life in peace.'

Φ   Φ   Φ

Impatient with nothing much happening, I wondered if there was anything I could do to push our investigation along. Graham seemed to be tied up with I didn't know what, Egg and Claudine busy at work and Harry involved in some project at the university. On the investigation front we seemed to be simply waiting for Paul Vachon to be caught. I phoned Hélène and asked if she was free to have a chat.

'Rebecca, I am desolée, was it anything important? I take a class at the university in an hour.'

Explaining my thoughts it occurred to me a big hole in my ambition was that I had no idea who or what to prod. Hélène filled the slot for me unintentionally.

'I suppose you want to tidy up some of the loose ends like these odd gold bars that have been mentioned from time to time. I can understand Coutard, Vachon and Duval having a share, but not why Claudine and Egg think the gold is hidden in the mountains.

'Exactly Hélène. Would you like to meet me for a coffee sometime so that we can make some sort of plan.'

She readily agreed, but we made no immediate arrangement.

Φ   Φ   Φ

'Penny for your thoughts,' the offer came from Harry when he found me idly doodling with papers spread on our dining table.

'Oh it's just something I discussed with Hélène.'

'And?'

'We were wondering if any of the gold was still tucked away in hiding places and forgotten now the crooks are dead.'

'Aren't we all?'

'More specifically, I was wondering if there is any lost gold, where is it hidden?'

'Aren't we all?'

'Oh! Funny, I'm being serious.'

Well! I dare not say, "Aren't we all" again, so what's on your mind?'

'Simply wondering if Graham and his crowd are looking at this aspect. They seem to be happy the gold is shared and gone, but take Duval. If Coutard, Duval and Vachon split their loot three ways and had, say, a million each, Graham's traced barely half of that in various bank accounts. They found Duval dead with six gold bars, where's the rest of his nest egg. Then there's Coutard and Vachon's share.'

'Coutard's share was found in the wood yard by Sam.'

'And Coutard moved it pronto, where is it now?'

'I see what you mean. Why don't you ask Graham?'

'I will, but he already thinks we are too interested in the gold so I might get a dusty answer.

Which, when I phoned Graham that evening was exactly what happened.

'Rebecca, don't worry your pretty little head about it. There's a team of people working on analysing the gold movements and bank accounts.'

'Don't pretty little head me.' I snapped, 'You condescending ......ooh!'

'That's not a ladylike discussion, Rebecca.'

'After I'd put the phone down I resolved to talk to Egg about his information that they had seen Duval on the mountain Leizar Athéka. Seen him there more than once. I decided to ask Egg what he thought about Duval's gold and was he taking it to the mountain?

Φ   Φ   Φ

Hélène and I met at the Artisans for coffee while we discussed our progress to date and what was the best investigation for us now that Graham had called us Holmes and Watson.

'Rebecca, you once mentioned a connection with Leizar Athéka, surely that's a possibility if someone has been hiding something it might be there?'

'Possibly, but Sam and the Musketeers thought the public footpath over the mountain was the route the crooks used to take gold backwards and forwards. Taking gold ingots out to be melted down and bringing amateur gold bars back in a form that could not be identified.'

'How was it organised?'

'Apparently, there is a horse ranch up there and that may have been a staging post; a sort of swapping place. Egg mentioned the couple who own the ranch, Philippe and Maria. He said they were good people at heart and Graham decided to do nothing about them.'

'So they could still be involved, or holding a gold stock that no one knows exists.'

'I suppose so, yes. I did ask Egg yesterday about the couple who run the ranch and he said they had been cleared as ok. He admitted they where slightly involved with the gold smuggling, but were not prosecuted. He suggested arranging for us to meet them sometime and I agreed it would be a good idea.'

'No, Rebecca, I don't think we should wait. We will go and have a look as soon as possible.'

Chapter Nine
A Close Encounter

Waiting until Harry was out; I telephoned Egg at his place of work. After an exchange of greetings I opened with an apology. 'Sorry, but thinking about it I want to go against our agreement of last night and follow up Claudine's story about the drugs. Is it safe to discuss this on your line, or should I pop up to see you this evening?'

'Both' Egg chuckled. 'This is not my phone, so would you hang up and I'll call you back.'

It seemed an eternity before he phoned with an apology of his own for keeping me waiting so long, although he did not explain the delay.

'What is your concern?' he asked.

'That the only direct clue we have that might lead us to whoever has taken the place of Coutard and company is the men wearing black. I think we should follow up Claudine's information. Just you and me, for it's likely to be a dangerous thing to do. Sorry to suggest this for it was your idea we stood back and left it to the authorities.'

'The only reason I said that was because of the risk. Graham said we should not seek to solve the mystery because we might put ourselves in danger.'

'That's why I suggest we go to St Jean on Saturday without Claudine and Harry.'

'Rebecca, our little group formerly faced danger all the time, so dangerous, Sam was killed. You have no need to worry about Claudine and I am sure that Harry can look after himself. We are already in danger because they know who we are and we don't have that same advantage.'

'You're not keen on the idea, then?'

'No, thinking about it, I think you are right, we can't just sit and wait, especially as it's you two girls they have targeted so far.'

'I hadn't registered that.' I replied. 'Was there a reason for that do you think, or did it just work out that way?' My thoughts went into overdrive.

After a couple of minutes Egg asked, 'Are you still there?'

'Yes, just thinking about what you said.'

'We knew who the enemy were last time,' Egg replied, 'and that made it easier to try and keep out of tricky situations. By the way Graham's back in London. I told him about the Casino in an e-mail last night and he was back on to me in minutes. He asked me for your e-mail address, living so near, we have never seen a need to exchange it.'

I gave my e-mail address to Egg and made a note of his and asked, 'What are we going to tell Graham about the Men in Black?'

'If you agree, I will tell him the four of us - I'm certain Claudine will join us - are going to do a bit of careful investigating of the drugs on Saturday. I warn you we will both then have an e-mail back from him telling us to take up something like boules instead.'

I laughed, 'If he asked for my address, it sounds as if I'm in for a wigging anyway, no doubt for visiting the Casino.' I laughed again as a thought struck me, 'At least I can say it was your idea. Egg, will you come down later with Claudine for a bit of supper and we'll have a chat about it. By the way, I followed up your suggestion and asked Jean to join us for a meal and he said he was too busy.'

'I can't say that I am surprised,' Egg said sadly, 'I don't think he is going to change his mind about our plans. That does not worry me, but I am concerned he will try to pursue our investigation on his own. Acting in isolation will almost certainly be dangerous and put him in peril of his life.'

'I don't see that there's anything more that can done. Do you think it might help if I went to speak with him?'

'I think it might make him worse.'

Φ   Φ   Φ

We guessed wrong about the e-mails for the phone rang ten minutes later and it was Graham. 'What's going on Rebecca, I don't like the sound of any of this?'

Neither of us had anything very new to say and he took my point that we were more at risk by knowing nothing about the Men in Black than by embarking on a little careful investigation. He was adamant we should not go back to the Casino and said he would try to fly out in a few days so he could assess the situation. 'We will go and check it out,' he explained. 'But it may be a good idea to tell Ramel what we are doing first.' He gave me a telephone number, which I fortunately wrote down as he spoke because he would not repeat it. 'If something unusual crops up and you really have to go to the Casino before I come, do not go alone. Phone that number and discuss what you intend to do with Marius first. He will almost certainly fly down to join you.'

Of course, Claudine and Harry were all for the trip to St Jean. 'We do not seem to be doing so much with gathering knowledge of who hides the gold that must still be hidden somewhere,' Claudine said while agreeing. 'Perhaps these Men in Black have a different scheme and are nothing to do with our search?'

'Not likely,' Harry argued. 'Remember they shot Coutard.'

'What seems strange? Egg mused, 'is that they would look for attention by all dressing in the same clothes.'

'I think that's to frighten people,' I added my view. 'Especially simple country people who tend to be superstitious.'

'I had a lecture this afternoon from Graham,' Egg replied. 'He doesn't seem to think we are frightened enough.'

I added to Egg's comment, 'He phoned me to say we should stay away from the Casino, but if we did go back to phone Marius first. He gave me his number.'

Claudine expressed surprise, 'Is Comte Bertin still here? I thought he must have gone back to Paris.'

Egg looked at the number I had written. 'This is a Paris number.'

Considering the short notice, the meal I produced was described as excellent and, in view of the wine we consumed it was fortunate we all lived in the same block.

Claudine, who still had the car she shared with Jean, insisted she would drive the next day. She explained the car was useful for commuting to Pau and she had not seen Jean for a while. With an unusual obstinacy that may have saved our lives, Harry was even more positive that he would drive, softening his determination by explaining our hire car was more powerful than Claudine's.

I joked to Claudine, 'Surely you and Egg are more used to a tough four-wheel-drive for your adventures? Our car can't match that, but it is nearer to a tank than yours.' Of course, I also had to explain comparison of their car to a tank. Egg suggested "La char" for the next time we wanted to insult their car.

Behind the banter, I think that secretly Claudine was happy Harry insisted on driving.

It was yet another beautiful day as we drove to St Jean. The distant mountains had a slight blue haze and looked almost as if they had been painted on the sky. Normally a fairly quiet road that had once been part of the route to Compestella, on this day the road was virtually deserted by other traffic.

Claudine, sitting in the car beside Harry, produced a request that unknown to me showed a marked change in her mood since the funeral when she asked, or rather stated, 'Harry, can we go to the Kakouétta if there is time this afternoon?'

'Why?' I asked, not knowing this was a question she had almost always asked when Sam was driving in this direction. Claudine, I discovered, had a theory the Cathar treasure was hidden in the area of the Kakouétta but had made no attempt to visit since Sam died.

Egg replied to my question for her, 'You and Harry should be interested because the Kakouétta is a wild, remote Gorge that's Claudine's favourite as a place where the Cathar treasure might be hidden, and might be one of the places where the wartime "Gang-of-Four" hid the gold.'

'Sounds a good idea then,' Harry said, 'we'll see what time we have, perhaps we should have brought a picnic. Tell me, who's the "Gang-of-Four?" Obviously something to do with your past adventures!'

'Oh!' Claudine replied, 'this is one of the matters that will occur in our searches. Matters about past events that we should have explained but we forget.'

'It is inevitable,' I leaned forward in the back seat. 'Everything you did must be so clear in your mind, that you think we also know. Being a woman and more intelligent than Harry, I can guess it was Coutard, Duval and Vachon, but who was the fourth?'

Egg laughed, 'I will ignore your assessment of men. Otherwise, the guess is very good but wrong by a generation. It was the fathers of Coutard, Duval and Vachon who were in the Gang of Four and the fourth was a man named Pierront who fled to England after the war.'

'Fled?'

'Yes, he inherited the Manoir after his father was murdered during the confusion at the end of the war. It is believed Pierront also had been threatened; possibly a settling of old scores left over from the war. Whatever the problem Pierront thought it best to leave. More recently, Graham, while in Dorset, shot him dead when he threatened Sam.'

'Wow,' I exclaimed, 'You did tell me Graham shot Perront, but there is a lot we don't know. No wonder you refer to your past activities as an adventure.'

'Look out,' Harry interrupted, 'we are approaching St Jean. Where do you want to go?'

'The Uharte car park, of course.'

Harry parked and we walked round a little, but saw no car with men dressed in black.

Egg dived into a shop saying he would ask a friend if he knows anything, but came back with a long face. 'He says he has heard nothing, but I'm sure he is not telling the truth. I hope my guess is wrong for I counted this man as a friend.'

I consoled him. 'Don't be hard on your friend, Egg. If you are right it means he's afraid and if that's the case we are on the right trail.'

We spent a merry hour touring the shops, with grumbles from the men when Claudine and I explored a ladies clothes shop. We settled, for lunch, in a riverside restaurant with a balcony that also had a view of the car park.

As we lingered over coffee discussing what to do next, Coutard's widow, Arlette walked in. Harry jumped up immediately and asked her to join us, at the same time introducing her to Claudine and Egg.

Arlette smiled a little longer at Egg as she asked, 'An unusual name?'

'It's from Thunderbirds.'

'Don't ask,' Claudine interrupted.

Arlette laughed, 'I will leave you to be a man of mystery,' she whispered to Egg.

A pink-eared Egg sat down as we ordered more coffee.

While we chattered away, I introduced a tricky question as an experiment to test Arlette explaining to her, 'A puzzle the other day when a complete stranger knew who we were, yet almost no one knows we are here.'

'I know who you are,' she replied. 'Do you think I told someone?'

Avoiding answering her question I asked instead, 'This person was someone who knew where we lived.'

'Where do you live?'

'The Emile Zola flats in Orthez.'

My silent companions looked a little wide-eyed at my questions as Arlette responded, 'Ah! I see a connection with the troubles your friends had with my husband. Is this some kind of test for me?'

'No, Arlette, not exactly. I am certain you are as good as your husband was bad. It was just a clumsy fishing trip for information.'

'Then you should ask your questions directly, Rebecca. Really I know nothing of the past activities. Perhaps you already know the connection I just mentioned is that your flats are partly owned by Yoland Ferrand who also owned the cottage rented by your friend who was killed. Another link is that the son of Yoland married the daughter of the late Bertrand Duval.'

That was a possibly important piece of information that at least Harry and I did not know.

Egg filled the following silence, 'You said Yoland Ferrand was part owner of the flats. Do you know who owns the rest?'

'Yes, I do.'

As we parted company, Arlette gave me her card. 'Call to see me any time and welcome, but there is not much I can tell you. I have spoken several times with the police.'

Φ   Φ   Φ

We walked slowly to the car park, our next move undecided.

'All the time we discover how much we do not know,' Claudine said in a sad voice.

Suddenly, I shouted for Harry who was trailing behind still talking to Arlette, 'Come on,' I cried. 'The driver of the white car that's just gone past was dressed all in black.'

'Go,' Egg assessed the situation immediately. 'Get your car. I'll wait here to see where he turns.'

Claudine and I ran across to the car and I spun the wheels pulling away, but remembered to stop for Egg to climb in the back and Harry to jump in the front seat left empty for him by Claudine. The move went smoothly without comment. 'We are a team!!!' I registered as we streaked up the road. No hesitation, in spite of the surprise. We all knew what we had to do and did it quickly. I smiled with satisfaction; we had a chance of success.

The white car took the road south.

'Heading for the Spanish border,' Claudine observed.

I lost sight of the white car occasionally as the road twisted and turned and once Egg had found a map, dropped out of sight completely a couple of times. I thought my timing perfect for not alerting the men we were following until our car swept round a long bend and we saw the white car waiting at the side of the road.

Harry said 'Damn!'

Egg said, 'Drive straight past without going slow.'

Something I would have done anyway, but I acknowledged Egg's help.

'What do we do now?' Harry asked.

'I think in Volcarlus, which comes soon,' Claudine explained, 'they often have market stalls. Tourists which we wish to copy would stop to look.'

'Right,' I replied.

'Have we a camera?' Egg asked. 'We could pretend to take photos.'

None of us had a camera.

Harry had an idea, 'My mobile phone is bigger than some. I will hold it like a camera. Should be enough to fool someone in a passing car.'

Our luck was in and all went to plan. Harry was ready to fool the men as he stood facing Egg, Claudine and me as we posed by a colourful stall. I said in a singsong voice, 'The white car comes now.'

Then, as I saw the car swish past us I sang, 'It is slowing up, take another picture.'

Harry called for another pose from us models and crouched down with his fake camera as I have seen newsmen do with real cameras.

'The car has driven on,' I sang.

Claudine laughed, 'Will you be making a record of your song?'

'I think I should.'

Harry told me later he thought he could see why Graham is concerned that we do not respond with fear when we are in danger, but all blessings for that.

As we returned to the car, Harry and I had a minor dispute over who should be driving, but I insisted that having started the chase I would finish the job. Secretly I was enjoying myself.

Egg was back to his study of the map as I drove after the white car taking care not to catch up with it too soon. 'There are two chances to see them ahead,' he explained. 'Near Casa Guardiano the road climbs the side of the mountain and we should be able to see their progress.'

'And they ours,' I observed wryly.

I saw Egg grin in the rear view mirror.

'And at Roncesvalles we may be able to stop on high ground and watch where they turn at a road junction down on the plain. That will be the next turn we reach so we can't lose them.'

'Except in Roncesvalles,' Claudine reminded.

A lighter thought occurred to me to balance the tension. 'I suggest that we can't keep saying, the men, it, them, the white car and so on. Let's call our quarry what they are, "the thugs.'

'Yes I agree, Rebecca,' Claudine replied with a laugh, 'Les voyous.' Then she leaned back, smiling, 'Ils ont l'air un peu voyou.'

As we approached the mountain pass we had another stroke of luck, there was a large lorry parked in just the right place. I pulled up tight behind it, out of sight of the road above. We all jumped out and peered round both ends of the lorry looking for les voyous.

We saw they were just driving clear of the trees near the start of the climb.

Next, the lorry driver climbed down out of his cab, holding a truncheon, clearly intent on finding out if he was about to be hijacked.

Three of us watched as Claudine charmed the Spaniard from aggression into submission, then we climbed into our car and I drove off, sped on our way with a cheery wave from the driver.

'What did you say to him?' I asked.

'That is my secret,' Claudine replied.

Hopefully making up lost time, I roared up the steep climb, tyres protesting on the hairpins, while Harry grumbled about women drivers from the passenger seat. Then, taking advantage of a long stretch of straight road and a lesser incline, I climbed faster, racing the car into a bend below Casa.

'Hell!!!' I exclaimed.

On the road ahead, just across a deep cleft in the mountain and directly opposite us, the white car was just climbing out of a long hairpin then it disappeared round another bend.

'Did they see us?' Claudine cried.

No one knew.

I drove on more cautiously, concentrating on not, unexpectedly, catching up on our adversary.

We approached Roncesvalles, where Egg had forecast there would be a spot where we could see the road down on the plain, so I stopped. There were three turns les voyous could take on the road ahead. Egg acknowledged that was correct, pointing out he had seen from the map we would be able to see all three junctions from our vantage point. He even added the information that the village down on the plain was called Burguet.

We watched as les voyous drove through the village and took the next left turn from the road we were on, and headed east.

'I don't think they could have seen us,' Egg said hopefully.

I took off immediately, for we were now a long way behind our quarry, then made the same turn east, putting on a bit of speed as we raced along the valley floor. We passed through a village and Egg explained we were approaching a junction where he thought left was the best guess, but perhaps Harry ought to have a quick look at the map.

As I stopped, ignoring Egg's chauvinist comment, and Harry studied the map, he explained, 'The right turn goes south so unless they are going somewhere local, why turn off the main road?'

'So you think the most likely direction they took was, towards "Arive?" Egg answered.

Claudine leaned forward from the back, 'Arive sounds familiar, can I see the map?'

Egg traced his finger across the map. A pale Claudine leaned back in her seat, 'I thought so,' she explained, 'see just up the mountain from there is "Aria."

Egg explained so quickly he fell over his words a little, 'Aria is where Vachon took Claudine after he kidnapped her.'

'So, we are on the right track.' Harry replied. 'Get moving, Rebecca, let's get on and have a look at Aria.'

I had already reached between the front seats and taken Claudine's hand after her first mention of Aria and upon Harry's words I said, 'Men have no feelings at times.'

Harry looked round and seeing my hand with Claudine's, cried 'Oh! sorry, sorry,' he turned, red faced with mortification. 'I was just carried away with the chase.'

Claudine smiled wanly, 'I'm fine, Harry, go ahead Rebecca, we must do this.'

A car passed us so slowly it almost stopped, then sped ahead.

'That was les voyous,' I said grimly.

'How?' Egg exclaimed. 'How? We didn't pass them.'

'Only one way,' I replied. 'They must have stopped in the village.'

All were tense as I drove on. We were outwardly unafraid, even though the area and the road were completely deserted, offering no chance of help if we found ourselves in trouble. No one voted to go back. I grimly drove on into the unknown, but I did decide to give Aria a miss on this visit.

Arive was deserted and we roared through along an empty road, but a shock waited round the next long hairpin when the white car shot out from shrubbery at the side of the road and stopped broadside across the road in an attempt to block our way.

My passengers had a fright when I shouted "bastards" and swerved round the back of the white car as lurching and crashing, I managed to scrape between the car and the edge of the road, scattering a welter of small rocks and bits from the bushes.

'Bloody hell!' Harry gasped, 'I didn't think you would get through there.'

'You weren't alone,' I replied and although shaken, Egg patted my shoulder.

There was a jolt and a bang from behind. The white car had caught up with us and les voyous had demonstrated their arrival by ramming the rear of our car. I put the accelerator to the floor and was pulling away from our pursuers when a crack came from the back of our car and something hit the roof lining.

Claudine gave a little scream.

'That was a bullet,' Egg explained in rather a tense voice.

Try as I might it was impossible to shake the Men in Black off as the narrow road twisted and turned. Twice I saw spurts of dust in the road, which I took to be bullets and Egg, reported another crack in the back as a bullet in the boot.

I noticed a track to our left as we raced round a bend, then with horror, realised the road ahead was wider and more dangerous for us. On impulse, I slammed the brakes on, surprising the driver behind who shot past us before braking. I jammed one foot on the accelerator and the other on the brake while making a screaming turn in the road. I could hear Harry shouting 'Rebecca, look out! as we roared back round the corner and I turned the wildly leaping car onto the track, gunning the car up the slope, round another corner and through some trees. 'I hope this track goes somewhere,' I shouted at my shocked and speechless passengers. It did, into a quarry.

'We would have raised a cloud of dust going up the track,' Egg shouted. 'They must have seen the way we went.'

I did another squealing turn to head back.

Egg was right. The white car appeared up the track and was almost into the quarry when I drove straight towards it.

We all screamed together as our car hurtled towards a head on collision.

For a split second I could see the other driver's white face.

Our car tore on, until only yards away. I was shaking all over with fear.

The other driver lost his nerve, wrenching his car off the road into some bushes to avoid us as Harry was shouting at me, 'You bloody idiot!!'

Not until we had racketed back down to the road did I spare time to shout back, 'If I had stopped, they are armed, they would have killed us, we had nothing to lose.'

Egg, his voice shaking, called, 'They are catching up with us again, Rebecca.'

All our faces were as white as death masks, and the others were hanging on grimly as they continued to shout warnings of the crooks' continual attempts to pass. My fleeting glances behind showed the white car swinging from side to side seeking an advantage, as I did the same to block them off. 'Just waiting for me to make a mistake,' I thought with a shiver. Once they almost made it and the two cars ground together and it seemed everyone was shouting. Again the other driver lost his nerve as a bend approached and he dropped back.

Our high-speed chase changed to the even more dangerous situation with the road skirting the edge of the large lake. This made our pursuers more aggressive, forcing their car along inside of ours intent on pushing us in the lake. I could hear their tyres squealing from the powerful thrust of the white car's engine as they rammed their car into ours. The cars banged and scraped against each other as we literally fought a duel, slithering and slipping at high speed on the lakeside road. Almost they got through at one stage and I could feel our car being pushed remorselessly towards the edge overhanging the lake.

'Hang on,' I shouted, not knowing why, then came a harder lurch when the other car hit a roadside rock which literally threw their car in the air as it leapt our way, half falling on our roof and pushing us towards the lake. I held on to the steering wheel with all my strength, fearful sweat running down my face as I thrust my foot down on the accelerator as hard as I could causing us to skid violently sideways as we tore free of the other car. I looked back in a haze as, violently shaking, the white car dropped back and all was suddenly quiet.

Seeing nothing in what was left of our mirrors, I braked to a halt.

'What happened? I asked.

Harry leaned my way. 'Take this calmly, Rebecca. They went out of control and into the lake.'

Chapter Ten
Problems Galore

Shaking a little, I opened the car door and stepped out to find we were barely three feet from the edge of the drop into the lake. I stood dumbly watching the water lapping just below the level of the road. My eyes scanned the surface, but I didn't know what I expected to see.

Harry joined me, putting his arm round my waist. 'Are you alright?' he questioned anxiously.

'Yes,' I replied with a slight tremor in my voice. 'Egg, Claudine,' I called.

'We're OK,' Egg answered. 'You hadn't told me you were a stunt driver.'

'Don't joke,' Claudine reproached, 'I was terrified.'

Indeed, we all looked badly shaken.

We walked back along the road and found some scuff marks we assumed to be where the car plunged in the lake. With a feeling of horror, I could just make out the fading circle of ripples from the white car's impact with the water.

There was a battered piece of white painted metal trim lying in the road nearby. Harry picked it up and threw it in the lake after the car. I felt relief that his action had destroyed the sinister pattern.

No one commented.

'You would think there would be oil or something,' Harry said, waving towards the clear water. As we stood there a couple of ducks flew from the bushes behind us and landed in front of us on the water. I watched as they indignantly ruffled their feathers at this violent intrusion into their world.

'What are we going to do?' was Claudine's practical comment.

My thoughts were still on the other car. 'Those poor devils down there.'

'Are you crazy Rebecca,' Harry said angrily, 'minutes ago they were trying to kill us? But for your skilful driving that would be us down there.'

We walked back to look at our car, badly dented and scored on the left hand side, dents on the roof and side and the back bashed in.

'And at least two bullet holes, Egg added.

An inconsequential thought occurred to me. 'Egg, how did you know we took a bullet in the boot of the car?'

He put his hand in his pocket and produced the bullet. 'It came through the seat and hit me in the back,' he explained.

Claudine gave a little cry, 'You must be hurt, take off your jacket.'

We all inspected Egg's back, but none with more concern than Claudine. She kept repeating, 'You were nearly killed, I can't believe it.'

'Is someone going to tell me how nearly killed I was?' Egg asked plaintively

We all laughed, easing the tension.

'You have a fine bruise just below your neck,' I explained. 'But Claudine's right, you will never come closer to death than you did today.'

Claudine hugged him, 'Oh! Egg,' she repeated a couple of times.

'I think it's time I phoned Marius.' My voice was reluctant.

'No,' Claudine replied emphatically, 'let's get away from here first. I never want to see this place again.'

In fact, once we climbed in the car, no one wanted to stop anywhere, they were content to slump in their seats with their thoughts. Harry had offered to drive us back and I made no objection feeling a little shaky after all the excitement. When we arrived at Louis's garage, Harry pulled into the forecourt where he carefully parked with the badly damaged side of the car away from the road.

Louis came out of his garage concern clearly visible on his face.

He did not mention the car, but asked, 'Are you all in a good state?'

Claudine laughed and wrapped her arms round his powerful torso. 'Oh Louis, thank you for that, you asked exactly the same thing when we had a near miss before. I feel better already.'

He looked a mixture of mildly embarrassed, pleased, and, well! Claudine is a beautiful woman and I don't suppose many of those throw their arms round him. He gruffly suggested we moved to his office. He had already sent a mechanic to put a saucepan of water on for coffees.

Louis recovered his sense of humour as we settled on a variety of seats with the very welcome hot drinks. 'I won't ask any questions. We at Le Rendezvous des Agents Provocateurs accept that what looks like a motor destruction rally to the rest of the world is part of an ordinary day for the tourist.'

'Louis, my friend,' Harry responded, 'we keep no secret from you.' and he gave him a brief run down on the day's events.

'We have a saying about first things,' Louis replied. Would one of you make more coffee while I deal with first things?

I made the coffee while watching Louis and a mechanic bring our car in and park it in a corner of the voluminous garage. They then thoroughly checked over the car, finishing by covering it with a tarpaulin.

He came into the office and gave Harry another bullet. 'Your car was hit four times,' he explained.

'Louis,' I answered,' I have to speak to Marius and Graham before Harry and I can make any arrangements for the car. Perhaps I may use your telephone?'

'Bien sur,' he replied. 'Would you wish to speak privately? My house is behind the garage.' He took me round and opened the door into his house, showing me where he had a telephone in a small cluttered office. 'I will find a car for you to use until something is arranged.' He told me, 'Just pull the door shut when you have finished.'

Praying Marius was there, I dialled the number. He answered the phone personally and after greetings, I told him the story.'

'Are you all unhurt?'

'Yes, Egg has a bruise from a bullet ricochet, and we are all a bit shaken.'

Marius issued instructions, 'I must discuss this with Graham and that may not be until this evening. Do nothing about the car in the lake; I will arrange for that with Commissaire Ramel when I have finished speaking with you. Of course, it's important none of you speak of this until we have investigated who these men dressed in black are. Their associates will not know what has happened to their compatriots and the dead men will simply be missing as far as they are concerned. They may think the police have them and Ramel might make use of that. Now, it is important I speak with Louis rather than give you a message. Are you happy about that?'

'Yes, I'll fetch him for you.'

Still feeling mildly shocked, I walked back to fetch Louis. Marius's use of the words "dead men" brought home to me the enormity of the incident. I realised my actions hadn't actually killed them, but certainly my every move had unintentionally played a part in their death.

Later, Louis provided us with a red Peugeot, while having his usual joke, this time about the colour assuring us that other drivers will have a better chance of seeing us. He took me to one side and said Marius had left it to him to sort out the damage to the hire car. Louis rubbed the side of his nose. 'I have a friend in Bordeaux who specialises in difficult cars and he will have it like new very quick.' He gave a couple of red roses from his garden to Claudine and me, telling us we were with the wrong sort of men. 'Such ladies as you two should be worshipped, not engaged in a dangerous activity like tourism.' Then he looked serious, 'Take very great care,' he added. 'If anything happened to either of you it would fill me with sorrow.'

Φ Φ Φ

Egg suggested we all went to his parents in Labaraquette to relax and talk. 'It's a place far away from our activities,' he explained.

Of course, he was right, the psychological warmth of the farmhouse immediately enveloped us and we relaxed to the ministrations of Brigitte and Albert. All the horror of our afternoon receded, and our brains became more orderly, the tensions in our muscles slipping away.

We did not elaborate on our chase while telling Brigitte and Albert we had been trying to evade two of the Men in Black, but did say the bandits skidded into the lake while chasing us and the police did not want it discussed until they finished their investigations. That was more than enough to put Brigitte in a flurry, which led to her telling Claudine it was time she found a husband and did normal things like starting a family.

'That's a non runner, I'll wager,' I was smilingly musing to myself when Harry startled me out of my reverie.

'Obviously Brigitte thinks you are too far-gone to be saved,' Harry joked with me.

Claudine sat down to dinner and said, 'I can't believe it. How many people in the world are shot at in a car and that's happened to me twice.'

'It's not so rare,' Egg answered. 'It's happened twice to me as well.'

His humour helped to make a reasonably merry meal as the conversation steadily increased; a conversational hum silenced when the phone rang.

Albert answered and offered the phone to Harry with one word, 'Graham.'

The rest of us had to be content with half a conversation.

'No! We are all fine, the only injury a bruise on Egg's shoulder.'

'No! We've spoken to no one except Marius and Louis.'

'Louis is dealing with the car. He has a friend in Bordeaux.'

'No! Louis said he would remove the number plates before he took the car in.'

'They must still be in the car. There was no sign of life and we were there about 20 minutes.'

'No! It was very hot and they had their windows half open when they passed us. The car will have filled quickly and they were probably unconscious in any case.'

Both Brigitte and Claudine stirred at this comment.

'We have no idea who they are except you remember they came to the Casino and also threatened Louis. We had a report they were selling drugs in St Jean, but I think this was a side line, making money for themselves without the boss knowing.'

'You think so? It is certainly a possibility and would explain one or two things.'

'That's good, we'll look forward to seeing you in a couple of days.'

'I told you, Claudine's fine.'

Returning to the table I asked as he sat down, 'Explain what one or two things?'

'Oh!' Harry said, 'nothing important.'

I pointed my knife in his direction and said, 'Spill the beans.'

'Rebecca! It's bad luck to point a knife.'

'Well spotted, talk.'

Albert interceded to pour calm on our argument, 'don't ask Harry now. He will know when to tell you what you need to know.'

I hoped my face showed my feelings on that matter, but dropped the subject.

Gradually, as the evening progressed, we felt easier talking to each other about the chase, which was good therapy especially for dealing with the situation in the future.

Brigitte insisted we all stayed the night saying she had enough bedrooms.

No one argued and we all had another drink.

Contemplating my brandy, I remarked, ' We are going to have to go back to Spain and look into that area. At least try to find out where the Men in Black were heading before they became suspicious of us.

My comment unsettled Claudine. 'Thanks to your driving, Rebecca, we were lucky today. I don't want to risk going there again. But, as you say, we must. I really don't want to see that lake again. I'm sure I will have a cauchemar about it tonight.'

'We may both have a nightmare,' I answered, 'but I hope we both sleep peacefully instead.'

'They may not have been going to the lake,' Egg suggested. Their destination may have been somewhere else, but they followed us when we aroused their suspicions.'

Claudine fetched a map from some bookshelves and studied it. There is an old monastery somewhere up in the mountains between Roncesvalles and Leizar Athéka, that would make a good hide out.'

At my request Claudine agreed to search for more information on the Monastery at the Tourist Office in Pau where she is based.

'Of course,' she said. 'The road we were on also goes to Iraty and to within eight kilometres of Leizar Athéka.'

'What's the importance of Iraty?' I questioned.

Egg laughed, 'Very important to Claudine, it is close to the Kakouétta we spoke of earlier, but Holçarté is closer. Anyway if the Men in Black were going there it would have been much shorter to have gone through Estérençuby.'

We drifted back to musing on aspects of our day's adventures and our narrow escape.

Out of the blue, while making flattering remarks about my driving, Egg asked, 'I was not joking when I spoke about you being a stunt driver, Rebecca. Where did you learn to drive like that? You were in total control the whole time with not a hint of panic. We were all terrified.'

It was another question that could not be avoided but I remained silent and looked at Harry for help.

Harry shrugged, 'It's easily explained. Rebecca is an English woman driver, they all drive like that.

To laughter, I scolded Harry for not answering Egg's question. 'I'm sorry, Egg, I can't give you an answer. It just happened and once they started trying to kill us it made me so mad I responded with an anger that made me determined to hit back at them. I have never done anything as mad as that before.'

Harry added, 'And, I can tell you, Egg, that Rebecca is right about that. She is a very determined and brave lady.'

There was a chorus of support for my being brave.

Once again, only Egg looked dissatisfied with our answer.

Φ   Φ   Φ

Breakfast next morning was interrupted by another anxious call from Graham, but there was nothing to add since he was clearly being cagey about parting with information. Harry asked him what would happen about the car in the lake and he replied it would be better if we all forgot about it and left it to the authorities. He then added, 'I really ought to make a quick visit out there to tie up any loose ends. If any of this leaks to the papers it will be like the proverbial hitting the fan. I'll see what can be arranged and phone you late this afternoon.'

Harry gave Albert back his portable telephone and commented. 'Graham is telling us to forget all about the car chase.'

'That will not be easy.' Albert replied.

'Impossible,' I added.

'I think,' Brigitte paused for our attention. 'I think you young people should go off for the day and do things that are nothing to do with your investigations, so that you give your...' She paused turning her head to Claudine, 'Qu'est-ce que imaginations.'

'Imaginations,' Claudine replied to laughter all round.

Smiling broadly, Brigitte said, 'Leave them here and go out and enjoy yourselves.'

In fact, Harry and I had already decided it was time we went to Oleron Church and started our separate search for information about the Cathars. 'There's not much we can do until Graham lets us know when he is coming to France,' Harry added.

'Well! Thanks for getting around to telling us he's coming to see us,' I answered. 'I suppose we will all be told we should keep away from the crooks and leave it to the police.'

'That would be a bit difficult when they are trying to push us into a lake,' Harry protested.

'Do you want to come with us?' I asked Claudine and Egg.

'Thank you Rebecca, but I think we will go to the Holçarté,' Egg said in rather a thoughtful tone that attracted attention from Albert and Brigitte.

'No investigations,' Brigitte exclaimed.

'No investigations,' Egg agreed. 'But we think it would be a good idea to collect the wooden key and put it somewhere safer. Sam seemed to think it was important.'

He then asked Harry and me, 'Shall we meet for lunch in Mauleon? We will both be in that area. The Café Bon Vivant is open all day, we could meet at two if you are agreeable.'

Φ   Φ   Φ

Harry and I were surprised to find Oleron had two churches of note, the Cathedral Ste Croix being the oldest so we started there. From the west doorway there is a marvellous wall-to-wall view of the Pyrénées, but we could find nothing in the church we recognised as relating to the Cathars. Certainly, there were woodcarvings and we took many pictures, but they would have to wait until later for intelligent study.

'It's 11th century so the date fits,' Harry said, 'but we should have obtained more information from Egg.'

Moving on to the other Cathedral, the 12th Century Ste Marie we were immediately charmed by the carved tympanum over the door, but was there a Cathar connection?

We took a number of pictures there as well and decided to find out more before paying another visit to Oleron. By the time we had finished photographing I was impatient to move on to the shops of Mauleon acting on information provided by Claudine that the town was famous for its production of sandals or espadrilles. Harry groaned, complaining, 'No, no, Rebecca, not the dreaded shops'.

Chapter Eleven
Egg and Claudine

Meanwhile, Egg and Claudine drove first to her home in Rochenoir explaining their trip to the Holçarté Gorge to her parents. Saying nothing, of course, about the reason for their visit, the mysterious wooden key in the cave. As Egg repeated while on their way to the Pepin's house, they might as well collect the key and keep it somewhere safe and easily available until they found out what it was for.

When they had puzzled over the block of wood on their previous mission, Sam had said it was a sort of key and he might know what it was used for, but he had been killed, presumably, before he had a chance to seek confirmation of its use from a friend in England.

Claudine's mother answered the door and gave Egg an effusive welcome. 'So nice to see you Alain (using his proper name). When Claudine said she was going out I thought it must be with Jean, but you are always more than welcome as well.'

Egg sat, as instructed, on the sofa, and answered a mini flood of questions about his family and did he have a girl friend yet. He answered that Nicole had accompanied him a few times, but there was nothing arranged.

'What will she think about you having an assignation with Claudine?'

'Mother,' Claudine said sharply from the doorway. 'Don't embarrass Egg with your questions, we are just friends. We are not having an assignation.'

'Who is this other Englishman who has turned up, named Henry or something like that.'

'Oh!' said Claudine in exasperation, 'where do you pick up this gossip? His name is Harry and he is here on holiday with his wife, Rebecca. Come on Egg, let's go before Mother wants you to sign for me and return me by the hour of midnight.'

Egg shook hands with mother and whispered, 'I will have her back well before midnight,' and they left to the sound of laughter and Claudine tut-tutting.

Φ   Φ   Φ

Egg turned the car onto the track leading to the Holçarté Gorge and parked on the same spot that Sam had used on their previous visit. As they walked to the old cottage in the cliff, Egg remarked, 'So much has happened since that first day we all came here together. We were all united in our purpose then.'

'Yes, I can't believe it.'

'You always say that.'

'Always doesn't mean so much anymore.

'No! You are right there.'

They reached the cottage and were pleased to see everything about the cottage and cave looked exactly as they had left it. They turned to the cave in the cliff and stopped by the locked door that barred the entrance into the cave. Egg produced a screwdriver he had brought with him for the purpose and unscrewed the padlock and hasp completely. He opened the door and threw the lock onto the ground inside. 'Not much point in putting it back,' he remarked.

Claudine agreed. They had just come to take the wooden key away. They already knew from an earlier visit there was nothing more of interest in the cave.

Egg took a torch out of his pocket and went straight to the ledge where the piece of wood was hidden. He reached up, and then swept his hand right and left. 'It isn't here anymore!'

'It must be, no one has any reason to touch it and Vachon is dead.'

They searched the whole cave, even finding two high ledges near the back of the cave, they had not discovered before. Of wooden keys, there was nothing.

Egg raised his hands helplessly. 'This is impossible. Surely Vachon did not have time to return here before he died and Duval was already dead at that time.'

'Someone else came to take it away. But who?' Claudine wondered.

Then when Egg did not answer, 'I wonder what Sam would have done now. I don't know what to suggest, he was our leader, and he kept us together. We are not making much progress on our own, although that's not Harry and Rebecca's fault. We have to go to work and they are not familiar with all the events of the past.'

'Well!' Egg answered, 'for a start let's try to find the ledge with the fissure. You know the one on the cliff path in the gorge. I'm sure Sam thought that the wooden key had something to do with that ledge.'

'We must be quick,' Claudine said doubtfully. 'The weather is changing for a storm.' They left the cave and she looked again at the sky, 'It's not good.'

Indeed, the trees were restless and dark clouds drifted across the sky in a seemingly purposeful manner. There was no doubt rain was on the way and the area was notorious for its violent storms.

'Don't worry,' Egg replied, 'it won't take long to climb up to where we found the deep fissure in the rock.'

In fact it took them longer than they thought, some of the time wasted in searching for the right path. Then they wasted more when they strayed off the correct path and wandered into a wilderness of bushes they thought to recognise only to find themselves back at the point they had started from.

'Let's give it up,' Claudine suggested, 'the sky is ever more angry.'

'I have a compass in the car.'

'There isn't time and we might have trouble finding each other again.' She added, 'Be still' and put a finger to her lips while listening intently. 'That way,' she finally announced, 'I can faintly hear the sound of water.

They followed the path again and Egg recognised the spot where they had wandered the wrong way. 'We have to head for the slightly higher ground. We are misled each time because we know the path we want is lower and forget the approach is on high ground.'

At last they recognised the broken rocks that marked the spot where the false path started. The cleft looked just as they remembered it and the dizzy drop down into the side pool of the gorge was just as awesome. Claudine shivered, 'Let's be quick. I don't like this place and have a bad feeling about it.'

They looked around in an aimless way and found nothing they had not seen before. 'We are wrong I think, or need more information,' Egg said hopelessly. 'I can see no clue or anything strange. Even the marks in the moss that interested Sam have grown over. The moss!! Egg looked again and began to understand.'

Egg looked down into the stream and once more peered at the wall of the cleft as he ran his hands over the surface. 'Would it work,' he muttered, 'is it possible?'

Suddenly he turned, 'Tell me about the wooden key'

Claudine looked surprised at his question. Hesitating, not understanding what Egg wanted to know, she replied, 'You know it's a substantial piece of wood with a hole drilled through it. Because it's so strong it is heavy. That is, I suppose, why it was stored in the cave. So it was near to where they want to use it.' Her voice tailed off, with an intake of breath, as she spoke the last few words and realisation dawned.

'How long do you think the wooden key is?' Egg asked.

'Just under a metre.'

Egg took a measure out of his pocket and leaned across the crevasse to measure the width of the cleft.

'Eighty centimetres,' he said leaving a question heavy on the air.

They both stood staring at each other.

'Eighty centimetres,' Claudine repeated, 'but how would it work? Is it possible?'

'Why didn't I see it before,' Egg was woeful about his failure. 'Sam guessed.'

'Sam had seen something like it before,' Claudine was consoling.

'Jean knew,' Egg replied. 'Jean knew and it must have been Jean who took the key.'

As if to illustrate his comment a sharp gust of wind shrieked through the cleft.

'Quick,' Egg exclaimed, 'the storm will break any time now and that river will be a torrent. We can only guess how high it comes. It's well known how dangerous the gorge is. The flood of water may cover the lower path and block our way to the road.'

Again they lost their way in their hurry through the wilderness of trees and rocks. They had only just positively sorted out the direction they wanted when the sudden, moaning, rotary swirls of wind that closely precede a rainstorm scattered the leaves into whirling rings and the dust rose all around them.

'Hurry, over there,' Claudine shouted. 'See! A big overhang of rock with plenty of room for us to shelter.'

They just made it before a cascade of rain pelted down, the oversized droplets smashing into the ground. The wind shrieked again with greater intensity, leaves and branches tumbling. It seemed the whole of nature was angry. The friends were fortunate indeed for the deep recess in which they sheltered was almost a cave. A little afraid at the temper of the elements, they both moved right to the back away from the lashing rain. Claudine really was afraid of the repeated flashes of lightning and moved hastily to be beside Egg.

Standing close to each other watching the storm and torrential rain they were startled when a mighty clap of thunder sounded right overhead and the shock waves of sound caused dust to fall from cracks in the rock above them.

Claudine gave a little scream and instinctively caught hold of Egg as he just as instinctively put his arm protectively round her. She turned her face up towards him and he kissed her. A long, intense kiss as she relaxed in his arms. He didn't know why, it just happened. For a moment he held her as they searched each other's eyes and then both broke away, confused.

'What are we doing?' he exclaimed.

'I don't know,' Claudine replied softly.

They drove to Mauleon in silence, each wrapped in the turmoil of their private thoughts.

Revenge in Rochenoir

Chapter Twelve
Mauleon

'This looks like the place, Rebecca,' Harry said.

We were standing outside a small, but attractive restaurant bedecked with flowers and with the sheltered forecourt graced with tables each holding a colourful umbrella. However, the rainsquall that had swept the town while we were in the espadrille shop had made the seats too wet for use, so we entered to find that Egg and Claudine had arrived moments before us.

We settled into seats by the window and the waitress passed round menus. I could see Egg was bursting to tell us something, but ever the gentleman, he waited patiently until we had ordered and were armed each with a glass of wine.

Egg looking serious explained to Harry and me, 'We have said very little or nothing to you about the nature of the Holçarté Gorge so I ought to explain to you about the wooden key unless someone has already talked to you about it.'

Presumably we were supposed to agree or disagree, but Egg was clearly anxious to tell his story so he ploughed on.

In part of the gorge there is a difficult to follow path near the top of the cliff. At one point that path passes through a deep hollow on the very edge of the cliffs. In the hollow is a fissure that splits the path. It's only about a metre wide so it's possible for a walker to jump across. Down in the fissure is a sheer drop to the river of about twenty metres. At the bottom the swirling river has made a much larger pool inside the fissure. We think Vachon used some kind of winch to hide his gold in the pool or there may be a cave down there that can't be seen from above. We think what Sam called a wooden key is an important part of the winch. So,' he continued, 'the wooden key,' is part of some kind of hoist, perhaps to lower or raise the gold to a hiding place that no one would ever find in a pool down below. The winch part they had to take away because if someone found it in the cave they would know immediately what it was for.

'There would be two winches,' Claudine added.

Egg's face was comical in his surprised reaction to the interruption. 'Two!'

'Yes, you saw Vachon in that area and thought he had been there. Probably to hide some gold for we know they had to move it from the hiding place in the Manoir. He could do that on his own, by just tipping the gold off some sort of light winch into the stream. A winch for that would be easily carried in a bag. They would need a much stronger winch and at least two people to send a man down to hide the gold away, perhaps in a cave under the water.'

Egg looked at her with undisguised admiration in his eyes. 'You are right. It would make a perfect hiding place.'

'If you have a strong piece of wood,' Claudine and Egg laughed together at a shared joke.

'You mean just to tip gold bars into the river where anyone can find them.' I asked' Surely that would be too risky for something of such a high value?'

'That's just the point,' Egg answered. 'No one would find the gold. The bottom of the gorge is always under water and it frequently has flash floods. Almost no one has explored the length of the river, it's rocky and almost impassable in places. Even if someone did manage to wade along the river they wouldn't expect to find, or even notice, gold bars at the bottom of a pool in a fissure of the rocky cliff.

'Plus,' Claudine added, 'they couldn't reach the cave from above without climbing equipment or using a special winch. You would not have that sort of equipment with you unless you already knew the gold was there.'

'Well done,' Harry enthused. 'When do we go down and where can we find a winch?'

'Hang on a minute,' I protested. 'It's not the Klondike down there. Let a police squad do it or a Mountain Rescue team.'

My protest fell on deaf ears; my three companions had gold stars in their eyes.

Harry had an idea, 'I bet the bigger winch was kept at the wood yard. It would make sense; no one would think anything about a winch in a wood yard. I bet it's still there.'

'We must talk to Arlette,' I said in a triple harmony with Egg and Harry.

As we calmed down Claudine spoke only one word, 'No.'

She immediately had our attention.

Claudine explained, 'I hesitated to speak of this before because you all like Arlette and say she is willing to help. But, when you speak of sharing secrets like gold with her I must tell you that my instincts do not trust her. I cannot believe she knew nothing of her husband's activities any more than I can believe she has not been in contact with Paul Vachon. To put it simply, we really know nothing about her. She was living in Switzerland before Coutard died and Sam wondered if she was working with the crooks to smuggle gold.'

Φ   Φ   Φ

We all went back to Labaraquette about four o'clock to see if Graham had left any message as to when he would arrive and were astonished to see him sitting in one of Albert's armchairs drinking his cognac. 'What Ho!! Troops' he called genially, with a careless wave of his glass.

'Had one or two, have you,' was my thoughtful, but not outspoken response.

'Bit surprised to see you here so soon,' Harry replied instead.

'Had a chance of a lift from someone flying to Bayonne and – as something else had cropped up needing my attention - they dropped me off.'

'Small world,' my voice was calm, but my feelings were unaccountably sharper. Again I had that feeling that Graham knew more than he was telling us, although I said nothing to the others.

Graham put his half full glass down on a side table and leaned forward with a serious expression. 'I was most disturbed to hear about this car caper involving you chaps. Are all of you uninjured?'

'We're fine,' I answered cautiously, expecting a wigging. 'Egg collected a small bruise from a ricochet but, otherwise, we had a miraculous escape.'

'All thanks to Rebecca,' Claudine announced. 'I've never seen such driving. She was so cool and always in control.'

Obviously, she hadn't seen the perspiration pouring down my back as I was dodging the attempts to push us in the lake. I could feel Graham's eyes burning into me, expressing his concern, but I avoided contact knowing he would be either upset or angry about our near miss.

'How the Hell did you get into this insane car chase,' he suddenly blurted out.

We were all momentarily at a loss for words.

Egg answered first, 'We saw the Men in Black pass us in a car and we followed them. They realised what we were doing and unaccountably decided to attack us. In fact, when they tried to push us into the lake they were trying to murder us. They had no reason to be so vicious. I don't think they had any idea who we were, but simply thought we were an undercover drug enforcement team. Claudine had heard a rumour some men dressed in black had been trying to sell drugs in the car park. They had obviously attracted attention to themselves and were jumpy, thinking their choice was years in prison or to kill us. They decided we were expendable but they reckoned without the skills of Rebecca.'

I think we all looked at Egg in amazement. None of us had made the drug connection and fear of the law the prime mover in the reaction of the Men in Black.

'Thing is, old bean,' Graham answered, 'it's not your job to get yourself killed, it's mine.'

'Why do you want to kill Egg,' I asked innocently.

Even Graham had to laugh at his mistake.

He turned to me, 'You, young lady, had a lucky escape, although from what I've been hearing you did a brilliant job. I'm actually quite proud of you, old girl.'

Just wait until I give you a good kicking for the old girl, then you won't be so pleased.

Graham next addressed Claudine, 'I want to have a chat with you sometime tomorrow but I'm going to be busy all day. Would it be possible to see you in the evening?'

'How about meeting at my flat,' Egg suggested. 'Then Harry and Rebecca are not far away if you want to talk to them.'

'Top hole, old boy, that will be tickety boo.'

Egg laughed. 'Don't even try to tell me what that means. Just turn up when you're ready.'

We all sat down to a surprisingly cheerful supper considering all the circumstances. Then we had to give Graham every detail of the car chase. I noticed with relief that Claudine seemed to be easier in her thoughts about the subject and occasionally joined in. Once, she laughed and flashed me a knowing look, when I suggested, "Claudine seemed most concerned when she found Egg had been in the line of fire."

Each comment was answered by a groan or a sigh from Graham and missing my point, he said, 'Rebecca, I don't think any one of you knew what I meant when pleading you all keep a low profile in regard to the crooks. You seem to specialise in leaping into danger'.

He leaned back in his chair. 'Albert tells me it is just because you are all enthusiastic. I think you are all stark raving bloody mad.'

Φ   Φ   Φ

'I wonder if I should start looking out for a hat?' I knew there was a happy note in my voice. 'Problem is, we probably won't be here long enough although we can always come back if we're invited.'

'Rebecca, what are you talking about?' Harry replied.

'They're different, didn't you notice?'

'Who do you mean? Egg and Claudine? They're exactly the same.'

'They're more aware of each other, something's happened today.' I gave a little chuckle of delight.

'Of course they're aware of each other, they've known each other a long time. They see a lot of each other.'

'That's just the point. It's the girl next-door syndrome. You grow up together. Play together. See a lot of each other. She's a girl, but not a bad sort really, a good sport. She's always there so you don't realise that she's probably the first one you tell all your news and hopes. Then one day you look over the proverbial fence and realisation dawns. Wow! She's a girl!!! And life is never going to be the same again.'

Harry grinned as well. 'Well! Even if you're right it takes two to ring wedding bells. I shouldn't rush into buying hats.'

'Really, Harry, didn't you even notice how concerned she was yesterday over the possibility Egg might have been shot? Even fussed over a little bruise on his back. Oh! Men, don't they notice anything?'

Chapter Thirteen
Egg

U nusually for him, Egg could hardly contain his impatience to
settle with Jean the question of the wooden key. 'Jean,' his
voice sounding sharp even over the telephone, 'What have you done
with the wooden key?'

At first Jean procrastinated but finally admitted he had taken the
key away. 'No one knows what is hidden down there,' he finally
replied. 'It's best we are careful and speak to no one until we know
who we can trust. Have you spoken of this with your new friends?'

'If by that you mean Harry and Rebecca, yes I have.'

'Clonk,' was the noise from the telephone in reply as Jean had
clearly slammed down the handset.

Egg wondered whether to ring right back but decided there was
no point. He smiled ruefully as he thought, 'Good thing Jean wasn't
using his mobile or it would now be smashed on the ground.'

His phone ringing interrupted Egg's thoughts. He picked it up, 'I
hope you phoned to apologise,' he snapped.

'Why, what have I done?' Claudine's surprised voice replied.

'Oh! I'm sorry, I was just the victim of a few angry words from
Jean.'

'Me too, tell me your news.'

'Oh! It was only over him taking the wooden key away, which he
admits, but is unrepentant.

Claudine laughed. 'We can make another key. My conversation
was more to do with – as Sam would have said – the end of the
road.'

Egg noted the use of Sam as a reference, but didn't comment,
waiting for her to continue, assuming by her mention of Sam's name
that something had upset her badly.

Claudine continued, 'I have an invitation to stay a few days in
London next week with Lady Sophie. I've spoken to my boss, and

he is arranging for me to visit and be made known to the London Tourism Headquarters where Sam's friend, Peter Reynolds, is in charge. Peter - that is what he says I should call him - already telephoned me to ask whether I can spend at least a day with them. And, you won't guess this; I am invited for coffee at the French Embassy in London. I telephoned Lady Sophie to accept her invitation and asked if she would mind me doing these things while I am visiting her; do you know her reply?'

'No,' Egg replied dutifully, smiling at her excitement.

'Lady Sophie said her car and driver, Richard, would be available to take me anywhere I wanted to go. Can you imagine me, a poor girl from a small French town, arriving at the French Embassy in a chauffeur driven car?'

After Jean's angry and resentful words, Egg felt his good spirits flooding back with the warmth of her excitement. 'I'm very happy for you, Claudine. Enjoy every moment of your visit. I am sure all the people you meet will not only make you welcome, but be delighted to meet you. Can I help in any way?'

'Oh! Egg, you're so understanding.'

'Now tell me your bad news.'

'When I heard of my invitation from Lady Sophie I telephoned Jean straight away and found his attitude has not changed. He still does not want me to go. No, Egg, it's no use my hiding, it's worse than that.' She paused, hesitating over a form of words.

Egg spoke softly for her, 'It's the end of the road!'

'Exactement.'

'I don't know what to say to you, Claudine, except don't let this spoil your big chance for the future or your enjoyment of what I am sure will be a wonderful trip to London.'

Chapter Fourteen
The Wood yard

'Penny for your thoughts, Harry,' I remarked, noticing his furrowed brow.

'I'm worried, Rebecca, I've just had news from Egg that Claudine has been invited to London by Lady Sophie and I'm wondering if any risk is involved. We know nothing about this chap Graham shot, Pierront, or if he had any friends who might seek revenge or even if Paul Vachon fled to England. Although, I must say, Egg didn't seem to be bothered about her going and he knows more about the Rochenoir affair than we do.'

'Well!' I replied, 'you can talk to Graham and tell him about it when he comes to see Claudine this evening. He's the man with the resources and experience.'

Egg and I had made a loose arrangement to have a look at the Coutard wood yard, but in view of Graham's arrival, let alone his comments, during the previous evening, about keeping our heads down we put that on hold until it was seen what the next day produced.

Graham had told me he was going, with Ramel, to see the Spanish police and that he had arranged a meeting with Marius in the afternoon. He would not be drawn on either subject. Our latest plans were for a late supper in Egg's apartment in Orthez with the four of us and Graham attending.

It was therefore something of a surprise when I received a cheerful phone call from Graham in the late afternoon. Fortunately, Harry was out with Egg shopping for the evening meal and Claudine, rather anxious that present events would not impede her visit to London, was discussing her plans with her boss.

As stated, Graham telephoned and I felt a surge of confidence just to hear the cheery note of his voice. 'Hello Rebecca, nice to speak to you again. Just letting you know I will be there at six.

Everything has gone according to plan. I can't obtain a reply from Egg's number and I wanted to ask him if Marius could join us.'

'I'm certain it will be fine. I will speak to him as soon as they return from a shopping expedition to buy the makings of your supper.'

'Oh Lord! Tell them not to go to any trouble.'

I grinned at my reflection in the polished top of the table on which the phone stood, thinking does he really think we would not be pulling out all the stops when he was bringing a French Count, Comte Bertin for dinner with us. I explained the new situation regarding Claudine, her invitation from Lady Sophie and told him about Jean.

'Humm,' Graham mused, 'can't think what the matter is with Jean, he's been so reliable and helpful in the past.'

I answered to the effect that Harry and I hardly knew Jean and pointed out that although he seemed most upset about the risk of losing Claudine, he was acting in a manner that such a loss would be guaranteed.

'No, I don't think it's that,' was Graham's verdict. 'If he was really serious about her he would have married her long ago. Why wouldn't he? She's a beautiful, talented girl who would be a prize catch for any man. Claudine's future is assured and she will be moving out of his league now.'

'Well,' I replied, 'they always say that trouble goes hand in hand with women or money.'

'Right on!! There's been too much talk about gold and millions in cash. I suspect Sam giving away a gold bar was the final straw.'

'Giving away a gold bar? Who too?'

'Irrelevant, Rebecca. Just keep an eye open for any more gold. I feel it in my bones, something is going to break soon.'

We had a discussion about Claudine's pending visit and he didn't seem too bothered except for suggesting a task for me.

It was only after I had put the phone down and a digest of our conversation crystallised in my mind, a conviction formed that he had already known that Claudine was travelling to London.

Φ   Φ   Φ

Claudine and I were a little flustered to be preparing a meal for Marius.

'I don't see what the difference is Rebecca, you have prepared meals for the four of us,' Harry commented.

'No you wouldn't see a difference,' I answered.

'Don't forget,' Egg added. 'Marius is one of the French aristocracy.'

'They eat the same as us!'

'Just sort the wine out, Harry.'

In fact the meal was a great success, we girls having produced a dinner that would have defied some restaurants. I was a little worried when Egg made his usual announcement of "No talk of business while we are eating," but Graham and Marius heartily agreed with him.

Covertly I watched Graham and Marius and could detect the rapport between them. Our group was lucky to have those two on our side and I had no doubt Marius was a huge help to Graham. Marius, the mystery man. 'Gosh! He is handsome in a rugged sort of way.' I mused Certainly I wouldn't say no but he seemed to be a confirmed bachelor. I had fished for information from Graham who told me he had been married some years ago, but his wife died young. Any further questions generated a rebuff.

Over coffee, but no cognac. We were mindful that Graham and Marius had a police car waiting outside. We were told they were flying to Paris after dinner. Graham explained he had been refused a visit to the monastery but was certain it was on the level and the Spanish authorities were satisfied all was well. It seemed our Men in Black were simply operating under a disguise. Problem was from where were they operating?

He said Ramel had organised a watch on the empty casino and there was no activity there at all. Our mess – as he politely referred to our activities – was sorted out and we were to forget all about it. 'You chaps,' he added, 'are doing a marvellous job, but it's a very dangerous time. Whatever you do, keep your heads down.'

Harry answered, 'We, that is Rebecca, Egg and me are going to look round the empty wood yard to see if we can find the winches that Vachon used to lower the gold to a hiding place in the Holçarté.'

'Oh Lord! Not that old chestnut,' Graham groaned. 'Well! I can't see any harm in you pootling round an empty wood yard, but be careful. Marius, you wanted a word.'

Marius smiled. 'Without undermining what Graham has said, I think you did a good job in writing off a couple of the bastards.' He remembered the presence of Claudine and me and made a handsome apology for using the word, then continued, 'We think there are nine more possible members of the gang, but we can't touch them for lack of evidence and, in any case, their whereabouts are unknown. We have no idea where Paul Vachon is. Now that Graham has made it very difficult for them to sell the gold, we think they are taking it in small quantities to other countries and exchanging it for drugs. But there is no proof of any of this and you are to keep it to yourselves.'

As they were leaving Graham took both of Claudine's hands. 'Have an absolutely marvellous time and enjoy every minute of your visit. You have my number if there is anything you need or if you want to ask me anything at all at any time of day or night. You will not encounter a recording machine. If I am not available, a man named Peter will talk to you and you can trust him implicitly. I will be back in London tomorrow and I had thought of taking you out to dinner, but I don't think you will have the opportunity. Have a great time.'

And they were whisked away in the waiting car.

Claudine turned to me and asked, 'What does "implicitly" mean?'

Φ   Φ   Φ

Hélène telephoned Egg to say she had picked up a little information about drugs from one of her pupils and wondered if it had any connections with our investigations. Cautiously, Egg played down any interest and almost lost a lead when Hélène apologised for troubling him saying, 'I'm sure someone said a man dressed in black was of interest.'

The result was a meeting between them and me for coffee at the Artisans Restaurant. And, an exchange of information, which involved a story about the very shop, run by Gaston, a friend of Egg's, who had denied a few weeks ago any knowledge of drugs being sold.

'What do we do about this Gaston man? I asked.

'Leave it to me, Rebecca, I will go and see him before informing the police,' Egg announced.

'Then I must come too,' Hélène, answered firmly, because it involves one of my pupils. I can come with you both tomorrow morning at ten.'

I was horrified by her suggestion. 'Supposing we run into trouble?' I demanded. 'Hélène, you are equipped for all sorts of skills including making men's hearts race to the danger of their health. But if someone comes at Egg with a knife, I'm the girl he needs.'

But Hélène was not dissuaded, insisting she could look after herself

Harry's possible participation was dismissed without discussion.

Egg's friend, Gaston, surprised me and I soon had him marked down as unreliable. He was short, slightly stocky with black hair and about thirty. He lacked self-assurance and would not look me in the eye. When Egg started questioning him about drugs, he was embarrassed and frightened, but denied everything; even after he was told a witness had named him.

Egg threatened to call the police immediately, but said he wanted for the sake of an old acquaintance to give his friend a chance to redeem himself by sending the suppliers of the drugs to prison.

Still Gaston denied.

Hélène, suspicious of his actions and in an attempt to fool an eavesdropper, suddenly interceded, asking Gaston in German, 'Why do you keep looking at that door,' indicating with her head the back of the shop.'

Gaston looked as if the floor had been kicked from under him.

Being more of an action person, I tried a different sort of kicking. I moved swiftly to the door, kicked it open, then flattened myself against the wall to one side so efficiently that when a man dressed in black stepped through the wreck of the door pointing a pistol at Egg and Hélène, he had no comprehension of the hate and rage then poised behind him.

The Man in Black didn't know what hit him as I jerked the pistol up out of harm's way and using karate skills, systematically demolished him until he was a whimpering heap on the floor. 'Tie him up,' I called to Egg. Then vaulted the counter shouting to a terrified Gaston, 'This is for Hélène's pupil and any other innocent children you have hurt.' Then I hit him in the stomach with all the strength of my arm at such a force the man was sick. Pulling his head up by the hair, I spat 'Die you wretch, die' and started banging his head on the side of the counter.

'Let him go Rebecca, please,' Hélène, shouted.

I reluctantly let Gaston drop to the floor and walked round the counter to join her and Egg.

'I've used my emergency number for the police,' he said and sure enough a police car pulled up outside a few minutes later.

The leading Gendarme looked round and exclaimed 'Sacré Bleu and this is with only two of the Charley's Angels.'

'How do they know Harry called us that?' I asked in wonderment.

'Graham, who else' Egg replied.

A van arrived for the two prisoners and a gendarme was detailed to wait at the shop while Egg phoned Gaston's wife, Celine, and asked her to come and take charge or lock-up the business. Egg was upset about his friend but there was nothing we could do for him.

Later Ramel phoned to say neither man would talk because they were afraid of Paul Vachon and they were keeping them in custody.

Φ   Φ   Φ

Harry and I, a few days earlier, had taken the opportunity, while in Rochenoir, to drive past the Coutard timber yard and found it locked up and apparently deserted.

Egg had also discussed with me whether to ask Arlette if we could look round the premises but were put off by Claudine's opinion that we should not be too trusting until we knew her better. However, our agreed provisional arrangements to meet so that the three of us could go down and have a look round on our own, had been cancelled for Graham's visit -

After he left it seemed a good time to reinstate the postponed visit. It also happened that on our chosen morning a phone call from Louis confirmed an execution of that plan.

'Hello Monsieur Harry I have a new hire car for you,' he called to say. Then added the company in Pau who had supplied his original car had decided that changing it was the best course of action. The new car was ready for collection any time that suited him. Then he said, 'They have sold the car you wrecked to me, for a very good price.'

'I think you mean a very low price.'

'I see Monsieur you understand French commerce.'

'No, Louis, that's commerce the world over.'

A call to Egg elicited the information that he would not, after all, be able to join us for he would be heavily involved with the company he worked for because he was helping with an earlier production run of the magazine. 'Rebecca, you two go without me, then if you find a wooden key or keys - you know what they look like - you can bring them away along with the winch.'

'Egg, Graham has asked me to make up some kind of excuse to go to London so that I can accompany Claudine.' I asked, 'Perhaps describing it as a shopping trip so as not to worry her. He obviously thinks there is some risk because he remarked we would have no concerns once she is in London at which time he would take over. What do you think, will she mind and how should I play it?'

'You should play it with a straight bat,' Egg answered and I could imagine his broad grin at finding another leg-pull.

'We would describe your answer as you having a little dig at me.' I replied.

'Why dig.'

'You have me there, perhaps because we sometimes prod people in the ribs when we make a joke.'

'I won't ask why you do that, just say oh! those Anglais. Your conversation with Graham confirms an assumption I made when Claudine told me about Lady Sophie's car. I assumed some security operation had swung into place. That is why I have no concern about her going.'

'Why should you think that?'

'You forget, Lady Sophie's chauffeur was a security guard for her diplomat husband.'

I had not overlooked that point, it was unknown to me, and it generated another thought that filled me with fear. I hoped fervently that Graham and his pals were not using Claudine as bait, but said nothing of that fear to Egg.

Harry and I discussed Egg's comments as he drove us to Rochenoir. I explained the extra information they had not previously given us about the chauffeur.

'I don't think that makes any difference,' he replied.

'It makes me wonder if Lady Sophie was more involved in all this than appears,' I replied. 'I would like to meet her and sound her out.'

Φ   Φ   Φ

Louis was all smiles when we pulled onto his forecourt and made a big show of inspecting the car he had loaned us to see if there was any damage. He was less happy about our plan to inspect the wood yard. We trooped into his little office for the black coffee and a lecture.

'Perhaps I should come with you,' he announced. 'That you arrive with la femme concerns me when you are about to embark on an activity dangerous. You speak of a désert!!! – What word is it? – ah! An empty wood yard will do, but I think it is unlikely no one at all is there.'

I was about to say no when I saw Harry nodding, so acquiesced, accepting that he may have his own wish for Louis to be with us.

So it was that Louis drove the three of us, in the car he had just taken back and after parking round a corner from the wood yard, we arrived at the chained and padlocked gates of the yard.

Louis produced a pair of bolt cutters from a plastic bag he was carrying. 'Hold on Louis,' I said hastily, 'cutting open this gate is a bit obvious, let's look round first.'

He scratched his head, 'Qu'est-ce que obvious?' he asked me.

'Never mind, come on,' Harry said and marching off along the perimeter fence with the Louis and me following.

On the far side of the yard, near the river, we found just what we were looking for, a small gate opposite a landing stage. A gate overgrown with vegetation, out of use, and no match for Louis's cutters.

Egg had recounted to us the story of Sam hiding from Coutard's guards in the sawpit and finding bars of gold at the bottom of the pit under the sawdust. Naturally, we wanted to see what had happened since, so made straight for the spot. The pit was completely empty, not even any sawdust.

'That must have been a hair raising ordeal for Sam,' Harry acknowledged.

'I guess what you are saying,' Louis replied. 'I can tell you Sam was a brave man.'

Presumably the police removed the gold,' I mused, 'wonder what happened to it?'

"I think, maybe, Paul Vachon was here first,' said Louis.

'Where did it come from?' Harry asked.

'I don't think anyone knows.' Louis answered. 'It was said the gold went back to the war when agents and Germans fleeing to South America used gold to hire guides to escort them over the border into Spain.'

Louis hesitated, then rubbed the side of his nose using his characteristic signal of evil doing. 'I tell for something for your ears only and for Egg's ears when you tell him.' He hesitated again then went on, 'I heard a rumour many, many years ago that the Gang of Four became very rich after looting a bombed out bank during the war. But such knowledge is dangerous knowledge and best not reported. Tell the wrong person what you have heard and' – he drew a finger across his throat in a graphic and somehow terrifying illustration.

'Thank you for trusting us with that information, Louis,' I replied, 'it may answer the puzzle as to why Duval and Coutard tried to kill the Musketeers when they asked questions about the gold. We thought it must be because they stole it.'

'My puzzle,' Louis was shaking his head, 'is why Arlette Coutard has not sold the yard. She must now own it. What can be the reason for closing down a working business? What about the jobs of the men? It can't be because of the police because there are no notices to keep away. Do you know anything about that, Mr. Harry?'

'I'm sorry Louis; I know nothing about the yard. Let's split up and have a quick scout round to see if there is anyone here.'

I protested at this, 'If there is anyone about it would be better to keep together.'

'Don't worry about that, Rebecca I brought some whistles with me so that we can keep in contact.'

I asked Louis if he would stand guard on the small gate and keep a lookout for anybody while we searched to see if there were any winches suitable for using in the Holçarté Gorge.

Harry gave us each a whistle and said, 'Don't hesitate to blow it if in doubt and all converge to help if you hear a whistle blown.'

Louis asked, to some amusement, 'Mr. Harry, before you go, what is a scout and how do we converge?'

Harry and I did a circuit of the yard keeping as low a profile as possible by using the stacks of timber as cover and moving as quietly as possible.

'Do you know,' I said hesitantly. 'I feel there is someone here and that we are being watched, yet I've seen no one.'

'Rebecca, every time we go somewhere creepy you say that.'

'Yes, and I'm usually right.'

We continued to explore, noting a car parked beside the office block and shop but all was locked and in darkness. Returning to Louis we reported our findings. He was convinced there was someone there if a car was there, but he had not seen or heard anyone.

Harry and I decided to go to the main equipment stores on the far side of the yard and split up to double our chances while searching a number of smaller sheds that were within sight of each other.

The signal on the whistle, when it came, I knew was from Harry for it was a very short peep. That told me it was no emergency and that he had found a winch. I was soon by his side, closely followed by Louis. We were standing in a big, roofed timber shed with partly open sides where there was a mass of assorted, ancillary equipment like band-saw blades. It also included several winches of different sorts. Only two of which had a long bolt and nuts as a means of attaching. Both had a very long, fairly lightweight chain on the winch winder. Also in a sacking bag were two stout pieces of wood with bevelled ends and several shorter wood pieces, all with a hole drilled through them.

'Yes,' I acknowledged, 'these must be the objects of our search, but why are the chains so long?'

'Great!!' Harry exclaimed, 'we don't have to make some more wood pieces.'

'These are Sam's wooden keys?' Louis queried.

'Yes,' I answered, 'apparently Jean has the one they found at the gorge. Let's get out of here now we know what they are.'

We were interrupted by a loud crash on the far side of the wood yard.

Startled, Harry questioned that we had seen no one in our exploration so what could it be except the car parked near the offices, but asked, 'Were the front gates still locked?'

None of us knew.

We set off in the direction we thought the noise had come from and arrived to find a pile of timbers had collapsed and blocked one of the yard roads.

Louis was looking at the base of the pile and picked up a long iron bar and held it up. 'The wood did not fall alone; someone used this to help it fall.'

'Just a minute,' I exclaimed anxiously, 'where's Harry?'

Louis dropped the iron bar and rushed to my side. 'Rebecca, did he come with us?' he asked.

'I don't know, we were running.'

Louis gave a long blast on his whistle.

We both stood waiting.

Silence.

I suddenly felt drained and desperately worried.

Louis guessed or saw my concern. He patted my hand. 'We go back over the way we arrived,' he said urgently setting off without me.

We found nothing and more whistle blasts also produced nothing.

'Mrs Rebecca,' he held my arm. 'There is someone here; those timbers did not fall alone. It was a div…..'

'Diversion,' I prompted.

'Yes! To take us away from something they didn't want us to see. Maybe Harry realised and went in another direction. Even chased someone.'

We quickly searched the sheds where the winches were and found nothing unusual. I saw another ramshackle building that stood the other side of a mess of bits of timber and weeds. With Louis following closely behind, I reached the shed and heard a cry for help.

The door had a locked padlock on the outside.

I heard a voice from within, 'Rebecca, help me.'

'Louis,' I cried out frantically, 'Harry is hurt.'

The door was quickly smashed open with his powerful hands and feet, and then he threw himself on the ground and grunted with the effort it took to open a mantrap clamped round Harry's leg. As the tension on his leg was released, he slumped down on a pile of timbers where his pain eased to the bearable.

I ripped Harry's shirt from his back and, with Louis helping me, tore it into strips to bind his wounds.

While we were doing this, Harry explained he had fallen into a trap. He had seen someone run into the shed and chased after the man. He had just run into the shed when something seized his leg and he almost fainted with the excruciating pain. 'There was another door through which the chap must have escaped,' he explained. 'Then I heard him lock both doors and presumably run off to leave me to my fate.'

Louis suddenly let out a great roar, 'Batards, what manner of men set such traps. I am coming to get you Batards!' His eyes literally red with rage, he picked up an iron bar and roaring like a bull, rushed up the road towards the entrance.

Harry looked down at his leg still oozing blood and said, 'What now?'

Revenge in Rochenoir

Chapter Fifteen
To England

With the bleeding stemmed, Harry relaxed a little and calmed his shaking hands. Next he gingerly experimented with moving the injured leg.

'Help me stand, Rebecca.'

A wince or two followed by a few curses established his credibility as walking wounded.

I heaved a great sigh of thanks there were no broken bones.

We heard a car start up in the distance, a roaring of the engine and screaming tyres. I even thought the roar of Louis was mixed in somewhere, but we had no idea what was going on and there was very little we could do about it anyway. Supported by me, Harry managed to hobble outside.

Just then we saw Louis limping back down the road towards us.

'Is your leg in a good state?' Louis asked as he bent down to inspect my handiwork.

'I think I can walk.'

'I will take you to hospital.'

'Did you see the men?' Harry asked.

'Yes, they were dressed in black and made no attempt to conceal their faces. They are not afraid to break the law. Those men think they can do what they like. But, they are not brave like a warrior. When I dashed towards them shouting my family war cry, they ran away and jumped in the car. I started beating the car with my baton and breaking the windows, but they had already opened the gates and after trying to reverse over me, drove away very fast.'

I had a mental picture of an enraged Louis running down the road, roaring with rage and waving an iron bar. "Anyone would run away," was my conclusion.

Then concern rose in my consciousness. 'Louis I'm sorry not to ask before, but are you in a good shape?' Copying his previous question to us.

'No blood,' Louis waved dismissively, 'just a bump here and there.'

I spoke with a tremble in my voice. 'I've just realised what the Men in Black were trying to do. They knew nothing of Louis on the far side of the yard. They just thought it was the two of us. All they had to do was wait for you to step on the trap, and then the two of them could concentrate on what they assumed to be a helpless woman. You were out of action, they expected quickly to have had both of us overpowered. They were going to kill us. We were saved by Louis.'

'If they shot us someone would hear,' Harry objected.

Louis grunted. 'They would have cut your throats.'

Both Harry and I shivered.

'I better get you two to hospital,' my voice was concerned.

'What a fine army we are,' Harry exclaimed as he hobbled off towards the gates.

When we neared the entrance a car drove in and Arlette emerged. She looked us over and briefly inspected Harry's leg without speaking, then said, 'No explanations for the moment, I am taking you all straight to Pau hospital;' opening all her car's doors.

By the time Harry emerged from the treatment room, I had given Arlette the basics and Louis had joined us. As he said, his problems were simply bruises and Harry explained his luck in avoiding serious injury. Indeed, we were all surprised that only seven stitches were needed to hold him together.

'The doctor told me that people usually tear the wound and make it worse by trying to pull away' Harry explained. 'I told the doctor I was too paralysed with fear to move.'

I interjected, 'Louis thinks you were lucky because in their hurry they set the mantrap clumsily leaving the safety chain on. And then you were unlucky because the rusty old safety chain broke. Then lucky again when the weak springs on the old trap lacked the momentum to move the heavy jaws fast, limiting the damage from the teeth and there was not enough pressure to break a bone.'

'So many lucky and unlucky,' Harry groaned, 'what's the final score?'

'Not luck, but a miracle.' The voice was Nicole's. 'Harry could so easily have lost his leg.'

'Nicole has been helping to patch me up,' he explained.

'It is my job,' Nicole said as she wiped his brow with something and checked his pulse, which was, of course, racing from her proximity alone.

Harry continued, 'The doctor insisted on telephoning the gendarmes and reporting my injury and he let me talk to them as well. They put me through to Commissar Ramel when they realised who I was and he wants to see you, Rebecca, and me at four o'clock tomorrow afternoon. I didn't mention your name Louis so you are not involved.'

'Thank you Mr Harry, but if they do want to speak to me, I am happy to do so.'

I turned to Arlette and asked, 'What brought you to the wood yard?'

'The security guard in the factory across the road telephoned me to tell of the commotion at the yard. He asked if he should call the police and I said no. Because of the past happenings, I wanted to check the situation myself first.'

Harry asked Arlette how many sets of keys to the yard there were. 'I ask,' he explained, 'because the Men in Black had keys to unlock the gates. They had their car inside the locked gates when we arrived.'

Arlette shrugged. 'I have not bothered to change the locks because I am selling the yard. I have no knowledge of how many sets there are or who has them.'

I watched her as she spoke, trying to make up my mind if she was telling the truth. My conclusion was probably, but I was uneasy. She professed to know so little of her husband's business. I asked her if she had ever worked in the yard. Her no was quite positive.

Arlette looked over the sorry bunch comprising Louis, Harry and me with a serious expression, and announced, 'Rebecca, I am not going to ask you why you are in my wood yard let alone starting a war here.' Then she smiled. 'I assume it was something to do with the past operations, but I would be happy to listen if you wish to offer any explanations.'

Harry and I looked at each other and he decided on a partial reply. 'It's not really anything to do with me directly, but becoming friendly with Egg as a neighbour, Rebecca and I offered to help Egg and Claudine to find out if they were in any danger because of their accidental involvement in what appears to have been a gold smuggling operation. It would appear from today's events their fears were justified, but we have no idea who these people are or what they want from us unless it is simply a matter of revenge. Louis is nothing to do with it all and is just a good friend who is worried about our safety.'

'Thank you for your explanation,' she laughed. 'I'm sorry, your problem really is not funny, but it amused me that you carefully avoided explaining what you were doing in my wood yard.'

Harry grinned back. 'We were looking for some hand winches that we thought might be there and they are. Just as we found them the Men in Black attacked us. Does their wearing black mean anything to you? Are they your employees?'

'They are certainly nothing to do with me and I don't know why they were in the wood yard. I should tell you this is the first time I have visited the yard since my husband's death. I have no interest in the wood business and I asked my late husband's executors to sell the yard. I have already told you how I came to be called. Are you going to tell me about the winches?'

'I would prefer not to at this stage and I hope that reply does not mean you will say no to my request that we are allowed to take them away with us.'

She laughed again, a soft musical laugh. Harry told me later he was growing to like her, and it was something to resist if he was to remain objective.

'I see you are a man of mystery. Of course you may take them. When we leave the hospital, I will take you back to the yard so you can collect them and your car. Perhaps, Louis, you could secure the yard gates for me.'

After Arlette had dropped us off at the wood yard and departed, Louis stood scratching the back of his head. Recognising the signs, I asked, 'what are you thinking, Louis?'

He turned back to me giving his deep chuckle. 'Rebecca, all I will say is that I was only wondering if the time comes yet when she is maybe tired of being a widow.'

Φ   Φ   Φ

Taking my bloodstained husband home, I settled him down in a comfortable chair and, feeling as limp as a wet rag, sat down for a moment myself. When I had recovered from my shock, I poured a stiff scotch for each of us.

Of course, I was as cross as I was concerned at Harry's carelessness in walking into a trap, then relented and fussed over him. It seemed a good time to broach the subject of Claudine embarking on a visit to stay with Lady Sophie in London.

'It still seems a bit silly,' I mused, 'but I feel uneasy about her making such a trip at the present time. Particularly when things here seem to be moving faster. In common with Graham, I think both Egg and Claudine are too casual about the danger they are in. If you think it out from the point of view that Paul Vachon could be living a life of old Riley on a tropical island somewhere without any money worry for the rest of his natural and, instead, he is risking everything for petty revenge on a young woman he has never met. Think of it like that and you realise Claudine is in deadly danger.'

'God! It frightens me as well when you put it like that, Rebecca, but it works well with my fears if you feel such terrifying concern because Graham asked me as well if there was any possibility of you inventing some excuse for flying to London with Claudine. He says that once you have checked through customs in England he will take over responsibility for her safety.'

'Of course I will go if you are alright with your leg.'

'Don't worry about me. All that matters at the moment is yours and Claudine's safety.'

'One thing worries me; I hope this isn't some whiz idea of Graham's to use Claudine as bait to catch a criminal he already knows is in London. I don't know if she could stand up to another incident. She's not completely over Sam's death.'

'I had the same thought, but doubt that very much. Surely it would finish his career if he did that and it went wrong.'

'I just hope you are right. But, you can rely on me to be there with her if I am needed.'

'Graham suggests we say nothing about any potential dangers so not to spoil her natural enthusiasm and excitement over this big chance.'

'Of course, I agree. I'll phone her now.'

So it was arranged. We were booked to fly in two days with promises of a dual shopping trip in London that in scope would eclipse all shopping trips in London.

'Spare my wallet,' Harry groaned.

'Your wallet!! It's Graham's idea, I'll send him the bill!'

Φ   Φ   Φ

Harry and I – as requested – presented ourselves to Pau police headquarters at the required time and were asked to wait a few minutes.

I told Harry that Egg had mentioned he and Sam had been through such an interview with the police before. "You know, Rebecca," he said to me, "you and Harry are so different from Sam yet I like you both very much."

"Of course, they thought Sam was a Special Agent at first and even after his death and all the explanations they still had lingering doubts." Egg explained,"You generate similar speculation Rebecca. We wonder if you are both agents, Claudine thinks you are who you say you are and Jean thinks you are a spy for the opposition. Claudine and I are in agreement on one thing, that we feel safer with Rebecca and you on our side and we thank you for your help."

I told him we respected him so much I would admit to keeping a secret from him and will explain when the moment is right. I also told him he must believe we are on their side and added you are not any kind of secret agent. Any latitude awarded to us by the police is solely because of our association with Graham.'

At that moment we were called into Commissaire Ramel's office.

We were requested to sit down and offered coffee, which we both accepted.

Ramel tapped a number of folders on his desk and said, 'All of these relate in some way to your case. I read through them and wonder what will happen next? Would you please tell me why you invaded the Coutard timber yard.'

I told him the truth.

'Did you not think that was a matter for the police?'

'There is no proof that what we found so far is related to any criminal activities. All we have are our theories.'

There is no proof of any crime connected to the monastery in Spain either, yet Graham is pressing me to investigate.'

I shrugged.

Harry leaned forward, 'Can you tell us anything about the Men in Black? Surely there is evidence there. After all, some of them tried to kill us in Spain and others attacked us in the wood yard. They threatened Louis at his garage and you arrested one of them in a shop in St Jean Pied-de-Port. Surely there is enough there for you to work on?'

Ramel shuffled through his papers. We knew he was creating thinking time so we sat without speaking while he decided what to say.

Eventually Ramel lifted his right hand and let it drop back quietly to his desk. 'I tell you this in confidence. The Spanish police visited the monastery at Graham's request and reported back that all was well.'

'What does that mean exactly,' I asked.

Ramel made the same hopeless gesture with his hand. 'The new workers at the monastery, who have yet to be accepted, wear black trousers and what you call sweat shirts in black, but the Abbot vouches for them all and he has an impeccable reputation.'

'Are any of them missing?'

'I know what you are thinking. The men who tried to force you from the road have not been identified nor have they been reported missing.'

I asked the Commissaire if any of the Abbot's men could be indulging in criminal activities, as a sideline, without the authorities knowing.

Ramel, as I might have expected, understood my inference perfectly. 'The religious order is so strict any subterfuge would be detected very quickly.'

'None the less, Commissaire, there must be a connection somewhere.'

'I agree!'

And that was it.

I helped Harry down to a Café on the Boulevard des Pyrénées and ordered black coffees with cognac.

Harry guessed this was somewhere the others went with Sam and I was seeking inspiration. For some reason this made Harry feel he had let me down by not coming up with ideas, so snatched at straws. 'It could simply be that there is a criminal gang who dress up in black to throw us off the scent.'

'You forget we followed them to the vicinity of the monastery.'

'So! They're holed up in the catacombs.'

We laughed together.

Φ   Φ   Φ

Harry drove Claudine and me to the airport and insisted on escorting us to Departure saying he wanted to wave us off. He fooled me not a scrap and I appreciated his concern. I noticed, but was not surprised, a gendarme with a machine gun standing nonchalantly in Reception and was aware Harry had seen him as well. Claudine was already on cloud nine and noticed nothing.

'Have a fantastic time,' Harry told her. 'I don't know what you have arranged with Rebecca, but try not to let her lead you astray.'

While Claudine was in the ladies, I thought of something and asked Harry, 'How did the Men in Black at the wood yard drive through a chained and padlocked gate?'

'They must have had keys to the padlocks!'

As Claudine and I walked through to departures the gendarme with the machine gun saluted and gave me the briefest of smiles.

I mouthed "Thank you," as we passed while wondering how the gendarme knew me.

'My respect for Commissaire Ramel increases all the time,' I thought to myself with an uplift of confidence.

The plane swept up into the sky and banked slightly to turn for England and only then did I uncross my fingers.

Chapter Sixteen
London Adventures

That evening I phoned France from the privacy of my room. 'We can all relax, Harry, no sign of any trouble this end and I have picked up nothing on the grapevine. Richard, Lady Sophie's chauffeur, collected both of us from the airport and had the very good sense to phone Lady Sophie from the car to explain I had flown over with Claudine with plans to meet for a shopping expedition. Lady Sophie immediately insisted he persuade me to accompany Claudine to the house and I'm now staying here with her.'

Harry told me that was a load off his mind and it was certainly a load off mine as well.

Almost as I put down the receiver I received an unexpected call from Graham.

'Hello, Rebecca, old girl.'

'No too much of the old girl unless you want your shin kicked the next time we meet.' I warned him, and then told him where I was.

'Good, that helps my security arrangements. Bit of luck, what! Couldn't have arranged it better myself.'

I laughed, 'I'm quite sure you did arrange it.'

'Is that all you think I have to do? Look after a starry eyed cracker of a girl. By the way, some of the people she will meet think she's a bit of a hero. Anyway, that's not the main reason I phoned. I have had a chat with Albert and he and Brigitte are happy to have me as a guest yet again for two or three days, which I hope will coincide with your return so that we can all fly back together. But, that's by no means certain; so don't worry if I don't make it. Arrangements are in hand here so I'm more worried about the French end. Also I want to try and fix all this reasonably soon so I can have a chat with a police friend in Spain. Marius is meeting me when I arrive back in France. Between us we've picked up a bit of information about the Men in Black, but I don't want to talk about that on the phone.'

'We'll be more than happy to fly back with you if you do manage to join us.'

'Great, must go now.'

I sat down on the edge of my bed and put my mind to the vexed question of what on earth should I wear when I went down to dinner with a Ladyship.

There was a knock on the door before I had solved the conundrum.

It was Claudine. 'Lady Sophie came to my room for a chat and to explain that they are informal in all matters, unless it is an invitation dinner. We are to wear ordinary clothes and to call her Sophie.'

'Thank God for that.'

'Oh! Rebecca isn't it marvellous. I'm so pleased you are here with me.'

Richard served the dinner and there was also a middle-aged lady whom Sophie introduced as a cook, but who also helped serve at the table. Needless to say it was a fine dinner and we had a super and entertaining evening during which Sophie told us of some of her adventures as a diplomat's wife.

The next day Richard took us, first, to drop Claudine off at a tower block of offices where she was to spend the day with Peter Reynolds, the tourism chief, and then he drove me round some of the tourist spots of London. He was a mine of information and I enjoyed it very much.

I had a light lunch with Sophie who afterwards showed me round the house and explained some of her art collection. It was such an interesting talk and hobby; I wished collecting works of art came within my financial horizon. I hardly noticed the afternoon slipping away until just before five, Richard asked me if I wanted to go with him to collect Miss Pepin.

Claudine, of course, was full of her day and explained that Peter wanted her to go back to tourism headquarters after her visit to the French Embassy in the morning 'What shall I wear in the morning?' she asked in anguish.

I laughed, 'You're in the best place to find out, ask Sophie.'

Over dinner I mentioned exploring a few shops in the morning and Claudine protested I couldn't possibly go shopping without her, so I agreed to wait until the next day.

Lady Sophie suggested that instead I went with Richard and Claudine in the morning and, if I didn't mind waiting during the visit to the French Embassy, Richard would take me on a surprise visit she would arrange.

Of course, I agreed instantly.

Φ　　Φ　　Φ

There was a discreet tap on my door immediately after we retired for the night and I thought it might be Claudine but when I opened the door it was Richard.

He came in and accepted my invitation to sit down. 'Mrs Tilsley, I am sorry to have to report this, but today I twice saw a black Volvo following. It may be two different cars; I was not able to take a number. Do you want me to speak to Mr Graham or would you prefer to watch the situation tomorrow?'

Immediately I said, 'We will both be on the lookout tomorrow, Richard. Perhaps you will give me a signal if you see the car behind you tomorrow. I will take a camera and perhaps have an opportunity to take a photo of the car while pretending to be a sightseer.'

Of course we had our ears batted off when Claudine came out of the French Embassy. It was a delight to see the enjoyment shining out of her eyes. 'They treated me just like a Princess,' she said. 'I will never forget it.'

Fortunately, it was after we had been to the French Embassy and delivered her to Peter Reynolds that Richard suddenly said 'now' and pulled into the kerb.

No slouch, I had my window open almost before the car passed us and fired off three pictures in rapid succession. I looked at the digital display. 'Perfect,' I said to Richard and handed him the camera.

'I don't think they had any idea you took their picture,' he replied. 'Let's hope they now make a mistake. I will return the camera later.'

I sat back in the soft, leather seat, relief flooding through me. At last we had a target.

My outing was lunch with some of the cast at a London theatre followed by a conducted tour backstage and introduction to some other artists followed by sitting with the producer while watching them rehearse. I have never enjoyed an afternoon so much.

Just before we went down to dinner I had a phone call from Graham.

'Don't you dare call me "old girl" again,' I warned him before he started talking.

He laughed, 'Actually I was going to congratulate you and Richard on a superb piece of work today. The car you photographed was stolen two months ago in Southend so it looks as if we are on the right track. I understand you and Claudine are touring the shops tomorrow.

'Yes, it's a girls day out so keep away.'

'I must insist you go with Richard and don't travel any other way. This is even more important now that we have the information about the other car.'

'We don't know for sure it is anything to do with us.'

'Sadly, Rebecca, we can't take a chance on it. You can be sure if it turns up again tomorrow it's all stations go.'

In the evening we had a sherry with Sophie before dinner and it took only a couple of sips to unlock the news Claudine was bursting to tell us. 'Peter Reynolds has asked if I would consider working for him in London,' she announced.

'Why, how wonderful,' Sophie replied.

'The problem is it would mean leaving Egg,' she said in a rather sad voice.

'Egg!!!' I thought, 'just a minute, what about Jean and Nicole, have I missed a beat somewhere?' but said instead, 'Well! you will have to give it a few days to think it over carefully.'

'Yes, I agree,' Sophie backed my comment. 'Claudine if you want to stay longer while you consider this offer you are welcome to be my guest for as long as you like. It's been wonderful having the two of you here, even though it's only been a couple of days.'

Of course, I said nothing about my talk with Graham and Richard, but realised Sophie must know about our conversations. Richard would not have kept such an important matter from his employer.

Φ   Φ   Φ

Next morning, while Claudine was getting ready, I sat in her bedroom chatting about her visit to the embassy. She suddenly exclaimed, 'Oh I don't want to wear my red coat for another day, I wore it yesterday and the day before.'

'I think it's a beautiful coat.'

'Yes, I love it, but three days running.'

I had an inspiration, you know as they say, "A bolt from the blue." 'Why don't we swop? You wear my camel coat and I'd love to have your red coat for a day.'

'Oh! Rebecca, what a good idea.'

On our way downstairs, I made an excuse to go back to my room and rang Graham. I prayed he would answer the phone and he did. I explained about the coats and my idea.

'Rebecca, I can't let you take this risk.'

'Better I do this than for Claudine to be in danger. She's just not made to cope with that sort of situation Graham, don't worry, I'm completely confident. I'll ask Richard to try and keep to big stores so it's difficult to isolate us.'

'I don't like it but all right. Any messages through Richard so Claudine doesn't know.'

The first two stores were great fun and I almost relaxed, but after Richard parked outside the third, his whisper confirmed my worst fears. 'The car picked us up as we left the last store, it is now parked a little way up the road behind us.'

'Sound the alarm,' I whispered back.

I kept Claudine exploring for underwear, something ladies out together like to do, as long as possible and when we finally made for the doors, a handsome young man approached us and smiled, handing me a piece of paper. I read it and turned to Claudine, 'I have to make a quick visit somewhere, would you mind if I asked Peter to take you to the restaurant for a coffee until I return?'

She looked appreciatively at Peter and laughed, saying how could she refuse.

I walked out of the door and towards Richard pushing up the collar of Claudine's coat. When I was almost there he mouthed 'Be careful.' then opened the car door.

Suddenly, a man violently pushed his way partly between us, snarling to me, 'Get in the car!' and to Richard, 'don't do anything stupid.' Neither of us argued he had a stiletto type knife pressed to my ribs.

'Drive ahead, until I tell you to turn right,' he ordered Richard, adding, 'and don't try anything funny or she's a goner and believe me I mean it.'

He turned his face to me and growled, 'Your lot have been a damn nuisance, Claudine whatever your name is.'

'My name is Rebecca Tilsley.'

'You're what?' He pulled my collar down at exactly the time Richard shouted 'Now!' and slammed the car brakes on.

As the intruder was flung against the front seat, I grabbed his arm and twisted his knife round and pushed it into his leg causing him to explode into a great cry of pain.

Everything then happened at lightning speed. I was aware of Richard leaning over the front seat and dragging the man's head back as all the car doors opened and there seemed to be police everywhere. One of the police helped me out of the car and there before me was Graham wearing the broadest grin I had ever seen. He hugged me and kept saying 'Well done Rebecca, well done Rebecca.'

Richard pulled up again in front of the store and I fetched Claudine from an animated conversation with Peter. He declined a lift and we went on our way. Back in the car I said, 'I see you're preparing the ground in case you move to London.'

Claudine laughed, 'He's very nice and it's a bit of a coincidence his name is Peter.'

'Why, how many Peter's do you know apart from your possible new boss?'

'The one Graham told me to phone if I was in trouble.'

'Oh shit!!!'

She squeezed my hand. 'Whatever you have been doing, Rebecca, thank you.'

'I'll tell you about it one day,' I replied, 'but you don't need to know now.'

We hugged each other like a couple of schoolgirls and I saw Richard in the rear view mirror grinning, and then giving me a thumbs up.

Φ   Φ   Φ

I had what was becoming a regular before dinner call from Graham. He explained that he had been concerned if one of the men had been Paul Vachon it would have been necessary to call Claudine to identify him, but it was not. The man who drove the car is a known crook who is part of a drugs gang. With his record he will go down for 20 years so that's the end of his evil career. The man who held the knife on you is the man you photographed and he is something of an amateur who refused to say who he is but is daft enough to carry a driving licence. It says his name is Christopher Pierront. We think he is the son of Daniel Pierront, the thug I shot, but we are continuing investigations.' He added that he would stay in London for the next two or three days to make sure the London end was now closed.

'I did ask if you two were available to fly to France with me next Saturday, so we can all go together, but because of the success of your operation, I will probably go the day before. My plan is to see Marius and bring him up to speed.'

'We understand,'

'Rebecca, all we need now is Paul Vachon.'

'I'll bring you his head on a plate one day.'

'Don't be melodramatic, it's not ladylike.'

A discussion over dinner confirmed we were happy with Graham's plans. Lady Sophie suggested we spend our remaining three days in a flat she owned in Bath. A generous offer we accepted with great pleasure.

We learnt over breakfast that Richard would not only drive us down to Bath, he would stay to look after us during our visit. 'He is also a very good cook,' Sophie explained.

Richard drove out of London and for some distance on a motorway which I recognised as the M4 and turned off to detour and stop in the interesting old town of Marlborough. I had never been to Marlborough and, of course, it was all new to Claudine. We had coffee, then moved on to stop at the stone circle of Avebury. Lady Sophie said Avebury had many happy associations with her teenage years, but did not explain.

Not long after, we stopped at a country pub for lunch and I was surprised when the Landlord came from behind the bar to greet us and lead us to a reserved table with a view over the garden.

'You obviously made sure of a decent table for us,' I half foolishly commented.

'I leave that sort of thing to Richard,' she replied. 'I do know the hostelry well because it is owned within my family.'

'But, of course,' I secretly thought.

After what else but an excellent lunch, joined at Sophie's invitation, by Richard, we moved on to Bath arriving in mid-afternoon.

The flat was close to the Royal Crescent and was as big as a house with Claudine and me sharing an enormous bedroom with twin beds nearly as big as doubles. 'It's another world,' she said in wonder.

It was indeed and my gratitude to Sophie increased by the hour. Not only for her invitation to stay with her in London, but also for the delight of the trip to Bath - a light year away from the Men in Black – and something so new and entertaining it was just the right medicine for Claudine.

Richard managed to serve us an excellent four-course meal without effort, but did not join us at the table.

After, we relaxed in chairs soft enough to send us to sleep. We all three accepted a port from a decanter. I slowly twirled my glass while watching Claudine talking animatedly with Sophie. Noticing her confident and relaxed manner speaking to Lady Sophie as an equal, I saw a Claudine so different from the girlish devil may care from Rochenoir. Unaccountably, Sam came into my mind. He had seen there was another layer under the attractive girl who stole hearts so easily. I realised then the reason she had wanted to go to the Roman bridge to say good-bye to Sam. They were closer than I thought with Sam becoming a surrogate father. I was just thinking, 'She must miss him like hell,' when I realised Sophie had directed a question my way.

'Sorry Sophie, I think soporific would describe my state of mind.'

She smiled, 'That's good you are able to relax after all your adventures. I asked if Graham had much to say about his activities?'

I realised Sophie was hinting that she thought I ought to pass any information I had to Claudine, but I was also of the opinion I was a better judge of what she should know, although accepting my attitude was bound to be over protective.

Mindful that Graham must have discussed the situation with her, I chose my words very carefully but at the same time sending a signal back that I did not agree with her.

'Graham told me that in some sort of sting operation they had picked up a man named Christopher Pierront, who is the son of the late Daniel Pierront. They knew who he was from an undercover photograph that I took. There was a man with him who is a known criminal and he is talking so freely they are satisfied there is no organised group in this country that is anything to do with the French group we are after. Christopher Pierront only flew to England the day before we did and the French authorities are seeking his extradition.'

Claudine had been listening quietly and asked, 'You took the photograph the day you left me with Peter?'

'Sort of!'

'Thank you, Rebecca.'

Claudine turned back to Sophie and said, 'Thank you for your concern, Sophie, I realise you were prompting Rebecca to tell me more of the information that Graham told her. I really understand you believe it is safer for me to know these facts than to be kept in the, how do you say, kept in the dark. What you may not know is that I trust Rebecca implicitly (I saw a twitch of her mouth aimed at me when she used the new word) and am perfectly happy with her account.'

She added, 'It's marvellous to be here and I cannot find enough words to thank you.'

Sophie smiled, 'I hope you will not just come again but visit me often.'

Listening to the exchange my thoughts were overwhelming me in the certainty that there was so much strength to Claudine that it seemed impossible she was bothering with the sulky Jean when her perfect mate was so close to her. Her next words reassured me.

'I was talking to Peter, the boss here, about Egg and he suggested I might like to use the office computer to email him to say all was well with me. So I did mail him telling how much I was enjoying my visit and how much he would have enjoyed seeing the up-to-date computer equipment they use.'

'He replied that it seems quiet in Rochenoir without me.'

I relaxed. She talks to her new boss about Egg; sends him an email on the office computer; he sent a reply. 'All is well and on course,' I smiled like a contented cat.

Lady Sophie asked us if wanted to explore Bath on our own or if we would like her to organise a tour of the more famous sights during which she would be our guide.

We had no need to consult and accepted in unison.

'I am so pleased,' Sophie replied, 'it's not often I am blessed with two such young and charming companions. Do you know anything about the Authoress Jane Austen? She stayed in Bath in this very Square in number 13.

I had read a couple of Jane Austen's books as a teenager and Claudine had heard of her but read none of her works.

Sophie explained Jane Austen had lived only 41 years spread over the 1770s to the 1810s during which she wrote six great novels, four of them anonymously and two of them published after her death. Sophie thought it sad that Jane had not enjoyed in her lifetime the acclaim her books later earned.

At Sophie's words Claudine had sat erect and listened attentively. 'Had she a family?' she asked.

Not of her own,' Sophie replied. 'She never married. Her father was Rector of a church in Hampshire. There were seven children, Jane was number five. She was very close to her sister, Cassandra, and they wrote each other many letters, some of which have been published.'

'Oh!' Claudine exclaimed, 'I would love to read them.'

'They have been published several times. Perhaps I have a copy.' We all explored the bookshelves, but we were out of luck. 'Maybe it's in London,' Sophie said. 'We will be visiting the Jane Austen Museum tomorrow, we may find one there.'

After Claudine had gone to prepare for bed, I apologised to Lady Sophie. 'Sorry not to pick up your suggestion, Sophie, but there is more that I don't ever want Claudine to know. When Pierront eventually talked he said he had been sent from France by Paul Vachon, not just to kidnap Claudine, but to kill her in revenge for his brother's death.'

Φ   Φ   Φ

Next day, Lady Sophie turned out to be an excellent guide for a well planned tour with much input from Richard the Chauffeur. Sometimes we strolled, sometimes Richard appeared with the car just when we wanted him. We passed through Trim Street, which Sophie said was named after George Trim, a Clothier.

Did we think that was where "to trim" came from?

On foot we inspected a 15th century teashop Sally Lunn's, in what used to be called Lilliput Lane. Sophie said the teashop was named after a woman who sold cakes there in 1680. Then to the Roman Baths and to the elegant Grand Pump Room where Sophie had reserved a table for us. We enjoyed a leisurely lunch while a "Trio" of musicians played to entertain.

The afternoon was spent in the Assembly Rooms and the wonderful Museum of Costume. I absolutely loved the myriad costumes and Claudine was not far behind me. She specially liked an evening dress of white bead-embroidered muslin.

'Can you see me in that, Rebecca?'

'Yes, it would look great on you.'

'Do you think Jane Austen wore it?'

'Possibly,' Sophie replied. 'If not I'm sure she would have had something similar, she loved dancing.'

'How about Egg in that,' Claudine laughed, pointing to a male mannequin dressed in skin tight brown trousers with a cut away jacket and a shirt with lace ruffs

I chuckled. 'Actually I think he would look great in it, but I doubt he would wear it.'

It was a tired but happy trio who collapsed into Sophie's armchairs while a seemingly inexhaustible Richard plied us with hot tea and bath buns.

Sophie looked at us a little wistfully, 'I will miss your company when you return to France. You must come again whenever you want.'

'I would say the same to you, Sophie,' I answered, 'but I don't know how much longer Harry and I will be in France,'

Claudine looked quite shocked. 'Rebecca!!! I had quite forgotten you were only on holiday and would be going back to England.'

'Intuition tells me I might be back for a wedding,' I replied.

Claudine only smiled, but I read enough into her reaction to start planning my outfit.

When we went upstairs to bed we both found a book of the letters of Jane Austen on our pillows.

Revenge in Rochenoir

Chapter Seventeen
The Monastery

Claudine and I arrived at Labaraquette well before Egg and Harry and what a deluge of questions we had to answer from Albert and Brigitte.

'We have been wondering and hoping you were enjoying yourself and Egg has been pacing the carpet hoping you were well.' Brigitte said. 'I told him of course you were well. You were on holiday in England and meeting new people.'

'Yes, that's true,' Claudine gave me a smile.

Egg and Harry arrived at the rambling old farmhouse to the usual effusive welcome and Marmite, the brute of a dog, rushed into the room making straight for Harry, to his slight consternation, then stopped just short and growled.

He crouched down, 'Marmite, is this some form of acceptance?'

Their eyes were almost on a level in a mutual communication. Harry sensed Marmite was testing his nerve so kept perfectly still, holding the dog's gaze. After a few moments, Marmite just turned and walked back to the kitchen.

The others, silent up to that point, all thought it a good omen. 'He hasn't growled at anyone since Sam died, perhaps he will adopt you,' Brigitte seemed delighted.

'Is it an honour to be threatened by the family dog?' Harry asked of no one in particular. Which was just as well because no one answered when, at that point, Graham and Marius arrived.

Graham went straight to Harry, 'Tell me about this injury to your leg.'

'It's not too bad. They set a mantrap to catch one of us, but it was old and rusty so did not work properly.'

'So we can expect you to die of blood poisoning instead of fainting away.'

'I'm not the fainting away type.'

Graham grinned and turned to Egg, 'Thought I told you to keep out of trouble?'

'We did.'

'I see I'm still wasting my time.'

Harry shook hands with Marius, not having met him before. 'How is life in the Compagnies Républicaines de Sécurité,' he asked.

'Quiet compared to working with Graham,' Marius answered.

'Come and have wine,' Albert announced. An offer no one refused

When we had settled down with comments of appreciation in regard to Albert's very fine rosé, Graham explained that the Spanish police were still satisfied all was well with the Monastery Izlariette.

'Have they searched the place?' I asked.

'They have no reason to do so.'

'Then we'll have to bust in.'

To the amusement of Marius, Graham protested indignantly, 'Rebecca, so far you have "busted in", as you call it, to the Casino and the wood yard and done more harm than good. Can we start applying a little science and co-operation?'

'Meanwhile they shoot at us.'

Marius interceded, 'The Men in Black you have encountered seem to be a separate group who have imitated the monks as a cover. What we don't know is where their base is.' He shook his head to stop Egg interrupting and continued. 'We don't think it is possible for them to be a cell within the monks because the order is too strict and they would be found out. They must be hiding somewhere nearby and the Spanish are looking into this, but without success so far. There is a possibility of concealed caves in the area and that might be an answer. One thing is certain and that is they have, in a manner of speaking, gone to ground since the car went into the lake.'

'If you're looking for caves, you have a geologist and an archaeologist already on your team,' Harry pointed out.'

'Come and eat now,' Brigitte announced.

There was much talk of Claudine and her trip to London during the meal, but with coffee the conversation switched to the subject that had brought us together.

I started by telling them I had unproved information from Louis that he felt just knowing it was potentially dangerous and to speak of it fatal. 'In fact, he made me promise to keep his identity secret if we felt it necessary to pass it on to anyone else. Of course, I made that promise.' Unsurprisingly, Graham and Marius were happy to make the same promise so I told them the tale of the wartime rumours that a bombed out bank had been looted by the Gang of Four and their accomplices. 'He doesn't know where the bank was or even if the gold was thought to have been destroyed by the bomb,' I finished.

Graham gave a little whistle, 'It would certainly explain a lot,' he agreed. 'Good job the perpetrators, if it happened, are dead for looting was punishable by execution by a firing squad. Possibly, it's the same for possession.'

'It seems,' he said cautiously, 'more than probable that it has become too difficult for the smuggling gang to dispose of the gold legally or without attracting attention and your new information may have a bearing on this. They have turned to using the gold to buy drugs for resale in order to turn it into cash. What better way of disguising its origin. This has obviously opened a door for the more crooked members of the gang to start up their own sidelines by stealing from their compatriots. Hence, a cover up over the men who died. Remember also they have now lost at least three men and there can only be a handful of them left. Events are moving into our favour.'

'Why did you say "at least three men?"' Harry asked.

'Let me answer,' Marius said to Graham. 'We must assume the man Rebecca dealt with in the Casino is out of action and Christopher Pierront may have been part of Vachon's gang.'

'Are you going to arrest me?' I suggested.

'No, I was about to ask you to join my team in Paris.'

'I'm tempted, when do I start?'

Graham snorted, 'No chance. Marius has something to do of his own for the moment so those of us who are fit will go and have a scout round the Monastery and see if we can produce any ideas.'

'Just a minute,' Harry protested. 'Why am I left out? Earlier, you suggested a need for scientific help.'

'Your not fit.'

'Only a bit stiff.'

'Harry,' Graham said a trifle sharply, 'If there was any kind of chase we would have to abandon you.'

'Agreed!'

'Very well! But I mean it; if you come with us you can expect no special treatment. We will not put this operation at risk to save you.'

Φ   Φ   Φ

Next day immediately after one of Brigitte's marvellous breakfasts, I drove Harry, Egg and Graham along the route over the mountains from St-Jean-Pied-a-Port to the location where the crook's car had crashed in the lake. Graham had expressed a desire to visit the spot, but had explained he would understand if we would rather not.

Harry remembered my saying that I had no wish to go there again, but as far as he was concerned, the men were trying to kill us and deserved what they got.

'Good man,' Graham replied. A comment that produced a smile all round.

When I could get a word in, I acknowledged my previous opinion, but was all right now.

In the event, it was Harry who admitted to me it gave him a strange feeling to stand gazing at the still waters. Egg came to us and said quietly, 'It could so easily be us at the bottom of the lake and no one would have known where we were. Possibly for ever.'

This gave me a slight shock for I hadn't thought about that. Our visit was unplanned and to our families the four of us would simply have been missing, while we were really... No!! I mentally shook myself, best not to think about that. Suddenly, I wanted to be as far away from the lake as it was possible to be. 'Are you ready to move on, Graham?' I asked abruptly.

He gently took my hand. 'Yup.' he answered in a sympathetic tone. 'They're not down there you know Rebecca. It's all been sorted out. I think you have been an absolute brick.'

'Oh! Graham,' I answered, 'then I really would have been sunk.'

For some reason we all felt better about the event and relaxed a little. I could see Egg felt the same. We turned as one and walked to the car.

Before leaving the farm we had studied a large-scale map of the area around the monastery and had selected a spot where we could park the car as if we were tourists. The plan was to walk up round the mountain to reach the monastery from behind. Harry was desperately hoping he could make it and had taken a couple of painkillers in case he had difficulty. He was equally anxious not to be left behind, but Graham wouldn't hear of him joining on foot.

'Keep with the car,' he ordered, 'then if I need you, drive round and come up to the Monastery by the front drive.'

'If he had tried walking with us I would have been giving him hell,' I confided in Egg.

He laughed. 'I would have the same problem with Claudine.'

'But you tell me you are just good friends. Why should your activities concern her?'

Before he could answer Graham asked, 'What's this Egg, old chap, you're not mixing dangerous gold hunting with pleasurable activities, are you?'

'No, not until we have caught the last of the killers.'

Graham raised his eyebrows in my direction and I guessed the reason. Egg had not actually denied the question of an association with Claudine.

When we came in sight of the Monastery, the whole appearance and layout was totally different from all our expectations. As the expression goes, we stopped in our tracks.

'What's up?' Graham asked, as perceptive as ever.

I responded, 'From the way people spoke, Egg and I visualised a sort of church on top of a hill scenario, but this is nothing like that.'

Indeed it was not. The surrounding mountains were quite rugged and although we had climbed a fair height, they still dwarfed the Monastery. Only about a hundred metres away from the buildings there were cliffs that were higher than the Monastery. Massive outcrops of rock just about everywhere else. The whole scattered with trees and assorted scrub. True, there were views from some places and the area vast, but the general feeling was claustrophobic with a hundred and one hiding places.

'Surely a gang could hide out here?' Egg exclaimed.

'Difficult, but yes,' was Graham's view.

'If they had a hidden access for supplies, it would be easier,' Egg commented. 'Don't forget they have plenty of money to make whatever arrangements they need.'

'It's going to take some time to search even this area,' I observed.

'Well! Let's go and bang on the door,' Graham answered. 'And remember, none of us can speak French or Spanish.'

The first door we found on the side facing the cliffs produced nothing because nobody responded. We had better luck with the front door when our knocking produced a recorded voice making an announcement in Spanish.

'Well! We can't understand that funny foreign language telling us to go away because this is a closed order,' Graham said quietly, 'So, we better knock again.'

Egg pointed to a notice in Spanish beside the door. 'That says that they do not accept visitors and all communication should be in writing.'

'As I said, what a pity we don't understand it,' Graham responded with a grin, as he banged and thumped the door again.

'Actually, I really don't understand any of it,' I offered.

'Best you talk to them when they answer then. Tell them we are English walkers who are lost and in need of sustenance.'

I looked at his well-nourished form and said they would never believe that.

After another battering on the door it was slowly opened and a monk eyed each of us in turn before asking something in Spanish. I didn't understand it and my two companions who appeared to know more Spanish than I had previously credited, remained silent.

I explained to the monk in English that my name was Rebecca and that we were lost. He paused for a moment then shut the door without comment.

We stood looking at each other for guidance and eventually I asked of no one in particular, 'Is that it?'

The door suddenly opened again and an older monk appeared who was wearing a different coloured habit. 'What do you want?' he asked me in English in a peremptory tone.

I went through my routine.

The monk pointed down what was obviously an access road and said, 'Down there is a road where in time a car will pass. Signal you want to be transported.'

'Is there any possibility of some refreshment. We have walked a long way and are tired and thirsty.' Even as I said this, my realisation was that the comment was a non-starter. We simply didn't look tired and thirsty. The monk clearly thought the same; he slammed the door shut without replying.

'There're not many windows on the building,' Graham commented. 'If we're careful we should be able to have a look round without them knowing.'

'You've already seen the size of the place,' I said dryly. 'Do you think we'll be finished by Christmas?'

Egg, who had walked a short distance away called, 'This may help.'

We walked over to him and he pointed out a faint track in the ground where it passed between two large rocks. 'Many feet have passed this way,' Egg explained.

We followed the track, which sometimes petered out on the hard rock as we wound our way through a wilderness of scrub and rock. Our steps took us ever closer to a rocky cliff, something the eye was unable to resist. I paused looking up at a clear blue sky. A sky that was more than blue, it was impossibly blue. A momentary flash from the cliff then caught my eye. The sort of flash I had seen before when binoculars caught the sun. I passed my opinion to the others.

Graham agreed immediately, even without seeing the flash. 'No more than I would expect from a bunch of murdering crooks.'

Egg laughed. 'Graham is quite positive with his judgements. He would save the courts a lot of money if he was a Chief Justice.'

'I'm quite fair,' Graham responded. 'If they think they are innocent I will listen.'

We proceeded with a little more caution although if we were being watched from above there was little we could do to hide. The land flattened out a bit as we reached the base of the cliff and almost immediately I pointed out a smudge on the ground.

'What is it,' Graham asked.

'A tyre track,' I replied.

'Oh come on, how do you make a tyre track out of that?'

'I'm a geologist.'

'Rebecca, old girl, I hate to disappoint you but from Roman chariots to knights mediaeval to good old Queen Victoria there was not much call for tyres. Surely they do not figure at all in geology?'

'The principle's the same and I have already warned you what I would do if you called me "old girl" again.'

'I'll buy you some soft shoes, wait until then.'

We inspected the mark, which just about showed what might have been the tread of a tyre without offering any other evidence.

Suddenly there was a slight puff of dust in the ground near Egg's feet and he stepped back exclaiming, 'What was that?' As he began to speak there was the sound of percussion.

'A bullet,' Graham replied in a matter of fact voice.

We all shouted, "A bullet!!!" before diving behind the nearest rock.

'Well,' Graham came out with a pearl of wisdom. 'We are quite safe if the bandit is in front of us, but if he is behind our rock he is just lining up his sights.'

'Thank you for that reassuring information.'

Nothing more happened.

'I've seen this done in the pictures,' I announced, putting my sun hat on a stick and raising it just above the rock. 'The crook will fire and give himself away,' I added.

'He's already given himself away,' Graham had a sarcastic tone in his voice, 'When he tried to shoot Egg's trainers off his feet.'

'Move the hat along as if you are walking,' Egg suggested. Then added with a strained sort of grin, 'I saw that on television.'

I obligingly bobbed the hat along.

Nothing happened.

'He's long gone,' Graham sounded exasperated. 'Let's stop playing silly games.' He stood up, there was another crack and he hastily dropped down again. 'Bastard,' he said feelingly as he rubbed his ear.

'Good job he missed,' I opined.

'What do you think this is,' he held up a bloody hand. 'I'm bleeding to death.'

Egg checked his ear. 'The bullet just nicked the lobe,' he announced. 'You're ok unless you're thinking of wearing ear rings.'

'We're joking about our predicament,' I said with some concern. 'But this is serious. What are we going to do?'

'Well!' Graham replied, 'we can run away. Harry's the one in trouble with a gammy leg if they find him. Are we going to save him or leave him to his fate?'

The vote to save him was a predictable two to one.

Graham announced, 'When I stood up and the idiot fired it gave me a rough idea where he was. Mind you, he's a better shot than I expected.'

'So, how are we going to flush him out?'

'With this.' Graham rummaged in a little sack he had slung over his shoulder and as we watched, speechless, held out a hand grenade, pulled the pin, and gave it a powerful throw over our rock.

As the grenade exploded, he shouted, 'Come on,' and we did.

We found no trace of the crook and in minutes there was no trace of us.

Φ   Φ   Φ

Back at Labaraquette we recovered our composure over a brandy while Brigitte fussed over Graham's ear.

'For God's sake, 'I asked him, 'what on earth are you going to produce next, an armoured car?'

'We've proved they have something to hide,' Egg commented.

'Sadly, we've proved nothing,' Graham responded. 'We have no evidence of a shot and nothing to implicate the Monastery. We will have to try again early tomorrow morning.'

Brigitte and Claudine went off to the kitchen to prepare supper and Albert to look for wine. As soon as the door closed behind them Graham said to Harry. 'Would you excuse us for just five minutes old chap, I have something important to say to Rebecca while the others are in the kitchen?'

"Sure,' he replied, 'I'll go up to wash and change my shirt.'

Graham looked the most serious I had ever seen him as he said quietly to me. 'Rebecca, old girl, I want you to give everything you have into finding out how Vachon knew you and Claudine were going to London. Absolutely no one from my side breathed a word and I've spoken to Lady Sophie and Ramel and received the same assurance. Someone with access to us overheard something and spilled the beans. An action that nearly resulted in her death. I don't want to pre-empt your enquiry, but I don't see how it could have been anyone other than Jean.'

Revenge in Rochenoir

Chapter Eighteen
New Information

'What is the purpose of that?' Egg asked as Harry pinned a notice to the wall of our flat.

His enquiry was aimed at a sheet of paper whose content was quite simple-

Men in Black Gang	10
Minus one missing	9
One thrown down stairs	8
Minus two drowned	6
Minus one arrested	5

'It's obvious,' he replied. 'Yesterday Graham mentioned the losses they were suffering. This is our score against the Men in Black.

'I think Rebecca will say it's in bad taste.'

'Yes, I am going to say it's in bad taste. Take it down.'

'Why shouldn't we keep tally of our successes?'

'Rebecca appears to think like Claudine about many things and I will guess she also will say it's in bad taste,' Egg offered.

None the less the score sheet was left on the wall.

'It's almost five, we better go and pick up Graham,' I said

The phone rang it was Graham.

'You must be a mind reader,' Harry greeted him. 'Rebecca was just suggesting it was time to pick you up.'

'No!' he said. 'But you do need to be reading my mind because there is no way you are coming with us this morning. We were lucky yesterday. They will be waiting for us today.'

Harry protested he was looking forward to helping.'

The answer was painfully clear, 'No, you are not welcome in your present state. As I've already said, your presence with a bad leg could very easily put us all in danger. Rebecca, Egg and I will have enough on our plate without having to worry about you.'

Harry regretfully agreed he had a point, but Graham did relent and say he could join us as a back up providing and only if he stayed in the car. Harry acquiesced to the terms.

I drove over the border into Spain and headed for the mountain plateau where I parked in a different place on the western side. This was a precaution in case the Men in Black had seen our car the last time. Even though we had taken a different car on our visit the day before, Graham ruled we were to take no unnecessary chances, so we were in his car.

Harry had a very long face as we walked away without a backward glance.

Graham suggested we worked our way northwards to the higher ground allowing us to approach the Monastery via the top of the cliffs on the opposite side of the valley to where I had seen the reflection. This we managed easily and without encountering trouble or seeing anyone. Our position certainly gave us a grandstand view of the Monastery. However, any hopes of catching a Man in Black on the hop was dashed. Absolutely nothing was moving.

On such a clear day when the hot sun made everything stand our sharply the landscape looking like a brightly lit film set. The slightest movement would be easily detected. I thought, ruefully, the same applied to us. A man with binoculars would see us easily.

From our vantage point we could see with more clarity the unique position of the building. It was certainly protected from view on all sides by rugged cliffs; massive tumbles of rock and trees, none of which was really close to the main building. Between the cliffs and the buildings was some of the proliferation of greenery in varying sizes and smaller jumbles of rock. The road in from the south could clearly be seen from our new vantage point, except where it passed under trees. Another, smaller, road or track went away from behind the Monastery passing below where we were lying looking over the cliff. To our right the smaller road curved through some rocks before turning to the west as it cut down through a sort of gorge.

While we watched Egg was sure he could hear a vehicle approaching, but we saw nothing moving below. Then, from under the trees to our left, a quad bike towing a small trailer appeared. It passed along the road beneath us until hidden by the trees again.

'Where did that come from? Not the access road or we would have seen it before' I asked. 'That bike can only have come from the back of the Monastery. How can the monks claim no knowledge with that noisy thing chuntering around.'

'Something for me to discuss with the Spanish authorities,' Graham promised.

What the man on the quad bike was doing was something we were unable to answer. Although we watched for a while the bike failed to reappear.

As Egg remarked, 'The Men in Black are acting as if they own the Monastery.'

We worked our way down from the cliffs and round to the smaller road, having no difficulty with concealment for our route was mainly out of sight of the Monastery. Except, having seen the Man in Black from the cliffs we kept a sharp lookout for him and his bike. Of course, ever cheerful Graham commented as we passed a thick copse of trees, 'The crooks are hardly likely to call out "Good Afternoon" they'll just take a pot shot at us.'

We turned into the secondary road walking some distance trying to ascertain its purpose. Our exploration of the road availed us nothing for the tarmac track just seemed to go on and on. We stopped to consider what next and while quietly talking, sitting on wayside rocks, we heard the low sound of an approaching engine.

Only nothing came.

'I'm sure that was the sound of the same engine,' Egg ventured.

'Perhaps it's some kind of patrol, 'I asked. 'Maybe someone saw us approach and sent a warning or instructions to investigate. As Graham said, the first we'll know is when they do what they did last time, start shooting'

'Spread out a bit so as to make a harder target,' Graham ordered.

'Gee thanks, you certainly always have our best interest at heart. Let's skedaddle instead.'

There were no takers.

We moved on cautiously to investigate. As the road widened and dropped down below the higher rocks the route became bordered with a scattering of trees on each side of the road. 'We need a helicopter,' Graham grumbled.

'How about the noise?'

'Three bicycles then.'

We looked at each other, 'Three bicycles!!

Tomorrow?

'You know,' Graham growled. 'This might just be another road in and out. That's something Harry can check.' He dialed a number on his mobile phone.

'Who are you phoning?'

'Myself. On another number.'

Obviously he had an answer almost immediately.

'Oh Harry! Pleased you're not asleep. There's a large-scale map of the area in the door pocket. Have a look to see if you can identify the Monastery. It's ringed in red, that will be a help.'

'There's no need to be offensive.'

'That was a joke, old man.'

Harry did identify the road and reported it started some distance away and was marked as unsuitable for traffic.

'You'll be pleased to be driving my car instead of yours then,' Graham replied. 'I want you to find the road and drive up to meet us.'

I asked him, as he put the phone in his pocket, 'You don't think there is any danger in Harry driving up here? We don't know yet where the engine noise we heard came from and you said yourself, they'll shoot first and ask questions afterwards.'

'Danger?' The idea had clearly never occurred to him. 'He's a big lad,' was his ultimate verdict.

'Unarmed and remember he's only an archaeologist.'

Graham sighed and pulled out his mobile phone again, but before he could use it, a man's voice shocked us by shouting, 'Stand perfectly still and put your arms in the air.'

What we did was dive behind assorted rocks while several shots spattered around us.

'Crikey!!' Graham exclaimed. 'We seem to have annoyed someone.'

From our temporary shelter, he tried to phone Harry but there was no reply.

With his back to a rock, Egg looked around at the trees and then to more distant rocks and screes, 'they could be anywhere in this sort of terrain.' Then he saw a movement. 'Someone is working round to cut us off,' and at that moment a bullet hit the rock above our heads.

We scrambled deeper amongst the rocks.

Graham took a pistol out of his backpack. 'Rebecca, I'm going to try and work my way towards them. You two stay here and throw rocks about to distract them, but don't show yourselves.'

'Graham, there's at least two of them.'

'Can't be helped old girl, wish me luck,' and he was off immediately attracting shots, particularly when he once bobbed up to fire back.

I felt helpless; the Men in Black appeared to be taking little notice of our efforts to create a diversion by throwing rocks. They must have realised only one of us was armed.

Picking up a couple of heavy rocks, I called to Egg, 'Hold the fort,' and slithered down towards the road desperately looking here, there and everywhere.

I heard Egg scream a warning to Graham that one of the Men in Black was trotting down the road towards him, but out of Graham's sight. Egg, without any kind of weapon, was helpless to intervene.

I made it to a big rock that easily concealed me, conveniently right on the edge of the road, with splinters of rock showering around me as bullets smacked into the rock face.

It was at that moment Harry came up the road in the car and without any knowledge of the situation saw the man in the road. Knowing a running Man in Black was bad news whatever he was doing Harry drove straight at him.

The man managed two shots at the car's windscreen before he had to dive out of the way. Harry appeared untouched as he swerved past my hiding place.

As I heard more shots from further up the road, Harry tried to turn the car but the road was not wide enough and he became stuck and had to reverse with tyres protesting as the man he missed stood up and started shooting at him.

Hastily twisting my head, looking for any more trouble, I saw it in the form of the quad bike carrying two men coming straight down the road towards us. The man on the back of the bike was shooting wildly.

Harry told me later that although scared he was muttering to himself, 'We've been here before man,' as, having regained control of the car he drove straight for the bike and, fractionally, after his windscreen shattered in a hail of fire, the bike driver swerved violently away.

Harry was then astonished to see me jump up, a few feet from the bike, and hurl a rock that hit the driver, causing him to swerve again while still off balance from avoiding Harry's car.

The bike wobbled viciously then gave such a jolt the man on the rear seat, who had fired a couple of shots at me, was thrown onto the rocks. The quad bike then disappeared down the road; the driver abandoned his companion.

Graham appeared from nowhere, 'Come on,' he shouted, 'they're running. After them.' He ran towards the scree slopes.

I checked the man on the rocks, he was dead from a broken neck, and ran after Graham, at the same time seeing Egg hurrying to join us. Looking back Harry was laboriously hobbling along trying to catch up. 'Go back, I shouted to him,' and followed the others.

We saw no sign of our adversary and eventually stopped, panting for breath.

'Hopeless in this sort of terrain,' Graham spread his hands wide.

Harry hobbled up a few moments after. 'You're lucky to be alive,' Graham greeted him. 'If I hadn't winged the chap shooting at you, even a rotten shot like him would have eventually got you.' Then he peered at me, 'Is that blood on your arm?'

I looked down at a red patch in astonishment, while Egg was at my side in an instant, producing a snowy white handkerchief that he proceeded to ruin wiping and binding my arm.

'It's another miracle,' he said in wonder, 'a bullet must have just broken the skin, it might have killed you.'

'A miss is as good as a mile,' I joked, with a tremble in my voice.

'You don't understand, Rebecca.' He showed me a tear in the side of my cotton top. 'The bullet passed through the gap just below your armpit tearing between your arm and your body. An inch either way would have been serious.'

'What?' Graham exclaimed coming to me with concern written large on his face. 'No more Rebecca, that's enough, we can't have you taking this sort of risk.'

'It could have happened to any of us.'

Graham looked anxiously at Egg, asking if everyone else was all right and received an affirmative.

'The man who fell off the bike's dead, broken neck,' I reported.

'That probably saved at least one of our lives.'

'I didn't mean to kill him,' I answered.

'You didn't,' Graham answered. 'What those two men on the bike did was suicidal and if you hadn't acted so swiftly we would be looking at one of our bodies. Oh! By the way, well done, Harry. I hope you haven't damaged my car? Let's go and check out the dead murderer, with luck it's Paul Vachon.'

Only we didn't. When we returned to the spot where he had fallen off the bike, the body had gone.

Chapter Nineteen
Return to Leizar Athéka

After first aid in the form of a small dressing on my arm, we adventurers settled in Egg's apartment to discuss the day's events. First he surprised Graham by passing him a stiff shot of malt whisky. 'I remembered Sam once saying you liked this,' he commented.

'Good Lord,' Graham exclaimed. 'I never thought to see the like in foreign parts.'

Harry and I opted to join Egg with a cognac.

Suddenly Graham rose out of his chair and strode over to Harry's list on the wall. He studied it for a moment, took out a pen, made a note and went back to his chair.

Harry could not resist going to read what had been inscribed. It read, 'Minus one bounced, remainder four.'

'Now there are more of us than there are Men in Black,' Graham said.

'There may be people we don't know about,' I warned.

He pulled out his flashy mobile and asked us if we minded then punched the number of his contact in the Spanish police. A short conversation in Spanish followed.

Egg whispered to me, 'He is asking the police about the Monastery.'

The call clearly became more complicated and Graham resorted occasionally to a few words of English. Once he turned to Egg and asked the Spanish for "Quad Bike" but there was no need to answer. It seemed the Spaniard on the other end of the call knew. Eventually the call ended and Graham sat deep in thought.

'Whatever the Spanish police say,' he announced, 'the monks in that abbey are in on this operation.'

'That's not possible,' Egg replied.

'Today there was shooting and yesterday an explosion near the abbey yet not a word of it reached the ears of the Spanish police. If the monks are innocent, why didn't they report the gunfire to the police?'

'The abbey walls are pretty thick,' Harry answered. 'They may have heard nothing.'

'Tosh!!'

Egg laughed.

'All right,' I replied, 'what happens now? Do we smash our way in?'

Egg laughed again, 'I don't think that's an option.'

'Not yet,' Graham had a growl in his voice, 'but they are asking for it. My Spanish friend is going to pay them another visit and asked again for any definite evidence, which, of course, we don't have. I promised him we would not go back again until he contacted me after his visit. He is a bit unhappy I went there without telling him, so it's humour the Spaniard time.'

I stirred, 'If you're champing at the bit, we ought to have another go at the Casino.'

'Good idea! I've never seen inside it.'

I noticed the use of the word "inside" and assumed it meant Graham had already inspected the outside. I cursed silently to myself. Why did we have to hold back all the time? Why didn't we push on and sort it out?

He broke into my thoughts. 'Rebecca, I can see you are also champing at the proverbial bit, but we have to be patient and gather evidence.'

I suggested we did just that; gather evidence straight away, like tomorrow. 'Should be all quiet on a Sunday,' I added.

But Graham decided he ought to fly to Paris for a meeting with Marius and suggested we all went to the Casino on Wednesday and we had to be content with that.

I walked with him to his hire car so I could explain my answer to his question regarding the leak over my visit to London with Claudine. No matter which way I considered the matter there was only one tangible suspect.

'Jean,' I said. 'He was really angry about Claudine going to stay with Lady Sophie and it resulted in them breaking up. If his action was a flash of childish spite, he may have ended up with her death on his conscience.'

'What do we do?'

'I'll talk to him and if I think it was just stupidity, I'll suggest he leaves town for at least a year. Anything else I'll pass to Ramel.'

'Good girl, over to you.'

'Well! that's an improvement on "old girl". I still owe you a kick or two by the way.'

Φ   Φ   Φ

Harry, Egg and I got together to organise a picnic to take advantage of the currently gorgeous weather and phone calls to Claudine, Nicole and Hélène swiftly made up a party of six. Egg suggested Leizar Athéka, explaining to me the musketeers had picnics there before and it might reassure Claudine to go normally to places they had all been before.

We shared the passengers into two cars, Claudine's, and ours and departed to the mountains on a perfect day. Egg came in our car leaving three girls in the other. Harry joked the men were staying together for protection. 'They should be so lucky,' was my response.

As we wound up the endlessly twisting road through the forest it was so beautiful I was tempted to ask the others to drop me off, but it would have been selfish to disrupt the party by walking up on my own. Then there was another of those astonishing coincidences when Egg suddenly matched my thoughts.

'Rebecca, I would love to walk up through the forest, it is so beautiful, but not much fun on my own. I wonder if you and Harry would like to join me one day. Perhaps Claudine as well, although she is not as keen as I to embark on long walks.'

'I'd be delighted to do so. How about you Harry?'

'In a week or two when my leg has had a bit of training to reduce the stiffness.'

Just then we broke from the forest above the tree line and were silent as we enjoyed the majesty of the mountains. Approaching the summit of the col beside Leizar Athéka, Harry could see Claudine had pulled off the road so he came to a stop, calling through his window, 'You stopping here ladies?'

Claudine came to us and suggested we walk down the footpath to see how Maria and Philippe were. 'I have never met them,' she said. 'To me they are a missing link.'

Egg explained, 'Vachon wanted to take her to the farm when he kidnapped her, but Maria and Philippe refused to let him.'

'But didn't tell the police what Vachon had done,' I reminded him.

'Like so many others they were afraid of Paul Vachon.'

'Well! if you wish,' I replied and Harry expressed an affirmative as well. My private thoughts were that we owed the couple nothing. Sure they refused to help Vachon, but to my mind it was criminal they did nothing to try and save Claudine.

It was a pleasant walk down the footpath. We girls in summer skirts and a variety of tops, but Hélène elegant as usual in light weight tan trousers with a brown check shirt. The weather was glorious and the view over the countryside more than impressive with part of Spain spread out before us. No one would have known a low opening to the left would curve round and open up to a wider, cliff backed valley with an old farmhouse nestling with its sheds and barns. A tall, lean looking man with black hair opened the door as we approached and called, apparently in Spanish, 'Do you want to go horse riding?' He then recognised Egg, saying, 'I remember you walking here some time ago.'

I was then thrown into some confusion, realising from what I had read of Claudine's kidnapping, it was probable that none of us, except Egg, had been there before. This meant I didn't have a clue what to say to a man I considered one of the enemy. I was actually cross with Egg for not preparing us for the meeting. Perhaps the others felt the same for we were all silent waiting for Egg to finish his conversation.

He waved an arm towards us and said, in English to Philippe, 'These are my friends.'

'Come in and welcome,' he replied in English.

'Could I have a word with you first?' Egg answered.

Philippe opened the door wider and a middle aged woman stepped through holding out a hand to shake all of ours. 'This is my wife Maria. She will show you the horses. Have a trot about if you want.' He then disappeared inside with Egg.

We followed Maria to the corrals and I whispered to Harry, 'This is a rum do.' I was also very interested in a very long barn a short distance from the corrals. Apart from its size it had an unusual feature in that it appeared to disappear into the slope of the valley.

I asked Maria about the barn and she seemed a little reticent, answering with a shrug. 'Surely it must be buried inside the mountain?' I persisted.

'In the days before refrigerators it was a way to keep food cool,' she explained.

'Fine,' I thought. 'Why make a mystery out of my question?'

Despite the unexpected and unusual situation we found ourselves in we had an entertaining half hour patting and stroking what seemed to be a very friendly bunch of horses and two leggy, but adorable colts. Maria introduced us to each horse and Harry mounted one trotting it round the compound to clapping and cheers from us all.

Hélène asked if he was willing to race all comers and the fool said 'Yes,' adding, 'I warn you I am experienced with quite a bit of riding,' he boasted. 'Are you challenging me to a race?'

'Yes, how about for 10 Euros.'

'You're on!' Harry asked Maria to open the corral gate for him.

Maria clapped her hands with delight and suggested they rode to the top of the valley; round a post they would see put there for just that purpose, and back again to the corral.

Harry pointed his horse in the right direction and looked round impatiently for Hélène who, having looked over the horses, had selected a stallion. She lead him out of the corral, having fitted reins and a bridle and was standing by his head whispering sweet nothings in the animal's ear.

'Il est fougueux,' Maria said to her.

'Bon.'

Maria checked the bridle and gave the reins to Hélène. 'I will bring a saddle,' she said.

'Don't bother, he's fine as he is.' Hélène stroked her horse's nose and said to Harry, 'Are you ready?'

'What is fougueux?' I asked Egg.

'Spirited.'

'Oh no!' I exclaimed, 'instinct tells me Harry's in for a pasting.'

Still standing beside her horse, Hélène cried, 'Then go!!!'

While Harry hesitated, Hélène grasped her horse's mane with both hands and jumped up across him, swinging her leg swiftly astride in a continuous smooth movement that the horse seemed to understand as it took off like a rocket the second she was settled. I watched her full of admiration as in full control of the animal, with her fair hair streaming behind her; she disappeared from view with Harry lumbering after her. 'What a woman, who could possibly tame her?' I said to Claudine.

'I know who! If he is interested,' she replied, 'but I will not say.'

A little later they rode back side by side and refused to say who had won, but then we all knew that anyway.

Philippe and Egg had joined us as the riders arrived and Philippe gave Hélène a hand down as she swung her leg back over the horse and slid down towards the ground.

'His name is "Pétard" he said.

Hélène walked to the horse's head and breathed "Pétard" in his ear. Pétard nuzzled her as she stroked him and for some reason I had a lump in my throat as I watched them together.

Philippe was talking to Hélène and I heard him say, 'You can come to ride him any time, there will be no charge.'

'I would like to do that,' Hélène replied.

A chastened Harry asked Philippe if the horse's name had a meaning.

'Yes, in English, it would be "Firecracker".

'There is coffee and biscuits at the house,' Maria cried, 'all are welcome.'

As we walked back Egg told me he had a long talk with Philippe about the past and he wanted to speak to us all and apologise for our problems.

We sat outside with our refreshments and Philippe stood facing us a little self-consciously. 'You all know we were associates of Coutard, Duval and Vachon, but I ask you to believe we were never friends and were never part of their organisation. We were helpless in their power mainly from Paul Vachon who is an evil man. Believe me when Coulon, Vachon and Duval died we celebrated our happiness, a happiness made dim only because Paul was still a free man. We are at threat from someone like Paul with our isolated position in this remote spot where we can expect help from no one. I might have thought to shoot Vachon by accident with my hunting rifle, but I am a Catholic and could never do something like that. Then he found out our only daughter was in a clinic on a machine and he said if we gave any trouble he would arrange for the machine to be switched off in the night. We spoke to the hospital and they said it was impossible for that to happen but we were terrified and dared not take the risk. Now our daughter has died we will be able to refuse any demand from Paul for help, although we are still afraid of him.'

He walked over to Claudine and took both her hands. 'That is why we did not tell the police when the Vachon brothers came here looking for somewhere to hide you. We took courage to tell the brothers they were mad to even think of kidnapping you and we would have no part of it. I confess we did nothing until the police came here, then we told them where you might have been taken. Mademoiselle, can you ever forgive us?'

Claudine stood up and hugged him. 'I understand and of course I forgive you. Every man would protect his own family first before all others.'

As they say, there wasn't a dry eye in the house, except mine. I hated him for doing nothing to save Claudine and still do. Although I did feel a twinge of sorrow for Maria who had been in tears from the moment Philippe started to tell their story.

I don't know who suggested we had our picnic there but it proved to be a popular choice. Philippe, Harry and Egg walked back up to the cars to collect our picnic supplies and Maria produced her own cakes and a large pie. Wine was in abundance, although Philippe suggested we could all go for a pony trek later so to keep a cool head. Nicole said she had never ridden a horse, but didn't appear nervous and said she was willing to try. Harry promised he would keep an eye on her and I thought, 'So what's new?'

We sat around chatting over a coffee or two, enjoying the sun after eating in the shade of some trees. Hélène called for our attention and said, 'Philippe has spoken of something on his mind and I think it is always best to speak of your concerns so I will tell of something that troubles me. I had become very fond of Sam and tried to make myself brave to go to his funeral, but the day before my nerve failed and I ran away. I am certain that had it been possible for me to ask Sam he would have said he understood.'

Realising that Hélène was more than a little upset, I diverted attention. 'Perhaps we should follow Hélène and Philippe's example. Does anyone want to ask me a question?'

'I will ask Jean's question,' Egg announced. 'Why didn't you stay in Rochenoir which is much closer to Oleron than Orthez? You don't have to answer, perhaps it's none of my business.'

'I will answer,' I replied. 'We rented our apartment so that I could be close to you.'

Everyone laughed, but a smiling Egg said, 'I believe you.'

My eyes met his and his eyes were saying, 'I know' and my eyes were responding, 'I know you know.'

I added, 'News I can tell you is that it's Graham, who I think knows more that he passes on to us. He did tell me something when he explained the day we saw Marius in the restaurant, that he was on police business, working under cover. Graham explained it was nothing directly to do with our case so he wasn't informed. However, it may not have been a direct connection, but it did concern us. The two men with Marius were former members of the gang that operated before Paul Vachon took them over. I can see it is dangerous territory for the men to speak of those days and understand why they did not want us involved in that particular aspect.'

Claudine came up with an interesting idea, 'I think Rebecca, Hélène and I should go to the Pont du Rochenoir Restaurant and tell François Duval he is the only possible person who could have told the thief who tried to snatch my bag that we were in his restaurant that day and what has he to say for himself.'

That silenced the gathering for a moment.

'I agree,' said Hélène.

'Seconded,' I added. 'Let's do it tomorrow.'

Next came the time for us to be matched to our horses and here Philippe's experience in taking groups for rides came to the fore. We were quickly sorted and mounted with only Nicole a completely new rider. Of course she was able to rely on Harry for advice and the pair of them were soon lagging behind. I felt a bit sorry for him really; he knew I was watching him like a hawk. Claudine and Hélène rode together and what an eye catching sight to see the two beautiful girls riding effortlessly together in colourful summer clothes. Harry did remember me long enough to call me to join them for a picture and then another with Nicole making a foursome.

Philippe took us on a wonderful ride - Maria had stayed behind - We followed a track down to the GR65 with him calling, 'I will take you behind the pic of Athéka to see a side you never see from the road. I also keep us away from steep slopes which make me nervous.'

We all laughed at that for our route was clearly designed for our mixed abilities and Philippe was a consummate horseman. We continued towards Urdanasburu until we could see the wavy slopes leading towards the deep valley of Gorrichoneco. What a horse ride! I could see why people become passionate about it.

We turned and followed the road and footpath back to Maria where, after each of us dealing with our own horse under Philippe's watchful eye, we joined Maria for some delicious scone type cakes. It was truly a memorable afternoon.

Chapter Twenty
Carlotta

Convinced there was more to be learned about what happened to the gold than had been discovered to date, my cognisance of the situation would not rest. What had happened to Duval's share was never far from my thoughts. Then there was the question of Coutard's gold in the sawpit. So he moved the gold after Sam discovered it; where to?

It just happened late one afternoon I poured myself a glass of wine and with the first sip, for no particular reason, I thought of Hélène so I dialled her number.

'Hélène, sorry our proposed investigation was delayed by other events but I need help to try again and get something going,' was my opening, and then I reminded her of my previous thoughts and my current lack of a starting point.

'Carlotta,' she replied.

'Who's Carlotta?'

'Oh Rebecca, being bloodhounds on a trail could be fun. Can I join you on your mystery search?'

'I was rather hoping that you would.'

'Carlotta is the daughter of a very nice Spaniard, Carlos, who is caretaker of the Rochenoir Holiday Complex. The gites belonged to the late Renaud Coutard along with the Manoir ruin. Now, of course, they are owned by Arlette. The connection is that Carlotta was secretary to Renaud Coutard and she may well know about the gold being moved. She is a bit of a – what do you say – yes a bombshell, only not blonde. You understand, the type who are often the recipients of men's unguarded comments.'

Wow! Hélène, I understand perfectly. You are just the type to make a good Watson. I am delighted to have you join me in the hunt for the forgotten shares of gold.'

'Let me see,' she replied. 'Rebecca and Hélène in the "Hunt for the Forgotten Gold." 'Of course I will join you.'

'It might be dangerous.'

'What fun.'

I grinned into the telephone. She was certainly a girl ready for adventure.

When Hélène decided Carlos definitely still worked at the Holiday Centre it was decided we would start with him the next morning.

A promising start that only led to another destination. Hélène, after explaining to Carlos that we wanted to speak with his daughter, turned to me to say she no longer lived in Rochenoir. After losing her job when Coutard died, she returned to Spain and is now living with his brother and his family in Esquir.

'How far away is that?'

'About forty of your miles.'

'So?'

Hélène clapped her hands, 'So we go.'

Carlos had phoned ahead to pave our way so Carlotta and her uncle were waiting for us when we arrived.

Hélène had said she was a pretty girl, the reason Carlos was so protective, but that did not prepare me for the sultry beauty who welcomed us. Long, black, wavy hair that tumbled forward over one of her shoulders, dark Spanish eyes, and a figure, well! enough said.

I thought perhaps it was Sam who wanted to speak with me,' she said in English while shaking hands with us.

I looked at Hélène who shrugged.

'Sam was shot and killed while rescuing Claudine,' I explained.

Carlotta looked shocked at the news. 'I am sad, even though I only met him once. Did Paul Vachon kill him?' she asked.

'No! Paul's brother Gerard Vachon did. Why did you ask that?'

She spoke to her uncle in Spanish and he replied.

Hélène, who it appeared, could speak Spanish, intervened. 'Your uncle is suspicious of us and wants to know who we are. Tell him we are helping the French police to find some gold that Coutard hid before he died. We also came to ask if you know where it is hidden.'

This led to a long discussion between Carlotta and her uncle after she had translated Hélène's comments.

Carlotta turned to face us and took a few moments to compose herself, then explained-

'Renaud Coutard many times asked me to move into his house and live with him, but I didn't want to sell myself to an old man, even though he promised I would be rich. Yes, I know about the gold Renaud gave me a thousand Euros not to talk about it. I know where it is hidden but I have not touched it and will not tell where it is for fear of my own safety.'

'I don't understand, who would harm you?'

Before I left France and after Renaud had died, I was still working at the office to see what would happen and if I would be paid the wages I was owed. One day Paul Vachon came into the office and ordered me to tell him where Renaud had put his gold. When I told him he should speak to the Notaire who was handling all the arrangements, he said if I did not give him the gold he would kill me. I told him if he did that it would never be found. After that I talked to my father about it and my father, worried about my safety, sent me back to Spain to live with my uncle.

My uncle says I should contact the French police because there might be a reward, which would compensate for my lost wages, but I am afraid to tell anyone where I am.

'Carlotta,' I replied, 'tell your uncle that with his and your permission, we will discuss this difficulty with a high authority in the French police and agree a plan to deal with gold in the safest way possible. If you promise to remain silent and leave it to us, we will come and see you again with an answer. I am sure you will receive a reward. But, you must not do or say anything until we have caught Paul Vachon for he is a very dangerous man.' I gave her my and Hélène's phone numbers in case anything happened to concern her and Commissaire Ramel's to use in an emergency.

Hélène also told Carlotta that she could stay with her in her apartment until the gold was sorted out. All she had to do was telephone and we would drive over and collect her.

Φ   Φ   Φ

We drove back to Rochenoir cock-a-hoop at our early success. We also agreed to do and say nothing until we had spoken to Graham.

'Where do you think the gold is?' Hélène asked.

'My bet is that it is still in the wood yard somewhere,' I replied. The sawdust pit was probably just a temporary place while something better was prepared.

Graham's reaction to our news was typical. 'Rebecca, I can't have two unprotected women wandering around playing at Holmes and Watson. Leave it to the police.'

'You didn't even know there was some hidden gold until I just told you and nor did the police. If we hadn't acted the gold would have been lost or in Paul Vachon's hands.'

'I'm not going to argue with you. There is a team working on this, leave it to them.'

'So what has this team of yours discovered?'

'I'm not going to discuss it.'

'Well! Just bear in mind that the person who knows where this gold is has promised to speak to no one but us and we have promised, in return, that we will keep his or her identity secret. Let me know what you want to do. We are not idiots, Graham, in fact we are probably the two most astute people you have working on your side.'

About ten minutes later a penitent Graham called to say that Ramel was going to arrange a meeting in the next few days and I would be hearing from him.

I forgot to tell Graham the next item on the Holmes and Watson schedule was the Burnt Manoir. I did wonder, though, which of us was Holmes.

By mid afternoon we were invited to attend Ramel's office the next day at 4pm

Φ   Φ   Φ

Still flush with our early success, Hélène and I arrived at the Holiday Complex just as Carlos was brewing his first coffee of the day.

'Beautiful ladies, this is an honour for me. Will you have coffee?'

Of course we agreed, after all talk was the object of our visit.

As we sipped our coffee, I asked Carlos if he had any problems with the changeover of ownership. He said he had not and that Arlette Coutard was a kind employer who did not interfere and who discussed matters with him and had made two changes he suggested for the apartments. She had promised a bonus for the end of the month as a reward for his loyalty.

'After all,' he puffed out his chest, ' I have cared for these apartments for nearly three years and the only complaint was from Duval after Sam had punched Duval on the jaw.'

We both laughed and Hélène quickly explained we were not laughing at him, Carlos, but we kept hearing tales about Sam.

'Sam was my friend,' he said with pride. Then added that Madame Arlette would be visiting the flats later to discuss some redecorating.

I explained – through Hélène – the situation with Carlotta and he thanked us for helping. He confided, 'I was tempted to say to my girl we would keep the gold money for ourselves, but it would be too much. A gold bar must be worth very many Euros.'

I had to confess I didn't know how many it was maybe 15,000, and made a note to find out

Carlos then explained a little extra money is good to have, but if you have more money than your place in the community merits it brings trouble. Special trouble with people who are jealous. In a short time you find you have few friends and are not invited to other people's houses or to events in their lives. He would rather be poor, happy and respected by his friends.

I asked Hélène to tell him that his thoughts were worthy of him and that I respected him for them.

That merited another cup of his opaque coffee.

We explained we would like to look over the Manoir again and also the tunnel and wondered if we could get past the police tapes to do so.

Carlos said it would be no problem except for the tunnel doors to which only the police had keys.

We were conducted to the tower and Carlos soon picked the lock and opened the door for us to walk in. It just seemed a pleasant round tower to me but Hélène exclaimed, 'Good Heavens, who did this?'

A rapid-fire conversation with Carlos seemed to sort it out, whatever it was.

She explained to me, 'The walls used to be' – hesitating for a moment – 'adorned with distasteful pictures of torture, hate, sodomy and rape. There were also unhealthy mixtures of humans and animals. I was certain of a connection with one of these evil sects and roughly dated picture styles from the 17th to 18th centuries. I complained to Jacques Ferron the Mayor saying such a place would be bad for the town if a tourist saw such indecent art and the tower should be demolished. Instead, Carlos says, the Mayor sent workmen to paint out the pictures.

'Un moment, Rebecca, I will speak to the Mayor.'

She took a mobile from her small bag and dialled a number from memory. Judging by results she then no problem when she asked to speak to the Mayor. I didn't understand much of the conversation, but noticed she called the Mayor Jacques and spoke in a mildly demanding tone.

After, she explained Jacques thought knocking down the tower without permission of the owner might be beyond his powers, but painting out the pictures was covered by local regulations on obscenity.

This left me wondering, of course, why they needed regulations (plural) on obscenity.

'You appear to know the Mayor,' I asked cautiously.

'Oh yes, he married my older sister.

Carlos looked most impressed that Hélène could order the Mayor about and became even more respectful.

Hélène next showed me how to release the hidden catches of a wall panel and opened it, revealing steps going down to the tunnel.

As the panel swung open she gave a little giggle and explained that when Sam was trying to open it for the first time, she reached past him to help. 'We were very close to each other. I don't expect he noticed, but it was really quite sexy.'

I looked at her in astonishment, did she really think she could huddle up to a man and have no effect on him. 'What have I missed?' was my next thought, 'Sam certainly got around.'

We found nothing in the room below the steps and even Carlos admitted he could not open the door that covered the tunnel entrance.

We walked through the woodland area behind the Manoir and Carlos let us through a back gate into the grounds. He explained, but we already knew, we could walk out through the front entrance when we finished.

Hélène was surprised just how much of the overgrown vegetation had been cleared since she last visited.

I wasn't. My theory being that Ramel's boys were making sure there were no more concealed hiding places. The clearing work had continued inside and the suspected presence of a second stairway to the cellar at the east end of the Manoir had been confirmed. However, that also had a door blocking access. On an impulse I called Louis and cried help. I also told him the yellow police tapes had gone so it was, presumably, no longer a crime scene.

Louis was quickly there in a car with a few tools. He made-belief drilling his head with a finger saying, 'There were plenty of tools on his breakdown truck, but it also had his name on the side. 'I am here clandestin,' he said.

Hélène suggested "incognito" was a better explanation and wrote it on a piece of paper for him. He tucked the paper carefully into an inside pocket of his jacket. I smiled; sure he would keep her little note.

Of the two stairs and doors to the cellar, Louis decided the easiest to tackle would be the new one and he certainly had it open in a few minutes. I asked no questions, just hoped Arlette would not turn up while we were there. He also opened the door to the tunnel, but warned us once again of the danger from roof falls. He insisted he would stay to guard us and help if he could.

The broken open wine boxes were still there so Hélène and I listed all the inscriptions on them because Harry thought he could trace them. Louis, with his bare hands, easily tore off the side of what we thought the most important box, so that we could take it with us. We could find no trace of any hiding place in the cellar, so turned our attention to the tunnel.

The spoil heap we had been told killed Duval had gone and Louis was pleased to see a few new props had been put in to support the roof of the tunnel. We found nothing in the tunnel to interest us and had not really expected to.

'We are clutching at straws,' I told my companions.

'That is a new expression to me,' Hélène answered, 'but we have something similar.'

A gadget Louis has brought with him some kind of hand-held, electro magnetic device that searched for metal buried in floors and walls. He explained it was very good with water pipes, but doubted it knew what gold was. None the less, he was industriously testing random spots on the walls and looking pretty miserable at his lack of success.

Trying to help him, I also ran my hands over the walls and noticed a slight deposit of salts in one place. 'Try here!' I suggested. 'This,' rubbing my hand across the deposits, 'simply means water has somehow gained access to the wall, but it's worth a try. Trust me, I'm a geologist.'

He had an instant response and was gone for some tools in a flash.

Louis hacked away at the wall, patiently stopping from time to time at my request, while I carefully brushed the fragments into a polythene bag.

'What are you doing?' he asked when I first started.

'Harry is an archaeologist,' I answered.

We finally broke through into a small, square recess in which, amongst some debris, were a few coins. We later counted twenty.

Collecting all the bits and pieces in my polythene bag, I passed the coins one by one to Louis who gave them to Hélène. 'They were in some kind of wooden box that has rotted away,' I told them.

'Are they gold?' Louis asked with a trace of excitement in his voice.

'Sorry, Louis,' Hélène replied, 'but they are silver and quite old. I would say 17th century. If you agree to my taking them to show a friend at the university, I can find out for you what they are worth.'

'They are not mine, Madame Rebecca found them.'

'If you had not been testing the walls, we would not have found them,' I answered. 'As far as I am concerned they are yours. But you should talk to Arlette about your find, she doesn't own them but she does own the land they were found on and I don't know what the French law is in these matters.'

'I will find out about that also,' Hélène promised.

'And I will talk to Arlette,' Louis said. 'We are friends.'

Hélène and I exchanged raised eyebrows and smiles.

In great good humour, we climbed up the stairs into the shell of the Manoir and found Arlette waiting for us with a grim expression.

'Would you mind explaining just what you are doing here, Rebecca? 'Carlos told me you were here but he said nothing of you being one of the conspirators, Louis.'

Chapter Twenty-one
Answers?

I searched Arlette's face for some clue as to what her heartfelt reaction was to finding us in the Manoir and decided to apologise.

'I am truly sorry I didn't ask you before we came here to the Manoir, Arlette, but you must realise your view of our indiscretion is vastly different to our view of the situation. To you it is a possession; to us it is a wrecked building that is a subject of curiosity. Hélène and I made an impromptu decision to come, now that the police have finished their investigation, (fingers crossed at my white lie), and see if they had cleared the roof fall that killed Duval. You probably know, as a matter of public safety, the police covered the tunnel entrance with a new door. We asked Louis for help in reopening the tunnel so we could have a cautious look to see what action the police had taken to secure the unstable roof. I considered this in terms of our co-operation with the police investigation rather than interfering with your property.

While there, we also asked Louis to chip away a small area of the wall where I had observed strange behaviour of some sediment. You may remember I am a geologist. This led to the discovery of a small cache of old coins that had, in times long past, either been hidden or secreted as part of some pagan ceremony. Hélène has offered to show the coins to a friend at the university in an attempt to find out exactly what they are. Louis undertook to discuss the coins with you in order to find out their ownership and future. In England they would be submitted to a legal process that would either award them to the finder or committed to the national museum in exchange for a reward. We don't know what happens in France. As I have already told you, I am sorry we acted on impulse and repeat that Louis was involved only when we asked him to help us.'

'A pretty speech, Rebecca, and I accept your story and will listen with interest to the result of your enquiries. No offence has been caused to me mostly because I do not care much about the Manoir. You probably realise I will sell the site in due course. I will say again, something I have said before, you can talk to me anytime. Certainly I would prefer you did that.'

Φ   Φ   Φ

I was ushered into Ramel's office by an amused Spiro to be greeted with a smile from the commissaire and a sort of scowl by Graham. We all accepted coffee and Ramel said, 'We asked you to come in for a talk because we are concerned for your safety.'

His sentiment supported by a grunt from Graham.

I shrugged, 'I don't know why there is all this concern about our checking of overlooked detail. Our actions are no more dangerous than anything else we have done in the past while trying to unravel what events have transpired. You are not seriously suggesting that Carlotta is a threat?'

'Thing is old girl...!

'Graham!!!, I've warned you about that.'

'Thing is we are afraid that someone may feed you false information in order to lure you into an ambush.'

'You will just have to trust our judgement.'

'Rebecca, it's pretty certain from our information that Coutard's share is largely accounted for. This girl you found can't know where there is a big supply.'

'Are you going to tell me why you think this?'

'Because Coutard must have capitalised more of his gold than Duval and Vachon and salted more money away in various bank accounts. That's why he was so uptight about the accounts being frozen. We think he just showed your Carlotta three or four of their home made gold bars to impress her. If that's all she has we are not interested. She can keep them and do a deal with Arlette for some cash.'

In view of Graham's remarks, I didn't know the best way to deal with the questions that had arisen over our meeting with Carlotta and her admission to knowing where some of the gold was hidden. Talk to Carlotta first or to Arlette? The latter won.

My curiosity over where Arlette was now living was soon answered when I found it was the large house, just across the farm lane beside the Manoir. Egg, when he told me where she lived also retailed the story of how he and Sam had wondered if a tunnel existed from the house, under the lane, and to the Manoir. 'We now know there isn't one,' he added with a chuckle.

'How do you know there isn't one?' That knocked the smile off his face.

'I was told so, but you are right, my information could be wrong.'

Arlette showed me into the lounge, which overlooked quite a pretty garden. I looked at the chintzy curtains and upholstery of the largish room and remarked, 'Somehow, I don't see your taste in the furnishings.'

Arlette laughed, 'You are right again; my original furniture was changed by my husband to make the house more modern. You can decide for yourself if he succeeded. I think perhaps he had hopes of bringing Carlotta here.'

'Has she been in touch with you?'

'I spoke to her yesterday.'

'About the gold bars?'

'She also told you?'

'Not exactly. I asked her if she knew anything about the gold that had been hidden in the sawdust pit and she said Renauld had shown her where it was hidden.'

'You see Rebecca, as I am sure that you do, that makes my late husband incredibly stupid. If there is any gold still hidden - which I am sure there is not – he was taking a risk by telling her for he was not to know her family might have decided to take it away to Spain without delay.'

'They would have a problem with that. His name is Paul Vachon. We think she has seen only a couple of gold bars with which Renauld intended to lure her.'

Arlette laughed again, I think it time to help you with some misconceptions - is that word right? First, Carlotta really is a very nice girl from a church going Roman Catholic family. I don't believe they would have anything to do with dishonesty. She tolerated Renauld's wandering hands because she wanted to keep her job. I'm certain she gave him no encouragement. Yes, there was some gold but I am satisfied that after there was interference with the sawpit, Gerard Vachon agreed to look after it by storing it in the safe in the Casino. I should tell you that I had a share of the early gold payments, but have received nothing since I parted from my husband. My lawyers have served notice on the police and the Mayor that I want returned any gold that belongs to my husband's estate. Now that I have made myself open to you, what do you want me to do?'

'The question surprised me and took me off my guard. I didn't come to ask you to do anything, but to find out what you thought about the situation? Graham wants any odds and ends of gold taken out of circulation. He would be happy if Carlotta has access to any gold bars, and that you reach an agreement about their disposal with her. If you feel they are yours, reward her for their return. Say a reward for the return of lost property.'

'Yes, I'm happy with that. Shall we both go to see her in the morning?'

Later, I phoned Hélène to tell her what was happening. I also explained my curiosity about the long barn on Leizar Athéka and asked her she would join me in a trip to the mountain in the afternoon. 'Crikey,' I thought, 'what was that day when I said I was bored?'

Φ   Φ   Φ

Next morning the response from Carlotta was that she would meet us at the wood yard. 'My uncle will drive me,' she explained. 'He is interested in helping me but I am still worried about Paul Vachon.'

For all Arlette said, my reaction was, 'I'll bet her uncle is interested in the gold.'

However, I answered, 'The best way to deal with Paul Vachon is to dump the gold on someone who can handle it.' Crystal clear, I could see the predicament Carlotta's family found themselves in. They thought they knew she could access the gold, but did not have the means to steal it with the high security at the wood yard. I had also phoned Graham and he asked me to call him from the wood yard, whatever the situation.

I collected Arlette by car and we arrived about a half hour before we expected our guests. We used the time to make a minute inspection of the offices, surmising that was where the hiding place was likely to be. We found nothing.

When Carlotta arrived she immediately pointed out a large portrait of what I was sure depicted a young Arlette. When I posed the question, she agreed it was and said, 'I think it is meant to be some obscure joke of my husband's but I've never worked out what the joke is.'

The picture was fixed firmly flat to the wall and we could not move it.

Arlette telephoned for a carpenter she knew.

The carpenter succeeded in removing the picture from the wall and scratched the back of his head. 'There's nothing there,' was his final decision.

'There must be,' Carlotta cried, 'he always said everything he had of value was behind the picture.'

Arlette asked the carpenter, 'Remove the panelling behind where the picture hung.'

This produced a bare wall.

Carlotta was in tears, 'Why would he lie to me?'

On a hunch I tore the backing papers off the rear of the picture, but there was nothing there either. I asked Carlotta, 'Where did the gold he showed you come from?'

She tearfully pointed to a small safe let into the wall behind Coutard's desk. 'I don't know the combination,' she added.

'If it hasn't been changed, I do,' Arlette stepped forward and a few moments later opened the door of the safe and stepped away from it. 'Look please, Rebecca,' she asked me.

I took out a pile of papers, some keys and two gold bars. While Carlotta's uncle looked at the gold, I picked up the phone and dialled Graham's number. 'There's no secret cache' I announced, 'just two gold bars in a safe.'

'I told you so, but I won't crow' he replied. 'Well! Not much anyway. Let me speak to Arlette.'

What their conversation was about I don't know to this day.

Arlette told Carlotta she had arranged for her to be paid the wages she was owed plus a year's salary in compensation for the loss of her job. She also offered to pay Carlotta half the value of the two gold bars as an acknowledgement of her disappointment that the bars were not hers and her understanding of the sense of loss she was feeling. 'I apologise for my late husband's actions,' she added. 'If you wish to come back to France for work, contact me and I will help you.' They then hugged each other.

'I hope you take up that offer,' I said to Carlotta as she was leaving.

'My father would never allow it now there has been trouble.'

'How old are you Carlotta?'

'I am twenty-three.'

'It's time you left home and looked after your own affairs.'

I watched Carlotta and her uncle leave but was not hopeful she would take charge of her own life.

Φ   Φ   Φ

After my tense morning the drive up to Leizar Athéka with Hélène was a pure delight. Her range of knowledge and quick wit confirmed yet again to me that she would be the perfect match for the man I had in mind and I only hoped she felt the same although I did not broach the subject. It was a cloudless, hot day and the peaks all round us stood out in their majesty. We found the marker for the footpath not far from a flat area at the side of the road. An area that had the appearance of a provision for parking. We parked, but did not want to make a direct approach to the ranch. Instead, we walked up the mountain slope and headed in the direction we thought the valley lay. An hour later we had found no farm.

'I thought to ask Egg for some information,' I told Hélène as we walked across the slopes to the north of the footpath. 'But didn't because he is so protective of these people I'm sure he would have taken the day off and insisted on joining us.'

Then we saw it from our high vantage point, the farm and stable laying hidden away in the fold in the hills. We worked our way along to the part of the valley top opposite the farm and lay prone so that we could stare down on the complex comprising the main house and the collection of sheds and stables. Our point of interest was the long barn, the end of which looked as if it had been buried in the hillside. 'That may be a cold store,' Hélène remarked, 'or a wonderful opportunity for a concealed hiding place.'

I agreed, telling her Maria had said it was a good way to store food, but had not appeared to want to talk about it.

We could see no sign of life, but it was clearly impossible to approach the house without being seen from the windows.

Hélène commented on this then added, 'That applies to anyone approaching from both directions.'

"Both directions!!!" I hadn't thought about an approach from the top of the valley. Studying the layout it occurred that with no windows on the side facing the top of the valley, it was possible to approach the long barn type shed without being seen. Possible, that is, if it was also possible to climb down into the valley. I said as much to Hélène.

'Unless someone is in the shed,' she responded dryly.

We walked along the hillside but the valley slopes were too precipitous.

'We could get down,' I remarked. 'Getting back up again would be the problem.'

Unless?

We eventually found a dried up watercourse snaking down in what was, fortunately, the lower part of the top of the valley. 'What do you think?' I asked.

'Impossible in the wet.'

'It's not wet.'

'Let's try then.'

We carefully inched our way down for a few feet with me in the lead. 'How are you doing?' I called up softly.

'Climbing is ruining my fingernails.'

'Is that important?'

'Not in the context.'

I grinned and moved steadily down.

We both looked a bit scruffy when we reached the bottom, with scuffed shoes and broken fingernails. We moved cautiously and carefully down the valley keeping close to the slopes of the hidden side.

We stopped dead in our tracks when Hélène asked, 'Do you know if they have dogs?'

'You're good with dogs.'

'They still bark!'

That was true, but we were almost there. We had unbelievable luck when we found the long shed had a door on our side that was blind to the house. We slipped inside quickly and as our eyes adjusted to the change in light we found the shed contained all manner of equipment. We moved to the end of the shed that was buried into the hillside and found it was indeed used partly as a food store. At the furthest extent of the shed, where we must have been between 10 and 20 feet under the hillside, we found a stout door that was not only locked it too strong for us to force.

As we stared in disbelief at this setback we heard a door at the far end of the shed open and close, followed by footsteps heading our way.

We hastily dived behind a pile of filled sacks and pulled some straw on top of ourselves and held our breath. Well! we did for about twenty seconds then hastily held our noses to stop sneezing from the dust we had disturbed. We could hear the person who had entered moving about as he or she collected a few things together and froze when an arm reached up and tried to pull down a length of string hanging from a beam.

I sighed with relief when the steps moved away then chilled again at the unmistakable sound of a ladder or steps being dragged to and propped against the sacks hiding us. Lifting my eyes, not daring to move a muscle, I saw, through my light covering of straw, a man step onto the sacks and unravel the string. I prayed, 'Please don't look down,' as he stepped backwards onto the ladder. The footsteps retreated back to the door and we heard it swing shut. 'Don't move yet,' I hissed to Hélène,' exactly as the door opened again and the footsteps returned. The hand again reached up and this time yanked on the string more forcibly which released the string but dislodged something else that fell through the straw and hit my arm with a painful whack. Somehow, I stifled the appropriate reaction.

After the visitor had gone we crept away with our nerves a bit jangled. As we went Hélène whispered, 'That was great, Rebecca. Isn't this fun?'

We made it to the top of the gully and took stock.

'God, you look an awful sight,' I said, with some satisfaction, to the normally perfectly groomed Hélène.

She laughed and replied, 'Well! I think straw in your hair suits you in a Hill Billy kind of a way.'

We drove home wondering what was behind that door

Chapter Twenty-two
Pierront Talks

As lunchtime approached I drove first to collect Hélène, then on to the Rochenoir Tourist Office for Claudine. I waited outside so not to interrupt her work, mindful that we had taken the previous day off for the trip to Leizar Athéka. While waiting I complemented Hélène on her skilful handling of Pétard, her mount on the day of the picnic.

'I was the classic small child,' she explained. 'Wanting a pony of my own and fortunate in having parents who could afford one. As a young teenager I called it Bambi after the American, Walt Disney. Bambi and I were inseparable. When I moved on to grown up horses they were always from a stable for I could not part with Bambi. When he died I was heartbroken, he was my best friend.'

I was saved having to think of a reply by the arrival of Claudine.

'Are we all of a firm resolve?' she asked as she slipped onto the back seat. 'We take no nonsense from François?'

'In English we would say we take no prisoners,' I answered.

'I agree, let's give him hell!' Hélène added.

'Hélène,' I replied, 'for someone who is my epitome of ladylike, you do come out with the strangest remarks at times.'

She laughed, 'I will guess the meaning of epitome and thank you. Sometimes I let my hair down.'

I drove to the Pont du Rochenoir Restaurant and found a slot in which to park right outside the door. The restaurant was quiet and François Duval burst through his swing doors to greet us. 'Welcome beautiful ladies,' he cried. 'Such pleasure comes to me when I see you.'

'Not for long,' I muttered.

François brought us a complimentary Kir each and made excellent recommendations from his menu and truth to tell we had a superb meal including a bottle of Taval. 'I buy some Taval when I discovered you ladies like rosé,' he announced and I believed him.

After our happy meal it therefore came as something of a surprise to him when we invited him to sit with us for a moment and turned to more serious business.

I opened with, 'François, we hold you responsible for an evil deed. The last time we came to your restaurant, as you very well know, an attempt was made to snatch le sac à main of my friend Claudine.'

He looked absolutely stunned as he blustered and protested, with perspiration appearing on his face and his hands waving defensibly.

'Enough,' Claudine surprised us all by speaking sharply to François in what I must say was an authoritative voice. She continued in French and he seemed to wilt with every word.

As a miserable François sat quietly, Claudine explained to me that she had told him no one but ourselves and one other man, Harry, had known where we were going to eat so he must have telephoned the information or was personally responsible for the attack. 'I also told him,' she added, 'unless he spoke the truth I would speak with Celestine Capelle, Duval's daughter who now owns the restaurant, and ask her to take back his lease,'

François had recovered a little and asked us to accompany him to his private apartment.

'This restaurant is a good business,' he opened, 'so when Celestine told me she was not interested in running it herself I asked immediately if I could have a contract. It is a very good arrangement but one day Paul Vachon came and told me he was going to be my new partner.'

'Do you know Paul Vachon?' I asked.

'Yes, our families have a connection for a long time, but he is an unpleasant man and his dead brother was not much better. I told him to get out of my restaurant, but that night my windows were smashed and he was back in the next day to warn me again. I told him to leave and reported his threats to the police. It was then a quiet time until three men came in for a meal, refused to pay and turned over tables and broke things. Next morning Paul was back in, threatening unless I did a simple thing for him such a disturbance would happen all the time. He gave me a photo of you Mademoiselle,' he turned to Claudine, 'and said he wanted to know if you ever came to the restaurant.' François was visibly distressed at this and his bulky frame shook. 'It seemed such a minor request but if I had known he would try to rob you I would never have telephoned him. A thousand apologies mademoiselle. I have not seen him since.'

'Paul has other things on his mind now,' I remarked.

Claudine was as forgiving with François as she had been with Philippe. 'I can understand your difficulty,' she replied, 'but you should have warned me.'

'At that time I didn't know who you were.'

When we left François tried to say the menu was free, but I crashed in and told him we wanted no favours from him.

We all went back to the Tourist Office with Claudine and begged another coffee. We were feeling somewhat upset by the encounter even though it was much as we expected. She invited us all to Egg's for an evening meal so we could discuss it with the men. Before parting we were unanimous on one thing and each one of us agreed to a pact, "We would get Paul Vachon."

Φ   Φ   Φ

The six of us, plus Graham, gathered round Egg's ever hospitable table for supper. Over the non-stop chatter, I heard Egg's computer making odd noises that ended with a plaintive sort of bleep. He had taken no notice so I asked him if the signal meant anything special. He went to look and called over his shoulder, 'It is a priority message for Graham. Shall I leave it until we have finished eating?'

I don't know what he would have said if he had had the chance because Claudine immediately answered, 'No! of course we want to know immediately.'

Graham grinned and answered, 'Who am I to oppose the lady's wishes.' He rose from the table and went to the computer swiftly reading through a couple of pages with a chuckle or two.

Egg shrugged as he returned.

Graham sat down looking a little smug.

'Well!' Claudine asked impatiently.

'Come on, Graham,' I added my support, 'don't tease.'

'It was just conformation that the English police are on their toes. When they catch a crook, he talks.'

'Just as long as there's nothing funny going on,' I replied. 'You know my opinion about the tales we read of the British Government turning their eyes away from prisoners being tortured under what would otherwise have been a silly name like, "Extraordinary Rendition."

187

Graham looked quite shocked. 'As if I would be a party to anything like that. It is routine police questioning and dedicated investigation that has produced the information on this paper. As you already know, one of the two men arrested for complicity in the plot to capture Claudine is the late Daniel Pierront's son, Christopher Pierront. When he has been dealt with by the British courts, he will be extradited back to France where he faces a long sentence for an assault on a barman in Paris.'

Egg exclaimed, 'We had no idea he had a son.'

'Quite! Apparently he was ordered to do the job by Paul Vachon and he complied because he was afraid. Now in prison with time on his hands, he can see all that will happen in the future if he falls further into Vachon's grip. So, he asked for police protection in exchange for information.

It appears there were several men known to his father who had helped escaping Germans out through Spain as well as giving assistance to allied prisoners escaping. Plus a couple of allied agents helped in as well as out of France. Theoretically Pierront's men were fighting for the Allied cause. But, in reality, they were making a fortune in gold from payments for services rendered. Plus anything extra they robbed and murdered to obtain. Even so, young Pierront says his father told him his fellow gang members had reneged on an agreement they share the spoils equally. He claims that although paid well as guides it was nothing near enough money to buy things like a restaurant and especially the casino. He further claims his father didn't know where the extra gold had come from but it was much better quality and they wouldn't part with the ingots, but had them melted down first.

As the war ended and law and order was in a shambles these men formed a sort of gang to pool their resources under the leadership of the late Daniel Pierront.

We might never have known about them if they had just shared the money and scattered. They didn't because of internal quarrels that included Vachon's father, Caesar Vachon, who claimed control of the group and all its money. Apparently Caesar personally strangled Daniel's father and that was why Daniel fled to England because he would be killed as well.

From there what came to be known as the "Gang of Four", the fathers of Vachon, Coutard, Duval, plus Pierront, took control and did what they liked. After the war when Daniel Pierront had fled, the Gang of Four came to be the four sons of the gang members.

Christopher Pierront thinks there were only ten men in the gang and he had heard that one of those was missing in strange circumstances. He also confirmed that the group used some of their money as insurance for the future. Coutard purchased the Wood yard, Duval the Restaurant, Pierront had cash sent to England, although they cheated him by only sending a token 200,000 Euros, and – wait for it – the Vachons purchased the Casino.

They kept the purchase secret and had a friend run the Casino for a share in the profits. Then, disaster for them when Sam's Musketeers started nosing around and selling gold became more difficult. At first their extra gold was hidden in the cellar of the burnt Manoir, but afraid of Sam's interest in the Manoir, they moved it out to the sawpit in the wood yard. Sam accidentally found the gold in the sawpit and created a real emergency that could only be served by moving the gold to the Casino's strong room.

I would guess that because of the men they had lost there were not enough trustworthy members of the gang left to run the Casino so they had to close it.

Well! That's it for the moment.'

'Just a minute,' I exclaimed. 'Are you saying this Pierront doesn't know where the crooks are based?'

'No, I'm telling you he says he doesn't know. A bit more time in prison and a threat to seize all his assets might loosen his tongue.' His smile broadened, 'Christopher Pierront obviously doesn't know two of the gang drowned, that one is under arrest and another broke his neck so if he is right about his numbers, only four face us now. And, not only that, because of their past actions and brutality, they have no friends who will help them.'

When we were settled over coffee and cognac, Claudine announced that she had given much thought to taking the job in London offered by Peter Reynolds, but she had decided, after discussing it with Peter, on a compromise. 'All my family and friends live here,' she explained, 'so I will work from Pau, but go sometimes to London for perhaps a week.' She paused and added, 'and, maybe Paris. I will stay with Sophie when I go to London and she wants me to take Egg with me on a visit. She would like to talk to him some more.'

All Egg and Claudine did next was to smile at each other, but it was enough to remind me I should start looking for a hat.

My next task was to see Jean and I had phoned for an arrangement on Saturday morning.

We met at Les Artisans and after greetings he opened the conversation by saying, 'If you have come to speak with me about Claudine, it is too late. We have agreed to go our separate ways. Her behaviour made me very angry and it would not be a sound foundation for a marriage.'

'How long have the two of you been close to each other?'

He looked surprised at the question. 'I don't know, perhaps four years. Why?'

'Jean, if you had been madly in love with Claudine you would have been desperate to marry her after four years. Being possessive is not love.'

'We would have married one day, but that is a matter between us and nothing to do with you.'

'There is nothing between you except friendship, Jean, but that, as you say, is none of my business. I came to ask with whom did you discuss Claudine's trip to London?'

'I don't know, I was very angry about the trip.'

'Who was it?'

'Why!'

'Because whoever it was passed on the information to Paul Vachon. He sent one of his men who followed her to London and there he tried to kill her. If you did that on purpose I am going to beat you up right now.'

'I will talk to Claudine about it. This matter is nothing to do with you.'

I jumped up and walked round the table to him as he also stood, but the anger on my face clearly showed and he stepped back away from me. I positively hissed at him and may even have accidentally wet his face with spittle as I grated between clenched teeth. 'You have done enough damage, keep away from her and forget you ever knew her until our investigation is finished. Don't for one moment think that I can't sort you out for that would be a big mistake.'

Aware that people at other tables were looking our way, I walked back to my seat.

Jean, looking embarrassed, also sat down, saying, 'I don't know what the rest of the restaurant overhead. You had better leave.'

'I will leave when you have told me who you spoke to about Claudine.'

Eventually, after some procrastination, he admitted a possibility.

'I saw André in the car park after I had a row with Egg. I was angry and said something about her leaving me to work in London. I don't know exactly what I said.'

'Who is André?'

'He is the man who is janitor for the flats where you and Egg are staying.'

'Would he be André Ferrand?'

'Yes.'

'Yolande's husband. The Yoland who owned Sam's holiday cottage. How could you give such information to someone suspected of connections with the men who kidnapped Claudine? What sort of a friend would do such a thing?'

'I didn't think. I was angry'

I jumped up again and so did he stepping back away from me as I walked back round the table. I slapped his face as hard as I could. While he rubbed his cheek, astonishment writ large on his face, I practically snarled like an animal, 'I'm leaving now, not because I am finished with you but because I am so angry it worries me what I might do to you. Don't ever come near me in the future. Your action from jealous stupidity might have killed Claudine if I had not been there to help her. Don't ever be in any doubt about what I will do to you if she is harmed.'

I stormed out, but was so angry and upset I sat in the car for half an hour afraid of driving something as lethal as a car until I had calmed down.

When I moved it was to mutter, 'Now for André.'

Chapter Twenty-three
They search here and there

Although I would have dearly liked to sort out André next, there was an arrangement for me to meet Graham for the first part of a fast roundup of our potential targets. He needed to go back to England for a couple of days at least, but was afraid of what mischief we might make when left to our own devices. Learning we had one of Sam's wooden keys and two winches he determined to have me drive him to Holçarté.

'First,' he announced, 'I have spoken to Hélène and she is quite willing to join us today.'

'Why were you phoning Hélène?'

'To thank her.'

'For what? What are you up to?'

'Nothing.'

'Graham, don't tell me that, you are always up to something!'

Luckily when we called into our flat to collect the gear, Harry had caught the bus to Pau, leaving a note to say he had some research to do at the University. Apparently after remembering he was on an archaeological mission and his notes were, so far, pathetic.

'He should change his job to something more adventurous,' Graham responded unsympathetically.

'He has this reluctance to be killed before his time,' was my response.

Hélène was ready, but I sent her back for stronger footwear.

Pleased as I was that Graham had also put some sensible shoes on for the muddy path, I still resisted his attempt to foist the heavier winch on to me and picked up the wooden key handing Hélène two lighter items to carry.

There was no need to go to the cave and ruined cottage, but Graham wanted to see them. It was at this point I explained we all had one thing in common and that was none of us had been directly through the woods to the cottage before so we would have to be careful and look for it with the aid of Egg's directions.

'Rebecca,' Graham protested, 'you lured me out here thinking you are an expert guide to the place and now you admit you are potentially as lost as we soon will be.'

'It was your idea. Come on, I have Egg's notes; all we are looking for is a tree.'

Hélène laughed, 'That's easy, we are surrounded with them.'

None the less we soon found our way and had lots of fun trying to guess why the cave was wanted in the first place. Graham's idea that the cottage was built simply because the cave was there was undoubtedly correct but took us nowhere.

Curiously, despite Egg's warning that the crevasse was hard to find, I lead my small party straight there. We were undisturbed by the precipitate drop down into the pool, a drop that had made Claudine uneasy.

Graham quickly fitted the specially shaped wooden key into the rock sides of the fissure and attached the winch. We saw immediately why the cable on the winch was so long when we realised how far down it was to the water.

'So', I said, 'they are designed for a man to go down and be able to pull himself back up again. There must be another part to this, a platform to stand on. It also explains the four hooks on the end of the cable, they must be to hook into four eyelet's on the platform.'

'There's something else none of you noticed' Graham announced with a slight smirk. 'The winch cable is made of a high quality steel. Not something you would fit for expendable goods, this outfit is a human lift.'

Graham next tied an auxiliary rope to the framework of the winch. 'Just in case it slips,' he explained. He then volunteered to test the apparatus with his weight. No one argued, but Hélène suggested the three of us should be able to drag to the fissure a small piece of tree trunk she had seen a short way back along the path and use it to weight the winch as a safer test. It took half an hour to do this and lash it with a hanging loop to put over a hook on the winch cable. Graham then said in a very solemn voice, 'I launch you bit of tree as one small step for man,' and as we laughed, pushed the tree off the ledge into the fissure. It took very little time to reach the pool taking the winch and the wooden key with it.

'Damn,' he said. 'How fortuitous I tied a rope to the winch.'

'Except,' I replied, controlling my mirth fairly successfully, 'you just added an extra weight when you tied a zonking great lump of wood to it.'

'Damn.'

'You already said that.'

Rebecca, this is not funny.'

Actually, it was, but I kept quiet.

It was a disappointed and miserable trio that returned down the path after unsuccessfully trying to pull the winch back up using the rope; the lump of wood was just too heavy for our delicate hands and the difficulty of gripping the rope. Graham and I decided our omission was in not taking two winches with us, so we could have used the second to haul up the first.

Hélène's response was that the omission probably saved a life for it almost certainly would have slipped again.

'We can only risk someone descending when we have found out what keeps the wooden key in place,' Hélène pointed out. Then she surprised us with a suggestion. 'I have an engineer friend who might know what to do. Would you like me to ask her or do you want to keep it a secret?

'Her?' asked Graham with a huge question mark in his voice.

'Watch what you say,' I warned.

Hélène laughed, 'We already know he is a chauvinist.

'Why didn't you tell us you knew an engineer,' Graham demanded instead.

'Because you did not tell me you needed one.'

'Humph.'

Hélène and I exchanged a grin.

'We have extra time now,' she suggested, 'why don't we go to see Farmer Bruno again? He is not very far away if we go back through Iraty.'

All thought this a good idea and less than an hour later we were pulling up alongside the collection of sheds and watching Hélène doing her dog-training act again. We trooped to the door of the larger building which we knew was Bruno's living accommodation. The door was open, but he was not inside. He was standing behind us, his dogs by his side, and holding a shotgun. He walked towards us and said in Basque that he was looking to see who it was before he came out in the open. He invited us inside and I made some coffee while Hélène talked to Bruno.

I returned with the drinks and we all settled down.

'Tell me what he's been saying,' Graham demanded impatiently.

'In both England and in France it is the same thing we speak. It is small talk.'

We both laughed when he snorted 'Small talk' in an incredulous voice.

Hélène, speaking in Basque, explained to Bruno gently that his friend Gerard Vachon had been shot by the police during an attempt by Gerard to kidnap Claudine.

Bruno was quiet for a moment then asked if Claudine was all right.

'Yes.'

'I told you he was a bad man, but not as bad as his brother, Paul.'

'Paul threatened François Duval who took over Bertrand Duval's restaurant.'

We could not, of course, understand the response but Hélène turned to us at the farmer's reply to say his description of François had been rather vulgar and she would not like to repeat it but in its simplest form a fat lump might be appropriate.

'What a scholarly reply,' I answered, and she smiled.

'Will you two members of the ladies sewing circle get on with it,' Graham protested

'What does he mean?'

'He's being rude now!'

Bruno was continuing and Hélène was all attention and a short conversation followed.

She turned looking very unhappy. 'He has been threatened by someone, but he will not say who has been here. Nor will he say if it was because we came before. I have asked him to move for a small time if I find him somewhere to go but he just says this is his home.

'Ask him if I can arrange police protection for him,' Graham, concerned and alert, asked.

Hélène passed the message.

'He says no, he has no time for the police.'

'Is there anything we can do?' I asked.

'Nothing I can think.'

'Has he any friends or relatives we can ask to help him?' I enquired.

Hélène spoke for a few minutes then turned, 'no, there is no one. He says he is the last of his generation, except for Paul, and he wants nothing to do with him.'

Bruno was speaking again and I could tell she was agreeing, but Hélène neither turned nor translated.

'What does he say now,' I asked.

She looked round to us and I could see there were tears in her eyes, 'He asked me to look after his friends if anything happened to him.'

'I thought you said he didn't have any friends.'

'He means his dogs.'

Suddenly there were tears in my eyes as well.

Φ   Φ   Φ

We did what it seemed we always did when we were down, we headed for the comfort and safety of Labaraquette, calling Egg, Claudine and Harry to follow us there.

Brigitte produced some tiny cakes and pretty good tea, and we sat round a log fire Albert had prepared against what was going to be a cool evening. We felt better for their administrations but were all unhappy about Bruno.

'We are helpless,' Graham decided. 'You can't drag a man out of his own home and even if we could persuade him to go into some kind of sheltered accommodation, he would hate it and they wouldn't take his dogs.'

'The man is best where he is,' Brigitte also decided. 'He is content in his own home and you do not know for sure that he is in danger. It might just be a warning.'

I reported my conversation with Jean, toning down my angry exchange. There was no comment from the others except Albert said quietly, 'Perhaps it is for the best.

Graham had more to say about André saying he did not think it wise for me to approach him. 'There is no purpose in advertising your connection,' he decided. 'I'll give Ramel a ring in the morning. Let him deal with it by holding him in the pokey for a couple of days. That should put the frighteners on him. If we put enough pressure on the small fry, someone will crack and give us an anonymous tip to where Paul Vachon hides out. I must pay a visit to England, I'll fly back the day after tomorrow for a couple of days.'

When the others came we switched to wine and were soon in lighter mood. Claudine was disappointed we had been to see Bruno without her and vowed to see him at the weekend.

Somnolent after another of Brigitte's delightful meals we relaxed round the fire, each armed with a digestife.

Harry twirled his glass gazing into the liquid thoughtfully. 'You know what I would like to do tomorrow?' He raised his eyes to look around us.

'No! definitely not!' my answer was firm.

'You don't know what I was going to say,' a protest I waved away with my hand.

I saw out of the corner of my eye Egg and Claudine exchange puzzled glances,

We sat in silence for a while.

Egg coughed discreetly, 'Are you two having a silent argument?'

I laughed, but did not speak.

'Thing is,' Harry started.

'We promised Graham we would wait and be low key in our operations,' I said sharply. 'He knows better than you when we should go there.'

'Quite right,' said the man himself, although I am astonished to hear Rebecca is listening to me for once.

Enlightenment dawned in Egg's eyes. 'Oh!' he exclaimed. 'You want to go back to the Casino.'

'Hélène clapped her hands, 'Oh! I have never seen the inside, can I come too?'

'Do you realise they are talking about breaking in again,' I said to her.

'Oh! what an adventure that will be.'

'You are all barking mad.' Graham announced.

At least four crestfallen faces turned his way.

'But,' he added, 'I'm with you. Count me in.'

After making arrangements for the morrow, Harry and I took Hélène home. Before driving off, I slipping back indoors using an excuse I had (purposely) left my scarf and caught Graham on his own to protest about the proposed trip to the Casino. 'Do you realise there will be six of us,' I demanded.

'Five. Harry won't be with us, his leg is not strong enough for this kind of caper.'

'You'll be lucky if you can stop him.'

'I've arranged for the Professor he is working with to give him a morning call to ask for some help. He won't refuse such a request.'

I looked at him open mouthed. 'You must be the ace meddler in other people's affairs.

'That's rather uncalled for, old girl.'

I kicked his shin. 'Don't say I didn't warn you what would happen the next time.'

Φ   Φ   Φ

As predicted by Graham, five of us, without Harry, set off for the Casino, all squeezed into Graham's car. 'We mustn't be too long, I've some work to prepare before my flight to England,' Graham warned.

He drove into the Casino entrance, turned the car, and parked facing the entrance. 'That's for a quick getaway if the rozzers come,' he said to no one in particular.'

Hélène said, 'It's les flic in France', to Graham.

'What is?'

'Slang for the police.'

'Rozzers, isn't slang, it's an old English word.'

No one commented.

'Isn't the car a bit obvious,' I asked him sweetly, but he just grinned and took something heavy, concealed in a bag, from the boot of the car.

Suddenly guessing what it might be I thought, 'Oh no! he wouldn't dare.'

I soon found he would, when we reached the front and he unveiled an electronic ram that smashed the front door open in seconds. 'We outnumber them now,' he answered my astonished face,'

Claudine and Hélène, who had not seen the interior before, were impressed by the decor and repeated a remark Egg had made on his earlier visit, 'Why keep it closed, so much is invested here, why not open for gambling?'

'After all,' Hélène added, 'Isn't that what crooks do?'

'Not all of them,' Graham replied.

Egg and I led the way to the corridor and explained our theory about the strong room and the "odds board" being the door. We soon found the catch that opened the blackboard odds door but the steel one behind it Graham declared to be impregnable without an acetylene cutter.

Crestfallen, we went back to the two ladies who were exploring the gambling tables.

'I have seen such things in films,' Claudine told us, 'but these are the first I see that are real. It must be very exciting to play.'

'And can be very expensive,' I added.

We explored the upper floor, including the office where this time the computer was silent.

'Perhaps they have moved out,' Egg questioned.

'No!' Graham replied. 'If there was gold in the strong room, it's still there. They are at the end of their particular road. We are snapping at their heels. The game is up.'

'Then,' I answered, 'they are now particularly dangerous because according to your words they have absolutely nothing to lose.'

'We have to flush them out so we can get to grips with them.'

'That would be fine if you were on your own, but you have four other people with you.'

'Don't worry about me, Rebecca.' Claudine interceded to calm the escalating friction between Graham and myself. Egg and Hélène supported Claudine.

Graham insisted on a room-by-room search of the abandoned bedrooms on the top floor in the roof, but we found nothing and started down the stairs.

'I can smell smoke,' Hélène said sharply.

'I can see smoke,' Egg added as a coil of writhing smoke came up from the lower stairs and started to spread each way along the landing.

We ran to the top of the stairs, but the way below was opaque with smoke. 'We will never find our way through,' Egg cried.

'There's an emergency fire door each end of the landing,' I called and we all ran through the increasing smoke to the door.

I crashed the bar on the door down and was about to open it when Graham warned, 'If you let in fresh air it will fan the flames and make our situation worse.'

'What other options are there?' I answered while opening the door and stepping outside, followed by a rush of smoke. Smoke that may have saved my life when a badly aimed bullet hit the open door. My attempt to dive back in was thwarted by the others pushing their way out, all the time with me shouting 'Back, back, back, and more bullets whistling past. Suddenly, the bullets stopped and a slight breeze thinned the smoke. Even so, we could see nothing below. We stood on the fire escape platform wondering what to do with no volunteers to go back into the fire.

I noticed that Graham had produced a handgun. 'I will go first and silence whoever was shooting at us,' he announced confidently. First I will phone Ramel. He could not make his phone work. 'No signal,' he said.

'Impossible,' Egg answered, 'let me see.' Egg's next comment was that there was too much signal and that the crooks must be using some kind of jammer.

'I am beginning to be nervous,' Claudine whispered to me.

'Let's go.' Graham said abruptly. 'Let me go ahead while you all keep as close to the wall as possible. When we move down out of the smoke and become visible we may have to move as quickly as possible. Keep near me, don't split up.'

With that, he moved cautiously down the stairs.'

We moved only a short distance before there was the crack of a shot and two or three bullets whistled up past us. We all scrambled back.

'Why did I hear only one shot," I asked.

'I only fired one and then I missed.' Graham replied. 'Although they did run off.'

'They must be using silencers on their guns,' Egg exclaimed. 'Of course, they would not want anyone to hear. Graham's shot must have worried them.'

'Another bullet hissed past.

'They can hear us talking, get back inside,' I said quietly to the tune of another bullet.

We huddled by the open door to take advantage of the outside air, the landing being more dense with smoke.

'We must do something before the flames reach us,' I ventured.

Egg turned and walked a little into the smoke. 'There are no flames.' he ventured.

'And, I don't think this is real smoke,' Hélène announced. 'Egg did not cough and the smoke follows the carpet not the ceiling.'

'You're right,' Egg exclaimed, 'the smoke is too cold.'

Graham joined the discussion, 'You mean all this is to scare an intruder out of the building.'

'Yes,' Egg answered. 'And a single person or even a couple would probably have run straight out of the door into their hands.'

'Arms,' Claudine corrected and received a smile in return.

'Well,' I took the initiative, 'if we're not going to choke, all hold hands in a line and I will guide you to the back emergency door.'

Going down the stairs was hell because we all needed at least one hand free. We also found the dummy smoke very unpleasant and we were all a bit dizzy quite quickly. We collected at the bottom of the stairs and I asked, 'The front door is nearer, would it be better to risk it?'

I felt Graham's arm round my shoulders, 'No need, old girl, see the smoke is clearing. Lead on, Mac Duff!

We made it to the promenade then to the dining room doors and were able to stop and recover our breath. Once we had passed through the doors into the kitchen there was no smoke.

'Only in the open part of the building,' Graham commented.

'Who is Mac Duff?' Claudine and Egg asked almost together.

No one answered. Hélène was propping open doors to clear the smoke and Graham and I had gone to check the smoke had not been a diversion to cover the crooks opening the strong room. All was still locked but the place was not deserted.

Three firemen came in the front door and two Gendarmes escorted Claudine, Hélène and Egg to the Foyer.

One of the gendarmes had recognised Claudine and he asked with a broad smile, 'Are you organising a rave?'

Chapter Twenty-four
La Rhune

After the opening of the front doors, the smoke almost cleared from the Foyer. The senior gendarme indicated for us all to sit down on the chairs there. Graham automatically took out his phone and the gendarme gently took it away, asking him to sit down.

He did without protest and requested a call be put through to Ramel. We had already found on the fire escape that the mobile phone would not work; nor did the police radio, so the gendarme went outside to make the call with Graham following.

We watched as they both talked on the radio and then a crestfallen Graham came back in and sat down without a word.

'Well?' I enquired.

'It's all in hand.'

'And?'

Graham looked uncomfortable, 'Ramel is sending transport to collect us from here; he wants to talk to us.'

Perhaps it was the release of tension from our recent escapade, but I just burst out laughing.

The firemen gathered in the Foyer reporting to the senior gendarme there was no trace of fire anywhere in the building. The Capitaine des Pompiers then showed us a small machine under a table near the bar that he explained was made to make a smoke, adding proudly they had one just like it in their Caserne de Pompiers. In answer to a question from Egg, he answered there was an electronic device to switch it on, but declined to tell him where it was. Just then a Black Maria arrived for us with me laughing fit to burst on finding the French term for what we call the "Monkey Wagon" was a "Panier à Salade."

Ramel did not look at all amused when he walked into the police station waiting room and asked just Graham to follow him to his office. They were talking for some time, but both returned to us seemingly in good humour and Ramel shook Graham's hand. He then turned to us and said, with a smile, that he was fâché with all of us, but his men were amused by our activities.

A policeman drove us back to the Casino so we could collect our car and the gendarmes were still there waiting for two workmen to finish mending the door. The senior gendarme, with something of a smirk, gave Graham back his bashing machine suggesting he kept it for "noix" in the future.

Φ   Φ   Φ

Relaxing with a mid morning coffee, I picked up the phone to answer what sounded like a slightly flustered Egg, 'Rebecca, I'm so pleased you are there, could you possibly come straight up to my flat? I have someone here that I want you to meet.'

'Of course, I'll be with you in minutes.'

I almost raced up the stairs wondering what had gone wrong this time. Egg was waiting for me, standing in his open doorway. He stepped back, pulling the door open wide, revealing a young woman sitting on a chair drawn up to his dining table.

As I walked to the table, I could see she had a distraught expression and I sensed, dare I say, an air of desperation?

Egg introduced- 'Rebecca, this is Carine Dumont, the wife of my friend in St Jean. Conrad is still held by the police so Carine has come to me for advice on an urgent matter. It appears that her husband helped to support the financial burden of his shop by acting as a courier passing messages between Paul Vachon and the representative of a smuggling group in Spain. Carine has received a message that has to be delivered to a Spanish courier on the Rhune tomorrow morning. Although wanting no part of it she is afraid of what Paul Vachon will do if she refuses. She is horrified at what Conrad has been doing and wants him to pay whatever penalty he deserves so they can then sell the shop and make a new start in another town when he is released from prison after serving his sentence. Carine came for advice, but Graham has only just gone back to England so I don't want to phone him unless I have to; what do you suggest we do?'

'First of all, what's the Rhune?'

'Of course, you would not know being a stranger to the area. It is a big mountain that is near to the seaside town of Biarritz. Really it is, as you might say, the Basque Sacred Mountain. It climbs 3,000 feet and is on the border between France and Spain. There is an electric railway to the top and that is where Paul Vachon wants to send a message. Carine will explain.'

As I sat down facing her, Egg added as an afterthought, 'She speaks very good English.'

'What's to be delivered?' I asked.

Carine opened a small bag on her lap and laid a gold ingot on the table.

'My God!' I exclaimed. 'What are you expecting to collect?'

She didn't answer my question directly, but explained, 'Whoever Conrad meets brings a package and they make an exchange. He goes up on the train at eleven hours and always sits with a table right next to the men's WC so that if the police come he can slip inside and put the gold in the citerne of a toilette.'

'Carine, I must know what is in the package to be collected.'

She went very pale and looked uncomfortable. 'No one has put it into words,' her voice faltered.

'You must tell me or I cannot help you.'

'I do not know for sure, but it can only be drugs.'

'Would you make us some coffee, Egg, while I find Marius.'

Carine was now deathly pale and visibly shaking so I pulled out a chair and sat beside her, taking her hand in both of mine.

'Listen to me, Carine. You have done the right thing to come here and we will look after you and sort out the trouble you have. I will make the delivery tomorrow so that you are not involved in the exchange. Don't worry; we will handle the arrangements from now on. You turn your attention to supporting your husband.'

Hoping as I spoke that I would be able to handle the swop.

As Egg passed round the coffees, I picked up the phone and dialled the emergency number for Marius.

The man who answered hesitated until I spoke my name, then said he would transfer me.

Marius seemed unfazed at my explanation. He thanked me for dealing with the news calmly and added, 'Of course, we will make the delivery. Fortunately I am in Bayonne and it will be perfectly possible for me to meet you at Le Rhune station. Hold please.'

I could hear the rattle of a computer keyboard. 'Your lady is correct; there is a train at 11 am. We also will make use of that train. Rebecca! I am assuming you will join me, but please say if you would rather not.

'Are you kidding, try and keep me away,' I replied,

He chuckled, 'I want you to travel on the train alone so that you can act as a back-up observer, and for you to keep contact with the quarry, if possible. We also need a woman to accompany me and she needs to be as attractive as you are, with a hope she will distract the courier. But for Graham's glowing praise of your other skills, which make you perfect for handling any difficulties, I would have asked you to join me. Who do you suggest instead?'

'Claudine would be very good, Hélène would be perfect.'

'The English have a saying that describes my predicament, I am spoilt for choice. Rebecca, can I leave it to you to arrange a hidden choice for me.'

'You mean a Blind Date.'

'I will look forward to your choice and my Blind Date. If the lady who brought the information is still there will she also speak to me?'

When I asked Carine if she would speak with Brigadier, Comte Marius Bertin of the Compagnies Républicaines de Sécurité she looked terrified, but did take the phone.

Her face gradually smoothed as she listened and even the trace of a smile appeared. She gave me back the phone and said, 'He is very nice. He has promised to discuss Conrad's case with someone named Graham and Commissaire Ramel. He also said that they would look after me and gave me a number to ring at Pau police station if I was worried about anything. He thought it very unlikely that I would hear any more from Paul Vachon, but if I had any concern they would put me in another house until all was settled. Oh Rebecca! Thank you so many times. I am so happy and relieved. Everything looked so hopeless. There was a darkness and it seemed to be the end of my world. I didn't know what to do.'

I rang Hélène doubtfully, not knowing how she would react to my proposal, but I had no need to worry. Even before asking a single question about what I wanted her to do, she said, 'Oh yes, of course I remember the handsome Marius. I would be delighted to join him for a mystery train ride.'

Later, Graham phoned me with what was becoming his usual cry of be careful. I explained what had been arranged for the morrow. He spluttered when I told him Hélène was going to join Marius on the train up the mountain. 'Lucky swine,' he grated. 'It was just the same when we were teenagers, Marius always got the girl. Nothing ever changes.'

My only surprise in his reaction was that he had known Marius for so long.

Φ   Φ   Φ

Next morning I stood "alone" alongside the train on the platform of the open plan Rhune station in St Ignace watching Marius and Hélène chattering. I had asked her to wear a dress for a Mata Hari part, as a sort of joke, but she couldn't have interpreted what was wanted better. If it's possible to have an elegant sun dress that's exactly what she wore, an elegant, cream silk sundress with a cream, wide brimmed sun hat with just the right sized, casually, but carefully, strewn, navy-blue decoration round the brim. With her long, fair hair hanging down her shoulders she looked irresistible. In fact, while I watched, two men walked into each other, their attention distracted.

The body language of Marius and Hélène illustrated they were attracted to each other and I felt just a little twinge of envy. I could also see why he wanted an eye-catching companion. Had I been tasked with finding an undercover drugs courier, the handsome couple before me would have been my last guess.

The train ride up the mountain on such a superb day was outstanding, as the little town disappeared behind us and the train slowly ground up to a kind of lay-by. This was the only passing place to make way for a train that almost immediately came down the single track. While we waited I admired the outstanding view looking back from our temporary stop but turning to our upward progress as we continued to climb took us to vistas that implied we would soon be able to see the whole world. Not having a tough, handsome Brigadier to talk to, I enjoyed the views with undivided attention.

Well! almost my undivided attention for I was looking out for other people who were travelling alone. My first reaction to the news of a courier exchange on the Rhune was to consider carefully what route the opposition might take. As far as I could see from an extensive study of large-scale maps there wasn't one. True, you could walk across miles of mountain, but there was little prospect of a decent track south from the top of the Rhune. In fact, there was nothing that was secure from a third party attack. After all, the courier would be carrying a valuable, and heavy, gold ingot. I decided the courier, Spanish or not, would disguise his route and come by train. He would probably even try going up on the same train as the person he was to meet so he/she could assess the situation. I also guessed whoever was coming from Spain would wait and go down on the next train after his quarry left to avoid any chance of his being seen in France by the person he had just met. And, I already had my favourite suspect.

Marius and Hélène did not wander too far on the top of the mountain and were soon in the gift shop inspecting the array of everything on sale that you couldn't possibly want to buy on top of a mountain. With satisfaction, I noticed my suspect, a youngish, good looking man wearing a green anorak and with a small brown haversack over his shoulder, was never far away from them.

It was part of my plan to make myself known to the courier before he spoke to Marius so I delayed no longer and accosted the young man asking for help in choosing a present for my father. I may not match Hélène in the seduction stakes, but I'm good enough to weaken the male will. We were on first name terms in seconds - although I thought his offer of the name Damien was inventive - and he only ducked joining me for a drink because he remembered his mission.

I selected a table for myself with the sun behind me so that it wouldn't be possible for me to be seen clearly and waited events. Damien spoke briefly to Marius then accepted an invitation to sit down. A long discussion followed and it was clear all was not going well and it even developed into an argument.

Eventually, while a waiter was serving them drinks, I walked across the middle of the floor to the Ladies. This was a prearranged plan and Hélène soon joined me. She whispered there was a hitch because Marius should have the gold bar in a haversack that matched Damien's so they could simply do a swop without opening either bag. Damien had become jumpy and very nervous and almost walked out without doing the exchange. Marius was calming him and suggesting they all travelled down on the train together and do an exchange of bags in the car park. At the moment Damien would not consider going down on the train, saying he had to go back to Spain. She gave me a number to ring and to ask for operation parapluie to be launched.

I walked straight from the ladies to the outside world and found myself a spot to sit on the grass where I could keep a close watch of the tiny mountain station. Dramatically, the station was perched before a wide panorama that stretched to the sea. Elsewhere mountains jostled each other to claim pride of place in what was really a wonderful scene. Just as I was thinking all it needed was for Julie Andrews to come flapping along singing "the hills are alive," my associates appeared.

Marius and Hélène walked slowly down to the train, Marius twisting round as if looking for someone. I kept still. Whatever had happened inside it would do no good to advertise myself.

Hélène boarded the train, but Marius remained on the narrow platform, still looking round.

I took a small make-up mirror from my purse and reflected the sun onto his face a couple of times causing him to look up towards me. He gave no indication of any kind but simply followed Hélène onto the train. It was flattering that he appeared to be concerned about my safety, I thought, then realised he might equally well have been making sure I was in position ready to follow Damien.

Eventually the train driver finished changing round the rooftop poles attached to the trapeze that fed the electric current to the train. After wiping his hands on a greasy rag he boarded the crowded train and it was off on its journey to the station at St Ignace.

I looked round as someone sat down beside me, it was Damien.

'You missed the train,' I ventured.

'I wanted to avoid someone on it, the next one will do for me.'

'My plan as well,' I replied, 'except that I stayed to admire this wonderful view.'

We stayed chatting for a while and I complimented him on his English. He replied that more Spanish men spoke English than French men. I laughed and asked how could he possibly know.

He told me the Rhune was popular with visitors long before the railway was installed and used to be called the Shepherd's mountain because so many flocks of sheep were grazed on its slopes.

'I hope you don't see me as a Shepherdess,' I replied.

He laughed and suggested a drink. As we rose to walk to the café I was thinking Damien was really nice and that maybe we had made a mistake somewhere, then noticed his haversack had gone and that he was carrying the camera case in which Marius had carried the gold bar.

After a quick look at a map on the wall of the lower station, I asked Damien if he was going in the direction of Sare, reasoning he would go that way back to Spain, and he said he was and asked if I wanted a lift.

I had no idea what my next move would be after that, for I expected at the end of our descent to the station it would be crawling with gendarmes who would pounce on Damien. Instead, as they say, you can never find a policeman when you want one, so I accepted his offer.

The mile to Sare was not enough for me to formulate any kind of plan, so I was still undecided. Not that there was much opportunity for thinking with Damien giving me a lecture on what a wonderful country Spain was. I have to admit his knowledge of the area, and of many other parts of Spain was extensive and his descriptions colourful and full of interest. I thought what a pity it was that he was wasting the possibility of an excellent career by associating with the wrong crowd.

My musings were distracted, when I realised we were entering the little town of Sare. I saw a police car in a lay-by but there was no opportunity to signal them.

Damien turned right and he remarked, 'It is a wonderful ride over the mountains to Bera. I have something to deliver not far from there and then I could drive you back to your hotel in Sare. Why don't you come with me?'

As he spoke I saw another police car parked in a side road and the penny dropped.

'Yes, I'd love to come with you to Bera.'

He was right about it being a lovely ride up the Col de Lizuniaga and I relaxed enjoying the wonderful views while my self appointed guide gave me a learned commentary.

'Damien,' I said, 'Why don't you look for a job in tourism? You are an ideal candidate for that field.'

He laughed, 'I do work in the tourist industry. But, I also earn extra money as a messenger. That was astute of you, Rebecca.'

I lapsed into a sad silence. What a pity.

Unknown to me there used to be a frontier customs post at the top and there still seemed to be some activity as we approached the old checkpoint. Damien became very fidgety and then suddenly rammed his foot on the car's accelerator when he saw police cars ahead. He increased speed, zigzagging between the cars until clear. But, there was nowhere to go; the road on was blocked with a barrier. He braked to a halt, grabbed Marius's camera case, jumped from the car and ran across a field towards some trees with me in hot pursuit.

Plunging after him through an aggressive hedge, I swore at the sound of my skirt ripping. A disaster that was nothing compared to sloshing through a muddy stream and tree branches tearing at my hair.

Catching up with Damien, I threw myself on his back and sent him crashing to the ground. 'Sorry, Damien,' I said sympathetically while twisting his arms behind his back to disable him and then sat on him until the gendarmes caught up.

He actually had the stamina and cheek to grin and say he was enjoying himself.

'Let me go and you can have this' he offered. He indicated with his head the black camera case that was lying beside him.

Back on the road, surrounded by rugged policemen, I was in my element for a while, but eventually Marius turned up to see me bedraggled and muddy and a cool, elegant Hélène attracted the policemen away.

I knew just enough Spanish to understand when one of the gendarmes asked her if she was a film star. Whatever she replied caused them all to laugh.

'Hélène is in perfect control,' I mused, 'she's wasted teaching history.'

'A centime for your thoughts,' Marius's voice broke my reverie.

He startled me, not having realised I had stood simply staring at Hélène and the police for so long. 'She's a confident, accomplished woman,' I replied. 'A woman yet to find her place in life.'

'I couldn't agree more. She put me at ease today, effortlessly.'

I looked at him speculatively. A tough Brigadier in the CRS and a Count to boot, probably with a mini estate somewhere. She put him at ease!! - What price Hélène the lion tamer? I already knew she had the world at her feet, now I knew her place in life. 'I wonder?' I breathed, as I followed Marius towards the group, the policemen standing aside respectfully.

'Attention men,' Marius spoke in a normal voice, but there was an instant hush. 'This lady by my side is Rebecca Tilsley. Rebecca has tailed our quarry all day and steered him into our custody, not to mention capturing this.' Marius held up the gold ingot.

There was a spontaneous and prolonged burst of applause from the policemen.

'Well done, Rebecca.' Marius kissed my pink, but muddy cheeks. 'I'm grateful you stayed with him and helped to chase him over the border so he was arrested in Spain. I didn't really expect you to conduct him there personally, but it saved us an embarrassment. The bug we planted on him failed to work, but the one I asked Hélène to plant on you in the toilet was fine.'

'It's all in a day's work,' I said laconically, as I quietly tried to hide the long tears in my skirt.

Φ   Φ   Φ

While we wound down over the appropriate beverage at Egg's that evening, Marius told us the switch was touch and go for a while. Damien had approached their table and asked if they had a message for him. Marius explained, 'I told him that I was acting for Conrad who was ill. That was a mistake because Damien knew he was in prison. He would have left at that, thinking I would have known Conrad was in prison if I had come as a messenger from him.

Fortunately, he stayed with us because he could hardly take his eyes off Hélène.'

'I was giving Damien smouldering glances,' she explained.

Still mildly miffed because she had attracted the policemen away from me I said, 'Show us an example,' but she just smiled and went on to say that Damien was unsure what to do.

'He became more agitated when he realised we didn't have the gold ingot in a brown haversack. It was apparently the system just to drop the two haversacks on the floor and each to pick up the appropriate one on leaving.

Marius joined in, 'I called a bluff by offering him my phone and telling him to call Paul, because I wasn't going to be responsible for making someone like Paul Vachon lose his temper. He was clearly afraid of him to such an extent he accepted my simply saying "Paul" as proof we were on close terms.

'The Spanish security service will have a little talk with him, then round up his contacts. I'm sure this end of the organisation will soon be, as you English say, put to bed.'

I considered "Put to sleep" would be a more appropriate remedy.

Marius rose from his chair. 'I must go,' he announced. Then to Hélène, 'Thank you for your company and assistance. I am sincerely regretful to be handing you back to your companions.'

She also stood. 'Perhaps then I could prevail upon you to transport me to where you found me, outside my apartment.'

Marius gave a little bow, 'It would be to my great pleasure Mademoiselle.'

Hélène performed a trace of a curtsey, and answered, 'Thank you Sire.'

'Oh please!' I muttered grumpily to myself.

Chapter Twenty-five
Secret of the Holçarté

Marius phoned me later the next day to say that Damien had co-operated fully and led two plain clothes police to the spot where it had been arranged to hand over the gold. A bonus gained, for there were two men waiting to take the gold ingot and both were arrested. One of the two turned out to be the senior man of the organisation and the Guardia are satisfied that is the end of the Vachon operation in Spain.

'Graham's worry now,' Marius explained, 'is that Paul Vachon will see how hopeless is his position and he may leave the area with his gold and disappear, so avoiding capture.

'I told him that from what I had seen and heard of the man, there was no doubt in my mind he will try hard to hit back. That he would want revenge as he demonstrated by sending Pierront to London to kill Claudine.

Marius then added, 'Graham is coming back to France in the morning and he will try and persuade both you and Claudine to go into hiding until this is all over.'

'About Claudine, I agree, but I also know she will refuse, but why include me?'

'Rebecca! Without your help yesterday the courier might have escaped with the gold ingot. If Paul Vachon knows that, then you also are on his revengeful list.'

Graham did not arrive the next day; he was waiting for me in our apartment upon my return from popping out for a few supplies. After greetings, he immediately embarked on his orders.

'You are to pick up Claudine straight away and the two of you fly to London and stay with Lady Sophie until we catch Paul Vachon.'

'No way!!'

'Rebecca, you don't realise the danger you are in.'

'I've already promised you that I will bring you Vachon's head on a plate. Catching him will not provide the kind of protection mankind needs. You very well know from your own words he is more dangerous than a wild animal and you cannot catch him on your own.'

'Rebecca!!!'

'You're wasting your time. I'm staying here.'

'Well, I'll speak to Claudine. In fact, I'll go up now.'

'Better we all go to Labaraquette and have a family conference,' I insisted. 'She might agree to stay there, but I doubt it.'

He uttered some sort of 'Humpf' and disappeared through the door. He was back about twenty minutes later with another 'Humpf' and the news that we would all meet at Labaraquette at six o'clock. 'It might be a good idea for you all to stay there overnight,' he remarked as he set off himself.

'Graham,' I called as he opened the door, 'you be very careful. Paul Vachon is no friend of yours either.'

Φ   Φ   Φ

As Harry and I drove Claudine and Egg over to Labaraquette in a rising storm, the visit did not seem to be such a good idea and I was thankful we had taken a few overnight things. The rain lashed down on the car in sheets as we left the flat's underground garage. And, leaving the shelter of the town's buildings, it quickly became apparent that the wind was at storm force as well. We were thankful to arrive at the farmhouse only slightly wet from running through the rain after leaving the car.

I was surprised to see Marius and Hélène there for Graham had made no mention of inviting them. They explained as we exchanged greetings that when Graham spoke of our meeting he had suggested all of us with an involvement should be made aware of the danger.

'I am very pleased that he did,' Albert called. 'It makes me happy to see you all here.'

Brigitte bustled about attending to food, with a wide smile on her face. She produced some little dishes of small biscuits and announced, 'Voilà! I find out the English eat the petite biscuit when they drink.'

We all laughed in appreciation of her kindness.

Considering the serious reason for our visit, we had quite a merry meal with not one mention of Paul Vachon. Indeed we did just what the English do and talked about the weather.

When the conversation did turn to thoughts of gold and whether it might now be hidden in the Monastery, Hélène asked if we meant the Monastery Izlariette. 'You speak as if you have been there. Have you been inside?'

'No,' Egg answered. 'The monk who answered the door told us he would not let us past the entrance.

'You say he spoke to you, that is strange, it is a closed order. Those Orthodox Coenobites are totally devout.'

I saw his head jerk up at her words.

Before Egg or I had an opportunity to ask what she meant, Albert inadvertently changed the subject when he remarked of our interest in the Holçarté Gorge and said. 'You adventurers would not want to be there on such a night as this.'

'Why?' asked Graham, who had only seen the gorge from the footpath.

'Because the river changes its mood from tumbling little waterfalls that delight the tourists to a raging monster that would devour all in its path were it not contained by the rocks and cliffs. This makes the river so angry it is effroyable' He looked enquiringly at Claudine.

'A horror. I think Rebecca and Harry would say fearsome.'

'How about this underwater cave you spoke of?' Graham asked Egg.

'Just what I was thinking,' he replied. 'It must be boiling like a cauldron.'

Harry, who I knew was feeling deprived after missing the assault on the Casino, quickly exclaimed, 'I could join you chaps tomorrow if you fancy looking to see if any gold has been washed down the river.'

'I think you would have to wait for the water levels to drop,' Hélène suggested.

'I'm sure that's true,' Egg answered. 'Its always a matter of wait and see with unpredictable mountain country.'

Albert was looking worried by our conversation. 'You are not planning to try walking in the river?' he exclaimed. 'You must not attempt to do that, it is very dangerous and in many places there is nowhere to walk except in the water. If high water comes there may be no place to hide from the river.'

'Don't worry,' Graham said to Albert, 'I will talk to Ramel about the river and see what he thinks is best.'

'I fly back to Paris tomorrow,' Marius said regretfully. 'Otherwise I would be tempted to join your river Safari.'

'If I am able to have time from work,' Claudine explained, 'I will join you. How about you Hélène?'

'I am also flying to Paris. Marius has offered to be my guide to the delights of the city. I have never explored Paris with a knowledgeable companion and I will enjoy the trip very much.

My quick glance round the table showed my face was the only one that was not displaying surprise at this news. I just smiled contentedly.

We had a long discussion about the threat from Paul Vachon with no one wanting to change their plans, but after some protesting, all agreed not to go anywhere alone. Marius gave us another surprise when he announced that Commissaire Ramel had agreed to supply an escort to see Claudine to and from work until Paul Vachon was apprehended and she had agreed, after protest, to make use of his offer.

I was slightly worried about the river when Graham told me he wouldn't bother Ramel. He explained he was certain all would be well if we waited for the river level to drop. He just wanted to reassure Albert.

When we eventually went to bed, Harry said to me, 'That was jolly clever of Marius to invite Hélène to Paris for a few days. That will keep her out of danger.'

'Yes! wasn't it clever,' I replied, with a broad grin.

Φ   Φ   Φ

It was two days before the weather had calmed completely and Albert rang to say the river levels had dropped.

Claudine was unable to join us, so Graham, Harry, Egg and I set out for the Holçarté armed with a long rope and two pairs of long waders to assist in recovering the winch.

On arriving, we looked at the still turbulent water and Graham insisted he took on the more dangerous task of exploring the river, while Harry and Egg took the path up to the cleft in the rock face.

'That puts me in the river with you,' I remarked but was unable to interpret his broad smile.

I explained to Harry, when he protested he should go in my place, it would be silly for him to risk being stuck up the gorge with a gammy leg. He, of course, insisted his leg was fine.

We donned the waders and braved the tumbling river.

I did protest immediately to Graham that although the river level had dropped to a reasonable height the water was still moving too fast for comfort and we should come back when the river was calmer. 'Albert told us it was dangerous. He was genuinely worried about it.'

'Don't fuss, Rebecca,' was all the thanks received.

The agreement was to recover the winch first, then the river party, or drowned rats as Egg suggested we should be called, would look for displaced gold bars on our way back.

Egg and Harry headed up to the crevasse to prepare for lowering the rope down to us when we reached the pool.

Graham and I had each armed ourselves with a pair of ski sticks to help maintain our balance on the uneven riverbed, and we needed them. It was difficult to find our footing for we soon found the fast moving water not only tried to push us off our feet, it was far from transparent and the violent ripples concealed the uneven riverbed.

'Fat chance to see any gold bars in these conditions,' I shouted.

Soon we were away from the open entrance to the gorge and progressed until the cliffs each side of the river reared high above us. We stopped for a breather and Graham finally agreed with my view that we should have waited until the water was calmer. Even so, we decided to go on and try to recover the winch. We continued splashing up stream with some parts easier than others and both of us took some spray into the top of our waders.

'We really need a wet suit,' I shouted, but such was the noise of the water I doubted he heard.

Then I saw a tangle of cable on the rocks and while making my way towards it, Graham looked back and realised what I was about and headed towards me. It was the winch, but what a tangle it was in.

The tangle prompted a barrage of angry words from Graham.

'Where's the crevice with the pool?' he asked.

'There's no sign of it here.'

'How much further do we have to go upstream?'

'Maybe it's nearer to take it back down to the bottom.'

'Then we could carry it up the path?'

I didn't answer but leaned on my ski sticks, smiling at his outburst.

'Humpf,' he snorted, then burst out laughing.

But, we had come some way up the river so decided to go on. First I cut free the rope that had been tied to the winch on our previous visit. Heaven knows what had happened to the log we used as a weight. Somehow we pulled the tangle of cable from the rocks. Then had a fight to recover the chain that snaked in and out of the rocks. Indeed, some of the rocks, rolled by the torrent, had settled on the chain. It took both of us to roll them off again. Rocks that had been effortlessly and carelessly tossed aside by the roaring water. After a useless attempt to make a coil of the cable so that it could be carried, we decided the only way was to wind the cable back on the winch drum. We detached the heavy, wooden key for me to carry and tied the whole bundle with the rope we had recovered, Graham manfully agreeing to carry the heavy bundle.

We finally managed, and although the day was warm, my hands were numb. Graham copied me when I tucked my hands under my armpits to warm them as we rested before continuing up the gorge.

Looking round as my hands warmed, I was astonished to see a broom in what appeared to be perfect condition, presumably dragged up from the welter of rocks by the winch cable. I waddled over to it with my hands still clamped by my arms, but pulled them out unable to resist inspecting the broom.

'What do you make of this?' I called.

'It's a broom, I never use them.'

'That doesn't surprise me. What do you think it's doing here, it looks almost new?'

Graham grumpily hopped over to me and inspected my find. 'Well! it's an odd place to find it but it could have floated downstream for miles.'

'It must have been mixed up with the winch cables.'

'So what!'

'So it's a bit strange.'

Graham would have thrown it high up on the loose rocks, but I took it from him and planted the handle in some loose, fine shale on the edge of the river, then added a cairn of rocks to reinforce it. Standing back to admire my handiwork, I remarked that it looked as if it was a sign and would puzzle any walkers looking down from above.

An impatient Graham, tiring of my activities, simply said, 'For crying out loud, come on Rebecca, we haven't come here to play games.'

It was more than an hour after leaving the bottom of the gorge when we arrived at the fissure and shouted 'Ahoy there,' to Egg and Harry.

They shouted they could see no sign of the winch from above.

'You wouldn't, we found it half way down the gorge,' Graham shouted back, while I tied their rope to the winch and called up, 'Haul away.'

We could easily see the water in the fissure pool was deeper than our waders were high, so Graham quickly abandoned any thoughts of looking for a cave, especially if it was underwater.

I edged close to the cliff on the upstream side of the pool and felt a surge of adrenaline. I called, 'There is a hole, I can just see the top but not how big it is. We can't just leave. I don't mind getting wet, I'm going to look.'

'No Rebecca,' he almost screamed. 'You could easily get into trouble and drown.' Then seeing I was determined, shouted up to Egg. 'Throw down the rope. This mad woman down here is going swimming.'

The rope came down, just missing us but did splash water over Graham. 'I knew you'd get me wet,' he said accusingly to me.

I tied the rope round my shoulders and waist in a cross harness as he fussed over me like an old woman.

'Please be careful, Rebecca,' he pleaded. 'None of your stunts.'

Kissing his cheek I told him not to make a fuss, that I knew what was involved and would be all right. Then added a message to tell Egg to light a campfire to dry me out afterwards.

I don't think that until my speaking the words "dry me out" that he had taken in the fact that I would be immersed, so I moved forward quickly before he had time to stop me.

The cold water was a bit of a shock when it came up above my waist, but I reached the hole without event and could even see the river bottom in the pool. Where I stood in the calmer water of the sheltered crevice, the water surface was much smoother. I moved to the opening and stubbed my foot on something, tripping and nearly diving into what turned out to be a mini cave. Of course it was too dark to see what was inside and I took one of those instant decisions one usually takes and regrets later.

Drawing a deep breath, I plunged under the water and felt my way into the hole, which was only about three times as wide as me. The floor seemed clear and almost by accident I discovered a further small chamber that would be invisible from the outside. With lungs almost bursting, my hands were sweeping frantically backwards and forwards. Then, as I hastily started pushing myself backwards, I felt something, with firm edges, that was heavy and which I just about managed to drag out to the cave entrance where my very cold hands forced me to let it drop. There was just time to thrust my head up for air before I drowned.

'For God's sake, Rebecca,' Graham was frantic and shouting. 'Get out of there before I have to come and fetch you.'

Instead, he again saw me plunge down after my hard won prize. My astonishment was complete when I saw the dropped gold ingot lying where it had fallen on the bed of the river. Next to it was the object that had tripped me, another gold ingot. I looked around quickly until my breath ran out, but there were no others that I could see. I rose up in the water as if staging an impersonation of The Lady of the Lake, holding aloft a gold ingot in each hand.

'Graham was speechless as I waded to him, then said, almost under his breath, 'My God! I would never have believed it.'

We all retreated to the cave and ruined cottage where the wooden key had been kept while we sorted out what to do about my wet clothes. Egg gave me his shirt, Graham his jacket and Harry his trousers. I thought my appearance was rather fetching in a grunge sort of way.

Everyone was delighted with our golden prize and Harry tried to inveigle Egg into borrowing the waders for a quick bit of prospecting up the river. He, fortunately, had more sense and then Graham killed any further delay by announcing the sooner I was in a hot bath the better.

We arrived back at our apartment to find on the doormat a note from Hélène with the instructions from her friend on how to set up the winch in the crevice so that it did not slip

Chapter Twenty-six
Farmer Bruno

I ignored the ring of my bedside phone and snuggled deeper under the bedclothes. My experience of telephone calls before nine am is that they are often the harbinger of bad news. A wasted attempt to avoid the inevitable when Harry shouted, 'Get the phone, Rebecca, I'm in the shower.'

I offered the phone a single monosyllable to illustrate my displeasure, 'Yes!'

'It's Hélène!'

Sitting bolt upright in bed I changed my tone, 'Oh, you are back, welcome.'

'Terrible news, Rebecca, Bruno Laurade was killed while I was away. Commissaire Ramel left a message for me before he went on holiday. He says it was an accident. I telephoned his office and they said Bruno was hit by a car while crossing the road in Rochenoir and, although the car did not stop and they are looking for the driver, they are satisfied it was an accident.'

'What was Bruno doing in Rochenoir?'

'Exactement, I worry about the dogs. If the police go to his farm before me the dogs will be angry and cause trouble. In any case there is my promise to Bruno they would be cared for. I must go up there quickly, is it possible one of you could take me?'

'Yes, of course, I will be round as soon as I've dressed.'

Putting the telephone down I registered the shock her news had caused me plus the realisation Hélène must be terribly upset. There was no question she was fond of the grumpy old man. 'Was he murdered?' I mused while showering. 'Yes, certainly he was murdered and by Paul Vachon.'

I intermittently explained the call to Harry while choking down some toast and he immediately phoned to cancel an appointment at the university explaining he would come with me in case we found any problems. He also phoned Graham who surprised us by saying he had to make an urgent trip to Paris to discuss, amongst other items, who legally owns the gold we had found. He hoped to be away not more than two days because it was urgent that Paul Vachon was found before he tried taking revenge again.

'Harry, old man, It's over to Rebecca, I have every confidence she will be able to cope with Hélène's situation. I will phone Ramel about it before I go, but I think he is on holiday from today of all days. It doesn't really matter; Spiro will have to deal with it. There's going to be some movement at last, but I can say nothing more until my return.'

Harry put the phone down and asked, 'Who's Spiro?

'I've no idea.'

'Well, he's the one left to deal with Bruno's death.'

'Oh no! they haven't put some PC Plod on the case, just because it's an old man?'

While Harry drove up the mountain, I sat in the back with Hélène and we endlessly and pointlessly discussed the terrible news. With no facts to go on there really was nothing to talk about except who killed Bruno. Of that she was of the same mind as both Harry and me, callous and pointless revenge by Paul Vachon. Well! nothing else with the exception of Graham's sudden departure. What was he up to in Paris?

Hélène said that Marius had a long telephone conversation with Graham while she was in Paris, but explained, with an apology, that she did not feel she could repeat anything she had overheard. Of course, I understood that perfectly.

As we approached Bruno's place our hearts sank further if that was possible. The farm buildings were a ruin of charred timbers.

Hélène gave a little cry and put her hands to her face, 'Oh no! the dogs would have been in one of the buildings.'

But they weren't as far as we could see without climbing into the almost ground level mess of charred wood and distorted metal.

'I don't think the fire would have been hot enough to burn all......' Harry stopped not knowing how to describe considerately what we were now going to be looking for.

'They burnt his car as well,' he lamely said instead.

'Bruno did not have a car and would have driven to Rochenoir in his old jeep. His jeep must be in Rochenoir.'

We inspected the car, it was just a metal framework and charred seats.

Harry saw something unusual a little way off and said, 'Wait here girls while I check an object on the grass over there.'

As he approached the spot I surmised what it must be and put my arm round Hélène. Turning to speak to her, I realised by the tears in her eyes she also knew so said nothing. Harry next walked to the left and we guessed both dogs were dead and ran across to the first. Hélène knelt on the grass by the dog and gently lifted its head. I stood back a little saying nothing to interrupt her grief.

Harry walked back to us and said quietly, 'They were both shot.'

When Hélène moved to kneel by the second dog, Harry told me he was going back to the burnt car. 'You can still read the number plate,' he explained, 'I'll phone Ramel's office and ask if they know about all this' - he waved a helpless arm – 'and have any information on the car. Don't say anything to Hélène yet, but I have a feeling that must be the car they used to kill Bruno.'

Not being a dog lover and neutral about animals I am ambivalent about other people owning dogs so, to me, Bruno's dogs were savage animals to avoid. None the less, influenced I suppose, by Hélène's distress, I too knelt by the animal and stroked its head. 'This is not fair,' I said to the dog's inanimate head. 'This was just someone wanting revenge that was nothing to do with you. You were ruthlessly killed just to hurt and warn us.'

Unaware that Hélène had returned while I was speaking to the dog, it startled me when she spoke from behind me, 'Thank you, Rebecca, I do not feel so alone now that I know you care as well.'

I stood up and we held each other. 'This was just pointless revenge by Paul Vachon,' I remarked with some anger. That old man had never hurt him and had said nothing harmful about his past relationship with the Vachons.'

Harry joined us, 'The burnt car is the one that killed Bruno,' he explained. 'The police are on their way. I explained about the dogs and they promised to bury them after they have examined them. They will have to treat Bruno's death as murder now.'

'I will wait for them and make sure the dogs have a proper burial,' Hélène said, 'Thank you both for driving me here and your support. When I leave it will be to walk alone in the woods and come to term with this terrible happening. You need not wait, I will have no problem obtaining transport in the police car.'

I was equally certain she would have "no problem obtaining transport" but all the same explained we would wait with her until the police arrived.

'I will find this Paul Vachon,' Hélène commented in a determined voice

'No!' I exclaimed in frightened alarm, 'no, no, no, you must leave it to us working together as a team. It would serve no purpose for you to be hurt by that madman. Hélène, I will guarantee you that Paul Vachon will not escape justice. I absolutely guarantee we will find him. Please let me act for you; promise me you won't go near him!'

She did promise, but using intuition, I also phoned Marius and warned him of the possible situation.

Φ   Φ   Φ

Harry and I called into Police headquarters in Pau and asked to speak to whoever was dealing with Ramel's affairs while he was away. By sheer chance the gendarme who attended the punch up when we girls were playing at being Charley's Angels was there and, of course, he recognised me and asked if he could help.

I explained about the farmer being killed and he took us through to Ramel's office and introduced us to Commissaire Tavernier, before discreetly leaving.

After shaking hands, Tavernier explained he was a relief for Ramel so would we be patient while he sent for the files on our case. I noticed when he accidentally knocked the edge of his computer screen and it turned slightly towards us he already had a display showing our names and a mass of smaller, print details.

A policeman came in with a tray of coffee followed by another of more senior rank who passed a wedge of papers to Tavernier. I noticed several places were marked with coloured strips of paper and guessed - correctly as it worked out - that someone had already marked important items to do with us. No one spoke while the coffee was poured and distributed, which gave me an opportunity to have a good look at the new arrival. A young Marius was an instant impression, tough of countenance for all his good looks, tanned, with deep brown hair and an easy way of moving. 'Where were you when I was riding up the Rhune in a train on my own?' I thought.

After the policeman bringing the coffee had gone, we were introduced to Lieutenant Spiro Bellec, as the senior case officer in charge of anything to do with Mademoiselle Claudine. Well! that took me down a peg or two.

At the wave of a hand from the Commissaire, Spiro pulled up a chair and sat down. He looked briefly at his boss who nodded his head. 'We have updated on the farmer,' he commenced looking at me, then hesitated. 'Is there something wrong Madame?'

'You caught me unguarded and read my expression, Spiro,' I replied. 'I am not a fan of the modern idiom and "updated" is one of my dislikes. And, please call me Rebecca.'

He grinned, 'I agree with you about current terminology and will say in my defence that my use of "updated" means I was already suspicious of the farmer's death for a reason unknown to you. On his person he carried a piece of paper with "Claudine, Tourist Office, Rochenoir," written upon it. I think he was on his way to see her and may have been killed to stop him talking to her. I have spoken to her and explained, also asking her to go into hiding for a few days. I regret to say she will not and tells me that she is not afraid to stand up to a bully. We have arranged for her to be guarded, but there is still a risk. We think Paul Vachon is somewhere in the immediate area and we are actively looking for him.'

'That's marvellous, you really are on your toes or should I say "with it."'

He gave me a gorgeous smile and said, 'You may say whatever you like, Rebecca,' and Rebecca was beginning to think that Spiro was a bit of all right as well.

After leaving the police station, we were about to go for a coffee while Harry and I chewed over our new knowledge when an idea struck me and that was to go and see Louis and bring him up to date.

Recounting my thoughts to Harry he was in complete agreement. 'Except, he added, 'I think you mean up to speed.'

He then learnt what a useful weapon a woman's handbag can be.

Louis was delighted to see us and we were ensconced in his little office in no time. I told him about Bruno and watched his face change from joy to sadness.

'I have not seen the man for many years. The last time was to visit his farm to repair a tractor. I told him there was a local garage close to him who could do the work for less, but he supported the workmen who had also supported him saying, "Ne pas romprez les liens avec le passé." At earlier times when we were young and I was svelte, we played Pelote together while our wives faite courir des cancans. Your news makes me sad. Who do you think is responsible?'

'Paul Vachon.'

'He is an evil man and it would be no loss if he were in prison for the rest of his life. I will spread the word around and gather the clues for you. Do you wish me to tell you, Rebecca, or to tell Ramel?

'Tell both of us, the more who hunt him the less chance he will harm Claudine.'

His face expressed shock at my words and he was silent while he seemed to be finding my comment hard to swallow. 'What has that kind and generous lady done that he would want to harm her?' he finally asked.

'He blames her for his brother's death and wants revenge. He sent Daniel Pierront's son Christophe to London to assassinate her. Fortunately he was stopped and Christophe is in prison.'

'My guess is that you saved her but you are quiet about your deed.'

'It was a team operation, I stopped him actually stabbing her, but Richard, Lady Sophie's Chauffeur, and Graham were there as well as a police squad.'

Louis came over to me and kissed my hand, embarrassing me slightly, 'Then I salute you, for risking your life - as you must have done - to save a young lady who is worth a thousand Paul Vachons. I don't mind admitting, as a grown man, that I would have shed tears if that evil man had succeeded in his mission. I will do all possible to help you.'

As we stood to leave, Harry - probably with all sorts of visions in his mind - could not resist asking Louis, 'Your wife used to dance the cancan?'

He looked puzzled, "danse," then enlightenment came and he laughed. 'Cancan is to have a big talk together.'

'We say "gossip" for a big talk,' I explained. 'Especially if it is talk about other people,'

'I will remember,' Louis promised with a big grin.

'At least you cheered him up a bit,' I remarked to Harry. 'He was quite upset about any possibility of harm to Claudine. But I'm determined it will not happen.'

We were well past lunchtime and food was calling but I wanted to make sure Claudine was not too upset by the news about Bruno. 'Are we too late to take you for a spot of lunch?' Harry enquired of her when we arrived at the Tourist Office.

'It is late but I haven't had a break because we were busy.' She looked doubtful, but the other two girls in her office encouraged her to join us. We climbed in the car and I suddenly realised what a man sitting in a car just up the street was doing and smiled. Spiro was keeping his promise and had a man on guard.

We went to Les Artisans and had a happy lunch although we were all sad about Bruno. 'Have you any idea why he was coming to see you?' I asked Claudine.

'None at all. If you remember I promised to call on him, but have not had time with the other things that we do. It's possible he had some information, but he would surely have spoken to Hélène not to me?'

'She has been away, he may have telephoned and had no reply.'

'I will ask her to check her telephone, she has one that logs numbers.'

I thought about that for a moment, then said, 'No, don't do that. It would serve no purpose and Hélène would be even more upset if she knew he wanted to speak to her and she wasn't there to help him.'

Chapter Twenty-seven
A little light engineering

Harry and I had our noses deep into books when there was a discreet tap on our door. We both kept our heads down, willing the other to answer and it was me who gave in and opened the door disclosing Egg and Claudine with unfathomable expressions on their faces. An invitation in and the production of four glasses of wine soon disclosed the purpose of their visit.

'We have been out for a surprise meal with Jean,' Egg explained.

'He invited us so that he could say good-bye,' Claudine added with a trace of sadness in her voice! He has accepted a transfer to the radio station's office in Pamplona.'

Egg added softly, 'They asked him to join them as a reporter some time ago.'

Claudine sipped her wine, then continued, 'I feel a little unhappy about it for I'm sure our breaking up had a part in his decision.'

'I'm certain of it,' I interceded firmly. And that was entirely down to him to do so. He has made a courageous and right choice. A new start away from his memories here is exactly what he needs. Of course you are sad, he is a friend and you will miss him.'

'Thank you, Rebecca, you always judge my feelings exactly.'

What she couldn't see, slightly behind her, were the traces of a serene smile on Egg's face.

After a little more chatter about old times, I asked if we were going to drop our hunt for gold in the Holçarté now it appeared to have been removed by Gerard Vachon before his death. 'I am certain there is nothing more in the underwater cave and the riverbed in the fissure had only the one ingot.

'I have been thinking about that,' Harry announced. You know we have no way of proving there was gold remaning in the small cave you found. The two gold ingots Rebecca found could easily have been washed in there in such a violent storm. Or even dropped from above during some long past visit by Vachon.'

We all stared at him - I won't say open mouthed, but pretty close to it.

Getting into his stride he continued, 'The hiding place could be in the rock on either side of the fissure. Higher, lower or anywhere accessible from the winch. It would make more sense than floundering in the water.

I threw a cushion at Harry, 'If the use of floundering is any kind of a reflection on my under water exploration, you are in trouble.'

The spontaneous laughter removed any last trace of tension left over from our discussion about Jean.

'I think we should go back,' Egg had a thoughtful frown. 'There may be an opening in the cliff wall on the way down.'

The note from Hélène's friend advised the wooden key was not enough,' Claudine said. 'There were some shorter pieces in the sack we found.'

When they had finished and looked to me for an answer I made a different suggestion. 'I think we should take all the parts to do with the winches to Louis and ask for his advice. He is an engineer after all. He may even be able to make a platform for us.'

'I vote for that,' Egg said. 'And, I have another thought. When we set the winch up properly, if the pulley chain does not reach the water, we will know the gold was hidden higher up.

We all sat sipping our drinks in silence as we absorbed this gem of information.

The reaction of Louis to my call for advice and help was, 'Come tomorrow morning. It will be a pleasure to forget cars for an hour or two.'

I explained about the platform and he offered to go to the wood yard and look for it. When I protested we could do that he said it was no trouble and that he knew what to look for. He would ask Arlette to let him in or loan him the keys.

I put the phone down with a grin. Louis had appeared to be very keen to invite Arlette to help. So, on Saturday morning we presented ourselves and our sacks of winch parts to Louis and found he had cleared one of his workbenches ready. His face lit with pleasure as he fingered the chains and he whistled under his breath. 'This is inoxydable, acier, very expensive.'

He was appalled that we had come so close to trying it out while supported by a single piece of wood however substantial it was. He explained there should be nuts on both ends of the long iron bar.

One of his engineers found some and they quickly assembled the mechanism.

He confirmed our theory about the four hooks, and said he found no trace of the missing platform. Speaking about it caused him to check the winch wires carefully. That provoked another whistle at which Harry and I chorused, 'Stainless steel.'

He also thought it unlikely they carried anything to the gorge when on a trip to the fissure for it was all pretty heavy. Much more likely they kept a complete outfit in the cave next to the cottage. 'Someone cleared the stuff out because it was finished,' he explained, 'but missed the support bar that you call a wooden key and caused you to think it was a simple supporting part. A bad thought that might have cost you your life.'

'Time for a coffee,' he announced.

Initially a disappointing comment for we were eager to test our new theories, but he was filling time while he sent an engineer on an errand.

A friend will make you a new platform,' he explained. 'I could make you a steel one, but it would be very heavy. We want a very light one made in good quality aluminium.

You also need an expert with you for which I offer myself, if you are going back to the Holçarté this afternoon.'

We accepted his suggestion and he accepted our invitation to Les Artisan's for lunch. Over coffee, prompted by some unexplained signal from my brain, I asked Louis if he had seen Arlette Coutard since the adventure in the wood yard.

I swear his eyes took on a slight glow. 'Arlette came to my garage for the service to her car and twice for essence,'

'And?'

'Well! she joined me for a coffee.'

'How often?'

Louis gave me a big grin, 'Three times.'

'Oh! Ho! Ho!' was our reaction and he went as near pink as his rugged face would allow.

'Next time take her for a lunch or dinner,' Harry suggested.

'Ah une problème, her world is higher than mine.'

'Oh Louis!' I practically stamped my foot. 'You will make me angry if you say such things. You are a fine, kind and loving man. I'm certain she will accept. She may not have had much to do with her husband as they drifted apart, but almost certainly his death would have reminded her how lonely life is on your own.'

Before he could answer, his engineer entered just inside the restaurant door and signalled Louis who waved him to our table. In his hands was what looked like the top of an aluminium step that was visibly a fine piece of work. In fact, I said so as I cradled it in my arms.

Louis smiled at the sight and said, 'I forget you are also an engineer, Rebecca.'

'No,' I corrected, 'I am a geologist, but I've worked with many engineers, all good men.'

Φ Φ Φ

Louis had visited the Holçarté before, as a younger man, so although familiar with the terrain, he hardly recognised the density of the woods and the established path up to the bridge. A surprise awaited him when, instead of heading straight up hill to the bridge I crossed the river over the shaky bridge and led the way through the woods to the cottage and cave.

Although Louis had been to the Holçarté before he had never seen the cave and cottage. 'It is not on a regular path,' was a thought he expressed.

We considered our search showed the cave was as we had left it from previous visits, but Louis showed us something we had missed. He produced a fairly powerful wind-up torch from his pocket and carefully inspected the floor below the ledge on which the wooden key had been stored. He showed us small traces of oil in the dirt, rubbing pinches of earth in his hands to demonstrate.

'The equipment was stored here,' he announced. 'It's absence must mean the Vachons have finished whatever they were doing.'

I next led them up through the woods with unerring skill and found myself in woodland so dense it had to be wrong. 'My usual method is to use the river,' I explained loftily. My second attempt was more successful.

Louis clearly knew nothing of the fissure in the river cliffs, but said he remembered a great opening in the ground somewhere in the woods. 'We came here a different way,' he explained. 'It was possible to find transport to Larrau and we walked from there.'

'How far was that?' Claudine asked.

'About six kilometres,'

'Each way,' I prompted.

He laughed. 'Yes, we always came back.'

Harry pointed out the the shape of the rock indentations that we assumed were for the wooden key and Louis quickly found more lower down that exactly fitted the slightly shorter wooden cross piece.

He assembled the winch in place with Egg's help, making sure the double sets of nuts were holding all secure, but he was not happy about the arrangement. 'It is not completely safe so is a type of ... he struggled for a word and continued, 'Installation de fortune.'

'They would say makeshift,' Egg explained.

'What does it mean it makes?' Louis asked.

'Something badly,' Claudine laughed.

'Surely it could move sideways?' Egg persisted.

'Probably not with a weight on the platform.'

Putting a heavy rock on the new platform and lowering it to the bottom showed it all worked smoothly. 'Sorry,' Egg said to Claudine. 'The cable goes down into the water.'

'Oh!' she said crossly. 'I thought we would find some more gold bars.'

Egg took off his outer clothes revealing a wet-suit he had said he was wearing. He put on a harness stored in his rucksack and clipped a carabineer onto the steel cable.

'Are you sure you want to risk going down,' I asked, supported also by Louis.

'Don't worry, Rebecca. I'm probably going to be alright,' picking up on the words from our previous discussion.

'I will operate,' Louis said, 'Just wave if you want me to stop.'

In fact Egg waved several times as he made a close inspection of the fissure. At the bottom, he stepped off the platform and looked around in the river, even exploring the small cave where I found the gold ingot, but he appeared to find nothing. He stopped again on the way up and gave us palpitations when he stepped off the winch platform and disappeared.

When safely back, he explained there was a kind of cave made by another fissure, but there was nothing there and no evidence it had been used.

With our help, Harry also went down on the hoist, but no one else was tempted.

Claudine had brought a small picnic, so we found a vantage spot overlooking the gorge and enjoyed coffee and cakes while deciding, regretfully, there was no more to be found in the Holçarté

'It's a wonderful place,' I announced. 'There is a footpath from there to the top of the Kakouétta, I would love to do that walk.'

'Me too,' Claudine supported.

'Egg told me you were not a keen walker.'

'That's probably because I walk faster than he does and he's too proud to ask me to go slower. When I walk with him some more as a companion, I will remember to walk more slowly.

I didn't know if Louis was hinting or just expressing interest when he said casually, 'We must be close to the Monastery where you saw the Men in Black.'

Whatever his intention it provoked an immediate response from Claudine, Egg and Harry.

Claudine appealed to me, 'Rebecca, let's have a little explore. You have all seen the Monastery. I've never been there.'

Louis raised his hands as if in surrender. 'I wish not to have asked such a question. It is not a place for you ladies. There might be serious danger.'

'Also,' I said firmly, 'we promised Graham we would not go there until the Spanish police had checked them out.'

'If we approached over the mountain,' Egg suggested. 'We could show them without going anywhere near the building. Anyway, we ought to keep an eye on the place. It's so remote anything could be happening there.'

'That's partly my point,' I observed. 'We were down the service road, nowhere near the Monastery, when we had a shoot-out with the crooks.'

'How terrifying,' Claudine pressed her hands together and her eyes shone with excitement.

Aware my companions were suffering a deflation of spirits at the inconclusive end to our Holçarté search, I relented. I also knew who would get it in the neck from Graham if he heard of our activities. However I agreed to a limited visit and Harry drove us towards the Monastery. This meant we passed the lake. 'Do you mind if I stop for Louis to see where our adventure nearly came to an end,' he asked.

All agreed, but I think both Claudine and I had another shiver at the sight of the water,

'I once vowed never to return,' Claudine said to me as we stood side by side, holding hands like children, looking at the mirror calm water. 'But now I want to see because it makes me very cross at what they attempted to do.'

'She has such a knack of understatement,' I considered. And kept my views of the Men in Black to myself.

Φ   Φ   Φ

Harry convinced us that there was a spot he remembered, about half way up the service road, where we could conceal the car under some trees. He argued it would be safer than a trek across the open mountain.

'It would be safer not to be there at all,' I pointed out.

Whatever, events were decided for us when driving up the service road and negotiating a long bend, we saw on a path through the trees two men putting something in a trailer attached to a red quad bike.

In shock Harry jammed the car brakes on, skidding to a halt, but the men had seen us. One jumped on the quad bike and roared off up the road with the other man shouting and running after him.

I saw another example of how fast Louis could move in spite of his muscular bulk, when he was out of the car in a flash running after the man. We followed somewhat more slowly walking to where the men had been. We had just realised the path led to a cave, when Louis returned.

In another display of his sheer brute strength, Louis was dragging the man, whose legs were bumping along behind him, by a fistful of cloth grabbed from the back of the man's shirt.

In spite of the trauma of the moment I smiled, wondering what the Man in Black, for that was his garb, thought had captured him. Louis dropped the man at my feet saying, 'Un petit cadeau for you, Rebecca.'

As the man struggled upright, Harry stepped forward and in an authoritative manner that surprised me, demanded, 'If you have a weapon, give it to me immediately.'

The moment was lost a little when the man did not understand Harry's English, but Egg quickly translated and the man meekly handed him a handgun.

We moved into the cave taking Jules - as we later found his name to be - with us.

Harry fetched the car and parked it in some trees near the cave while I dialled the emergency number Marius had given us. He was not there.

Captain Yves Jeovin, the officer who took my call, promised to ring me back quickly and said he would send help immediately.

I told him we were on Spanish territory.

'Thank you for that helpful information,' he replied.

Then silence from the phone, but what sounded like a tirade of protest from the prisoner. He suddenly shouted something to Harry and went to walk out of the cave.

He didn't get far this time; Louis took a fistful of the front of Jules's shirt and almost lifted him off the ground. 'Batard, you wait here while I wait to see if they want you strangled.' He drew a finger across his throat as an illustration.

There was no doubt the man understood.

'What was he saying before he tried to leave,' I asked Egg.

'You will be shocked to hear, the other man was Paul Vachon.'

I was shocked, 'We missed catching Paul Vachon,' I exclaimed.

'No Rebecca,' Harry replied. 'We missed the possibility of one of us being shot trying to capture Paul Vachon.'

Egg continued. 'Jules is furious that Paul abandoned him and says he is finished with him. He claims only the two of them will be left now that he is prepared to leave.'

'Tell him he's going nowhere,' I said grimly.

'They have lived the last few days in this cave and Paul has taken what's left of their equipment in the trailer. He won't be coming back.'

Egg was proved wrong when Jules, noticing the others were concentrating on following our conversation, jumped up and made to leave. A bullet from outside ricocheting round the cave persuaded him to return.

'Sorry,' I consoled, 'It appears Vachon's back.'

A voice from outside shouted in English, 'Send my man out and you can all go free,'

'I think that is the lie of the year,' Claudine spoke after a long silence.

Jules appealed to us to let him go, he had no quarrel with any of us and he would take Paul away from us so that we could escape.

'What do you want me to say?' Egg enquired.

'Tell Jules all Paul wants is for him to go out so he can kill him. He knows too much and Paul is moving on,' I replied.

Another bullet whined off the side of the cave and hit the rocks at the back of the cave.

Harry had inched towards the cave mouth, flat against the wall, and fired a shot outside.

This provoked a couple of shots into the cave, but no Paul Vachon.

The next shout from Paul was more chilling. 'I have a grenade, if you don't release your prisoner, I will throw it into the cave,'

We looked at each other, was it a bluff?

'Give me the gun,' I said to Harry, 'I'll settle this.'

He refused.

'I think we should wait, Rebecca,' Claudine suggested. 'We have been lucky in the past, you had a cut your side, Egg had his back bruised by another and Graham had a piece out of his ear by a bullet close to this spot. Harry's leg was caught in a mantrap. Our luck in avoiding serious injury will surely run out sometime.'

My phone buzzed softly. 'Hello Captain, yes it is Rebecca. We are fine for the moment, but are under siege from Paul Vachon who has returned. He has fired a couple of times into the cave, but I don't think he will come in because he knows we have a gun taken from our prisoner. Yes I'm sure we will be fine. Thank you.'

I turned to the others. 'Some Spanish police are on the way, but it will be two hours before Marius arrives. He says to go with the police and he will meet us at a secret, Spanish anti-terrorist headquarters. He asked if we could hold out until the police arrive and I said yes.'

As we stood staring at each other for inspiration, smoke started to roll into the cave.

'The bastard,' Harry exclaimed, 'he's trying to smoke us out.'

'That's it' I snapped, 'my patience is exhausted. Give me the gun.'

'No!'

'Right, I'll go without it.'

I turned for the entrance to a chorus of 'no's' and 'stop, Rebecca' then suddenly Harry was beside me firing a couple of shots ahead into the smoke. As visibility cleared we saw Paul Vachon not far away. He fired hastily but missed.

Harry shouted, 'My God I'm out of ammo!!' as he, fortunately, disappeared into the swirling smoke.

I lost my bearings and shouted frantically to Harry.

Thankfully, there was a blast of a siren as a Police van came screaming up the road. At the same time I heard another shot and something tugged my hair. I looked round and saw our quarry had gone. I shouted to the police and ran the only way Vachon could have gone, through scrub and trees on the opposite side of the road, but there was no sign of him. The police called for a back-up helicopter, but there wasn't one available.

Revenge in Rochenoir

Chapter Twenty-eight
Loose ends

The Spanish police were friendly, but firm. Of course they took the gun away from Harry. Then insisted two of us travelled in the police car and one of their officers climbed into the front passenger seat of ours. Jules went in a police van. They had already driven up to the Monastery and, one gendarme who had been there before to check them out came back and Egg told us he said all was normal there.

'Extraordinary!!' summed up my reaction to this report.

We were taken to a modern building that looked nothing like a police station, settled into a comfortable lounge and plied with refreshments. A senior officer came to greet us and apologise for an inevitable delay. He explained Marius had requested they did not question the prisoner until he arrived and they had agreed.

A medical man would look at my head very shortly. He sent an officer back with some magazines to help us pass the time. A kind thought, but the magazines were, not unexpectedly, all Spanish.

'What did he mean about my head,' I asked.

Egg looked at my scalp, after politely asking if he could, and remarked there was a little dried blood. At that moment a doctor arrived and after a brief glance opened his medical kit and started swabbing my scalp.

A little frightened, I asked the doctor what was wrong, was it serious.

'No,' he answered, 'I think here is more blood than injury, I will examine some more' and soon confirmed a slight laceration and some bruising of the scalp.

I remembered the tug in my hair after Paul Vachon shot at me and asked, 'Could it have been a bullet?'

The doctor acknowledged it could easily have been.

We all looked at each other with concern. Another narrow life and death escape.

'One day,' Harry said solemnly, 'our luck will run out.'

A little later a man and woman came who were clearly police, but were dressed in ordinary clothes. The man gave the trace of a smile, as he greeted us, but the woman's face was severe. Probably one of those involuntary personal dislikes, but when she looked at me, I couldn't help feeling the emotions of what I suspected a mouse might feel facing an open trap. Her first words did not reassure me.

'We will take you to separate interview rooms and speak with you all,' the woman said peremptorily.' Pick up your things and follow me.'

'No,' I said firmly, 'we have done nothing wrong. We are here as witnesses to help you.'

I stepped forward and we stood face to face. It was a contest of wills as, trembling just slightly; I glared at her and stood my ground.

She gave in first, when the man said in Spanish, 'We can interview them here.'

'Why did you go to the Monastery when you had been told to keep away?' she demanded.

I refused to answer any questions until Comte Marius Bertin arrived.'

The Spanish policeman actually smiled at this and drew the woman to one side. After a few words he came back to us and said he agreed to our request, but if we had any information that was urgent to their enquiries he would be happier if we told them now.

I explained about Paul Vachon shooting at us and running away and he acknowledged that the police knew and they were hunting for him.

We settled down again, but were all a little upset by the negative response we had received,

While we waited, Egg told us he had been having a long conversation with Jules who told him that after Paul assembled his gang some years ago, a few of them who had been sleeping rough, stayed in Farmer Bruno's sheds, until they moved to the Casino. He said perhaps that was what Bruno was going to tell us.

He added that none of the men had seen much of the money the original Gang of Four had amassed during the war. Jules thought it had probably been shared out or spent in buying off people who knew the gang had broken the law while collecting payments under threats. Fear at knowing the retribution that would follow if they stepped out of line, kept them quiet and, in truth, they were all as bad as one another. The remaining men had been fed up with the situation and looking for a way out of their predicament, explaining they were almost prisoners.

'Evil breeds evil,' I replied. 'I have not one iota of sympathy for any of them. Who knows how many were killed or terrorised in the confused last days of the war.'

Eventually, Marius arrived and laughed as he said, 'I never know what you adventurers are going to do next. How did they manage to involve you, Louis?'

'I am proud to be their friend,' Louis replied.

'So am I,' Marius agreed. 'You can all leave immediately if you wish or wait while I have a brief chat with the prisoner.'

'We'll wait to see what we have caught,' I replied. 'His name is Jules, by the way. Egg has a piece of information from Hélène he thinks is important and I agree with him.'

Marius looked enquiringly at Egg. 'Is it confidential? Do you wish to speak privately?'

'Nothing like that,' he answered. 'Hélène thinks the monks at Monastery Izlariette are Coenobites.'

'And she is an expert with languages and ethnological groups and would know. That is very interesting and makes it impossible that a genuine monk answered the Monastery door to you. I will discuss the implications of this with my Spanish colleagues.'

'Hope your communication skills are better than mine,' I responded.

That provoked another smile. He looked back on his way to the door. 'You had better work on what you are going to say to Graham when he arrives.'

When Marius returned it was to say Jules was talking freely and it was likely to be a very long interview. 'It appears their organisation fell to pieces after two of their men disappeared taking their car with them. Paul assumed they had deserted him and has been in a rage ever since. As he lost men, there were not enough he could trust to run the Casino so it had to be closed. In desperation they took over the remote Monastery. There were only five monks and they made no resistance and simply waited for Paul and company to go. The gang kept the monks in their own quarters and treated them well. The monks never spoke, but passed notes if they wanted anything. They made no attempt to contact the police, even after they had been released. There is no question of them making a complaint to the police.

We are arranging communication with them through an Abbot of the Brotherhood, but I'm absolutely certain they will refuse to press charges or make any kind of official statement. Even Paul Vachon would have seen the sense of not harming them. You all go home now and thank you for this breakthrough. If Graham comes tomorrow we will arrange a meeting, perhaps at your parents house,' the last directed at Egg.

Φ   Φ   Φ

Next day we did meet at Labaraquette, but without Marius who was busy elsewhere. Graham had suggested we met in the evening so Egg and Claudine could be there. 'The first good news,' he announced ' is that we have positive information that Paul Vachon is now on his own. There has been some undercover work that resulted in the arrest of what had been one of the Men in Black at the Monastery. Two men on the fringes of the organisation, realising the police net was growing ever tighter, surrendered and handed this man over to the authorities.

The bad news is that this means Paul Vachon is now completely on his own. We know he has money, but unaccountably he remains in the area. It's therefore assumed he still looks for revenge and it is absolutely imperative you go nowhere alone and take every possible care. I repeat my offer for you to go to England until this is over. I can see by your faces that such a practical solution is likely to be turned down again.

Better news is that Sam's estate has been settled - you may remember I am an executor - and he has left £10,000 each to Egg and Claudine and £5,000 to Jean. Lady Sophie and I are to be Trustees of a Trust compiled from the balance of Sam's estate, plus the assets of the late Josephine Sayers and Mark Billington. The Trust will build a Health Centre in Rochenoir.

I'm sorry to have to tell you that the responsible person that Josephine trusted was Mark Billington's brother, Jake, who not only failed to support and help Josephine as he had promised, he also contested and delayed Mark's will for purely personal gain. It seems he had ambitions to marry Josephine, but she was not interested, probably closer to Mark. After all, she did go to the Pyrénées looking for him at some danger to herself, as events subsequently proved.'

He sat down to an absolute buzz of conversation and a round of applause.

Sitting next to Egg I whispered; 'Now you have no excuse not to marry the girl.'

I went up to Graham to congratulate him on sorting out what must have been a complicated affair of the wills.

'You know,' he said, 'I expected some resistance from Lady Sophie over Sam's wish to do something for Rochenoir because, after all, that is where her favourite niece was killed, but she thought it a brilliant idea. Mark left a will in favour of Josephine and the brother unsuccessfully challenged that. Josephine left no will and Lady Sophie therefore inherited both lots. She signed the money over to the Trust saying that Josephine had loved her visits to the town and the people there, even though bad things had happened.'

'Now absolutely keep this under your hat,' he whispered, 'The police are going to raid the Casino at six am tomorrow, if you would like to come with me?'

'Now you're talking,' I replied.

Revenge in Rochenoir

Chapter Twenty-nine
Police raids

Harry wasn't best pleased by my, as he called it, preferential treatment. He found out only on the morning of the raid, in the early hours, that I was being taken by Graham on what he called some jolly junket that excluded him. He also grumpily wanted to know what we were up to and where we were going.

At which Graham became cross and told him sharply that he should very well know that security was paramount and he was no exception to the "Need to know rule."

Graham chuckled as we drove off, saying, 'You'll have your ears chewed off when you get back home.'

'If we get back'

'That's uncalled for, have you ever been killed while you are under my protection?'

'Nearly.'

'Humpf,'

We stopped a road away from the Casino and walked in the back way, the fence having a convenient section cut out. 'I bet you organised that so you didn't have to crawl under,' I said accusingly, but received no reply.

We hadn't seen a sign of life as we approached the Casino the grounds looking still and deserted It was therefore a slight shock when Commissaire Ramel suddenly appeared, looking at me rather dubiously.

'Rebecca's with me,' Graham said tersely.

'You must both pick up a bullet proof vest from Spiro.'

Looking round while they exchanged a few words, I realised with a start that the Casino wasn't deserted, there were police and gendarmes hiding everywhere.

We moved forward under cover of some trees to a spot very close to the Casino.

Spiro appeared, winking at me, and handed each of us a vest. He explained, 'We think it is very likely that Paul Vachon is inside the building.'

'What makes you so sure?' I asked.

'Where else does he have to hide?

Spiro checked my armour very carefully to make sure it fitted well.

'You're very attentive,' I said appreciatively.

'Who wouldn't be in my place?' he chuckled.

Any saucy reply I might have formulated was averted by Graham when he called in a low voice, 'For Pete's sake let's get on, Rebecca. Let Spiro attend to his duties.'

Spiro and I smiled, completely on the same wavelength.

Ramel looked at me again as if he wished I was anywhere but on his patch and said, 'When the first wave of police moves in, you must wait until the building is declared secure before you enter.'

I replied in the affirmative, but had not the slightest intention of holding back. If Vachon was there, the bastard was mine.

There was no blowing of whistles, or shouting of commands, but by some well executed plan everyone moved smoothly in on the Casino. Quite a number formed a cordon round the building while the rest piled in through the front door, including Graham, with me close behind. We made straight for the chips room to stand guard over the strong room to secure any evidence it might contain. It was still undisturbed and apparently untouched.

'We wait here,' Graham ordered firmly. 'No tricks from you, Rebecca.' He grinned. 'We want him alive, he's now the only one left with primary knowledge so he's the sole custodian of where the remaining gold is and who has helped them.'

'The gold's in there.' I replied, 'We'll find it soon enough once we are through the door into the strong room. It's the only place it could be. Perhaps Vachon sleeps in there to guard it. With a bit of luck they'll catch him in bed at this hour.'

'No chance, he's into electronic surveillance gear, remember, and the whole place is festooned with cameras. I bet he detected the police arriving and was planning his escape before you and I arrived.'

'I told you the gold's in there.' I pointed to the odds board, 'Just be careful because Vachon might be as well. If he is he'll be armed, desperate and dangerous.'

As my words echoed slightly in the passageway we had just left, three uniformed officers burst through the fake door from the foyer and crashed through straight for us. The first, a gendarme, pointed his pistol at Graham, shouted something in French and fired, the impact of the bullet throwing Graham back against the wall. The gendarme called an order to the two policemen with him and one produced handcuffs, stepping towards me as two more police, hearing the shot, came running through the door from the kitchen. Only their training stopped them opening fire on our group.

I practically threw the policeman with the handcuffs aside and, in a bit of a panic, rushed to help Graham.

'I'm O.K.' he said, just a bit shakily, pointing to the tear in his armoured vest. 'Bet I've got a corker of a bruise.' He lifted his radio to speak without success. 'The jammer's still on,' he swore.

'None of the radios work,' one of the policemen explained. One of the gendarmes had obviously whispered to the trigger happy one who Graham was and he tried to tell him he was sorry, but Graham impatiently brushed him aside.

'What the hell did you think you were you doing?' I demanded of the officer still holding the handcuffs?

'The senior gendarme, the one who fired the gun ordered us to follow him and be ready to shoot at a moment's notice.' he replied

'Which is the gendarme who shot you?' I exclaimed to Graham.

'He's gone,' another gendarme said, 'Must have left in the commotion.'

Graham and I exclaimed together, 'Vachon!'

At that moment four gendarmes pushed though the swing doors from the dining room, 'Where's the prisoner?' the leading one asked in French, 'we were sent in to collect him.'

I took off immediately, through the dining room to the end outside door. 'Of course' I muttered, 'only Vachon would have known about the fake door and that the far end, outside door was not screwed shut.'

I shouted to two gendarmes, standing casually, smoking a cigarette, near the door. 'Did one of your men just come out?'

'Yes, he brought a message to say it was all over and to send in a squad to collect the prisoner.' He waved his useless radio to indicate his radio was not working.

'Which way did he go?'

The man shrugged and turned back to his companion.

Swearing like a trooper, I returned to the chips room to find Ramel had arrived. 'He's managed to get away,' I said. 'No one would notice another gendarme leaving. After shooting Graham he just walked out. He must have had a uniform'

'His brother was a gendarme,' Ramel said. 'So, yes, we did not allow for the possibility he might have one of his brother's uniforms. But he would not have had the vest we issued this morning. Who are the two police officers who were with the man who fired the shot?'

They acknowledged and explained Vachon had commandeered them saying he, Commissaire Ramel, had sent him to form a guard on the strong room. In answer to a question asking, 'Had the missing man been wearing the approved vest,' the two gendarmes replied with a sheepish, 'no.' They were ordered back to the station to await Ramel's return.

'You were lucky today,' Graham said to the two policemen, 'His plan was probably to use you as cover while he collected whatever he wanted in there' - pointing to the strong room door − 'then he would have shot you when you were no longer of use to him. Our mistake was in thinking we could manage without the use of the radios. A single call would have blown his cover.'

At that point the locksmith arrived to open the strong room door.

He soon sorted out the large blackboard illustrating the gambling odds, which he removed completely, then tackled the steel strong room door and examined the inner steel door.

'Hang on a minute,' I cried. 'How do we know the inner door is not booby trapped?'

That stopped them all in their tracks.

After some discussion, and consideration of Paul Vachon's past actions, it was decided not to take any chances and a specialist army team was called in for advice. Ramel also released most of the gendarmes and police back to normal duties.

The building was cleared while the army did whatever they did and it included a small explosion. When we were let back in, the door had been blown open. There seemed to be no other damage in a small room behind the door that we soon found contained racks of documents and two large safes.

Graham, in newfound good humour, asked, 'Would Rebecca like us to blow up the safes as well?'

'You mock,' I replied, 'but Vachon is looking for revenge. If he thought the gold was lost to him he would go into "If I can't have it then no one will have it mode," and be happy to kill, not only anyone who was responsible for his deprivation, but also whoever helped in recovering the gold. While you open each safe I'll go outside.'

The army Captain backed my view saying if there was any kind of doubt we should not take the risk. He had two men with protective clothing and they were willing to blow the locks. He added they could drill through the locks to access the interior and pump in an inert gas first. That would minimise the risk.

Graham was all for going ahead, arguing, 'We have wasted enough time on unnecessary precautions already.'

All looked to Commissaire Ramel who showed the first decisiveness of anyone that morning. 'Over to you,' he told the Captain, 'good luck! Everyone else outside.'

Accompanied by a tut, tutting Graham, we waited in the police minibus hearing as time went by first a muffled explosion then a little later a slightly louder one.

The Captain sent one of his men to fetch us after the smoke had cleared. We trooped in observing the two safe doors standing slightly ajar. 'The left safe holds routine matters to do with the Casino,' he explained, 'but the right hand safe was a different matter. The young lady, here, probably saved life or injury for it did contain a trap. It also holds a secret.' He opened the door with a flourish to show it was more than half filled with small gold bricks. He took a couple out and passed them to us, one coming into my hand. 'Thank you, Madame,' he said to me, 'for standing on your ground and keeping to your belief.'

'Paul Vachon is a ruthless man,' I replied, 'there seemed to me no way he would give up easily.' I then gave him one of my best smiles.

'Sorry Rebecca,' Graham gave my arm a squeeze, 'you were right, we guessed wrong.' He waved the other gold brick the Captain had taken from the safe. 'This has been specially made, probably from melted down ingots.'

While he talked I had been looking at the stack in the safe, with the gold brick warm in my hand when suddenly so much seemed so clear. It was such a bolt of realisation I looked round for something blue. 'We have it all wrong,' I gasped breathlessly. 'Sam and his Musketeers misunderstood the plot and we did the same, failing to see the real story. To use an old saying, we have all been chasing our tails. Let's get away from the smell of cordite while I try to rationalise my thoughts.'

'No,' Ramel said. 'We will leave my men to clear up and secure the gold while we go to my office to discuss this morning's operation.'

Φ   Φ   Φ

Our discussions took in a break for lunch and after we were finished, it was decided we should call a meeting of our clan at Labaraquette. Arrangements were made for a barbecue there in late afternoon.

The ladies who collected round the barbecue in the lovely old garden at Labaraquette were, apart from Claudine, Hélène and myself, the men Graham, Egg, Harry and Marius. Our host Brigitte and Albert plied us with wine and food and Harry was in charge of the barbecue. Later, Nicole joined us.

Graham told them of our morning adventures and then said we had made a breakthrough in understanding what had passed before. He said many of our suppositions had been wrong, but that did not show any failing on our part. 'None the less we turned a corner when Rebecca had inspiration at the sight of the gold bricks.' He added it would be better if I told them all about it myself, since it was my idea.

With every eye on me, I felt more nervous than I had ever felt before and started by saying that, of course my theory might be wrong, but we had heard rumours from two sources so were confident the tale was probably true.

That produced from Graham a cry of, 'Just get on with it, Rebecca.'

I smiled at my supporter. 'When I saw the gold in the safe my first thought was, "Why are these bricks different from the others we have seen? There were none of the type of gold ingot we had seen before. Then my thoughts ran over the trouble the crooks had gone to in moving the gold about; the Manoir, the Casino, the Wood yard, activities on Leizar Athéka, caving in the Holçarté Gorge and even Duval who lost his life carrying gold in the tunnel.

Then realisation dawned that they hadn't kept moving it.

Obviously the gold store started in the cellar of the Manoir during World War Two. Later, it was shared between Vachon, Coutard and Duval with a token amount of cash sent to Pierront who had fled to England.

Next came the thought that if you added up the money frozen in the various bank accounts and added that to what has been spent buying Vachon the Casino, Coutard the Wood yard, Duval the Restaurant, plus the money to Pierront in England, and the gold we know was still in the Manoir cellar and in the Wood yard saw pit along with the gold now in the Casino plus whatever their fathers spent, it dawned on me that it must amount to millions. There was simply too much gold,

Yes, they may have earned a lot of money smuggling agents in and out of the country and even more guiding Germans out, but surely not that much money.

Also something that has puzzled all of us from the beginning, the activity was not criminal enough, even if they robbed refugees, for them to kill to cover their tracks, as they have again and again.

There's only one answer. Could it be that the bulk of the gold came from a wartime heist, perhaps a bombed bank in France or Germany or possibly gold in transit on a convoy. Maybe even go back to the Spanish Civil War. Any kind of robbery, particularly if anyone was killed, is illegal and restitution would be demanded. That was why the crooks were afraid of what we might find out.

I had accepted the theory of why the gold was taken both in and out of Spain through Leizar Athéka, but isn't it much more likely that they had found a goldsmith in Spain who would smelt the traceable gold ingots they had inherited from the fathers' robbery, into tidy little untraceable bricks? Bricks that would stack neatly into wine boxes in the Manoir and a big safe in the Casino. We know the wartime gang broke up in acrimony, distrust, robbery and assassination. Why should we think the sons of the fathers were any better? We saw ourselves how quick to violence they were. The gold ingots we have been finding, are, I am sure, a mixture of payments for services rendered and what they have stolen from each other. What's left of the robbery gold is now all smelted, untraceable and in the Casino.

Towards the end, Vachon tried to keep his men together and probably refused to hand out their shares in the knowledge they would abandon him the moment they had their money. At some point a long time ago, Vachon moved the few men he had left from Farmer Bruno's sheds to the Casino where they had a job running the gambling and guarding the place. He probably never had any real control over them except by violence and terror. And, as he lost men and we put up the pressure, he did not have enough men even to staff the place. He dared not take anyone on from outside. He then announced the Casino had been sold and closed it, moving the spare men to the Monastery to draw us away from the Casino. The Men in Black were not only a poor disguise as novice monks but did have the bonus of drawing attention away from the Casino. A ruse that rebounded when the Men in Black stole ingots to barter for drugs and in doing so drew more attention than they wanted.

Don't you see the cauldron that Sam and his Musketeers walked into? Vachon, Coutard and Duval must have been on a knife-edge, distrusting each other, fearful in the knowledge that at that time they still had a stock of traceable gold ingots.

Josephine and Mark Billington must have rung alarm bells and they killed them both. Remember, they didn't know for sure what had caused Josephine to go to the police. They didn't know who knew the story. They were cautiously selling the gold already smelted so they could disappear with the money.

Into that scene walks Sam and almost on his first night in Rochenoir, he truthfully answered a question saying he was a retired banker. That answer must have devastated the crooks. What, in their eyes, was a banker on his own doing in town asking questions about, of all places, the Manoir? He must be there investigating the old robbery. Sam must have put the fear of God into them.'

The buzz of conversation in response was rewarding with all supporting the bank theory.

Nicole joined us just as we finished talking but we didn't discuss much of my hypothesis, waiting to hear the result of Ramel's thoughts and investigation. And, of course, Paul Vachon was still at large and an ever present danger.

Φ   Φ   Φ

Harry was certainly making a good job of building up the barbecue. 'Pleased to have something to do,' I thought.

Nicole wandered over to watch him and they were soon in animated conversation. I watched for a moment then sighed; soon I may have to do something about that unless we finish our investigation quickly, too often they drift into each other's orbits.

Egg joined me, 'How do you like the thought of Nicole as a sister-in-law?' he asked with a smile. 'I can assure you she is a very nice girl.'

'I would have no objection at the right time,' I answered automatically. Then realisation dawned. 'Damn, you caught me out there. How long have you known?'

'I didn't know, but gradually assumed over a long time from so many little things. Words, gestures, responses, my own instinct. Don't worry, Rebecca, I haven't spoken to anyone about it; not even Claudine.'

'And, I am keeping your secret, Egg,' I smiled, 'that one day you will marry Claudine. I have never seen a couple more suited to the comment that they were made for each other.'

He didn't answer for a moment, then replied, 'I hope you are right. I haven't spoken to her about it yet. I feel she needs time for the parting from Jean to be lost in the past.'

'Well! don't wait too long. You are giving up quality time that you could be spending together. She gave up the opportunity of working in London with Peter Reynolds, an influential man in Tourism. Don't you think that sacrifice might have been so she could spend her life together with you?'

Hélène and Claudine wandered over to join us and you could literally feel an atmosphere of excitement about them. Egg quickly found chairs for us all and although no one asked the question we waited expectantly. Claudine asked Egg to quietly find some wine because she wanted to have a secret celebration. I was sure of what was coming, but waited silently, as I looked round our happy band. It suddenly really came home to me how much I would miss them all when Harry and I were finished and we went back to England.

It was Hélène who raised her glass slightly and spoke, 'My dearest friends,' she said. 'I tell you now something I wish you to keep secret for a few days. I just want you to be the first to know that Marius has proposed to me and I have accepted.'

Revenge in Rochenoir

Chapter Thirty
Revenge

As I raised my glass in celebration, I said to Hélène, 'Your wedding will make you a Countess.'

'Oh!' she answered with a slightly startled look, 'I suppose it will. Now, Rebecca, you really do make me nervous.'

'No!' Hélène, it makes you in love if all you thought about was Marius and not what comes with him.'

After we had quietly toasted our elevated friend, I remarked to her that in my opinion she would make the perfect Countess Bertin and I couldn't be happier for her and all agreed. 'Ever since I saw the two of you together on the Rhune station I thought what a wonderful match the pair of you would make. It gives me a warm glow and I wish every happiness for the two of you. I also wait with impatience for permission to spread the best news I have heard for a long time.'

After a second quiet toast just for the hell of it, Hélène said my mention of a Countess and the Rhune plus, no doubt, the amount of wine we were drinking, had reminded her of an old, but true, story. 'You bring back to me this story about the Empress Eugénie de Montijo who was the wife of Napoleon the Third. She had a big interest in the Rhune but had been discouraged by her advisors of trying to walk up the mountain. You understand there was no railway then because it was 1859 or 1860 - I think! Before the railway was built. One day the Empress became impatient and organised her own outing for a picnic on the slopes, insisting her Ladies in Waiting accompanied her. Of course, normally, her ladies only walked in well tended gardens so had nothing suitable to wear out of doors. They were protesting and crying as they stumbled on stones, tore their chiffon dresses on the arbustes and ruined their dainty shoes but they say the Empress enjoyed her day out.'

'Can we expect such treatment if you invite us to your château?' I asked.

'If I did, Rebecca, I'm sure you would reach the top long before I arrived on the summit with my dress torn.'

I laughed, 'It's simply beyond my imagination to picture you arriving anywhere with your dress torn.'

Φ   Φ   Φ

Claudine and I were absolutely dying to do something in the way of a celebration to mark the forthcoming marriage and hit upon the idea of using Graham coming back to us as a reason to organise a picnic. He looked doubtful. 'Graham, you love picnics and it's absolutely gorgeous weather. What better way to spend it?'

'I should stay near the phone, I'm expecting calls.'

'So put the phone in your pocket.'

Egg laughed and Graham looked a little uncomfortable. 'Egg, old man,' he suddenly exclaimed, 'Would you think it rude if I went outside for a word with Rebecca?'

'No! of course not. Would you rather I left the room?'

Graham was already on his way and I hastily followed him. He walked out of the farmyard and over to a little copse where he sat on a grassy knoll and I joined him.

'Obviously, something serious on your mind.'

'Rebecca, old girl....'

'I warned you about that,' I replied with an ominous tone to my voice.

'There's something big on. I will be involved.'

'Spill the beans.'

Graham sat deep in thought, while I sat silent without moving.

'We haven't been idle,' he commenced. 'Marius has been like a ferret the way he's gathered information. You remember I went to Paris, suddenly, for a conference. We have been keeping track of where Paul Vachon is most of the time and we've put together a Swat Team to smoke him out. That should happen soon.'

'Where is he now?'

'Here.'

'You want some help?'

'Well! you suggesting a picnic gave me an idea, but talking about it out loud convinces me it was a mad idea, so forget all about it.'

'You're overlooking I promised to catch him for you.'

'Rebecca, this is going to be really dangerous. I can't let you. Twice you have cheated death by a tiny margin. Enough is enough! Now I wish I hadn't mentioned it to you.'

'Start by telling me what has happened lately, you clearly know a lot more than you have told us.'

He stood up and paced fretfully backwards and forwards, an agonised expression on his face as he was torn between accepting my offer of help and fear that I might become a casualty.

'Graham, I know you well enough to know you have a plan and you want me to be involved. So stop hesitating. You should know I'm with you whatever it is.'

He sat back down beside me. 'We have been more or less tailing Paul Vachon for a while, but he's as slippery as an eel. The fiasco of his escape from the Casino makes me fearful that he might be too artful for the men we have available. We have sprung two traps from which he's escaped. But, in the last one in Pau, although he got away, we grabbed three men who were with him. They had been hired by him to do a job - he hadn't told them what - but they have been warned off and offered a deal in exchange for spreading the word that Paul is bad news. No crook wants other crooks with a bad reputation on their patch so they are doing a good job. We know for certain Paul is now completely on his own. We also know he's here in Orthez and we've laid a gold bait for him in the Holçarté Gorge. He apparently doesn't know his brother managed to move the gold out of the Gorge and he thinks their gold is still in the cave. Perhaps it included some of the stolen bank ingots that could be traced. Whatever, either through greed or concern he's hired a man to help him recover it. The man he hired has assured him that his brother, Gerard, was unable to move the gold before the police shot him.

'This man seems to be well informed.'

'He jolly well ought to be, I trained him personally.'

'Graham, as I've said so many times before, is there no end to your manoeuvring? So I get the picture, if there were police all over the wood Paul Vachon would do a bunk, gold or no gold. But he won't take so much notice of a picnic, especially if we are all dressed and acting like tourists.'

'Two of the police team will be with you,' Graham said, a worried frown on his forehead.'

'No! Graham, no police to be with us. We must be what we say we are. We will act differently otherwise.'

'We?' he queried.

'Yes, Hélène, Claudine, Egg, Harry and me.'

'No. I can't agree to that. It's too risky.'

'The more of us there are, the more we look like tourists.'

Graham took out his mobile and asked a surprised Egg to come out and join us.

'Not Claudine,' he said while we waited, 'It's too big a risk that Paul Vachon knows her.'

'I agree.'

Egg came and sat on the grass in front of us. 'You can count me in, whatever it is,' he said with a smile.

'Count you into what?' I asked.

'Come on Rebecca, you two are obviously plotting something and it has to be connected with Paul Vachon.'

'It might be very dangerous,' Graham said abruptly.

Egg rolled onto his knees so he was nearer level with us. 'Graham, if what we are about to do will remove that man so Claudine is safe, I don't care what happens to me.'

'Good man,' Graham leaned forward to shake Egg's hand.

I smiled knowingly to Egg.

He smiled back. 'I will ask as soon as Vachon is captured,' he said to me.

'Ask what?' Graham asked curiously.

'It's a secret,' I laughed, but my heart was beating with joy for the young couple.

Graham stressed the need for absolute secrecy and recited the whole story and plan. Egg was with us wholeheartedly.

I suggested they left it to me to tell Hélène, Harry and Claudine, but not until the morning of the operation. I would tell Hélène and Harry to keep the day free. I was worried about including Hélène, in view of her impending marriage, but could see no way of keeping her out of our scheme. I resolved to try asking her not to take the risk for Marius's sake.

'When is the day for operation Paul Vachon?' I asked Graham.

'Tomorrow.'

Φ   Φ   Φ

Graham and Spiro arrived to join us for breakfast so we made quite a crowd for Albert and Bridget to feed but they loved it. While they were busy in the kitchen, Graham explained the day's plans and it gave us a bit of a shock. 'There will be no police in or near the wood. 'We can't risk Vachon seeing them and doing a runner.'

When Harry protested and asked about protection for the women. Graham made a feeble joke that he didn't think we were in much danger from him. Then, when no one laughed, he apologised and explained he was trying to lighten the mood. The cavalry would not be far away and would move in to surround the area as soon as Paul Vachon was in the Gorge or the wood. We would all be wired for sound by Spiro and at the slightest sign of trouble the police team would move in.

When he mentioned our being wired for sound I grinned at Spiro and he smiled back, reading my mind I'm sure.

While we were finishing our coffee and before we were wired for sound, I walked over to Spiro who was standing alone.

'Good luck!' was my simple message.

'You too,' he replied. 'Be careful, Rebecca, I will look out for you if I can.'

I smiled my thanks, a little nervously for me. 'Before we go into this rather dangerous operation, there's something I want you to know. I'm not married to Harry. We are close friends, but just working on this together at Graham's request.'

'Thank you for telling me. I must confess that I did know. Graham told me in confidence when he warned me off my interest in you.'

'Warned you off!!! That man is impossible. The interfering...'

Came the voice of the man himself, calling, 'Rebecca, can we get on? You don't have time to gossip.'

Spiro next fitted us out with our concealed electronics, demonstrating how to switch it on and off and explaining, in very good English, that the additional emergency button was not only for speed but in case reception became difficult.

In view of where we were going, I asked if the stuff was waterproof and Graham said it was, but probably wouldn't work under water so I was to keep out of gorges and caves.

'Gee, thanks,' I replied

Albert and Brigitte had returned with the trolley for breakfast while all this was going on and Brigitte had concern writ large upon her face.

I walked over to her and gave her a big hug. 'Brigitte,' I spoke, steeling my voice to speak calmly. 'Don't worry, we are just helping and really will be having a picnic in the Holçarté woods. Claudine will explain when we have gone. I promise you; we will all be safely back this afternoon.'

'You have my word on that as well,' Graham added.

While we were having breakfast Louis arrived with Sam's English car. The idea was for us to use it so we looked more like tourists. A mechanic in a four-wheel drive pickup truck arrived to join Louis shortly after.

Louis looked woeful. He took both my hands, 'Rebecca, it fills my heart with terror that you good people are going into so much danger. Graham took me into his confidence when arranging about the car and I wanted to take your place, but he would not agree. He has asked me to stand by here ready to help if it should become necessary. I think maybe to watch for Claudine as well.'

'Louis,' I replied, 'Don't let Claudine persuade you to take her to the Holçarté. Don't come unless Graham says it is safe.' On an impulse I kissed both those hands that were so powerful but still held mine as gently as a baby's.

'You can rely on me,' he replied, looking at his hands as if he had never seen them before.

'I know I can.'

Claudine put her arms round me and held me tightly for a few moments without speaking. A grim looking Albert and Brigitte, who had guessed, despite all the preparations for a frivolous picnic, that something really serious was in the air, silently waved us away from the farm.

All was quiet when we parked on what had become our regular parking spot. Graham supplied English maps, guidebooks and odds and ends of apparel to make the car look as authentic as possible.

The others walked up the path to the suspension bridge relaxed in the knowledge that Graham's agent, and temporary guide, leading Paul Vachon had been instructed not to arrive at the Holçarté before eleven. So, at ten, we should be well ahead of them.

I set a pace up to the bridge that surprised them a little. Harry, who should have supported me, grumbled about the rush. I answered the sooner we were clear of the bridge area, the more relaxed I would be.

That was, in fact, the positive truth, for my companions did not know that Graham had called me earlier in the morning to explain he would have to call the operation off. He could not make contact with his agent and consequently had no idea where Paul Vachon's current movements.

My refusal to drop the expedition and declaration we would go without him put us all on course again and guaranteed me a telling-off later.

'That's if I'm still in the land of the living', I thought grimly.

We found the spot in the woods that Graham and Spiro had reconnoitred. They were right, it gave us a perfect view - with binoculars - of the bridge we had not long walked over. We set everything up for a picnic and did a little scouting round but all was still and quiet.

Hélène, who had insisted she would not let her friends go into danger alone, looked round a little nervously and voiced a worry, 'We haven't seen a sign of a gendarme. We could be the only people in the wood except for Paul Vachon when he arrives.'

We had a surprisingly merry lunch in the circumstances; maybe it was the wine although I noticed we were all being careful what we drank. I raised my glass, 'This is a tribute to the bravery of Hélène, Egg, and Harry who have answered the call to fight evil.'

Egg raised his glass to say, 'And Rebecca and Sam's car to bring us luck.'

Harry was a little uneasy that all was so still, not even birds singing. 'It's as if all the wildlife know that something evil is about to happen.'

'Oh! Thank you, Harry,' Héléne replied. 'You really know how to cheer us up.'

I explained to the others that he was right and I was going to creep through the bushes to the gorge and have a cautious look round because it did seem too quiet.

They protested, but could see I was determined.

Egg produced a super, small Walkie Talkie and gave me one of the pair. 'Call if you want me, Rebecca.'

'Good thinking, Egg.'

Grinning a reply, 'You didn't think I expected you to behave yourself did you?' he asked. 'There's a compass on the side, the gorge will always be north of you.'

We all ceremoniously switched on our sound systems.

No one had crossed the bridge and we had seen no one in the woods. I spoke this out loud; mindful that the back-up squad were probably wondering how we were getting on.

I moved fairly easily through the trees, bushes and scrub until I found the top of the gorge. I had never thought about the layout of the area, but realised the fissure must be further up stream from where we had our picnic. Puzzling over the maze of paths we had followed before, I wondered why we had never left the regular path and simply followed the top of the gorge. I soon found out it was pretty tough going. Suddenly I found a path of sorts and recognised from some trees it was close to where the rock path dropped slightly down to the cleft. Inching forward until I could see the cleft, I froze; Paul Vachon was already there. How was that possible, he hadn't passed us? Fortunately he had his back to me as he peered down the cleft in the rock.

I backed slowly out of sight and turned to return along the cliff a short distance. Speaking into my sound system I whispered, 'Graham, I hope you can hear me. Vachon is already at the cleft, but does not seem to know what to do. I don't think he knows how to get down to the cave.'

Spiro quietly acknowledged and said they would start blocking him off.

Next I called Egg on the Walkie talkie.

After speaking with Egg I crept back along the path with the intention of spying on Paul Vachon through the bushes. Bad mistake! This time Vachon was facing my way and I think he saw me. In any case something had alerted him. Maybe he heard me communicating with the others or had heard Egg's loud "Roger" in acknowledgement of my message.

As soon as Vachon started towards me I was off, but the thick scrub and foliage hampered me with its denseness. It was not too bad when I was walking slowly along the gorge and found Paul at the cleft, but a nightmare hindering any attempt to run while avoiding pursuit. I could hear my antagonist crashing along behind me and realised he must catch up with me eventually. I looked around wildly for an easier path or for somewhere to hide but to no avail. Suddenly his hands grasped me from behind as he tried to pull me over backwards. I twisted out of his grasp and used my unarmed combat skills to fend him off, then found to my dismay he was as good, or better, a fighter than me. We feinted a few times, then he simply made use of brute force as he crashed into me and threw his weight and power to get me down on the ground. He dropped on me trying to pin me down but I fought like a wildcat. Suddenly he thrust his hand into my hair, twisting and pulling, the pain in my scalp excruciating as I struggled. He dragged my head round and we were face to face for the first time. To my horror it wasn't hate I saw in his eyes, but lust.

'Oh no you don't,' I spat at him. 'You'll have to kill me first,' and went for his eyes. He jerked his head away leaving me a target. I grabbed both his ears, digging my nails hard into them, trying to tear them off. He gave a guttural snarl, just like the animal he was as he jerked his head to twist away. A move that gave me a chance, as I turned the other way and squirmed from beneath him, jumped up and dived into some thickly leaved trees so gaining a start as he recovered. I saw with satisfaction my fingers were bloodstained and even hoped he was trying to stick his ears back on. It seemed in no time I heard him crashing behind me again and desperately ploughing through some bushes, saw the yawning gap of the gorge in front of me and realised I was about to run off the cliff. My mad dash had taken me back, almost to the very edge of the gorge.

I whirled round as Vachon came through the same gap. We stood face to face with me barely six feet from an unknown drop into the ravine.

He paused and to my surprise, spoke in very good English, 'I think your day has come,' he leered. 'You have been a thorn in my side, Mademoiselle Claudine, but most of all I come to avenge the death of my brother.'

As he moved slightly forward trying to gain a more advantageous position, we both heard the distant sound of police sirens. My spirits soared.

Vachon shouted, 'Vous etes une rosse,' and flung himself forward in a temper.

I tried to dodge him, hoping his raging momentum would send him off the cliff but he managed to grab me and, wildly struggling, we tottered perilously close to the edge. I think he realised he was in danger of joining me in the gorge and started trying to drag me away from the edge and gain enough room to send me down on my own. Realising this, about the same time as he started to kick my legs, I thrust my leg between his in an attempt to trip him. He went down with a sickening thud with me on top of him. Again he used his brute strength to force himself up and dislodge me, but something went disastrously wrong when he overbalanced and slipped over the edge taking me with him.

I thought nothing during the seconds it took to fall down, my brain paralysed. I hit the water with a frightful whack, plunging the depths and bumping the bottom as well. I struggled to the surface, every bone in my body protesting. I realised as soon as my head broke into open air I had luckily fallen into the pool that Graham and I had walked past on our earlier visit. I half swam and half propelled myself to a large rock, hanging on while I tried to compose my body into some semblance of humanity.

Looking round, there was no sign of Paul Vachon. 'Good,' I thought, 'hope the bastard is dead.'

Briefly I wondered about looking for him but quickly realised he was more than a match for me and I had better get the hell out of there.

Dragging myself out of the water uncovered a few more aches, pains and bruises but taking a quick stock of the situation, nothing broken as far as I could tell. Now higher out of the pool I could see Vachon floating on his back in the water, but no sign of life.

Moving to make my way down the river for help, my legs certainly felt stiff while walking on the uneven riverbed and my progress was slow. I kept anxiously looking up to the cliff top hoping for some sign of the support team. I'd lost Egg's walkie talkie somewhere along my headlong dash so had no means of communication. I spoke into my sound system from time to time, but had no reply. I doubted it was still working.

Sitting down to rest for a moment, I looked back and saw with dismay Paul Vachon was now stumbling along following me. I watched him for a moment, and thought from the way he staggered he looked hurt, but he must still have been gaining on me. 'How had he survived and why hadn't I attacked him in the pool?' I thought with despair. I pressed on as fast as the river would allow, knowing keeping ahead was the difference between life and death. The thought came with a chill greater than the water that he might have a gun. If so, he only needed to get within range.

I stopped to look back and shivered, sure he was a little closer.

Egg was shouting from above but I could not see him. Then I realised he was throwing rocks down on Vachon. I could see the splash as two hit the water and heard an angry roar from Paul Vachon as one hit him.

'Good on you, Egg,' I muttered and almost raised a smile as I hurried on. Looking back yet again as the river turned slightly, and I was hidden from behind, I noticed a wide fissure in the cliff and sought it for a few moments sanctuary. I realised if Vachon looked back he would see me, but he had no reason to do that when he was intent on catching me up. For insurance, I also picked up a rock that fitted my hand perfectly.

My breathing became easier with the rest and I watched with satisfaction as Vachon stumbled past barely twenty feet away, then with dismay when I heard Egg's voice directly above me shouting at Vachon at the same time as one of Egg's missiles hit him in the back.

Vachon twisted round in anger and an evil smile distorted his face when he saw me. 'We meet again, Claudine,' he growled. 'This time you will not escape.'

As I watched him stagger towards me, I knew there was only one chance for me to survive; I had to get it right first time. To my consternation he pulled a gun out of his pocket. This wasn't in my plan.

'The police will hear the shot; you know they are on the cliffs; they will pick you off easily. Go ahead! Shoot me.'

Paul Vachon hesitated, then put the gun away. He picked up a rock instead. 'This is good enough to finish you,' he growled. He staggered on until he towered over me in my crevice.

'How about an exchange,' I said, as he lifted his rock.

'What sort of exchange?' He half lowered his rock.

'My rock for yours,' I screamed, bringing the rock from behind my back and wildly smashed it into his face. He staggered backwards, tripping and falling back half in the river. I jumped after him as he tried to pick himself up and thrust his face under the water using all my weight to hold him down. I waited until the bubbles stopped then limped on down the river almost out of my mind with terror.

Eventually I had to sit on a boulder to rest, wondering if I was ever going to get out of the gorge in one piece. Where was the end? I seemed to have stumbled along the river for hours. Unable to stop myself from repeatedly looking up the river, my heart filled with dread when I saw the unmistakable form of Vachon stumbling slowly down the river still intent on his mission to kill me. 'How did he survive?' I agonised. His movements were now so slow there seemed to be a chance I could outrun him, but after a while my strength seemed to be waning so fast I was becoming concerned about passing out.

Seeing ahead the broom I had, on the earlier visit, planted in the bank, gave me renewed hope. A potential weapon!! Hobbling up to it I snatched the broom and felt ten feet taller immediately. What quirk of fate or providence had made me secure it there with a cairn of rocks?

I shouted to no one in particular, 'you wait until I see you Graham. I'll tell you all about it. If you had thrown this away, I would have been helpless, now I have a chance.'

Feeling better for my shouting match with myself, I plunged on trying even harder. Although desperately tired, I noticed voices seemed to be coming from above again. Pausing for breath and looking back, I could make out rocks hitting the water round Vachon and realised it was still Egg and his helpers shouting and throwing rocks to distract him.

Smiling with renewed heart, even though I knew Egg could not do much to help me, I no longer felt so helplessly alone. Turning a bend in the river and finding myself in a short canyon like section, the idea came that if I quickly hid behind one of the huge rocks, there was every chance Vachon would go past me and into trouble when he reached the end of the gorge and found the police waiting.

I half crouched behind my rock, aware from the absence of shouting from above that we were out of Egg's sight. Controlling my breath as much as possible was not really necessary with the gurgling of the river, it just seemed I had to do something to try and help myself.

What I thought to be the scrape of Vachon's boots going past raised my hopes. How long should I stay hidden? I didn't want to emerge and catch up with him.

'Come out Claudine, I know you are behind the rock.'

My heart sank to my boots, it was Vachon, the man was invincible!

Approaching delirium, I grasped my trusty broom. I then did one of those silly things we do when under pressure. I saluted and addressed the broom as if a General before the battle. 'Now we are going into battle where all depends on you,' I told the broom, 'Stand by me today and you will have a cupboard for the rest of your life.'

I walked slowly round the rock and saw to my dismay that Paul Vachon was holding his pistol ready and that he was out of range of my broom. I also saw the gash on his forehead from my rock and his damaged eye. What was this man made of, why was he still standing?

'Pointing the gun towards me he asked, 'Who is that with you.'

In spite of the threat, I struggled to keep a straight face as I replied, 'You know very well I am alone.'

'Don't lie to me, I heard voices.'

'Just talking to my broom.'

'Don't treat me with disrespect, Claudine, you have not long to live and that could be even shorter.' He raised the gun.

'I'm not Claudine.'

He peered at me and looked just a little confused, 'I will finish with whoever is behind the rock and then you and I will settle our differences.'

I couldn't believe it when he walked past me and sloshed his way round the rock. I moved close to the rock and grasped my broom firmly.

As an angry man came splashing back from behind the rock, I swung the broom like a mallet with what was left of my strength and the broom head hit him squarely in the forehead. Paul Vachon tottered back into the rock and slid down to the ground, but he was not out. 'Drop the broom,' he mumbled a bit incoherently, pointing the gun at me with only a slight shaking of his arm.

I dropped the broom

'You are going to suffer for your interference, I will shoot you in each arm, then in each leg, and then kill you.' He put his other hand up to support the arm holding the gun which was now unwavering as it aimed at my chest.

'The police are on their way, you cannot escape.'

'Then all the more reason to kill you.' He struggled to raise the pistol higher as he aimed

'Laisse tomber le pistolet,' a voice shouted.

I watched as Vachon's arm tensed, and a shot rang out, but I felt no pain. Instead, I saw a disgusting splat as a bullet hit the side of Vachon's head.

I could stand no more and dropped weakly to the ground, leaned back against a rock and passed out.

As I came round, a strong arm was supporting my shoulders and someone was bathing my face with river water.

Lifting my eyelids, I saw a man's eyes of a heavenly blue were gazing anxiously into mine.

'Am I dead?' I asked.

'No,' Spiro replied, 'I hope you are very much alive.'

Revenge in Rochenoir

Chapter Thirty-one
Last Words

We had a party to celebrate the demise of Paul Vachon and his gang – where else – but at Labaraquette. Full of food and wine, we relaxed in the warmth of a late spring evening. Naturally talk soon turned towards the vexed question, is there still some gold out there?

Graham and Marius thought not.

There's no doubt in my mind,' ventured Graham, 'that even allowing for the funds Paul Vachon used to buy the Casino and the extorted or stolen gold in his safe, Paul has another cache, the gold that was hidden in the Holçarté. It won't be here for it is more likely to have been deposited in a bank based in whichever country he was going to run to after taking his revenge out on Sam's stalwart investigators. Those amateur Musketeers who spoiled his evil plans. Now it's hidden away you would probably have more chance of reward in finding the Cathar treasure.

'But your agent said it was still there?'

'That's what I told him to say. He's fine by the way, Paul just tied him up to keep him out of the way while he killed Claudine.'

'Or me, he thought I was Claudine.

'The good news is that when the courts have made a judgement on what should happen to the recovered gold, you will all be in line for a jolly good bonus. That is, all except the gold ingot Sam found and gave to me. That has been donated to the Rochenoir Clinic.'

Graham then stood, 'One last announcement that is well deserved and fills my heart with pride is that Rebecca will be recommended for a French gong for the part she played, including scant regard for her own safety, in bringing the crooks to justice.'

Recovering from the shock of the announcement and an embarrassingly prolonged round of applause, I stood up and remembering I had a glass of wine in my hand, took a quick gulp for courage.

'First I must admit to Egg, Claudine, Brigitte and Albert that I misled them slightly by telling them a little white lie in claiming Harry as my husband. And, sorry Egg, you were wrong in thinking he was my brother. He is not a relative but a dear friend who offered to help when Graham asked me to come to Rochenoir and protect Claudine. Everything else I told you is true. Yes, I am a Geologist; yes Harry is an Archaeologist; yes we met at university; and no, we are not special agents. Graham had a hold over me when he told me of the situation in Rochenoir and the shooting of Sam. It made me give up my job to help keep two people I had never heard of out of trouble. Two people that I dearly love today, Claudine and Egg. Gosh! Can I add that I never expected anything like an award for helping them? It was reward enough that we are all safe and alive today, albeit with a few bruises on some of us. Is this honour your doing, Graham?'

'No!' Marius's voice was loud and clear. 'The recommendation was from me and it's a well deserved tribute to your bravery.'

As the applause died down I called, 'It was not me alone, Spiro saved my life and at the same time he ended Vachon's. Where are you Spiro?

Suddenly he was there and taking my hand. He looked straight at me and said, 'It is my great honour to stand beside you.' And as he took both my hands, I don't think, as we gazed at each other, either of us could hear our small audience clapping yet again.

I did hear through a haze Claudine call out, 'Graham tell us what was the influence you had over Rebecca that you were so sure she would help you even at the risk of her life.

Graham laughed with delight, 'I say with pride because Rebecca is my one and only daughter. Can I add that not only is Spiro the French style Mountie who got his man, I hope he gets the woman as well.'

I think when Spiro kissed me he answered the question.

Last Words

Lightning Source UK Ltd.
Milton Keynes UK
23 December 2009

147863UK00002B/93/P